BOY OF FIRE AND EARTH

Comedian and writer Sami Shah has been profiled in *New York Times*, appeared on BBC Asian Network, and TEDx Melbourne. He has written and performed a two-part series for BBC Radio 4 – *A Beginner's Guide to Pakistan* – and has appeared as a panellist on *QI* with Stephen Fry. His autobiography, *I, Migrant*, has been nominated for multiple literary awards. He lives in Melbourne, Australia, where no djinns have contacted him yet.

BOY OF FIRE AND EARTH

Sami Shah

PICADOR INDIA

First published in India 2017 by Picador India
an imprint of Pan Macmillan India
a division of Macmillan Publishers India Private Limited
Pan Macmillan India, 707, Kailash Building
26, K. G. Marg, New Delhi – 110 001
www.panmacmillan.co.in

Pan Macmillan, 20 New Wharf Road, London N1 9RR
Basingstoke and Oxford
Associated companies throughout the world
www.panmacmillan.com

ISBN 978-93-86215-14-7

1 3 5 7 9 8 6 4 2

Typeset by Manmohan Kumar
Printed and bound in India by
Replika Press Pvt. Ltd.

For Taha Bhai

'mazaa aya'

'And verily, We created mankind from sounding clay of altered smooth mud and the jinn We created from smokeless fire.'

Quran 15:26–27

FIRE BOY

I.

Rehman Husain finished his Fajr prayer before his wife Mumtaz awoke, their room still dark except for the caramel glow of a small lamp. He folded the mat and placed it back in the bedside drawer, then cautiously picked his way across the room. His spine snapped a loud complaint when he bent to pick up his sneakers, but Mumtaz slept on. Carrying the shoes outside, Rehman sat on the stairway, laced them up, and threw on a light jacket over his shalwar kameez.

Karachi was an alien place at this early hour, startlingly noiseless when contrasted with the rest of the day. Arterial sprays of morning light spread above, yet the streets were dark, silent houses fringing them on either side.

Rehman had learned to enjoy his morning walks; they gave him time to prepare for the day's challenges in a near-meditative state, a clarity of thought only achieved at this lonely hour.

The commitment to a daily march through the neighbourhood had been initiated after a heart bypass surgery the year before, required to force open a pair of clogged arteries. He was a textile merchant, owning a sizeable garment factory that employed over a hundred workers. Plagued by unpredictable electricity outages and politicized unions, his days were filled with stress-induced migraines and fatigue. Despite this, he had been considering establishing a second factory. The heart attack put an end to those plans.

'You're just forty-two, Rehman bhai,' the surgeon had said, 'heart attacks shouldn't be happening to you yet. You need to reduce the stress in your life, not add to it.'

Besides, he would think to himself, *it's not as though I have anyone to pass the factories on to.*

Rehman did not blame their childlessness on Mumtaz. Early in their marriage, the doctors had diagnosed her with fibroids in her uterus. They had been told that the chances of conception would be slim and risky. They tried anyway and she miscarried in her fourth month. Over time they both accepted their lot and practised giving it barely any thought. But, like many men of his generation discovered, having your chest opened and your heart exposed to the outside world, even briefly, unearths all the old insecurities.

And so he walked, burying his melancholy under practical considerations of work. When this was done to his satisfaction, he would return home to Mumtaz, who would be readying his breakfast of toast and tea.

The trick, he had learned, was not to focus on the walking but to let it happen while his mind went elsewhere. He would list whatever jobs lay ahead in the day, allowing himself to plot their execution. When his mind was full of responsibilities, it held little space for other thoughts. Most days he managed an hour at a steady pace, returning home once the sun achieved full glare and radiated sticky heat like the pit of an overripe mango.

This day, however, he was exhausted after just a few minutes. His breath seemed just out of reach, slipping further away with each hungry inhalation. Sweat stung his eyes and he wiped it with a trembling hand. He pressed two fingers to his neck and felt the escalating flutter.

Rehman crossed over to the sidewalk and sat on the concrete with his head in his hands. A banyan tree extended over the boundary wall behind him, creating a thick canopy of convoluted branches.

Had he not been so focused on calming his heartbeat, Rehman might have noticed the peculiar absence of bird droppings on the ground around him. The length of the sidewalk was slick with the splatter of crow shit, except for a circle of clean grey concrete inside which Rehman sat.

The last of the cool morning breeze passed through the leaves overhead, creating a reassuring susurrus. Rehman sat there for several minutes, regulating his breathing, bringing his heart rate down to a more stable rhythm by visualizing a slow and steady pulse. He did not think to look up into the tree.

Deciding he felt well enough to return home, he stood up and began the short walk back. By the time he reached his gate, his kameez was transparent with sweat. He did not notice it, however, nor did he notice that his hands had curled into fists so tightly that he could barely grasp the key in his pocket and unlock the gate. He walked into the house and went straight up to the bedroom.

Mumtaz was in the kitchen and announced over her shoulder that tea would be ready soon, that he shouldn't take too long in the shower. The only response she received was their bedroom door slamming. It wasn't until the kettle was taken off the stove and its whistling drained of urgency that she heard the rough sounds from upstairs – hard thuds of furniture slamming against the wall, steady groans of wood threatening to splinter.

'Rehman?' she called up to him. Hearing no response, she walked out of the kitchen. 'Rehman?'

The sounds grew louder as she climbed the stairs, accompanied by a second noise that created an auditory current, pulling her faster towards the closed door – it was a continuous moan, unmistakably Rehman's.

'Rehman, what's happened? Are you okay?' she said, reaching the door. The handle resisted her attempts at turning. She knocked softly, then when there was no response, thumped hard on the door with her fists. The thudding continued, as did that wretched moan. Mumtaz bent down and peered through the keyhole, whispering a prayer to Allah that she would not see her husband suffering a heart attack on the other side, thrashing on their bed, out of her reach.

Instead, she saw Rehman sitting naked in bed, his head tilted back far enough for his face to be out of view, masturbating with both hands. His body rocked each time his hands pumped the length of his penis, the force of his rhythm causing the bed to violently shift and groan. Mumtaz gasped loudly and fell backwards. Then she rushed back down to the kitchen and returned to preparing breakfast with an intense concentration, her face flushing red-hot.

Later, Rehman only remembered feeling tired from the walk and returning home to nap. Mumtaz did not tell him what she had seen. She did seem oddly embarrassed around him that evening and at night when they made love she was more enthusiastic than usual. But he forgot those details the next morning and when he went for his walk again, it was as uneventful as ever.

Nine months passed and Rehman never once had cause to wonder about the morning his walk had been interrupted. If Mumtaz remembered it at all, it was with the amusement of a wife who decided her husband should be allowed his privacy.

Then on a clear, moonlit night, he was woken up by a persistent knocking at the gate. Mumtaz was snoring softly. He left her sleeping and walked out onto the balcony that afforded a view of the street. Looking down, he saw a lone woman, her tall frame wrapped in a white shawl.

'What do you want?' Rehman asked.

The woman continued to knock on the gate without looking up at him. He slipped on a pair of sandals and went downstairs, pausing to consider stories he had heard of women asking for help and the helpers being set upon by hidden thieves, once they had let their guard down. So, he detoured to the kitchen where he grabbed a knife.

He checked his watch to confirm that it was, indeed, well past midnight and then opened the gate, knife held behind his back. Standing in the street was the tallest woman he had ever seen. She was more than a full foot above him, his head level with the curve of her bosom. The shawl was wound tightly around her and Rehman couldn't help but admire how it shone. It was the finest cloth he had ever seen, luminous in the moonlight as it swelled and rippled. Her face – framed inside a cave of shadows – was dark and beautiful; skin so black it gleamed like onyx. But it was the eyes that frightened him, so much that the knife fell from his grip and clattered noisily onto the ground. Flames licked and danced inside them, and when she stared at him, Rehman felt as though he was looking into the grill of a furnace. The air in front of her face simmered with the heat.

'Allahu Akbar,' he whispered, awe and fear mixing in his voice, 'you are a djinn.'

'Yes,' she replied, her voice the deep roar of a distant inferno. When she spoke, her mouth opened enough for him to see the single curling flame that was her tongue.

Rehman struggled to remember the prayer that protected against djinns, its words slipping past him, leaving panic in their wake.

'P-please,' stammered Rehman, 'don't hurt us.'

She lifted her hands, black blades for fingers pulling the shawl off her head. Hair gushed down her back and pooled around her feet in an oil slick. The smell of burnt parchment filled the air.

He was paralysed, although he didn't know whether by fear or by some control she exerted over him. She reached up and ran a finger across his cheek. The skin seared where she touched it, blisters bubbling to the surface in a thin streak across the side of his face. He felt no pain, his mind devoured by terror. Then her shawl dropped to the ground. Rehman's eyes followed it, looking down at the mass of cloth puddling on the concrete. When he looked up, there was nothing. Where she had been, was a curl of smoke, a grey comma rising into the night.

He exhaled, thanked Allah and collapsed on the ground next to the cloth. Except it wasn't cloth at all. It had been when it fell, but now it was a baby, naked and asleep. Rehman stared at the infant, with pink skin and dimpled elbows and knees. Tiny feet kicked upwards and a large round face smiled peacefully. The boy – his circumcised penis small but very definitely there – farted once, then broke the silence with a shrill cry. Rehman suddenly spoke in a voice that wasn't his.

'His name is Wahid,' he said.

Then Mumtaz came down to ask why she could hear a baby crying.

Interlude a.

These stories always happen to someone's cousin brother's nephew. Muzammil Bangash was, unfortunately for him, just that. His entire family – all the cousins and brothers and uncles included – lived in the same tiny village in Pakistan's north, in the shadow of the Karakoram mountains. It was the combined crush of relations and oppressive topography that drove Muzammil away. Shortly after turning seventeen, he announced he was leaving home and moving to Karachi.

When he told his father, there had been violence. Even though Muzammil was taller, he did not dare protect himself from the thick leather belt his father beat him with. All he could do was let the old man exhaust himself, allowing the silence he offered in return as his only defence. When he told his mother, she retaliated with a marriage.

In a hurriedly arranged ceremony, Muzammil was married off to his first cousin, Mina, and had he been less obsessed with escaping the confines of their village, he would have been grateful for her. That night, when he took her virginity, she gasped, nails digging into his shoulder. He felt a spasm of sympathy for her, but it was quickly replaced with the need for release that sharpens a man's senses to a singularly focused point. Afterwards, as she slept next to him, he stared at the ceiling, forcing himself not to turn and look at her nakedness, so that the anger and bitterness may grow in him unabated. She was a part of his parents' plan to keep him from going away, from replacing the mountains that filled his horizon with the towers and structures of the modern world. And so, in the morning, after telling Mina he would return in nine months for the birth of their son, he left.

A year passed and he did not go back. Karachi swallowed him whole. He got a job working for a distant relative who owned several taxis and shared a small room on the fourth floor with three other men, their lives partitioned by bunk beds under a roof sagging with water seepage. Every morning he cleaned the old black Daihatsu he rented from his uncle and set out in search of passengers. His day would end once he had earned enough money to fill petrol for the next day and still be able to put away for the weekly payments for the taxi. Then he would drive to the edge of the city, where land gave way to ocean. There he'd sit on the rocks, looking out at the world ahead. He played at wondering how long before he would be able to leave even Karachi behind and travel to the rest of the world. He knew of another taxi driver who had managed to get construction work in Dubai and the idea of crossing to another country gave him a dizzying thrill.

It was while driving back from the beach one night that he saw the woman on the side of the road. The road leading from the beach was barren and dark; with thorny bushes on either side of a dirt track, lit only by the feeble glow his headlights threw a few feet ahead. Yet the woman stood out brilliantly in the gloom, wrapped in a shawl so red that she was like the flame of a candle.

Muzammil was speeding when he saw her and by the time his taxi came to a stop, he was well ahead of her. The car grunted loudly as he threw it in reverse, giving a teeth-rattling shudder whenever asked to do anything other than move in a straight line. He sped back towards the woman and braked just in time to come to a rest near her. He checked the meter and flipped the switch on top that reset the rotary dial. When he turned to look, she still hadn't moved. Just as Muzammil began to reach back to open the rear door from the inside, she started walking around the car. He could hear footsteps crunching on the gravel as she rounded past the trunk and all the way to the front seat on the passenger side. The wind increased, throwing fans of dust against the windscreen and pressing her shawl against her. A slim hand rose up and tapped the window, red nails clacking on glass. He almost threw himself at the door, cursing as hands that suddenly seemed large and unsteady struggled to pull up the small latch. He finally succeeded and yanked the handle, letting the door swing outwards. The woman manoeuvred herself into the car and sat next to him. Muzammil got his first proper look at her then. Straight black hair, utterly still and brushed so neatly he could make out each individual strand; her face was white, fairer even than the women of his village and they were renowned for their complexion; the eyes were bruised with mascara and the lips were coloured as red as the nails that had tapped against the window. All of it came together with such symmetrical beauty that Muzammil found himself staring. She turned to him, fixed him with deep black eyes and smiled.

He shook his head, resetting it to working condition, and then turned to look at the road ahead. Small whorls of sand were spinning like carousels in the light his car threw.

'Where to, baji?' he asked, patting the meter.

'Just start driving,' she replied, in a voice that laid phantom kisses across his mind.

Muzammil depressed the accelerator, trying to shift in his seat so that he could better hide the erection swelling under his clothes.

Needing to hear her voice again, Muzammil asked, 'Baji, it is not safe to be here so late at night. Why were you out walking at this hour?'

Hearing no reply, he glanced at her. She had shifted in her seat, so that her body now angled towards him. The shawl was lying in her lap, the blouse beneath the same deep red, curving over ample breasts and ending several inches above her navel. She looked at him with eyes that were not shy and soft like Mina's had been on the night that he had lain with her, but hungry and full of promise. Muzammil's foot lifted off the accelerator and the car slowed. His erection was an obvious tent in his shalwar, so hard that it throbbed painfully.

'Baji, I –'

'Stop here,' she said, reaching out and placing a hand on the side of his face. It was cold and he could smell roses on her fingertips. Muzammil turned the steering wheel sharply to one side and brought the car to a skidding halt on the gravel. He switched off the engine and darkness pressed against the windows.

Muzammil was now thinking of only one thing. His mind had already raced ahead to imaginings that drove out all other thought from his head. He turned towards her, desperate to press his face against her skin, and taste the roses and sweat that he could smell on her. And she was reaching down, her hands gripping the stiffness between his legs. He lifted her up, trying to pull her onto him, finding her almost weightless. She raised a leg, bringing it across his lap. Which was when he saw her foot.

Muzammil began screaming.

The erection, firm in her hands just moments before, shrank and his bowels loosened. He was still shrieking when she bit out his tongue with teeth jagged like shards of glass in a broken window. Her eyes filled with darkness, the contents falling backwards inside her skull. He stared into two empty sockets that swallowed his sanity. She pushed her fingers into his eyes, popping the eyeballs like soap bubbles. As he died, Muzammil's last thoughts were of Mina, lying there in bed next to him all those months ago.

The thing that had been a woman fed. When it was done and there was nothing left, it climbed out of the car and walked away, the footprints it left in the dirt facing the wrong way.

II.

Wahid was seven years old when he saw his first djinn.

Mumtaz had stopped thinking of him as anything other than her own son from the moment they had decided to adopt him. They decided keeping him would be better than handing him over to an orphanage and maybe it was Allah's blessing to the childless couple. She never understood why her husband was so adamant on a name that was, frankly, not one she would have chosen. But he seemed extraordinarily stubborn about it and so she had relented. Rehman convinced himself of his own story – the boy had been abandoned on his doorstep and he never really saw by whom – and besides, when you have to learn to change very real diapers filled with very real baby shit, it's difficult to take djinn women with eyes full of fire seriously, even if you saw them yourself.

Being an only child, Wahid never quite seemed to escape Mumtaz's obsessive concern, made all the worse by his perpetual illnesses. His body was constantly suffering the effects of allergies and flu viruses, as if it existed in an alien environment to which it could not adapt. He was on a diet of antihistamines and had to carry an inhaler with him at all times, never sure when he'd have to ward off an asthma attack. Tissues filled every pocket in his always-baggy clothes, and he left a trail of them wherever he went. He developed a preference for staying indoors, where problematic variables like pollen and dust could be controlled with closed windows and ritualistic cleaning. Where other boys his age had shelves filled with action figures and model cars, Wahid's displayed medicines, nebulizers and tissue boxes. Most of the time, he could be found sitting on a chair under those shelves, his dripping nose pushed deep in the pages of a book. Wahid had an insatiable appetite for reading and only seemed able to stop coughing when left alone with his books.

Which was why Wahid was miserable whenever Laila came over. Laila was the daughter of Rehman's first cousin Imran and his wife Batool. Imran was easy to love; a short man – verging on obese – with a small, neat moustache, on an impossibly round face, that drew attention to itself by being the only successful growth of hair on his head. Batool, a beautiful woman with a slender build, spoke with a soft voice and had a tinkling laugh. Laila had gotten none of her mother's looks and none of her father's good humour.

'Whatchoo reading,' Laila demanded, snatching *The Horse and His Boy* out of Wahid's hands and inspecting the cover before tossing it to the ground. As the elders sat in the dining room discussing politics over cups of tea, she had been sent upstairs to play with Wahid.

Wahid did not bother asking for the book to be returned, knowing it would not happen. He sniffled, pulled his legs up protectively so that only his head was visible over the bony knees and watched her cautiously. Laila then decided to take an interest in his medicines, but they were too high to reach, even when she went up on tiptoe. Wahid thought she looked very much like a walrus lifting its weight off the ground, and smiled. Then she spun around and pinched him hard on an exposed calf.

'Ow! Why did you do that?' he whined.

'I'm bored. You're boring. This room's boring. Let's go outside,' she announced, flopping down on his bed.

Wahid did not want to go outside. He wanted Laila to leave and he wanted to be left alone to finish reading about Shasta and Aslan.

'But Ammi says it's too hot to go outside.'

She sprang up from the bed and stalked towards him, fingers flexing like crab claws.

'Don't make me hurt you. Then you'll go crying to your Ammi and everyone will know what a baby you are.'

Wahid scrambled off the chair and out of her reach. Laila played at chasing him down the stairs and waited impatiently as he put his shoes on near the front door, arms folded and huffing loudly.

'Ammi, I'm going outside with Laila,' yelled Wahid. The dining room was right across the main entrance and he could not wait to be old enough to sit comfortably indoors with other adults who would not inflict pain. He heard his mother starting to say something and then being interrupted by Rehman.

'Okay, go, wear your shoes,' called his father.

Laila grinned at Wahid and, in a sing-song voice reserved for adults, said, 'Don't worry about Wahid, Mumtaz auntie! I'll take care of him!'

Wahid finished tying his laces and they both went out of the door. The Karachi summer smacked them in the face, all shade blasted away by the sunlight. Wahid blinked furiously as his eyes tried to adjust to the sudden change in brightness, focusing just in time to dodge a large ball thrown at him.

'You were supposed to catch that,' complained Laila. She was in the garden leading up to the front door, motioning for him to return the ball. Wahid retrieved the ball and crossed the small driveway, manoeuvring between the cars, and stepped onto the grass. He could already feel his body reacting to the outdoors, as if the air was so thick with allergens that if he looked down he would see large clumps of pollen attaching themselves to his arms and legs. Throwing the ball back at Laila, he used his free hand to pull out a tissue from his pocket and catch a sneeze. The ball fell a foot short of Laila and rolled to her feet slowly. 'You throw like a girl,' she said.

'Yeah … well … you *are* a girl' replied Wahid, instantly dissatisfied with this reply. He let out a rattling series of sneezes.

For the next half hour, Laila became a great deal more tolerable, mostly because Wahid did as he was instructed. They played catch for a while and then she chased him around the large lawn until they were both exhausted. They collapsed on the grass, finding it cool against their skin. As Wahid squinted up at the sun, trying to see how long he could look at it directly to make phantom squiggly shapes appear in front of his eyes, Laila got up again and made her way over to the corner of the garden.

'Hey, potty face, look at this!'

Wahid rolled over to see Laila standing under a tamarind tree, inspecting something at its base. The tree was the oldest and largest in the garden, thin branches twisting up and away from the house, clawing at the world beyond the boundary wall.

Wahid got up and walked to Laila who was studying a toffee lying in the mud, still in its shiny cellophane wrapper, gleaming like a ruby.

'It's a toffee,' said Wahid.

Laila punched him in the arm.

'I know, dumbhead,' she said, then snatched it up. 'It's mine! I saw it first!'

Wahid, who had no interest in eating candy that had been lying on the ground, looked up into the tree to see if there was an explanation for how it had come there. He expected maybe a crow or a cat to be sitting in the branches, staring mournfully down at the dropped treat. Instead, he gasped loud enough to make Laila pause in her archaeological dusting of the find.

'What is it?' she asked, peering up into the snarl of branches.

Wahid pointed, surprised that he even needed to show what he was staring at. High up in the tree was a man, perched with his back against the trunk, his legs crossed on a thin branch. He wore a white shalwar kameez, his chin resting on large fists. Given how high up he was and that the sun was behind him, Wahid couldn't make out his features. He could see the eyes though, staring down at them; the eyes were flaming red, bright as the toffee wrapper that was crinkling loudly as Laila unwrapped it.

'That man …' whispered Wahid.

Laila rolled her eyes and laughed triumphantly as she tossed the wrapper over her shoulder, holding the sticky candy between her fingers and examining it.

'What man? I don't see any man. Stop trying to steal my toffee.'

Wahid gave her an irritated glare and then looked back up. The man's face was still obscure, but the fiery red eyes seemed fixed on Laila. Wahid wasn't sure but he thought he could see a smile. He suddenly wanted to be back indoors. He didn't know who the man was, he didn't look like anyone Wahid had seen working in their house, and he especially didn't like the way the eyes glowed, despite the brightness of day.

'Laila,' Wahid whispered, starting to back away slowly from the tree, 'maybe the toffee is that man's?'

Laila glared at Wahid, still not looking upwards after having given that first perfunctory glance. Then she threw the toffee into her mouth and bit down on it.

'It's delicious,' she announced, between exaggerated chews.

Wahid looked at her in astonishment and then turned to stare up at the tree, continuing to back away from both it and her. The man was gone.

That evening, after Laila and her parents left, Wahid told his mother and father what he had seen. They gave him encouraging smiles, discussing how being an only child was probably what gave him his wonderful imagination. Wahid, who did not doubt at all the certainty of what he had seen, understood that they were not going to believe him. That night he read until the book rolled off his chest and by morning he had forgotten the man, the toffee and Laila's visit.

Two weeks later, Laila's father called Rehman and asked for help.

'Laila is very ill,' Imran said.

'What's wrong with her?' Rehman asked.

'I … Rehman, I can't explain it,' answered Imran, his voice low and frightened.

'Have you gone to a doctor?'

'Of course, that's the first thing we did. And the second and the third. None of them could find anything wrong with her. We even … Rehman, we even went to a … to a psychiatrist.'

'To a psychiatrist,' Rehman whispered in awe. He had never known anyone who had been to a psychiatrist. 'What did he say?'

'He said Laila had been traumatized. Trauma, Rehman. Why is my baby traumatized? What happened to her? She is just a child.'

Imran's voice sounded increasingly squeezed, as if speaking required some great act of will.

'So, did the psychiatrist give any medicines?'

'Something to calm her down at night. To stop the screaming. It worked for a few days, maybe three, then she started again.'

'How is Batool? Is she okay?'

'How can she be okay?' Imran almost shrieked. There was a long pause and deep breathing. Then, in a more controlled voice, he continued, 'Sorry. She is up all night praying. Doesn't leave Laila's side. Even when it gets too much for me, she doesn't leave our baby's side at all. Please, can you come over today? Please.'

'Of course, Imran. You don't even need to ask. Do you want me to bring anything? Should I bring Mumtaz?'

'Yes, it would be good to have Mumtaz there. For Batool. She needs someone to talk to. Also, there will be someone else.'

'Who?'

'I can't tell you right now ... I can't ... You'll see when you come.'

Rehman called Mumtaz as soon as Imran hung up and told her. She said she would check with her parents to see if they could babysit Wahid for the evening. When he got home an hour later, however, he was informed that the grandparents were unavailable and so Wahid would have to accompany them.

'Ammi, what's wrong with Laila?' asked Wahid on the drive over.

'She's not feeling well, so we are going over to see her. You'll have to behave yourself, as Imran chacha and Batool chachi are very upset. Okay?'

Wahid considered these rules and found them acceptable, nodding his agreement.

They reached Imran's house late in the evening. The gate was attended by the cook, who led them into the house and seated them in the drawing room before running off to fetch Imran. A minute later Imran entered, looking wretched. His eyes were ringed with creases and he hadn't shaved in days, streaks of stubble shading his cheeks. Wahid could see white in the moustache that hadn't been there the last time. His father got up and they hugged. His mother asked about Batool and then went upstairs to Laila's room to be with her. Wahid sat quietly, hands folded politely on his lap, trying not to be too obvious in his efforts to understand what was being discussed between the two men.

'I don't understand, Imran. What's wrong with her?' asked Rehman.

Imran looked as though he was about to cry. He glanced at Wahid, who was now staring fixedly up at the fan rotating overhead. Then he whispered, entirely too loudly to be ignored.

'Djinn. I think she's possessed by a djinn.'

Even through his peripheral vision, Wahid could see the shock on his father's face.

'A djinn!' he repeated. Then glancing at Wahid, he returned to a whisper, 'Are you sure? I mean, how do you ...?'

Just as Imran was about to offer an explanation for this tantalizing bit of information, the cook appeared at the door.

'Sahib, an old man is here. He says you know why.'

Imran stood up, discovered he was too unsteady to stand on his own and let Rehman hold him up by his shoulder.

'Bring him in. And tell Batool to come down as well.'

Just as the cook left the room, Laila screamed twice from upstairs. The first was the shrill wail of a girl in pain, the second unmistakably was a shriek of joy. Imran started to recite a prayer loudly and Rehman joined him in the recitation. Wahid suddenly wanted to run away, but he continued to sit, slowly whispering the same prayer himself.

The servant returned almost immediately, respectfully leading, what looked to Wahid to be the oldest man on the planet. His face was a coral mass of wrinkles under which he could barely open his eyes; on his forehead was the thumbprint bruise that marked men who spent all their time prostrated in prayer; an orange beard blazed from below his nose down to his stomach. He took one look at Wahid and clucked loudly, turning to the two men to address them in a voice so withered it was barely audible.

'The boy must leave here. He should not see this.'

At his father's command, Wahid was sent to the kitchen to watch TV with the cook. It was on the other side of the house, and he was no longer able to see the drawing room, nor hear Laila's screams. A small TV had been set up on a countertop next to the stove on which the cook and the family driver were watching the evening news. Or, at least, pretending to watch the news. Between them, Wahid caught a far more detailed and fascinating conversation than what he had just left behind.

'Why is the mullah here?' asked the driver, after getting a stool for Wahid to sit on and motioning to the cook to bring some snacks for the boy.

'I don't know,' answered Wahid. 'Maybe for the djinn?'

He wasn't sure he should have divulged this right away, but it was entirely too large to contain, a bubble of information bloating inside him.

The cook, who had climbed up on a stool to get to the box of biscuits at the back of the cabinet, jumped down and stabbed the box at the driver triumphantly. 'I knew it! I told you it was a djinn!' Then, less enthusiastically, he said, 'Poor little Laila bibi.'

The driver turned up the volume on the TV, the female newscaster was detailing a visit to Karachi by Prime Minister Benazir Bhutto. He stared at the TV for a few seconds, then said, 'In my village, a woman was once possessed by a djinn. We had to beat her with sticks to get it out. She almost died.'

'What happened to her?' asked the cook.

'She is still alive. The djinn left her. But no one will marry her now. She is ...' – he glanced at Wahid – '... ruined. The djinn, it marries the woman while she is under its control. So you see ...'

Wahid was shaking now. Despite their contentious relationship, he didn't want Laila to be beaten by sticks. So, when he heard her screaming again, this time loud enough to carry all the way to them – which meant she was downstairs in the drawing room he had been made to leave – he began running towards it even before he realized what he was doing. The cook and driver didn't follow, instead broke into loud prayers.

The scream had been pained. But it had also been in a voice deeper than Laila's. Wahid processed all this by the time he reached the door. When another scream began, he pushed the door open and went into the room.

Then he peed himself.

Wahid didn't notice the stream of hot urine coursing down his leg, staining his jeans and filling his socks. All his attention was consumed by what was in the centre of the room. His father and mother were standing in the corner closest to him. Batool chachi stood with them, her hands covering her mouth, trapped in the process of screaming, the sound not making it out. Her cheeks were shiny with tears. His mother had her arms around Batool chachi, holding her tightly as she herself tried to control her tears. His father's hands were cupped at chest level, his mouth miming what must have been a prayer.

On the ground ahead of them, in the centre of the room, was Laila. Imran chacha was holding her down, hands pressed tightly against her shoulders. She was writhing and shuddering, her body contorting into nearly impossible positions as she struggled to lift herself off the floor. Laila's face was ... not Laila's. It was darker, as though a shadow was falling over it. Her eyes were the white of a skin of fat on raw meat; her lips had curled back, showing teeth longer and yellower than any that Wahid had ever seen before. She wore a shalwar kameez that was sweat-soaked and stuck to her skin. Over her stood the old man, no longer feeble and stooping – he was standing with feet on either side of her, in his hands he carried a Quran, reciting from it in a loud and forceful voice. He seemed not to notice the girl suffering on the ground.

For Wahid, however, the only thing in the room worth seeing was the new man. He was as visible as everyone else in the room, except for the way he seemed to occupy the same space as Laila. He was taller than her, much taller. Her entire length fit in the space between his collarbone and his navel. He was naked, a long penis flapping between his legs. He seemed to be somehow running through Laila. The exposed parts of his body that she didn't occupy were completely tangible. But where she started, he ended. His face was also alternating between rage and pain, just like hers. Wahid stared at him, not quite understanding what his eyes showed him. The man was darker than anyone Wahid had ever seen – a shadow given depth and weight. His arms were crooked at the elbow, hands disappearing inside Laila's head. Fingers surfaced from her brow, like dorsal fins cutting through water.

'The man,' gasped Wahid. Then his legs stopped supporting him and he fell backwards. His father heard him and ran over, trying to block Wahid's view with his body.

'Wahid, you can't be here.'

Wahid looked up at his father and then back at the man who had grown around Laila. One hand emerged from the side, erupting out of the matted hair. It came slapping back down and Laila shrieked hard.

'The man,' gasped Wahid, 'the man … inside … inside Laila.'

His father looked back at Laila, the confusion he expressed bringing realization to Wahid. No one else could see him.

Then, as if he felt the force of being seen, the man twisted and stared at Wahid. He stopped moving, stopped wringing his hands in Laila's head and looked directly at Wahid. That was when Wahid saw the flames in his eyes, just like the man who had been sitting in the tree. The force of recognition staggered Wahid. The man blinked once and then was gone. He didn't get up to leave, nor did he slowly dissolve. He was there and then he wasn't.

Laila fainted, and her father collapsed next to her, exhausted. Her mother broke free of the grip that Mumtaz had on her and rushed to her daughter, collapsing on top of the unconscious body. The old man continued to pray. And Wahid began to cry.

On the drive home, no one spoke. Wahid sat silently, staring at his hands folded in his lap. They let Wahid sleep in their room that night, understanding that he might be too frightened to sleep on his own. He had moved out, into his own bedroom across the hallway, when he was three. His parents' bed seemed a lot smaller now. He squeezed in between them. As his father began to snore progressively louder and his mother joined in with her own nasal whine, Wahid found it impossible to relax. He kept seeing the man entwined with Laila. Every time he closed his eyes, he could see the face looking at him from the floor of the drawing room. So, when he looked up and saw the same face form out of the darkness over him, the same eyes staring down at him, he thought he had finally fallen asleep. It was only when the man spoke and he heard the voice clearly that he realized he was still awake.

'You can see me,' said the man, his voice deep and full of menace.

Wahid, not knowing what else to do, nodded. Then fingers, large and hot, wrapped themselves around his throat. Wahid tried to scream, but his lungs couldn't push the sound out. He closed his eyes so that he wouldn't have to look at the flames that licked at the man's eyelids. The grip on his throat was so hard, he could feel the hands meeting in the middle, palms pressing together with his crushed neck between them. His parents' snores seemed further and further away, still continuous and unbroken. Then his own eyes started to burn. Heat built up inside Wahid's head and the darkness filled with sunspots. Wahid thought he was dying, until he heard a gasp. The hands were gone. Air slammed into his throat, filling his chest as he breathed in large, hungry gulps. He opened his eyes and saw the man, standing at the edge of the room, holding up large hands that glowed red hot, like the ends of lit matches.

'You burned me,' whispered the man, staring at his hands. 'What are you?'

And then, he was gone.

Wahid didn't wake his parents. They continued to express their sleep in mournful snorts and whistles. He couldn't even find the strength to keep his own eyes open. His throat burned and his vision swirled. He lost consciousness and didn't wake up until his father shook him the next morning.

He didn't tell them anything. The ability to describe it all seemed beyond his capabilities. In the mirror, he could see no evidence of the attack. His neck was free of bruises and the fingers that had seemed scalding as they wrapped around his throat had left none of the blisters that Wahid thought they would have. When he joined his father and mother for breakfast in the kitchen, they both sat next to him and glared at each other until his father finally spoke, his voice breaking the silence.

'Wahid,' he began cautiously, 'I want to talk to you about what you saw last night. Do you understand what had happened?'

Wahid froze between bites of scrambled egg. He hadn't told them about what happened during the night, so how did they know? It took a great deal of processing for his mind to rewind past the attempt on his life and remember Laila. He looked at his father, then at his mother and nodded slowly.

'What do you think you saw, beta?'

Wahid swallowed and then, looking down at the last few bites left on his plate, said, 'A djinn, Baba.'

He didn't need to look up to see that his mother was on the verge of crying. She cried easily, especially when it came to Wahid. He could tell that tears were threatening to flow just by the shift in her breathing.

'Yes, Wahid. Laila had been ... taken control of by a djinn. What are djinns?'

Wahid tried to remember what he had learned from his Islamiyat teacher in school. He regurgitated the lesson in one quick burst.

'Djinns are creatures made by Allah just like man, except they are made of fire and not earth like us. The Devil, I mean Shaitan, is a djinn who was too proud to bow down to Hazrat Adam and sometimes djinns possess humans but there are good djinns and bad djinns.' He took a deep breath and looked up at his father. He said, 'The djinn that was controlling Laila was a bad djinn, Baba?'

His mother ruffled his curls; they wobbled around her fingers.

'Yes, Wahid, it was a bad djinn,' answered his father. 'But it's gone now. The maulvi prayed to Allah to save Laila and the djinn left.'

'Can the djinn come back?'

His father squeezed his hand reassuringly, scooped up the last of the egg with his spoon and ate it all in one bite. Then getting up he smiled at his son and said 'No, beta, once they are forced away they can't come back. Laila is safe.'

Interlude b.

These things happen. They happen all the time, in fact. And they care not a whit whether we believe in them. What happened to the two men on their drive back from a village in the interior of Sind, for example, really did take place.

Tariq and Parvez left Karachi just before sunrise and drove all morning on roads that were nothing more than gravel pressed flat by the passage of trucks. Through larger villages where every building was concrete and every house had electricity, to smaller ones with houses made of packed mud and lanterns in the windows, Tariq steered and Parvez sang songs and told stories the entire way, each containing more poorly constructed puns about sex.

They hunted till sunset at a friend's farm, shooting at wild boar and quail and managing to hit neither. The two reluctantly put their guns back in the jeep only once the first stars appeared in the purple sky. Still, with enough hash to last them the drive back and Parvez's cache of stories not yet fully emptied, they were looking forward to the long journey back.

As Parvez and Tariq took turns exhaling sweet, thick smoke, their stomachs began grumbling loudly. Parvez searched the back seat in vain for forgotten bags of chips or half-full biscuit boxes, but found only wrappers and cigarette packs. And so, with hunger growing, they drove on through the dark, hoping for a shop or truck stop around every corner and cursing loudly when they found none. They were passing through long stretches of darkness, with the headlights of the jeep casting stretched ovals of halogen white on nothing but gravel and trees.

Soon the hunger grew so intense that both fell silent. So, when Tariq saw a man pushing a cart in the distance, a tiny figure pecked out of the dark by a solitary street light, he pushed down on the accelerator with a whoop of joy. They stopped just a few yards away and bounded out, loudly thanking Allah and praising the cart vendor for finding his way into their lives. That the vendor didn't turn in their direction was something they did not notice. He was an old man, bent and tired, a grey shawl draped over his head like a burkha, splattered with dried mud. A thick, white beard spilled from inside the hood. As Parvez drew closer, almost running in his enthusiasm, he saw the cart was not carrying any vegetables or fruit, but was laden with four large rolls of cloth, their ends drooping over the side like softening candles. He slowed down, disappointment replacing elation.

Parvez walked up to the man and gestured at the cart, 'Assalam o Alaikum, Baba ji, we are starving. If you have any food, we will gladly pay you for it.'

The old man didn't reply. He just stood stooped over his cart, as if inspecting the wares, his face completely hidden in a puddle of darkness. Parvez glanced down at the cart, taking a closer look at the cloth. Each roll was white as ivory and almost as long as he was. An old rusted metal weighing scale lay on top of the spool furthest from him. It was this scale that the old man was giving all his attention to. Moving closer, Parvez saw the ends of the spools were leaking, a dark liquid dribbling steadily from whatever was wrapped inside. Each droplet made a *plip* sound as it splashed in its respective puddle. 'Baba ji, what is –'

From behind him, Tariq began stuttering loudly, Arabic words hiccuping out of him. Parvez recognized them as the words from the last chapter of the Quran. Words that offered protection against the Devil and against evil. And against djinns. He turned to look at Tariq who was still crouched, staring straight ahead at what was on the cart. His eyes had widened, tears streaming and flecks of spit flew from his mouth as he struggled to get the last words of the prayer out. Parvez turned back and was startled to see the man was standing closer, somehow having moved silently out from behind the cart.

The droplets were falling faster. *Plip, plip, plip.*

The face that emerged from inside the cavern of the shawl confused him at first. The eyes were too low on the head, just above the chin. Then he understood and with understanding came a terrible shriek. The beard was not a beard, but was in fact hair. A thick white tumble of hair hanging down from a head oriented the wrong way up. Black eyes stared out at him from just above the wrinkled brow, a nose curving upwards above that and a twisted scar for a mouth on top. The shawl began to pull apart, revealing two arms, naked and thin with pink skin sagging off them. They ended at the wrist in blunt, red stumps. Parvez stared stupidly, taking in the jagged shards of white bone that stuck out of the rotted ends. Then he looked back at the face. Torn and blistered lips parted and a line of drool tracked down over the cheeks and around the eyes below, disappearing into the coarse matting of hair.

A single sentence was said. It made Parvez wail and Tariq screamed like he hadn't screamed since he was a child. They turned and ran, back to their jeep that had been mercifully left running. Both jumped in, knowing better than to look back, Tariq not even waiting to close his door as they accelerated away. The man was still standing, blunt arms outstretched as the jeep rocketed past him, the question he had asked ringing in their ears even when they finally stopped the hysterical crying much later.

'How will I weigh them?' he had asked.

III.

In the same winter that Pakistan once again entered a dictatorship, Rehman died. His passing was not connected in any way to the coup, it just happened to occur two days after it. A fire had broken out in the factory – Rehman had been away for a meeting when it began and by the time he reached, an hour later, it was raging. An arm of black smoke punched upwards from the squat building, visible from miles around. He ran towards the factory and was met by a cluster of soot-blackened workers staring impotently at the inferno.

'What happened?' Rehman had screamed, shielding his face from the heat.

'We don't know, sir,' said one of the men, squeezing out the words between ragged coughs, 'it just started.'

'Is everyone safe?'

'Most of us made it out in time, but there are still a few inside, I think. Maybe when the firefighters –'

'Fuck the firefighters! By the time they get here, there'll be nothing left.'

He broke through the gawping mass of spectators and ran towards his factory. As he leaped clumsily through a whorl of flames to reach the inside, his face felt as though it was broiling off his skull. Crashing hard on the ground of the factory floor, he looked up to see his life's work drowning in fire. The walls were awash with rippling splashes of flame and the blaze had chewed through hardened concrete pillars. Flakes of denim flurried around him like autumnal leaves, glowing red-hot as they caught in his hair and clothes. He batted at himself and called out for survivors. The roar swallowed his voice and so he tried to edge further inwards but found the heat too much to bear. It already felt as though his lungs had grown heavy with smoke and so he reluctantly turned to make a dash for the exit. He had almost begun sprinting for it when he saw someone standing at the back of the large room. Veiled by curtains of drifting flame, visible only in the gaps between them, was a single dark figure.

'Run to me,' screamed Rehman. 'Come on! Fast!'

There was no one. Just a smear of ash on the far wall. Rehman cursed and ran towards the exit. As he made his way through the door, the heart attack struck. An icicle of pain stabbing through his chest. He collapsed outside the building, dead by the time his factory workers reached him.

Wahid, though a teenager by then, was still too young to know what was required of him at the funeral. So, his father's friends and relatives let him grieve as they made all the arrangements. He sat with his mother, trying not to cry around her, letting himself do so only when alone. It was, he had been informed by adults, how the 'Man of the House' must behave. He took his turn shouldering one corner of the metal coffin as the men carried it to the mosque, prayed with all the mourners and then thanked them for their condolences. Then he sat next to the coffin on the bus as they were all driven to the graveyard. He watched his father's body, cocooned in white cloth, being lowered into the ground, and recited the prayer for the deceased with his hands raised just as everyone else did.

As they closed the grave with concrete slabs, Wahid turned to Imran and asked why they did so. It was the first burial he had seen and in movies people were always lowered in a casket.

Imran smiled. 'That is the Christian way, Wahid. In Islam, we leave enough space for your father to sit up on the day of Qiyamat so that he may be judged by Allah.'

Wahid turned back to see the third and final square slab being put in place and felt claustrophobic. The thought of his father trapped under an unbreakable roof made his throat close and he began finding it hard to breathe. Taking a blast from his inhaler, he looked up and away, which is when he saw the woman standing at a distance looking down at them. She was tall, very tall and enveloped in a cloud of shimmering black cloth that pulsed and undulated despite there being no wind, like a blot of ink suspended in clear liquid. She was too far away for him to see her face, but he could tell she was looking in their direction, seemingly at his father's grave. Mud was being shovelled over the grey concrete by two labourers, although Wahid barely noticed, his focus entirely on the woman and breaking off only when Imran had to raise his voice to be noticed.

'Sorry. I was looking at someone,' mumbled Wahid.

'It's okay,' his father's cousin replied with a smile. 'Let's go back to your Ammi. She needs you now.'

Wahid looked down at the large mound of wet earth, tried to imagine his father underneath it and bit his lip so hard he winced. Then he and all the other men walked back to the bus. He turned back to see the woman one last time, so he could wave to her, but she too had left.

Interlude c.

There was a ring given by Allah to Hazrat Sulaiman bin Dawud, who was both a prophet and a king. It granted him dominion over man and over djinns and all that lay in between. Allah favoured him with it because of the wisdom and devotion he had displayed in his years as ruler of the Jewish tribes. The sons and daughters of Adam greeted him as the best amongst them, and those of smokeless fire that we know as djinns, served him loyally and faithfully, for the ring took control of their will.

To the djinns, Hazrat Sulaiman gave the task of constructing great monuments and houses of worship. For forty days and nights, he watched over their work, having learned never to fully trust the djinns. So immense was their labouring that when he died they did not even know it, for he remained standing upon the great rock, his weight borne by a cane. For forty days, the djinns below laboured on his works, believing him still alive. Then Allah sent a host of termites and his cane was eaten through. When Hazrat Sulaiman fell, the djinns were much chagrined by the deception, but they also rejoiced in their freedom. They left him there for his followers to bury and none thought to return for his ring.

None except one. And that was much later.

The ring sat on the ocean bed for a thousand upon thousand years. The salt did not erode it, nor did the continuous shifting of sand and silt over its surface dull its gleam – it shone in the darkness like the eye of a predatory fish. When the belly of a shark raking over it finally dislodged it, the currents caught it and it rose up. Eventually, it was swallowed by a fish, which was itself swallowed by a dolphin. The dolphin migrated with its pod to the Indian Ocean, never truly appreciating the value of what it carried in its belly. It was trapped in a fishing trawler's net and dragged out of the water, dying a thrashing and painful death on the deck of the boat. When it died, it vomited the contents of its stomach, spewing a mess of fish scales, pink fluid and a single ring onto the wooden floor. The captain of the boat was furious with his crew and so they were set to cleaning it up. It was one of the fishermen who found the ring. He wiped it on his sleeve and pocketed it before any of the others could see it. And so, Hazrat Sulaiman's ring, the very ring with which he had been granted dominion over all of Allah's creations, was taken back to land.

By the time the fisherman returned to his village the next week, he had forgotten about the ring still buried deep in his pocket. His home was a few miles outside Karachi, one of about two dozen small confusions of thatch, mud and brick in his coastal village.

His wife took the clothes from him and set to washing them while he played with his four children. As she cleaned his pants, scrubbing them with a thick bar of soap that had roughened her hands until they felt like dried pomfret, the ring rolled out onto the floor with a metallic tinkle. She picked it up and held it to the light. Then she slipped it on her finger, smiling at the perfect fit.

When, later that day, she asked him about the ring, he shrugged and told her he had found it on the deck of the boat. Then noticing how it seemed to please her, he changed the story of it being vomited out by a dying dolphin into it being dropped by a passing seagull. She asked if she could keep it and he decided there could be no harm in that, as long as she was willing to get it valued the next time they went to the city.

The next day, as she walked from their small home to the vegetable shop in a village nearby, the fisherman's wife was too busy sheltering her face from the whipping sand to notice the dogs. Had she looked around, she would have seen a pack of mongrels, all of them little more than bones in thinning sacks, flanking her like soldiers. They marched in rhythm to her steps, padding along obediently, three on each side. Foam bubbled around their muzzles but they did not attack, simply followed with their red eyes fixed on her back. She did not see them and by the time she neared the shops, the dogs had disappeared.

On the second day, she did notice the confluence of crows and gulls. They sat, wing to wing, on every surface around the house, silently watching her with black beady eyes. She did not have time to find their presence unnatural, choosing instead to fly into a rage over the vast quantities of shit they had deposited on her drying laundry. She ran at them with her arms flapping and her children came out to see why she was making loud shooing noises. They applauded in delight when they saw how their roof and walls were feathered with stubborn birds and joined in, eventually managing to frighten them all into the sky.

On the third day, nothing happened. That night, however, the fisherman rose from bed to drink some water. He walked into the small open courtyard behind their room and drank from cupped hands filled by cool water lifted from a clay pot. When sated, he turned to see his wife standing and watching him. She was in the doorway, lit cold blue by the moonlight, even though she had been snoring impressively when he left her side. There was no sleep in her expression, nor any lethargy in her posture. She stood as upright and solid as the door next to her, eyes gleaming like coins. Then she turned and walked back into their room. He followed her in, then frowned in confusion upon finding her asleep on the bed, still snoring loudly. Choosing not to wake her, he too went to sleep.

On the fourth night, the couple was woken up by the children. They claimed to have seen their father walk into their room, stand over them and then leave without answering their calls. They had followed him as he walked into the bedroom and were now asking why he was pretending to sleep. The fisherman and his wife sent them all back to bed and then he told her of the night before and how he had followed her into the room, only to find her asleep as well. Though they were both Hindus, like everyone else in their village, they too believed in the stories of djinns and prayed to Bhagwan for protection.

For two full days and nights, nothing happened. The fisherman went to his work and his wife tended to the children.

On the following night, she killed him.

Or rather, he thought it was her. As she pushed the blade into his chest, he stared in her eyes. Only they hadn't been eyes at all, but twin flames flickering in her head. The creature that was not his wife then walked into the children's room and crushed the air from their throats one by one as they slept, leaving large burnt handprints around their necks. Finally, it went to the fisherman's wife herself, sleeping soundly in her bed next to her dead husband. The sheets between them were dark with his blood. More splashed, spilling from her throat as the knife sliced through skin. She died with a gurgle, red bubbles filling her mouth.

Then the ring was taken from her finger.

IV.

By his eighteenth year, Wahid had grown into a lanky accumulation of elbows and knees with a mop of curls and a deep, dark complexion. A month away from the exams that marked the end of A levels, his days were packed with school, tuitions and study sessions.

He drove to school every morning in the small green hatchback Mumtaz had bought for him the year before, along the way picking up Arif and Hamza – two friends who lived in the same neighbourhood, with whom he shared most of the day's educational pilgrimages.

'Are we playing D&D today?' asked Wahid, as Arif pushed his seat back and stuck his feet up on the dashboard. In the back seat, Hamza unrolled a newspaper; a daily ritual he insisted provided him with adult authenticity.

'No can do,' said Arif, 'tonight is party night. You aren't coming, I take it?'

'I wasn't planning on it,' replied Wahid, letting his disappointment be plainly visible.

Hamza and Arif had been friends before they met Wahid, the three congregating only when their separate seventh grade classes had combined into one larger eighth grade. His father having died in the summer vacations, Wahid entered eighth grade with a sullen quietness about him. He would sit at the back of the room, the only evidence of his presence being the soft hiss of his inhaler going off at regular intervals. For the first few months of school, he ate his lunch in a solitary corner under a tree, oblivious to the din of hundreds of other boys and girls running around in the allotted half hour, and reading whatever epic fantasy series he had recently discovered. He had finished most of Michael Moorcock's *Eternal Champion* series, at least the ones he could find in second-hand bookstalls and Sunday bazaar searches, inhaling all the connected adventures of tragic heroes like Elric and Dorian Hawkmoon in tattered paperbacks. The *Corum* books were harder to find, but he had managed to discover a stack of them in comic form. Arif had first approached him as he was lost in the pages of a comic, perched on the edge of a long bench, shaded from the midday sun by a roof of branches.

'Cool! You read comics? Which one is that?'

The intrusion was so sudden that Wahid was wrenched out of his reading at a disorienting pace. He looked up to see a boy standing over him, as skinny as he was, but almost a foot shorter. Another boy was standing next to him, also a jumble of bony elbows and knees. Wahid recognized them from his class but couldn't put names to their inquisitive faces.

'Um … it's a … comic, yeah. *Corum*. He's an eternal champion,' said Wahid.

A half-eaten egg sandwich sat next to him and Arif picked it up, flopping down on the bench.

'Neat. I haven't read that one. You read *X-Men*? I have all the *X* titles,' said Arif.

'He collects anything with an X on it,' declared Hamza, still standing. 'The more Xs, the happier he gets.'

'Oh, fuck off, bhenchod,' said Arif, eyes still fixed on the comic in Wahid's hands. Wahid guffawed so hard at this that he spat bits of bread onto the pages of the comic.

'Classy,' said Hamza. 'I'm Hamza. That's Arif. You're Wahid, right?'

A chattering chorus of girls drifted past and all three paused in their introductions to affect dramatic levels of cool disinterest.

The next day, Wahid brought a stack of *Corum* comics to school and swapped them for a bunch of *X-Men* issues with Arif. A week later, the three of them had declared the bench under the tree as the headquarters of their private reading group, exchanging comic books and sandwiches as they argued over the merits of each superhero adventure.

Mumtaz had been thrilled when, a month later, Wahid asked her if he could spend the night at a friend's house. He had never really had any close friends before, preferring to spend his time indoors with his books. Once, a few years before Rehman died, she had encouraged Wahid to go outside and play cricket with some boys setting up a game in the lane in front of their house. He returned half an hour later when his complete lack of athletic skill had expelled him from the game.

'He's so lonely,' she had said to Rehman.

'I don't think he feels lonely. He seems happy actually and that's all that matters, doesn't it?' Rehman had replied.

The plan for the night had been for Wahid, Hamza and Arif to gorge themselves on chips and Pepsi while playing Xbox. Arif's elder brother had been given one on his birthday the year before and he had left it behind for Arif when he went to college in Lahore. But, while perusing shelves groaning under stacks of comics, each obsessively wrapped in protective plastic, Wahid had come across the large Dungeons & Dragons board game. The box was still sealed, lying half hidden behind more comic-book towers. Wahid pulled it down and stared at the cover – a dragon bathed in fiery red, clawing its way out of darkness.

'What's this?' asked Wahid.

Arif glanced up from a struggle to untangle the Xbox cables, 'Oh, that's Dungeons & Dragons. It's a board game. Role-playing stuff, you know. Like World of Warcraft, but with paper. One of my cousins brought it for me when he came from Chicago last year.'

Hamza walked over to Wahid, swigging Pepsi from a litre bottle, 'I remember that. We tried playing it a few months back. But it's no fun with two people and Arif was a shit dungeon master.'

'Dungeon master?' asked Wahid, pulling off the lid, 'Oh ... wow.' He was looking at a dungeon floor plan on folded paper, a thick book filled with the statistical strengths and weaknesses of everything from an elf to a werewolf and dice-shaped precious stones from a lost world. For the rest of the night, while Hamza and Arif battled with video-game characters, alternating between hurled abuse and tactical advice, Wahid sat on the bed, hunched over the rule book.

The next weekend had been their first game. Wahid served as conductor, having spent the week plotting a fantastical adventure for his friends in which they would battle orcs and win gold. That first game was a formal affair, with regular consultation of the rules and minor acts of imagination. The next week Wahid changed the game. He abandoned the constricting authority of the rule book and developed a game of his own – dragons battled with warrior magicians under twin moons. Treachery lurked in taverns where honest adventurers stopped in search of pints of mead and missions that would end in gold. In Wahid's world, Hamza was an elven thief named Barslow who could pick your pockets from the shadows and shoot an arrow through a ring. Arif had settled on a scantily clad barbarian woman named Chantilly. Guiding them was Wahid, the god of their world, who decided with a roll of a dice whether the dragons they encountered were friend or foe, or whether the army of the undead had just been disturbed. He filled a scrapbook with world maps and city maps and road maps, pulled from a slush of fantasy novels in his head.

With the exams approaching and Hamza's and Arif's imminent departures, the weekly games had become a rock to which Wahid bound himself as he tried to struggle against the tidal pull of change. He had been creating a single continuous adventure for the last five years, an epic saga that he knew had to finally be brought to a close, all laid out in encyclopaedic detail in his mind and on the last pages of his pile of journals. Which was why his disappointment at losing his friends to a party was so plain.

'He wasn't planning on coming to the party, Hamza,' said Arif.

'Aw, say it ain't so!' wailed Hamza from the back seat. 'A party isn't a party without you, Wahid! With your wild and crazy antics like staying up past nine-thirty!'

'Finishing all your homework,' said Arif.

'Sometimes saying the F word,' said Hamza

'Yes – Fudge. Besides, Maheen will be there,' offered Arif.

'So?' said Wahid.

'So, I thought you loved her?' said Arif

'I don't love her,' said Wahid, flashing Arif a glare, 'she's cool, that's all.'

The gunfire snapping of a fleet of autorickshaws careening through the traffic forced the boys to roll up their windows, unable to hear each other otherwise. At an intersection, a truck painted in gaudy splashes of purple and green ignored its red light and brought a dozen cars to screeching stops as it hurtled across their paths. Horns bleated and middle fingers stabbed upwards. The morning sky was already beginning to look like worn leather, creased and brown, as the city sent up drifts of exhaust.

'You know,' said Arif, 'when I think I'm falling in love with a girl, I just masturbate to her.'

'What does that do?' asked Hamza, hidden behind a wall of newsprint.

'It stops me from being in love. Once you do nasty, nasty things to them in your head, you don't see them the same way. Works every time!'

'You're a real gentleman,' said Wahid. 'One day you'll make some unfortunate girl very unlucky. And I am not going to masturbate to Maheen.'

'Seriously, man, it won't kill you to come to a party,' said Arif.

'How do you know?' answered Wahid. 'I've never been at one long enough to test that theory. Therefore, the possibility of my actually dying from prolonged exposure to a party does exist. Dammit, what's this now?'

A traffic policeman – dressed in a sweat-stained white uniform, shirt straining over his immense belly – was blocking the road and motioning for them to pull over. The three boys groaned as Wahid slowed the car and brought it to a stop next to two motorcyclists who were in various stages of negotiation with other policemen.

As the cop strolled over, Wahid reached into the glove compartment to retrieve the car papers and his wallet. 'Anyone have any cash?' he asked. 'I have just a five-hundred-rupee note and I'm not handing that over.'

'Yeah, I have some,' said Arif, pulling a wad of tens out of his pocket and handing it to Wahid.

'Please get out of the car,' said the policeman, bending to peer inside the car, his gigantic, curled moustache framing teeth the colour of polished wood.

Wahid sighed and stepped out, standing a full foot taller than the officer. At over six feet, he was used to towering over most people, a self-conscious stoop chronically curling his shoulders inwards. The cop didn't bother looking up at his face, instead motioned to the other boys to get out as well. Arif did as directed, while Hamza followed the instructions as slowly as possible, hoping to avoid it altogether if the negotiations could be conducted fast enough.

'Licence?' said the policeman, looking up at Wahid. A gush of traffic roared past them, ululating bus horns and the roar of trucks drowning out the policeman's voice almost entirely.

Wahid handed over the licence, putting on his friendliest smile. The policeman stared at it, then returned it, annoyed by its authenticity.

'You broke a red light back there,' he said, pointing to the intersection just behind them, yelling to be heard over the din of traffic.

Wahid knew he hadn't, but he also knew that explaining this was useless.

'Sorry bhai,' he screamed back, 'can I just pay the fee here?'

The cop looked as though he was pondering this egregious breach of protocol. 'Okay,' he finally offered with a resigned sigh, 'but only because I am in a good mood. Otherwise I would have taken your licence.'

'Thank you so much, officer sahib,' Arif said, his voice thick with sarcasm.

Wahid handed over most of the notes Arif had given him, taking his licence back as he did. The policeman pocketed them, then leaned in close, his eyes fixed on the few notes left in Wahid's hand.

'In these long days,' he said into Wahid's ear, exhaling rank breath onto the side of his face, 'a little extra for tea would also be appreciated.'

Wahid sighed and pushed the rest into the waiting hand. The policeman shoved the money into the same pocket as before without bothering to count it and started walking back into the middle of the road, hailing an approaching van, his interest in the boys already over.

Wahid and Arif got back into the car.

'Say it! Say! It!' chanted Arif.

'Bloody fudger!' said Wahid as he pulled back onto the road, smiling as Arif laughed. The motorcyclists were not having as much luck with their negotiations and one of them was waving his helmet at the policeman attending to him.

'Why the hell are they checking here?' asked Wahid.

'Like they need a fucking reason. I think there's some strike or something,' offered Hamza. 'The truck drivers' mafia is protesting. It's in the papers.'

'I think we're the only people in Karachi without a mafia of our own,' said Arif.

Hamza ignored him and returned to the newspaper. 'Corruption, corruption, bomb blast, drone attack, corruption,' he said, summarizing the headlines.

'If they got rid of corruption and terrorism,' said Arif, 'the paper would be as small as a Post-it note. I'm so sick of this place. When I go to America, I'm not coming back. I'm going to find a hot white chick with blonde hair and big tits and marry her and get a green card.'

'Don't forget, she needs to have low standards,' said Wahid, grinning, 'or at least some sort of brain damage.'

Arif had already gained admission into two American universities. He was due to leave four months later, in time for the fall semester and thus had completely lost interest in the A-level exams. Hamza had chosen to pursue law in London, his university of choice granting him a place conditional upon his exam results being up to a certain standard. Wahid was the only one of the three planning on staying in Karachi for university. He hoped to get a place in one of the better business schools so that he could learn the skills needed to restart the shuttered textile factory.

'Man, it's going to suck when you guys leave,' he said.

'I know, man. You'll miss all the hard partying we used to do together. Getting drunk and laid and stuff,' said Arif.

'Oh, this is interesting,' said Hamza with a snort, 'check this out. A physics professor in Karachi University thinks he might be able to harness the power of djinns to fulfil our energy needs.'

'Idiot.' Arif sighed.

'No, seriously, listen to this,' continued Hamza, reading from the paper. 'Professor Javed Kamal Rahim, a physics teacher in Karachi University, recently published a paper detailing the practical applications of using djinns as a source of energy. "We know from the Holy Quran that they are made of fire, so why not use them to replace the dwindling coal resources," says Professor Kamal. He is confident that if his experiments are successful, then Pakistan's energy shortage will finally end.'

'You know,' said Wahid, 'if he can stop the load shedding, then sure. We're spending a fortune on petrol for the generator at home. Gentlemen, we have arrived.'

Their school occupied most of a large block, the whole lane glutted with uniformed teenagers stamping out cigarettes and peeking at their phones before a chorus of bells summoned them inside. A row of small shops had erupted around the school, shelves stocked with tobacco, chocolates and soft drinks. Their shutters were still drawn, not needing to open until school let out in the afternoon when an army of hungry students would advance on them.

The three friends made their way to the back of the building, where everyone assembled to sing the national anthem, after which they went off to their respective classes, meeting up again during the half-hour lunch break at noon.

'C'mon Wahid,' said Arif between spoonfuls of biryani, 'the party will be awesome. Everyone's going. Are you sure you won't come?'

Wahid had attended a couple of parties a few years back and had despised every minute of each one. He found he was too awkward at dancing due to his height, always apologizing for his elbows and knees, and he had no interest in drinking, since alcohol conflicted with whatever cocktail of antibiotics he was on at the time.

'No, man, you know me. Just not my scene.'

'That's if the party even happens,' Hamza said. 'Isn't this the same one that got postponed because of the bomb blast last week?'

The week before, a suicide bomber had detonated outside an old Sufi shrine in the city, killing over a dozen people. The blast had been so loud that, even though they all lived several miles away, their windows and doors had shuddered.

'No, that was another party, and it anyway happened the day after the blast. Plus, that one sucked. This is being organized by different people. Lotsa hot girls.'

'Yes,' said Hamza, 'all of them just dying to have sex with three geeks, none of whom has ever had a girlfriend.'

The conversation continued in much the same vein for the rest of the lunch break, with Wahid watching Arif's enthusiasm and Hamza's cynicism being volleyed back and forth. After the last class of the day, Hamza and Wahid began the first of the day's tuitions, Arif managing to drop out of all since his college admission was confirmed.

In maths tuition, conducted by a thin man with a pencil moustache and grey hair, in a cramped apartment living room, Wahid and Hamza sat with seven other students from different schools and honed their ability to solve complex differential equations. One of the students in that class was Maheen Janjua. Maheen had black hair down to her waist, which she tied in a ponytail that bounced when she walked. Maheen chewed her lower lip when concentrating and smiled with perfect teeth. Maheen never even looked at Wahid and he was quite sure she didn't know his name. He would sneak glances at her when he was confident she wasn't looking.

On the drive to English literature tuition, he and Hamza stopped to pick up roast-beef burgers from Boat Basin, an arc of restaurants and fast-food shacks facing a vast sewerage canal. They parked the car in front of a megalith of stacked chairs and tables and signalled to a waiter. Ten minutes later, he ran up with a bag full of grease and chips and was generously tipped. The whole transaction was conducted fast enough so that only a few dozen flies managed to get into the car.

Literature was taught by an old lady who would often break off from teaching T. S. Eliot and Blake to tell stories about her many romances. By then their school uniforms were sweat stained and creased. After debating Prufrock's supposed impotence and practising how to identify iambic tetrameter, they headed to the final tuition of the day.

Business management instruction was delivered by a thin-lipped serious woman who also taught the same class in their school. To reach her apartment they had to squeeze the car through a narrow lane rendered two-way by the expanding fortifications of Bilawal House, the President's Karachi home. Flocks of policemen cordoned off the road and immense containers created labyrinthine diversions. To get around them, Wahid had to take a circuitous route through fractured side lanes, his car grunting and crackling as it bounced across hidden ditches and steeply rising speed breakers. Since this lane was the only one not swallowed by walls of blast-proof concrete, it was permanently in gridlock and by the time the boys reached business management, they were exhausted and foul-tempered.

Halfway through the class, Wahid suffered the teacher's glare when his phone trilled. Seeing his mother's number flashing on the screen, he excused himself and went out into the hallway to take the call.

'Beta, it says in the news that some shooting is happening where you are. When will you come home?'

Wahid could hear none of the familiar popping sounds of distant gunshots and told her so. She made him promise to drive carefully and he went back inside to have more glaring inflicted upon him.

By the time they left for home, dusk was settling. News vans with satellite dishes on their roofs blazed past them, followed by a single ambulance. They were assaulted at every traffic light by coordinated task forces of dirt-coloured children armed with squeegees, and buxom transsexuals firing scattershot rounds of flirtatious praise. Wahid waved them all away, pleading with the children to leave his windscreen unwashed and apologizing to each brightly ornamented hijra for not having any money to give.

Wahid dropped Hamza home, told him to have a good time at the party, then drove the short distance to his own house a couple of lanes away.

His mother was sitting in the lounge, curled up on the old sofa, reading a magazine. The large TV showed muted footage of protesters burning tyres in some distant part of the city. Her hair had turned white in the years since Rehman's death and the television's glow silvered it.

'Salaam, Ammi,' he said, collapsing on the couch next to her.

'Oh, you're home,' she noted, putting her magazine down and flexing her fingers to restore circulation.

'No, Ammi, I'm still at school. You're hallucinating,' said Wahid with a wise-ass grin, grabbing the remote from between them just fast enough to avoid her swatting hand. He began cycling through the channels, rapidly moving through news bulletins and political talk shows until he finally got to a rerun of *How I Met Your Mother* and turned up the volume.

Just as Wahid was letting the television lull him into a non-thinking stupor, his phone rang. He reached for it and saw a number with no name attached.

'Hello,' he said, answering it.

'Hi, is this Wahid?' said a female voice.

'Uh, yes.'

'Hi, Wahid, this is Maheen. From maths tuition. I'm not sure if you remember me?'

Wahid almost threw the remote at the TV trying to mute it. Mumtaz glanced up and raised an eyebrow at the stricken expression on her son's face.

'Yes! Maheen! Of course!' he yelled, then regaining some composure, 'Of course I know you. From class. I mean, I've seen you. I mean …' Wahid felt an overwhelming urge to beat his head with the remote until it could relearn how to form coherent sentences.

'You know,' continued Maheen with a giggle, 'there is a girl in class who would kill me if she knew I was calling you.'

'Really?' Wahid's eyes widened as though he had just heard something that defied the very laws of physics. 'Who is she?' His mind raced to remember the other girls in his maths tuition. He knew there were three in total, but all he could think of was the one who had just called him.

Another laugh. 'Sorry, can't tell. Listen, I was just calling to ask if you were coming to the party tonight.'

'The dance party?'

'Yeah, not the dinner party, nor the sitting-around-and-staring-at-one-another party. Although that might still happen. The dance party. I was going and I thought it would be nice to see you there, if you were coming.'

'I, um, I wasn't ... I mean to say I wasn't planning on it because I was busy with a family thing but I can come ... I mean I might drop by.'

'Well, if you do, find me.'

'I will,' said Wahid, finally feeling like he could control the speed of his tongue. 'I'll look for you.'

'I'd like that,' she said and then hung up.

Wahid stared at the phone like he had seen people do in movies. Then he turned to Mumtaz and told her he was going out.

Interlude d.

The red house had been empty for as long as anyone could remember, and some of the people living around it had been there for a very long time. It was a tall building surrounded by walls that had collapsed in places to reveal thick knee-high grass. Many cricket balls had disappeared in that grass over the years, the unlucky players too frightened by the stories they had heard to try retrieving them. Windows were webbed with cracks and looking through them from a distance – always from a distance – showed darkness inside.

The story, often repeated to anyone who would ask and shared by children even when not asked, was that the owner had been a rich man who brought home a beautiful bride. On their wedding night, the bride had been reluctant to share in the drink her new husband enjoyed and in a fit of rage he attacked her. She died with his hands around her neck and he with the smashed half of a bottle embedded in his. Since then, if you listened closely on the night of their wedding anniversary, you could hear her crying in pain and him roaring in anger.

One family, the story went, had moved into the apartment building across the red house and their window overlooked it. A month later, the family moved away. Their young son had seen a woman standing outside his fourth-floor window, her face stretched into a silent scream. His mother claimed to have felt hands wrap around her throat at night. No one remembered when that had happened, but everyone knew it to be true, just as no one could remember the exact date of the wedding anniversary but everyone claimed to have heard the wailing and screaming nonetheless.

Of course, nobody went into the red house.

Except this night. Under a moon gleaming like a polished skull, a man walked up to the front door, pushed it open and went inside. No one saw him do so because he made sure the street was empty when he did. The interior smelled of dust and rat shit and he had to pick his steps carefully, the dim light of his cell phone casting a pale glow on the ground as he walked. The front door opened onto a cavernous hall, lined with doorways barricaded by layers of cobwebs. A staircase at the back rose upwards, but the wooden steps were slick with excrement and some had cratered with age.

The man cursed as he almost lost his balance, his foot colliding against a loose panel of marble raised a few inches higher than the floor. He held up the phone and tried to find a clean place to sit on the ground but saw none. Carefully stepping over to the closest door, he tried to push against it, but he was no longer of an age when he could put a meaningful amount of weight behind his efforts and so it did not open. The ring on his finger was loose and it almost slipped off as he struggled with the handle, so he stopped. Instead, he walked back to the centre of the room and turned off his phone light, letting darkness rush back in. Then he waited.

After a few minutes his legs started to cramp. The house was cold, even though the night had been humid and thick with heat. His knuckles hurt in the chill and he massaged each hand in turn. He wished he had brought a coat with him.

After an hour, he almost fell asleep standing. His eyelids were closed and his mind filling with the nonsense reality of dreaming when he forced himself awake through sheer force of will. He opened his eyes and smiled. The darkness in front of him had congealed, forming the silhouette of a man, blacker than its surroundings. The figure was taller than him by at least two full feet, standing still with its head cocked sideways, as if studying him. The man touched the ring on his finger, reassuring himself of its presence.

'Assalam o Alaikum.'

The shape held still. Seeing no response to his greeting, the man tried another tack.

'Come on, you fucking piece of Shaitan's shit. I piss on your kind.'

That got a response. He felt, rather than heard, a roar. A heat gusted against him, like the exhaust of an old air conditioner. His skin felt like it had lost all moisture. The man coughed and spat, finding it difficult to work up enough phlegm. The darkness rushed at him, hardening as it did, the blurred edges sharpening as the figure seemed to gain weight.

The man did not turn and run as anyone else would have, he did not even flinch. Instead, he simply raised the hand with the ring on it and let the darkness slam against it. The force of the impact travelled through his arm, up his shoulder and lifted him off his feet entirely. He collapsed backwards, arm still held up, taking the weight of the fall on his hip. It took all his effort not to cry out in pain and he knew instantly that his bones would regret the fall for days to come. But that was for later. Right now, he stared in marvel at what he saw in front of him. The darkness was burning. The figure was thrashing on the floor, red-hot with thick smoke curling off it. The man stared in fascination, still sprawled on the ground just a few feet away. The heat baking off the figure was intense and he felt as though it would burn him were he to get any closer. And then it was over. Where there had been fire and smoke and a writhing form, there was nothing. Just the thick smell of charred meat.

The man lay down on the floor, feeling the coolness of the dirty marble against the back of his head. Then he began to laugh, a rasping sound that drifted through the room like a ghost.

This had never happened before.

V.

Wahid could feel the reverberating bass one lane away. On the sidewalk in front of the house where the party was under way, a group of men in white shirts and ill-fitting waistcoats sat around a table with a large 'valet' sign pasted across it. He got out and handed the keys to one of them.

Not knowing quite how to dress, he had decided on dark blue denim and a black shirt that hung loosely on his skinny frame. A pair of girls he didn't recognize entered the party ahead of him and he followed, only to be stopped at the gate by a woman seated at a table with a list in front of her. Two private security guards, dressed in blue uniforms with shotguns slung over their shoulders, flanked her on either side, a large grey metal detector standing behind them. He gave the woman his name and she scanned the list, then told him he was not on it.

Wahid pulled out his phone and dialled Arif's number. It rang several times until finally he answered.

'Wahid!' Arif yelled over music that made him almost inaudible.

'I'm outside!' Wahid yelled back.

'What!'

'I said, I'm outside!'

'Oh!'

A minute later, Arif was standing at the entrance, grinning too widely to be sober.

'He's with me!' he slurred to the woman with the list. She took Wahid's hand and pressed a stamp to his wrist, marking him with a blue smudge.

Arif grabbed Wahid by the shoulder and pushed him through the metal detector, then followed him inside. The party was in an enormous garden, covered with a black tent. In the centre was a raised wooden platform, crowded with teenagers dancing to music blaring through pillars of black speakers. A strobe light rendered their movements into a zombie feeding frenzy. Smoke machines hissed and the dancers disappeared in thick white fog. Around the dance floor, sofas had been arranged with low tables in front of them, each blanketed with an assortment of bottles, cans of Red Bull and ashtrays stuffed with cigarette butts.

'There must be two hundred people here,' yelled Wahid in Arif's ear.

'I know! Isn't it awesome?'

Arif led Wahid to a corner sofa, farthest from the dancing throng, and pointed to an empty spot. Hamza was also sitting on the sofa, attempting a conversation with another boy from their school. Both had half-empty glasses of copper liquid in front of them. Hamza gave Wahid an enthusiastic thumbs up and went back to whatever debate he was currently engaged in.

'What will you have, Romeo?' screamed Arif, entirely too loudly in Wahid's ear.

'Just a Coke,' said Wahid.

Arif flipped him the middle finger and then disappeared. Wahid sank uncomfortably into the sofa and began scanning the crowd for Maheen.

He sat there for an hour, looking for her. He hoped that every girl with long black hair would turn around and reveal herself to be Maheen, but was repeatedly disappointed. Twice he got up and walked through the clusters of people, repeating 'excuse me' and 'sorry' every few seconds as he would invariably bump against someone or knock cigarettes out of their hands. By the time he finished his second circuit, he found it hard to pretend as though he were anything but bored and decided to tell Arif and Hamza that he was leaving. Hamza had abandoned the couch by then and was nowhere to be seen, but Arif was sprawled across it, snoring loudly. Wahid hung his head and sighed, then walked over to Arif and pulled him upright, shaking him until his eyes opened.

'Time to go?' asked Arif, yawning loudly and exhaling directly onto Wahid's face.

'I'm leaving. You should too. You can't drive. How'd you get here?'

Arif leaned on Wahid's arm, letting his friend carry his weight and managed to communicate that Hamza had brought him.

'Well, stay here so I can find Hamza and tell him that I'll drop you off.'

Arif smiled weakly and crawled back onto the couch, covering his eyes with his forearm. Wahid began a new search for Hamza and found him by the bar trying to order a drink. Wahid pulled him away and yelled the update in his ear. Hamza nodded and hugged him goodbye before turning his attention back to the bartender.

It was on the return trip to Arif that he finally saw Maheen. She was standing with three other girls and talking animatedly. They spotted each other at the same time. She waved excitedly at him, and then gracefully glided between the maze of people standing between them. He suddenly became very self-conscious, deciding his height, physique and clothes had all conspired to make him look ridiculous.

'You came!' she hollered, leaning forward to be heard over the seismic blast of music.

'No, I'm still at home and you are hallucinating!' was what came out of Wahid's mouth, too fast for him to stop it.

'What!' she yelled.

'Nothing!'

She pointed at the speakers and rolled her eyes, so Wahid showed her the sofa where Arif was passed out in an uncomfortable configuration. She followed Wahid over and then pointed at Arif, miming holding a glass and drinking it.

Wahid nodded with what he hoped was a rueful smile. Then he leaned forward to be heard. 'I have to drop him home! I'm so sorry!'

Maheen pouted dramatically and then walked over to Arif, grabbing one arm and straining to pull him up. Wahid rushed over and grabbed the other arm, lifting Arif off the sofa and into a standing position. Arif opened one eye, surveyed his two crutches, then turned to Maheen and shouted, 'You found her!'

Maheen giggled and Wahid resisted the urge to drop his friend right there. The two of them half walked and half dragged him to the gate, finally making it outside where the music was less overwhelming.

'Sorry,' said Wahid, looking at Maheen over Arif's drooping head.

'Well, I was planning on leaving too. Can you drop me home on the way?' asked Maheen. Wahid did his best impression of a fish gasping for breath, then managed a nod.

They were both exhausted by Arif's weight by the time the valet brought Wahid's car and threw him onto the back seat a little too enthusiastically. He landed hard enough to jolt him awake. He lifted his head and winked at Wahid before going back to sleep.

Wahid turned to open the front door for Maheen, but the valet had already done so. Wahid ran back around to his side, pausing at the rear of the car where he was sure she couldn't see him, pulling out his inhaler and puffed deeply on it once. Then he got in and smiled at her before turning the wheel to set them on the road.

It was nearing on midnight and the streets were mostly empty. They drove for several minutes in silence, Wahid desperately trying to think of something to say, considering everything that came up and rejecting it. Then he realized he didn't know where to drop her.

'Sorry, I don't know where you live.'

She gave him her address and he decided the fact that it was so close to his own home was of cosmic significance.

'You know,' she said, turning in her seat so that she sat angled towards him, 'you could have asked me out.'

Wahid glanced at her and then heard himself saying, 'I … that is, I mean … I … the thing is –'

'Then I thought,' she continued, 'before tuitions finish and God knows when I'd see you again, I might as well do the asking-out myself.'

Wahid breathed slowly, trying to force the air into his lungs and holding it so that his heart rate might slow. 'Thanks,' he said.

'Arif said you were too shy, so he gave me your number. We were in physics tuition together.'

Wahid turned to shoot a glare at his friend who was snoring softly in the back.

He tried to speak, then stopped, slowed his breathing, then tried again. 'Thank you. I guess I was just worried you would say no.'

'How would you know if you never asked?'

Wahid turned off the main road, remembering the side lane he needed to take just in time. It was a long curving road, painted flat blue by the street lights overhead, with houses lined on both sides. The moon, full and white, gleamed ahead.

Wahid laughed. 'I suppose so. How are your studies going? How many subjects are you taking?'

Maheen groaned. 'Uff, too many. Everyone in my family has gotten straight As and since I'm the youngest, the pressure is full-on. I've got maths, physics, chemistry, literature, world history and English. So sick of studying.'

Wahid whistled, then remembered his mother once telling him it was rude to whistle and apologized.

Maheen smiled. 'You don't need to say sorry all the time.'

'Sorry. I mean okay,' he said with a laugh, then realizing his hand had brushed her leg when he changed gears, he apologized again.

'You know,' said Maheen, her voice dropping to a whisper, 'you still haven't done it.'

'Done what?' asked Wahid, navigating the car around a turning and into another lane, identical to the one they had just driven through. They were less than a couple of minutes away from her home now and he desperately wanted to turn the car around and start driving in another direction.

'Asked me out,' said Maheen.

'I ...' Wahid started, embarrassed. Just then, all the street lights went dark, as did the lights in all the houses around them. 'Shit,' said Wahid, 'electricity's gone.'

Maheen turned to look at the darkness and sighed. 'Fourth time today. You were saying something?'

Wahid was about to continue when the view in front – a road lit only by his car's headlights – twisted on its side. He tried turning to look at Maheen but found the weight of his head wouldn't let him. Instead, it tilted the other way and slammed against the side window. He heard her scream, but from farther away than she should be. The view twisted again, the moon now somehow below the horizon. A weight crashed against him, strands of hair whipping his face. Through them, he could see the sky, black and hard, rushing down towards him. Maheen screamed again, her voice closer now and he screamed with her. Then the solid mass of darkness slammed into the windscreen, exploding it inwards. Wahid tried to lift his arms to shield his face but they didn't respond. Tiny glinting comets hurtled towards him and he closed his eyes. He felt them slicing the skin on his face, the pain forcing his eyes open. Flares of white and yellow flashed in front of him like fireworks. Then it all stopped.

The car was upside down. It took Wahid a few seconds to understand that. The car was upside down and he was too. His entire weight was on his head, which pressed against the roof, now the floor. He tried calling out to Maheen and Arif, but his lungs felt like they couldn't gather enough air to push out words. All that came out was a hoarse bark and then a gurgling cough, wet with blood. The air became too heavy to drag in using the feeble breaths he was employing. He tried gulping it but not enough of it was passing into him. Trying to move his arms caused a detonation of pain that filled his vision with a searing white light. He blinked hard against the brightness, forcing it to fade.

A blur of tangled shapes slowly pulled into focus. The windscreen had shattered, jagged moonlit claws of glass lined the edge of the metal frame. Beyond it was the hood of the car, crumpled like a sheet of paper. He turned his head, felt repeated stabs of pain in his neck, until he could see to his right.

The door that should have been there was gone, giving him a clear view of the sidewalk edge just a few inches away. He tried calling to Maheen and Arif again and instead only managed to expel what little air he had left in his body. He tried to breathe it back inside him, but nothing came. He forced his arms to move again, ignoring the agony that it brought. He needed to get out of the car and breathe somehow. The view of the sidewalk blurred as tears filled his eyes, tracking onto his forehead. He forced one hand out towards the sidewalk, reaching for it with a hungry desperation. His fingers felt glass and concrete as he explored the surface for something to grip to pull himself out. His chest began to burn, heat boiling up inside it. He turned his arm sideways, elbow screaming in agony, and gripped the edge of the windscreen. His hand closed around the gnarled metal and he pushed against it with whatever strength his panic gave him. His head slid sideways and his entire weight landed on his shoulder and the other arm. He felt his knees collapse against his chest and tried to look down at them attempting to locate the pocket with the inhaler. Sweat and tears had diluted his vision completely, all he saw was dark smudges. He felt around where his hips should be, feeling for a pocket. A moment of relief as he felt the raised bulge of the inhaler. He pushed it out of his pocket and brought it up to his mouth. A surge of air blasted into his throat and forced its way into his lungs. Oxygen flooded his body and Wahid pulled it in through his nose and open mouth in big hungry gulps.

He lay there for a few seconds, just breathing deeply and relishing the taste of the air. Then he tried to call out to Maheen again. This time his voice was clear and loud. He said her name once and then waited for a response.

'Fuck,' was what he heard in response. It was neither Maheen's nor Arif's voice. It belonged to a man and seemed to come from outside the car.

Wahid took another regenerative hit from the inhaler and then tried to yell out for help. He got most of the word out before two hands grabbed his shoulder and he felt himself being pulled out of the car and thrown sideways. His back smacked against the concrete sidewalk and what little air he had just recovered was forced out of him again.

'He's still alive,' said the voice. Wahid wiped his eyes clean and looked up, straight into the interior of the car in front of him. It was an abstract jumble of metal and glass. Maheen's seat had been ripped from its position and lay on its side, with the back towards him. He could see the top of her head and a hand peeking out from one side. Both were covered in blood. The back, where Arif should have been, had completely caved in. It was as though the rear of the car had been crushed by a large weight. The whole thing looked like a grotesque sculpture of a bell lying on its side.

'Arif!' he screamed. 'Maheen!'

'Finish it then,' said the man's voice and Wahid remembered that someone else was there. He turned his head and scanned the area around him, seeing no one.

'Please, for Allah's sake, help us!' he screamed.

'Do it quickly,' was the response. Wahid peered into the darkness around the car, finally making out two shapes. They emerged as if night itself was taking form. Moonlight seemed to disregard them, leaving them filled with blackness. One was pointing at him with a long arm and the other had started moving towards him.

'Who are you? Please help us … please, my friends …' whimpered Wahid.

The figure that had started walking towards him stopped abruptly. Then it turned towards the first. 'He can see us,' said a female voice.

Wahid rubbed his eyes again, pain stabbing up his left arm when he did. He looked down at it to see a large gash, running from elbow to wrist. Blood had soaked through the remains of the shirtsleeve and pink muscle was exposed in thin strips. He looked back up at the figures, trying to separate them from the darkness that surrounded them.

'Please,' he managed through deep breaths, 'please help my friends. Maheen and Arif are in the car. Please.'

The figure with the woman's voice turned to him and moved closer. The head tilted as she considered Wahid. He stared back at her, not quite understanding what he saw.

'Your eyes,' he whispered.

'Kill him and be done with it,' roared the man from behind her.

Ignoring the urgency in the order, she knelt forward slowly, raising one hand and extending a long finger of pitch black. It looked like a knife that somehow sliced the light out of the world. Wahid continued to stare at her eyes, mesmerized by the small flames that licked outwards. She touched his cheek, pressing her fingertip against his skin. It felt like being jabbed with the edge of a hot knife. Then she hissed and withdrew it, eyes narrowing as she looked down at her finger. It was glowing red, smoke rising from the tip in thin grey wisps.

'I cannot touch him,' she said.

The male considered this, then disappeared behind the car. There was the sound of metal screaming and the car sprang upwards, spinning in the air before crashing down the right way up. The only tyre still attached to the car shot out and bounced off the curb. Wahid scrambled to his feet, pain roaring up his back and legs as he did.

The front seat had shifted when the car spun and Maheen was now lying with her upper body draped over the dashboard, her head resting on the broken steering wheel. A veil of blood covered her face entirely, thick and gleaming. The nose had been crushed flat and lips torn to show broken teeth. Wahid groaned and pulled himself fully up, taking his weight on his functioning foot and hopped towards her. He still couldn't see Arif. The only evidence of his being inside the car were threads of blood unspooling from under the back door.

'Use this,' said the male of the two. There was a terrible rending, metal being ripped like paper. The male creature stood upright, the whole door in his hands. Wahid stopped moving, stared as it lifted the curved sheet of metal over its head. Had his ankle not chosen that moment to surrender his weight, the door would have sliced into his chest and perhaps kept travelling through him. Instead, he landed on the ground, whole but wincing from the sharp pain in his leg, and the door punched into the wall behind him with explosive speed. Wahid screamed.

'You missed,' said the female one, her voice sing-song and taunting. Wahid lay on the ground, every attempt at movement spotlighting a new source of pain. Through tears and sweat, he could see her moving towards him.

A low mechanized rumble began as a generator was brought to life inside one of the surrounding houses. Across the road, bulbs over the gate and inside the house flickered on, throwing jagged white angles against the darkness. Wahid could see the road clearly; the car horrifically smashed; Maheen's face still obscured by blood; Arif's leg, twisted and broken, inside the car, the rest of him still buried under a boulder of metal. He looked away, back at his attackers. It was as though the light was bending around them, leaving their forms in the dark. The female was moving towards him, hands curved into claws. The male said, 'I'll take care of the lights,' and leapt up, his form smudging as he became less a man and more a dark cloud, streaming over the boundary wall of the lit house.

'Damn this,' said the female, 'let's see if you die faster than I burn.'

She leapt and landed on top of Wahid, her weight smashing into him. Large hands wrapped around his throat and began to press together.

A memory exploded in Wahid's mind, of being strangled by hands he could not see and a face in the darkness.

'Djinn,' he whispered, the word crushed in his throat. His torso was pinned under her knees, she was sitting on him as though he were a prayer mat. He stared up at the fiery eyes, thinned into slits. Then she started to growl. Smoke rose from around his neck as her hands began to sizzle on his skin. She didn't release him though, and in fact, increased the pressure on his throat. Wahid, his view completely obscured by grey smoke growing around him, put his last remaining strength into a push to free his good arm. Fortunately for him, she chose just that moment to shift her weight backwards and his arm swung free. He thrust his hand blindly towards her, hoping to push her off. Instead, he felt it pass through air. For a moment, he thought he had missed, but then her growl turned into a shriek. The hands lifted off Wahid and once again air flooded his throat and lungs. He stared up at her as drifts of smoke began to part. He didn't quite understand what he was seeing.

She was still sitting on him, knees pressed together on his chest. But she was no longer just blackness. His hand had passed into her chest somehow, submerged up to the wrist. The area around it looked like the surface of a lava bed, with cracked black angular wedges lit from below by a deep red flame. Glowing arteries were spreading outwards, dividing and bisecting her body into smaller and smaller patches. Her scream was deafening, like the siren of an ambulance stuck on a single high note. Wahid could feel heat emanating from her body and the air between them shimmered and danced. The darkness that composed her was almost entirely gone, her entire form had turned into a molten mass. Her scream stopped abruptly. The eyes turned a cold electric blue and then were swallowed by the supernova that seemed to have filled her. She didn't explode so much as dissipate into a mass of glowing embers that drifted apart, leaving Wahid lying on the ground with his hand held up in front of him.

'What did you do to her?' growled the male. Wahid hadn't seen him return. He was standing next to the car, still and straight.

Wahid tried to articulate a thought, but none formed and all that came out was a stuttering. 'I … I … I …'

'You killed her,' the djinn said, still standing there, the house behind him dark again. 'That isn't possible. She cannot die. We are Marid. We cannot die.' Then again as if to convince himself, he said, 'You killed her.'

Wahid forced himself to sit up, staring at the male and readying himself for the attack that was sure to come. But it didn't. The male turned and walked around the car, placing it between them. 'You took her from me,' he said. Then he reached into the car and pushed his large hands inside Maheen's body. They entered her like the keenest of knives entering meat. With an effort, he began to pull, straining like a fisherman retrieving a net laden with catch. Maheen seemed to emerge out of her own body, as though he was splitting her into two separate but complete copies. The first lay in the car, her body covered in glass and blood. The second, being pulled from the first, was whole and clean, only less dense. The Maheen that he pulled out was cloudy, like a glass replica that had been filled with smoke. The djinn's fingers were passing through her, yet somehow she stayed in his grip. First, her head appeared, her face undamaged and clean. Then her shoulders, bare and translucent, which was where his hands held her. He made one final, wrenching pull and ripped her entirely free of the body that still lay in the car. She was completely naked and lay across the djinn's forearms, glassy head hanging over his arm with translucent hair trailing down to the ground. Her eyes were closed and through the lids Wahid could see black smears of the road behind her. He sprang up and screamed her name, throwing himself into a run towards them.

'Now I take yours from you,' said the djinn. Then they were both gone. By the time Wahid had circled the car, there was just night and the smell of petrol. He screamed her name again and then spun around to look at her body still lying in the car. A large gash had split open the skin across her forehead and the blood was mostly from there. One eye was swollen, eyelashes buried entirely in a knot of muscle like the seam of a tennis ball. Her nose had flattened and small bone chips protruded from the skin. The rest of her body seemed almost pristine in comparison. From the neck down it seemed as though she were simply resting on the front of the car. Even the glass chips covering her shone like large clumps of glitter as they caught and reflected the light from the moon. Wahid leaned forward, gripped both sides of the empty doorframe and looked in the back. He could see Arif and what he saw made him retch and vomit. He staggered away from the car and bent over, spewing until there was nothing left inside him and then dry-heaving some more. Wahid stepped back into the middle of the road as the street lights began flickering on one by one, each one bringing the grotesque tragedy into sharper focus. That was when he looked down and realized his arm – that had been broken before with bone and muscle exposed – was fully healed.

VI.

Security guards rushed to help Wahid. They had been sitting outside the houses where the car crashed and so should have seen the whole thing unfold, but they had all been consumed by deep sleep at the same time. When they did awake, simultaneously, it was to find a boy covered in blood and vomit trying to pull the shattered form of a girl from inside a car that had been smashed worse than any they had ever seen. One of them vomited as well when he looked inside the car, but the rest were older and so more experienced with dead bodies and severed limbs, in the way that Karachi makes you. Someone called the emergency number that brought two ambulances. By the time the police arrived an hour later, one ambulance had already left with Maheen strapped to a gurney. The other had Wahid lying inside, an IV drip attached to his arm.

In the emergency room of a hospital, the young male doctor who examined Wahid told him that Allah had saved him that night and it was a miracle that he hadn't a single cut or bruise on him. Wahid nodded silently, tears tracking down his cheeks. One of the nurses managed to extract his home phone number from him and half an hour later Mumtaz charged into the emergency room crying hysterically. Behind her, Imran chacha and Batool chachi listened to the doctor advise bed rest for the next few days once Wahid was released in the morning. Wahid asked about Maheen and Arif. Imran chacha left to find out about the girl who had been brought in with Wahid. By the time he located the room she had been placed in, her family had arrived. Her mother had fainted when she saw the state of her daughter. Her father, a man Imran recognized from the news, stood silently in the middle of the hallway outside the room, face pressed into his hands and shaking. Imran spoke to the doctor attending to her and then returned to Wahid, asking him if he knew the girl well. Wahid nodded in a way that made it seem as though he were himself unsure if that was the right answer. Imran told him that the girl was unconscious but that the doctor had said her vital signs were stable. Then Imran held the boy close and told him, 'Arif was dead before they had even pulled him from the car.' Wahid didn't cry at this, just continued to stare down at his hands silently. He didn't answer any questions about how it happened nor did he respond to his mother's persistent hugs and kisses. The most movement he displayed was to turn his left arm sideways and touch the forearm, tracing a line with his finger over a wound that should have been there.

A few hours later, Wahid was lying in bed staring up at the white tiled ceiling of the room he had been admitted into. The doctor had insisted he be kept at the hospital for a few more hours. His mother, Imran chacha, and Batool chachi were asleep on chairs and a sofa in the small room. A banging on the door woke them all and when Imran opened the door, Maheen's father charged in. His face was red, eyes swollen from crying and spit flew from his mouth as he hurled abuse at Wahid. Imran struggled to restrain him physically, preventing him from attacking the boy who didn't flinch even when he was almost struck. Wahid just kept staring blankly as the man was dragged from the room by orderlies, wailing hysterically and promising to avenge his daughter's condition on Wahid. The doctor discharged Wahid shortly after that, allowing him to be taken home.

Once in his room, he sat at his desk all night, staring at his partial reflection on the darkened screen of the computer monitor. In the morning, Mumtaz brought breakfast and placed it next to him. He ignored the breakfast but undressed once she left and washed himself slowly. There were no scars on his body, no bruises. Even his breathing seemed clearer, as though the gauze that had filled his lungs his entire life had somehow cleared. By the time he was done dressing himself in an old T-shirt and jeans, Hamza was at the gate.

They sat on the bed. 'They're saying you were drunk,' said Hamza, who had clearly spent the last few hours crying. His eyes were like bloodied knuckles. 'I told everyone you don't drink and that you weren't drinking when you left. But they're saying it anyway.'

Wahid nodded slowly, not sure what he was agreeing with.

'What happened, man? I went to Arif's house before coming here. His brother said they found his arm completely ripped from his body and that bits of his head were missing. How can a car crash so badly? Did a truck hit you?'

Wahid slowly looked up at Hamza, his eyes focusing on the person in front of him for the first time in hours. 'Djinns,' he said softly.

'What?'

'Djinns,' said Wahid louder, as if saying it would somehow force it all to make sense.

'Djinns?'

'Yes.'

Hamza stood up and took a few steps away from the bed, then turned and looked at Wahid again.

'What do you mean djinns?'

'We were … attacked by djinns.'

'You were attacked by djinns? Djinns killed Arif and Maheen?'

'Maheen is dead?' asked Wahid.

'No, they're saying she's in a coma. That and she has a lot of injuries. Broken bones and stuff, man. What the fuck do you mean by djinns?'

Wahid breathed in, trying to organize the events into a coherent sequence and then let it all out in one rambling stream. He described the car overturning and the two figures that attacked him with red eyes and black hands. Then he described killing one of them and the other doing something to Maheen. He told it all and then he started to cry.

Hamza paced around the room, then walked to the desk and pulled open a drawer. Fumbling around inside, he retrieved an almost empty pack of cigarettes he had left there on a prior visit and lit two together, handing one to Wahid. Wahid took it, inhaled the smoke and for the first time in his life, didn't erupt into a coughing fit.

'There's another thing,' he said, wiping away tears from his cheeks with the back of his hand, 'I was hurt. My arm was ripped open and I could see the bone. My ankle was … it felt like it had broken. When the doctor saw me, he said I didn't have a scratch on me. I think killing that djinn woman did something to me.'

'Killing the djinn woman,' repeated Hamza slowly.

Wahid leaped off the chair, almost screeching. 'You think I don't realize how fucking ridiculous this sounds, man? You think I don't see that? But it fucking happened! How will I get anyone to believe me?'

Hamza, who at first took a few hurried steps away from his friend, raised his palms outward and said carefully, 'Okay, okay, it happened. But that doesn't help you, man. Arif is dead and Maheen is … we don't even know. Her father is a retired general, man. He comes on TV and shit. Did you know that? They say he wants you dead.'

Wahid slumped, shoulders sagging in exhaustion.

'They?'

'People at school. It's all over Facebook, man. People are on Arif's wall …' Hamza tried to continue but his voice hitched and he started to cry. The two friends hugged one another, weeping onto each other's shoulders.

'They're burying Arif today,' said Hamza, once he felt that he was done crying.

'Should I –'

'No. I don't think it'll be safe for you to come. Besides, everyone thinks you might be injured as well so it's okay for you not to. Arif's family won't want to see you right now. Just wait a few days maybe?'

'But I need to come. I need to see Arif one last time.'

'Look, I'll go over there. If I think you should come, then I'll call you, okay?'

'What should I do?'

Hamza considered this, burning through the last cigarette in the pack as he did. 'You need to find a djinn.'

'How will I do that?'

'We'll think of something. There must be a way. Just rest, okay. I gotta go now but I'll call you later.'

They both hugged again, then Hamza left. Wahid turned on the computer. It came alive with a beep and the soft whirring of the internal fan speeding up. Once the monitor lit up, he opened the browser and went to Facebook. Arif's wall was already full of condolence messages. All of them were from class friends and relatives, most just saying 'Rest in Peace' or 'You are with Allah now'. Wahid closed the browser and stood up, deciding it was time to talk to his mother.

Mumtaz was sitting in the TV room, talking on the cordless phone with every second word punctuated by a sob. Her cheeks glistened like wet paper. She saw Wahid coming down the stairs and said, 'I have to go, Batool,' and hung up. Wahid went to her and wrapped his long arms around her as she buried her face in his shoulder and cried. He held her tightly as her body shook, until she finally looked up at him, her face swollen with grief and misery.

'How are you, beta?'

'Okay, Amma,' said Wahid, sitting down with her and placing a hand over hers.

'What happened? You didn't say anything last night. How did the crash happen?'

'Amma …' began Wahid, intending to tell her everything. He knew his mother wouldn't doubt him – complete faith in her child was a mother's lot. But he wasn't sure that telling her would serve any purpose other than to frighten her.

'Amma, I don't know. We were driving and suddenly the car, it just flipped and crashed. Maybe I hit something or a tyre burst. I don't know.'

Mumtaz looked at her son, eyes still full of tears, and then asked if he had had anything to drink. Alcohol was not something she herself had any experience with, nor had Rehman ever had a drop to drink, to her knowledge. But she knew that teenagers were prone to do things their parents forbade. Neither she nor Rehman ever smoked but she often recognized the smell of cigarettes under a heavy layer of cologne or air freshener when Wahid came home after spending the day with his friends.

Wahid sighed and told her he hadn't been drinking. That he did not drink. For her, this was now the only truth she would allow and was relieved that she could confirm it to Imran and Batool.

'Wahid, that was Batool on the phone. She said Imran has been asking around and the girl who was with you, her father was a general.'

'I know,' said Wahid.

'Was she your girlfriend?' asked Mumtaz. Yet another question she had hoped not to have to confront her son with, although it now seemed like a trivial concern. Boys his age could have girlfriends, often did too. She wasn't naive. But she preferred ignorance of his potential relationships.

'No, Ammi,' said Wahid, 'she was just someone I knew from tuitions. I was dropping her home, that's all.'

'The doctor said it was a miracle you weren't hurt. You should read a prayer of thanks.'

'I will,' said Wahid sullenly. 'I just don't feel very thankful at all. Arif is dead and I can't go to his funeral.'

'I know, beta,' said Mumtaz, squeezing his hand, 'but you're alive. And for that I'm thankful.'

VII.

Hamza came over the next day. He hadn't called from Arif's burial, just sent a text message that read: *U shouldn't come, sorry man.*

Sitting in Wahid's room he described how Arif's mother had to be sedated all day to keep her hysteria from swallowing her. During the burial, Arif's elder brother had tried climbing into the grave and had to be pulled out by Hamza and the other men there. Everyone was saying the same thing: that Wahid had been driving drunk and crashed the car.

Wahid offered up no more defences. Instead, he stared at a picture of the three of them that he had pulled out of his cupboard the night before. It was lying in an old, dust-covered photo album that was buried under a pile of textbooks. It had been taken two years ago, when the three were finishing their O levels and were worried they might end up in different A-level institutes. They had dressed in suits and gone down to a professional photography studio that specialized in portraits. It showed three skinny boys in jackets that none of them wore well, with ties knotted with varying degrees of expertise. All three were grinning at the camera, arms draped over each other's shoulders.

'Listen,' said Hamza, 'I've been thinking about the djinn thing you said.'

Wahid turned to Hamza, girding himself for criticism or ridicule. Instead, Hamza walked over to the computer and pulled up the browser, typing out a search query. Hamza scanned the first few results, then clicked on the second link, redirecting the browser to the website of a local English newspaper where an article had been excerpted.

'Look, maybe he can help,' he said to Wahid.

Wahid walked over and bent closer to the screen, reading what it displayed.

It was the same article that Hamza had been reading in the car a couple of days before. The article detailed the physics professor from Karachi University, who claimed to be searching for a means of harnessing djinns to fulfil Pakistan's energy needs.

'Yeah,' said Hamza. 'Maybe he knows where to find djinns? He must if he plans on using them, right?'

'But you said he was crazy,' said Wahid, still reading the article.

'Yeah, but then I thought djinns were only something you found in ghost stories and Islamiyat class. You say two attacked you. So this should help, right?'

Wahid turned to Hamza, looking closely at his friend's face to make sure he wasn't mocking him in some inscrutable manner. He saw only sincere belief looking back at him.

'But how do we find him?'

'Well, he's at Karachi University, right? Here, let me see.'

Hamza took the mouse from Wahid and copied the professor's name from the article. Then he pasted it into the Google search bar. After a few seconds of loading and then exiting pages, he found what he had been searching for. It was the page for the Karachi University physics department, with the professor's picture on top: a smiling man in his fifties with a wreath of black hair, small round spectacles, and a neatly trimmed white beard.

'Let's go talk to him.'

'What, right now?'

'Sure, why not?'

They drove out into an oppressively sunny day. The university was across the city and between them and it was a universe of traffic. Wahid sat on the passenger side, chewing his nails, while Hamza navigated using a combination of aggressive driving and hand gestures.

'I read up on djinns last night,' said Wahid after several minutes of silence.

'Oh,' said Hamza, concentrating on overtaking a donkey cart that was managing to block two lanes of traffic. 'What did you find?'

'Well, Wikipedia has the same stuff that we have been taught. Quran stuff, like, made of smokeless fire, can change shape, live in abandoned places and all that.'

'Yeah, I remember having to research them for an Islamiyat test once in seventh grade, I think. Scared me shitless for a while. I thought every cat I saw was a djinn.'

Wahid ignored this and continued. 'I found more stuff on blogs and other sites. There are message forums discussing djinns all over the place. But most of them talk about how we shouldn't be scared of them and that the Quran will protect us against them. I even found a YouTube video of a man supposedly possessed by a djinn.'

'Did he look like the ones you saw?' asked Hamza. Then he yelled at the donkey cart, 'Fucking let me pass, you sister-fucking madarchod!'

'No,' continued Wahid, 'no, nothing I found was like them. And no one mentioned being attacked by djinns either. Some said that girls with long black hair can be possessed by djinns if they stand under trees. Then there's the thing the djinn did to Maheen. I couldn't find anything about that online.'

'From what you said, it sounded like it pulled her soul from her body? Maybe? I don't know. Can that be possible?'

'I don't know. That's what I've been thinking, but it's stupid, right?'

'Well, if you were attacked by djinns and you killed one by touching it then anything can happen now.'

'I guess.'

They drove the rest of the way in silence, Wahid staring out of the window at the city sliding past them. He had never been to Karachi University before. It sat on a side of the city that he didn't avoid so much as have no cause to visit. Everything he needed – the friends he had, the shops they went to and restaurants they ate at – was all within a few minutes' drive from his house.

'We're here,' said Hamza finally, bringing the car to a stop in front of a large iron gate. Two guards sat outside, one of them getting up and walking to the driver's side window. Hamza rolled it down and told them he needed to meet with the professor of the physics department. The gate was pulled open and Wahid and Hamza drove inside.

It was the first time that either had been to Karachi University and the sheer size of the campus amazed them. On either side of the narrow road they drove on were empty tracts of land, overgrown with wild bushes. Twice they had to pull over to make way for buses barrelling in the opposite direction, leaving rooster tails of dust in their wake. Soon students began appearing, young men and women carrying books and walking in clusters. They reached a row of brown buildings, featureless concrete monoliths, each one dedicated to a separate field of study.

They parked outside the department of physics and walked into the building. On the ground, someone had drawn an American flag in chalk that had to be stepped on to reach the entrance. They entered a small lobby, shadowed and gloomy, in defiance of the harsh brightness outside. Against the far wall, behind a desk, a man sat slowly pecking at the keyboard while glaring accusingly at the computer monitor. At first, he ignored the boys, fingers stamping on keys eroded clean of letters. It was only after Hamza raised the volume on his query that they were finally provided with the minimal amount of information needed to find the professor – he simply waved in the general direction of a flight of stairs behind him. They climbed up and found themselves standing in a corridor with doors on either side. Reading the names inscribed on each door, they finally found the one they were looking for.

Neat black letters painted onto a glass plate declared that the office belonged to Dr J. K. Rahim, PhD. They knocked, and then hearing no reply, tried the door handle. Finding it locked, they returned to the front desk and asked when he was due back. 'Don't know,' grunted the man, still staring at his computer screen as though it had offended him and he was waiting for an apology. They walked back to the locked door and sat down on the cool marble floor outside it. A few minutes later, they saw the professor entering the corridor from another room several doors down. Wahid and Hamza stood up as the professor walked towards them. He was a short man, wearing a white shirt and brown pants, the latter fitted around an immense belly with the help of honest-to-god suspenders.

'Sir, Assalam o Alaikum,' said Wahid, stepping aside to let the professor unlock his door.

'Walaikum,' said the professor in a cheerful voice. 'If you boys are here for admission to my class, that is not for another month.'

'No sir,' said Hamza, 'we wanted to talk to you about … about djinns.'

'Ah, the article,' said the professor, unlocking the door with a key he retrieved from his shirt pocket and motioning for them to follow him inside.

The room was a great deal smaller and more cluttered than they had expected – scabs of brick visible under peeling strips of light blue paint, metal bookshelves stacked with files and sheaves of papers, an accumulation of plaques and shields on one shelf, all faded to a uniform dull brown. In the middle of the room was a desk with an old computer monitor next to a picture frame showing the professor and a bird-like woman with a shawl around her head. The professor pressed a pair of switches on the wall next to the door. A tube light buzzed alive and filled the room with forensic light, a ceiling fan shuddered and whined as it began exerting itself. The professor sat down in a black leather chair, yellow foam leaking from small rips in the side and motioned for the boys to sit on two low-backed plastic chairs across from him. The room smelled of dust and old paper, and Wahid reflexively reached for his inhaler, surprising himself again when he realized he didn't need it. They both sat down and watched the professor boot up the ancient computer.

'So, are you here to make fun of me as well?' asked the professor, smiling as he looked at them. The computer beeped and whirred as it struggled to rouse from what must have been a very deep sleep.

'What?' said Wahid, 'No sir. Not at all.'

'You look too young to be in college. What department are you in? I've never seen you in the science building before.'

'We aren't college students, sir,' said Hamza. 'We are doing our A levels. We just –'

'Would you like some tea?' interrupted the professor. 'At my age, the brain does not work unless fuelled by heavy doses of caffeine.'

'No, thank you,' they both said.

'Ah, you're probably addicted to your Red Bulls, yes? Once you grow older, you will appreciate the true value of tea.'

He dialled a number on the phone lying next to the keyboard and asked for a cup of tea to be sent to his room along with a plate of biscuits. Then he turned back to the boys.

'A levels,' he said, rubbing his chin thoughtfully. 'It's not very often that I get to talk to students with actual brains. Most of my students have been in college long enough to have their intelligence squeezed out of them. Tell me, if you're not here to make fun of me, how can I help you?'

Wahid leaned forward slowly, trying not to telegraph his desperation, and said, 'Sir, have you ever seen a djinn?'

The professor burst out in a single laugh, then composed himself and seemed to consider the question, then laughed again. It was a soft sound, contagious and sweet. 'Ah son,' he said finally, 'why are you asking? Do you hope to help me for some extra credit in your physics exams? Or are you researching djinns so you can use them for some other purpose? Perhaps to fuel your car? Maybe run the generator in your house?'

'What?' said Hamza.

The professor gestured for them to pause the conversation as a man walked in with a tray of tea and biscuits. The steaming cup was placed in front of the professor who scooped two spoonfuls of sugar into it and stirred. The biscuits, old and crumbling, were put down in front of the boys. Once the man left, the professor held up his hand as though stopping traffic and sipped the tea carefully, slurping loudly as he did.

He sighed.

'You young people can have your coffee and your energy drinks,' said the professor with a satisfied smile, 'but a true Pakistani knows that there are few pleasures in life comparable to a cup of hot tea.'

Hamza, who was clearly not charmed by this digression, said, 'Professor, in the article in the paper, you said you had found a way to use djinns to generate power.'

The professor blew softly on the surface of the cup, his breath indenting the curling steam. 'I never said I had done it,' said the professor, 'simply that I thought it could be done. And you have yet to tell me why it is of such interest to two young men.'

Wahid scrambled for a reason. Up until then, it hadn't occurred to him that they might have to justify their curiosity.

'We think we saw a djinn,' said Hamza, a little too loudly.

The professor laughed again. 'Really? Tell me about it. Was it a cat? Or perhaps a woman on the side of the road asking for a ride at night? Or are those chudails? Witches, different from djinns, no?'

Hamza coughed nervously, turned to Wahid and glared at him. Wahid looked nervously down at his feet, his mind racing to edit out parts of what had happened so that he might present a more sanitized version.

'I was attacked by a pair of djinns, sir, a night ago. I was driving home at night and they attacked me. My car crashed. I saw them. They were black, completely black with red eyes, sir. Their eyes were made of … I think they were made of fire.'

The professor tutted loudly. 'It's bad enough having to worry about motorcyclists and trucks while driving in Karachi, now we have to worry about djinns too. Tell me, boy, which of the other professors put you up to this nonsense? Was it Bilal from the commerce department? If it was, tell him I figured out he was behind this and that he –'

'I'm telling the truth!' Wahid said in a strangled voice, catching the scream in time.

'Please, sir,' said Hamza, 'we're desperate. You have to understand. Our friend. He died in the accident. And another friend, we think the djinn did something to her. Please. You have to help us.'

The professor pushed himself back away from the table, rolling his chair until it thudded against the bookshelf behind him. He stood up and looked down at the two boys, eyes moving from Hamza to Wahid.

'What do you mean, did something?'

Wahid sagged in his chair, then described what he had experienced. He explained how the djinn had pulled Maheen into two different forms, one less substantial than the other. He even told of how he had somehow killed one of the djinns, rolling up his sleeve to show the place on his arm where the wound had been.

'Please,' he said at the end of his telling, 'you have to believe me. I need to know what happened. I need to find a djinn.'

The professor pulled off his spectacles and wiped the lenses with a handkerchief. He narrowed his eyes to focus as he did this.

'So you came to me. Why do you think I would know how to find a djinn?'

'Because of the article,' said Hamza. 'You said you could turn djinns to fuel. So we thought you must know.'

The professor perched the glasses carefully back on his nose, then turned away. With his small hands clasped behind his back, he stared at the medals and plaques.

'How old are the two of you?'

'I turned eighteen a month ago, sir,' said Wahid.

'The same, almost,' said Hamza. 'I'm a couple months older.'

'So you were born after Zia died?' said the professor. Then, without waiting for them to reply, he said, 'Yes, probably in the previous democracy, yes? But you have studied history maybe?

Do you know about the decade of Zia-ul-Haq's dictatorship? It was different from Musharraf's recent few years as dictator.'

'Sir?' said Wahid.

The professor turned towards them, smiling slightly in a way that looked less joyful than before and more embarrassed.

'Most of these medals you see are from the Zia years. Two of them I got from him directly. This small man with mad eyes and terrible breath pinned them to my chest and told me that I was doing the work that would make Allah and the Prophet proud. He told me I was making Islam stronger. Do you know what I did to make Islam stronger then?'

'No sir,' said Hamza.

'I was working on that nuclear bomb of ours. I was part of the team that got it to work. A technology that those Americans created in the '40s, took our top scientists decades to recreate in the '70s and '80s. We could have worked on such great things instead. Pakistanis have wonderful minds. Such wonderful imaginations. That Hadron Collider in Geneva, did you know it is based on principles set down by a Pakistani scientist? He won the Nobel Prize for his work, did you know that? A Pakistani. Do you know what we did to him?'

The professor picked up the half-empty teacup, looked down at the remaining contents and then drank it all in a single noisy gulp. He then picked up a biscuit, considered it for a second and put it back on the plate, patting his large belly with a sigh.

'We killed him. Not with a bullet or a bomb, the way we kill people now. But we killed him, yes. We decided he was not a Pakistani because of his religious beliefs and so forced him to leave the country and he died of a broken heart. In Pakistan, religion will always be stronger than science.

'Under Zia, religion was strongest of all. Unless science served religion, it was of no use to him. So, my colleagues, good scientists, committed acts of blasphemy against their profession. All of a sudden, it wasn't hydrogen and oxygen that created water, it was the will of Allah.'

The professor collapsed back in his chair, snorting loudly in disgust. 'A friend of mine, a talented physicist who could have done something great if he wanted to, was angry at the way the country was changing under Zia-ul-Haq. So he protested. He was arrested and beaten. When they released him, he announced he was going to focus on studying the speed at which Heaven was travelling away from earth. So they gave him a medal.

'In those days, I was a teacher struggling to find students. No one wanted to study science and those who did were only interested in using it for ridiculous reasons like finding the temperature of Hell. Three students actually wrote that as their thesis. The temperature of Hell! And if I had failed them I would have been branded a heretic for standing in the way of Islam, so I gave them As.

'By the time Zia died, the field of science in Pakistan was pathetic. In the years after, it didn't improve. No one wants to be a scientist in a country where you can earn money by being corrupt. And so, all the students become businessmen and bankers.'

The professor spat into a dustbin next to his desk, as though this last part had soured the taste in his mouth.

'So now, with my department getting no money and the number of students enrolling falling every year, I stole a trick from my old friends. I said I was going to use djinns for energy. Complete nonsense, I know it. And you must have laughed when you read it. Many did. But do you know who didn't laugh? The majority of the country. All those mindless idiots who will believe anything as long as you say Allah demanded it or that a hadith said it. They and their government. They would love me for such bullshit. Excuse me.'

The professor looked at the boys and spread his hands, as if revealing the inner workings of a magic trick.

'So I lied. And since I lied, I have had calls from the religious affairs ministries and half a dozen TV channels. And all have pledged money to the science department. Most will not pay – Pakistanis love to promise money that they will never give. But if even half do, I will have money. Money I can use to upgrade equipment and pay researchers' salaries with. But I have seen no djinns. I think it's safe to say I have never seen a djinn. As for what happened with you, sorry, but it's something I don't see how I can help you with. To be honest, I'm still not sure I quite believe you. You seem like decent boys so I don't think you're lying to me, but I can think of many different reasons, all perfectly rational, for what you think you saw. Most of them involve concussions of some kind, of course.'

The professor finally took one biscuit, cupping a hand under his chin to catch crumbs as he bit it in half. The boys looked at each other, then back at him.

'Thank you sir,' said Hamza finally.

'I wish I could have been of more help,' said the professor.

They both got up, shaking his hand in turn and then made their way to the door.

'Oh, when you pass the reception, tell that idiot there I want more tea,' said the professor. 'In Pakistan, there must always be more tea or we shall all go crazy!'

VIII.

By the time they drove out of the university campus, the afternoon sun was searing the road. Next to the gate, a man was selling cloudy glasses of lemon juice from under a cloth stall erected on a rolling cart and heat-dazed customers crowded in front of him. Hamza turned the air conditioner inside the car on full, but sweat still stuck their shirts to the vinyl seat covers.

'What now?' asked Hamza.

'No clue,' said Wahid. 'It's not like we can just drive around hoping to spot a djinn.'

'You know, while the professor was talking, I thought of something,' said Hamza. 'Djinns are religious creatures, right?'

'How do you mean?'

'Well, they're in the Quran. Even the professor doesn't seem to really believe in them. He's a … man of science, I guess. Djinns aren't scientific, they're from religion. Does that make any sense?'

'Kind of. I suppose. I mean, yeah, I guess. But how does that help me?'

'Well, why are we talking to a scientist about djinns? Shouldn't we talk to, like, a mullah or something? Someone who studies religion? Don't they say that religious people, like really religious people, can even see djinns sometimes?'

'So? Should I just go to the mosque near my house?'

'Well, I can drop you off there. Or, and I just thought of this, how about the mazaar? That's a really religious place too, right?

It's on the way and there are all kinds of stories about how djinns go to that place. My cook used to tell me how people say that sometimes they see tall figures wrapped in cloaks praying at the mazaar and everyone knows they are djinns. I can easily drop you off there. I need to be back home or I'd come with you, but there are tons of rickshaws and taxis outside the mazaar so you shouldn't have any problem getting back. What do you think?'

Wahid wanted desperately for Hamza to stay with him, but didn't say so. His cell phone rang and seeing *Home* flashing on the screen, he answered it.

'Beta,' said his mother, 'where are you?'

Wahid told her he was with Hamza and that they were just driving around.

'Okay,' she said, 'but come home before it gets dark. Imran and Batool will be coming over in the evening and Imran wanted to talk to you.'

Wahid told her he would be back in time, then turned to Hamza.

'Listen, any chance you can check on Maheen? Please? Maybe she's recovered?'

'I'll call a friend of hers I know,' said Hamza. 'I don't think I can go to the hospital. I barely knew her from tuitions.'

'Thanks, man,' said Wahid.

As they drove back across the city, Wahid pulled up the last dialled section of his cell phone, scrolling through the last few days' worth of phone calls he had received or made. Arif's name was repeated on that list over and over, the most recent call being the one he had made standing outside the party just two days before. Wahid stared at the name.

They passed through Shahrah-e-Faisal, the vast stretch of road that cut through the middle of the city and connected its far-flung edges. Hotels and office buildings rose up on either side, catching the sun in their glass surfaces and blinding everyone below. At every traffic light, children threatened to clean the windscreen, while hawkers displayed stacks of foreign interior decoration magazines and the day's newspapers. They ignored all of these with practised ease, finding their attention consumed instead by the struggle to find something to talk about that didn't involve djinns or dead friends.

Hamza pointed at the mazaar when it appeared on the horizon, silhouetted against the sky. Perched on top of a hill with the Arabian Sea stretching behind it, the shrine of Abdullah Shah Ghazi was a confusion of geometric patterns under a parrot green dome. Strings festooned with small triangular paper flags stretched from the height of the dome all the way to the ground, and a staircase led up to the interior. The sidewalk in front of the mazaar, where Hamza slowed to find a spot to park, was thronging with beggars. Some slept on the sun-baked concrete with their folded arms as pillows, while others just sat on their haunches and stared at passers-by.

Wahid thanked Hamza and got out of the car, nearly stepping on a sleeping man with clothes so thickly covered in dirt that he seemed to emerge out of the concrete underneath.

A week before, a lone terrorist with a bomb strapped to his chest had charged the gate. Finding his path blocked by a lone policeman, he detonated his burden just short of the entrance. The brave policeman and the attacker had been rendered down to their atomic substance but the casualty count could have been much higher had the attacker made it inside the mazaar. The local government had responded to the attack by installing a metal detector with a table next to it. Now a policeman sat behind the table collecting cell phones, while another tried to organize the visitors into an orderly line in front of the detector. If the terrorists had hoped to dissuade people from visiting the shrine, they had failed. The policemen were mostly being ignored as a mass of people pushed and shoved their way through and around the metal detector.

In the courtyard past the gate were half a dozen beggars, clustered together. They were taking turns injecting one another with a syringe, each one helping the other roll up a sleeve and stabbing it in the gaunt forearm offered. No one seemed to mind them and Wahid realized he was the only person staring. He turned to the mazaar in front, seeing the path to the stairs blockaded with shoes. Sandals, slippers and sneakers of all sizes were placed side by side in the hundreds. A little boy with freckles and dirty blonde hair approached him and offered to watch his shoes for a small fee. Wahid, understanding that paying him was the only way of guaranteeing that his shoes would still be there on his return, removed his own sneakers and placed them next to the rest, then gave the boy ten rupees. The boy saluted and sang, 'Thanks boss!' and sat down on the ground cross-legged, staring at the shoes as if their care was his only concern in the world.

Wahid stepped onto the marble platform that led to the staircase, the surface pleasingly cool under his feet. The stairs were wider than they had looked from a distance, divided in half with people climbing up on the right and descending on the left. He squeezed into place with a crowd of pilgrims and let the tidal movement pull him upwards. The smell of sweat rising off heat-baked bodies was intense and he managed to pull one arm up and buried his nose in the crook of his elbow. At the top, he was pushed into a cavernous hall, much larger than he had thought it would be.

The high ceiling was decorated with streamers and flags, the walls covered in tiles, each with a white flower painted on its ceramic surface, bound by hard symmetrical lines as though it were planted in a star-shaped pot. The tiles were seamlessly linked to one another, so that each wall became a painting of an immense angular garden. Old women, with gaily decorated shawls in splashes of green and pink pulled over their heads, sat leaning against the walls with hands cupped in front of them as they recited prayers. Old men with ivory beards circumambulated slowly in the centre of the room. Younger men sat on the ground, all facing the centre of the room and reading from Qurans, reciting prayers loudly in voices that rose and fell in a sing-song rhythm. Between them all, the focus of their prayers and devotion, was the shrine of Abdullah Shah Ghazi, the Sufi saint who, it was believed, protected the city from tornadoes and cyclones and granted the wishes of the most devout. A mound of packed earth and fresh mud rose from the centre. It had a rectangular wrought iron fencing and had been covered with a green blanket. As people approached it, they grabbed fistfuls of rose petals from troughs on the sides and showered the grave with their offerings. Then they raised their hands in prayer and began to make their respective pleas.

Wahid moved to one side, not wanting to block the way for anyone trying to enter the hall, and found an empty spot against the wall. He sat down between an old man who was weeping as he prayed and a small girl, not more than eight years old, who was watching everyone with interest. Her legs were drawn up against her chest as she chewed absently on a rose petal. She looked up at Wahid, offered him a fresh petal she had harvested from the ground and then popped it in her mouth with a shrug when he refused.

'What are you praying for?' she asked after observing Wahid for a few minutes.

'I'm not praying,' said Wahid softly, not wanting to disturb the meditative state of the old man next to them.

'Then why are you here? *He* is here because his son can't get married,' she said pointing to the old man still lost in tearful prayer. 'I heard him ask Baba ji for help.'

The old man ignored this publicizing of his private concerns and continued to sit with his face pressed into his hands. Wahid frowned at the girl, trying to appear as though he were not interested in what she had to say.

'Baba ji helps many people. He helped my mother. She is sitting near him now. There she is in the black dupatta. She wanted my Abba to stop drinking so much bhang water and get a job.'

'Did it work?' asked Wahid, despite himself.

'Kind of. My Abba left. But that is good says Ammi. Ammi says that Baba ji sometimes helps in ways we don't expect. So she comes here every week to pray for more help.' She nibbled on another petal. 'My name is Rukshanda. What's yours?'

'I'm Wahid.'

'So what are you here for if you aren't here to pray?' she said, staring at him expectantly.

'I need to speak to someone,' said Wahid. 'You shouldn't eat so many rose petals. They will give you a stomach ache.'

'That's okay.' She smiled, finishing off the latest one. Her lips were stained red, as though she had been chewing betel nut all day. 'I like them. I'm used to them. So Wahid bhai, who are you looking for? I come here all the time with Ammi and I know everyone. Maybe I can help you?'

Wahid looked at her, seeing a face that was pretty under the smudges of dirt that covered it. He sighed and told her she would not be able to help. Then, seeing no harm in blending in more effectively with everyone else, he got up and walked to the centre of the room. The tomb smelled of roses, a scent that went from sweetly refreshing to overbearing in the space of a few seconds. He manoeuvred into the rotating mass of worshippers and found himself standing next to the grave. Around him, people were softly mumbling their prayers, their voices accumulating into a constant buzz of need. Wahid looked around self-consciously, then realized that no one cared about him or what he prayed for, so he closed his eyes and prayed for Maheen to be safe and for Arif to forgive him. Then, almost apologetically for being so selfish, he asked for help. He opened his eyes, touched the green cloth covering the hill of damp mud and brought his fingers to his lips and kissed them lightly, mimicking what he saw others doing once they were finished with their prayers. He extricated himself from the crowd and returned to the spot by the wall, winking at the little girl who smiled back at him.

'What did you pray for?' she asked, patting the ground next to her.

'I prayed for help,' he replied, refusing yet another petal that she then chewed and swallowed.

'I know *that*,' she said, rolling her eyes with exaggerated annoyance. 'I mean what *exactly* did you pray for?'

Wahid sighed.

'I'm looking for someone who knows about djinns.'

Rukshanda considered this, thoughtfully scratching a faded scar on her cheek. 'You should talk to the mullah who sits in the office there,' she said, pointing to a doorway across from them. It was behind the tomb and so he hadn't seen it, but could glimpse it whenever the congregation in the centre parted just enough. 'I think I saw a djinn once,' she offered.

'Oh?'

'Yes. It took the shape of a goat with three legs. It used to sit outside our house until we shooed it away. Then one day it got angry at my father for chasing it away and it called out his name before running off.'

Wahid smiled at her.

'Was your father's name Baaa?'

The girl laughed so hard she frightened the old man who had been silent all this time. He jerked suddenly, his trance broken and he turned to Wahid and Rukshanda and glared. Wahid quickly got up, thanked her and made his way across the hall towards the door, turning once to see her giggling as she waved at him.

The door was simple and unmarked, incongruously set against the decorated wall. Wahid knocked once and hearing no response, tried the handle. It gave with a turn and so he slowly opened it. Turning to see that no one was trying to stop him, he went through and found himself in a narrow well-lit hallway. There were more doors, three on each side. None of them seemed to have any markings or signs and the first two he tried were locked. From behind the third, he could hear the sound of someone talking and so he knocked on it.

'Come in,' said a male voice from inside. Wahid opened the door and poked his head in – a bearded man in a pale blue shalwar kameez sat behind a small office desk, across from him were two other men, similarly dressed. All three wore green turbans and sported black, unruly beards.

'Assalam o Alaikum, beta,' said the man behind the desk. His eyes – thickly outlined with kohl behind a pair of wire spectacles – looked inquisitively at Wahid and he motioned for the other two to pull up a chair.

'Walaikum as Salaam,' said Wahid, entering the cramped room.

'How can I help you?' said the man behind the desk. A television placed on the corner of the table was showing the news and the images glowing on the screen were reflected on the lenses of his glasses.

Wahid looked nervously around at the other men in the room. The man behind the desk took the hint and asked the others to excuse them. They thanked him for his time and took their leave, closing the door behind them.

'Now, beta, how can I help you?'

Wahid was about to start on the details of what had brought him there, but he froze before the first word left his mouth. Reflected in the man's spectacles, the image distorted by the curve of the lenses but recognizable still, was Arif's picture on the television. Wahid's mouth felt like a cavern sealed off for too long. He motioned towards the television with a hand that shook visibly. The man arched an eyebrow and then obliged by turning up the volume.

'... killed in a car crash yesterday. Arif Rehmuddin was returning from a gathering late at night. In the car with him was another friend, currently hospitalized. A third friend, also in the car at the time, has been discharged from the hospital with minor injuries only.'

The reporter's voice was bored and monotonous, as if listing these events was some great exercise in futility that was forced upon him. Thankfully, no picture of either Maheen or Wahid was shown on the screen. The man looked from the TV screen to Wahid, then asked if the boy who had died was someone he knew.

'We went to the same school together,' said Wahid in a trembling voice.

'I am sorry,' said the man, following his condolence with a recital of the prayer for the dead, declaring the recently deceased as belonging to Allah and asked that they be returned to Him. Then he asked Wahid again, 'Is there anything I can help you with? I doubt you came here to watch the news.'

'I'm looking for djinns,' said Wahid.

The man stared at Wahid for a moment and then burst into loud laughter. It clattered in the tiny room, seeming to come from everywhere at once.

'And why are you looking for djinns? Is there not enough excitement in your life already? Do you wish, perhaps, to use a djinn to help you win a girl's heart? Because if you do I should warn you, they are quite useless at that.'

Wahid controlled his frustration, forcing himself to chuckle at the joke. 'No sir,' he said, 'I am curious about them, is all. I've never seen one and I had heard that they can be found here at the mazaar.'

'Oh?' The man laughed. 'Is this supposed to be where the djinns gather? Perhaps you should ask the addicts outside. They see a great deal more of djinns than you or I do. Although … I am sure that any djinn that used to be here have probably been frightened away by the bomb blast, don't you think? Even they would be horrified by an attack on such a holy place.'

'I … I don't …' stuttered Wahid. He wasn't sure how to continue, not wanting to break into a monologue of explanations.

If his discomfort was noticed at all, it was ignored, as the man scratched his beard and continued talking.

'It's true, you know. Only true monsters could attack such a respected shrine. They threatened to do so, but I never thought they would go ahead with it. No wonder all the djinns have left!'

'Sorry,' said Wahid, finally finding a footing in the one-sided conversation. 'The djinns left? They were here?'

'Oh yes. Even they know better than to stay at a place targeted by those Wahabi Deobandi sons of swine. You know, they threatened to kill me too. But I am not frightened. If I am to die for Baba ji, then let them kill me. There will be others to take my place.'

'Sir –'

'Call me Maulvi, or just Karamdaad.'

'Sorry, Maulvi sahib, I am genuinely interested in djinns. Could you help?'

'I told you,' said Maulvi Karamdaad, leaning back in his chair and smiling kindly once again at Wahid, 'there are no more djinns in the mazaar. They all left, I haven't seen any in days.'

'You could see them before?' asked Wahid, his voice rising with excitement.

'Oh yes, I have seen the djinns since I first started living here at the mazaar over two decades ago. I was a young man then, assigned by my madrasa to help with the cleaning and maintenance. I would sleep in the main hall at night, and pray and read the Quran all day. Would you like some tea? No?'

Karamdaad pulled a yellow kettle out of a cabinet under the desk, then found a porcelain cup and a tea bag. He plugged the kettle into a power outlet and set it to boil, talking throughout this ritual.

'They used to come here all the time, sometimes as many djinns as people. I could see them praying to Baba ji as well. They are easy to spot once you recognize them. They are very tall and have dark skin. And their eyes –'

'– are filled with fire,' said Wahid.

'Yes! That's right. So you know what they look like.'

'I … I've read about them.'

'As had I. But the first time you see them, there is nothing like it. Their eyes are red and burning with endless flame. Al-hamdu lillah, it was quite a sight. They never talked to me, but they would acknowledge my presence. Sometimes they would look in my direction and nod. My teacher though – who worked here before I did until the day he died of old age – they spoke to him.'

Steam was funnelling out of the kettle spout. Karamdaad unplugged it and poured hot water into the cup. He then placed the teabag inside the water and bent over double to pull a cup of sugar out from the same cabinet. Pouring a heaped spoon into the mug, he began to stir it with the precision and care of a chemist. Finally, milk was poured from a small cardboard container, also pulled out from beneath.

'They would talk to him and pray with him and wake him in time for Fajr prayers, even help him with his tasks. He was a truly holy man, you see. Oh, how he would have wept to hear of the attack. I thank Allah that he is not here to see what they tried to do to Baba ji's shrine.'

'So, there aren't any djinns any more?' asked Wahid.

'No. Until a few days ago, they used to come here all the time. Then they stopped. I haven't seen any in, oh, a week now. I think it must be because of the blast, although I saw a few in the early days after. Then a few day ago, poof, disappeared. Of course, I still get people claiming to be possessed by djinns, but they are not telling me the truth anymore. I know it is so.'

'Possessed?'

'Yes, possessed.' Karamdaad sipped the tea. Then he got up and motioned for Wahid to follow him. They left the room and stepped into the corridor. Karamdaad walked towards the furthest door on the right and pulled it open. Behind it was another door – this one was grey steel, with 'La Ilaha Ilallah' written on it in large curving Arabic letters. Above the letters, at face level, was a small rectangular panel cut into the door. Karamdaad slid this to one side and peeked through, then moved back and asked Wahid to look. Wahid squeezed past him into the small space and bent slightly at the knees to better look at what he was being shown.

The room inside was much darker than the hallway and so it took Wahid's eyes a few seconds to adjust. The interior slowly came into focus, details coalescing to reveal a room the same size as the one he had just been in. There was no desk or chair inside, just a low bed in one corner. On it was a girl – Wahid could not make out her age, but she seemed too tall to be a child – whose arms and legs had been tied to the corners of the bed. Her body was covered with a thick grey blanket and only her limbs and her head were visible outside it. Her face was hidden by what Wahid first assumed was a shroud and then realized was hair. It lay thick and black across her, extending down past her chin and under the blanket. She would moan loudly every few seconds, her voice guttural and deep, not much like the voice of a girl at all. Instead, it sounded like the voice of an old man with a severe bronchial condition who was having to pull sounds from a deep place within himself. Next to her, sitting on the ground with a white shawl pulled over her head and a Quran open in her hands, was an old woman. She was rocking slowly in place, reading from the text in front of her.

'Is that girl possessed by a djinn?' he asked, turning from the door and looking at Maulvi Karamdaad.

The maulvi rolled his eyes and started walking back towards his office. Wahid followed, closing the first door behind him. Once they were sitting again, an explanation was provided.

'That girl is not possessed,' said Maulvi Karamdaad. 'There have been possessions. I have dealt with them myself. Djinns can be lustful creatures who fall in love with women, especially if they have long black hair. It is why, after all, Allah has decreed that women cover their heads. A woman's hair can drive a man mad with desire. The effects on the djinns can be much the same. They are brought to me, speaking in voices that are not theirs as the djinn declares his possession over the girl. Sometimes I pray over them and sometimes, if it is persistent, I beat it out of them with a stick. Most times though, the girls are lying.'

'Lying? Why would they lie?'

'Because the only thing more powerful than a horny djinn is a girl who does not want to get married,' declared the maulvi, raising his cup of tea in a salute to these women. 'They claim to be possessed and copy the signs of possession that they have heard of. That way they are safe to reject any and all suitors, for who would marry a girl that has been claimed by a djinn? That girl inside is just such a case. Her mother can pray by her side for a year if she wants, but there will be no effect. Every few hours the girl will curse and spit and howl in that voice you heard.'

'It didn't sound like a girl's voice,' offered Wahid.

'Ah, but with some determination and imagination, even you could make that sound. And none are as determined nor as imaginative as these girls. But, if her mother was to say to her, "You can marry whomever you choose!", then you watch! That girl will be miraculously healed, the djinn will have left her body in an instant and she will never display such signs and ailments again!'

This final statement was followed by a long and slow sip of the tea, punctuated with a satisfied sigh from Maulvi Karamdaad. Once the ecstasy had passed, he looked at Wahid and was a bit surprised to see the disappointment on his face.

'I am sorry that there are no djinns here for you today, beta. Maybe, once the damage has been fixed and the shrine is safe from such attacks, maybe then the djinns will return. I hope so too. Until then, there is nothing.'

IX.

Kamran regretted not bringing a handsaw with him, his knife being too small to sever the woman's neck. After several minutes of exerting himself, his annoyance at his own absent-mindedness had turned into anger at the woman's corpse. Sweat dripped from his forehead, stinging his eyes and tracking into his thick black beard. Kamran made one more attempt at cutting through bone, but found it infuriatingly unyielding. There was a loud snapping sound, followed by a string of curses from the man. The blade had broken off inside her neck and embedded itself in cartilage and muscle. He pushed the body backwards and let it slap down on the ground, wiping his hands on his apron as he stood up.

The room no longer resembled the bedroom of a small house, the splashes of blood on the floor – dark and glistening – giving it the appearance of an abattoir.

Kamran looked around the room and spotted a low stool in front of the dressing table with ornate, curved legs and he sat down on it tentatively, not sure that something so spindly could support his weight. Patting his hands dry on the underside of the apron, he reached into his pocket and pulled out a pack of cigarettes. The weight of the pack told him he had, at least, not left his lighter at home and so he pulled out a cigarette and lit it. Leaning back to rest his elbows on the dressing table behind him, hearing make-up and perfumes clatter as it shook, he looked down at the body.

The woman was sprawled awkwardly, one arm twisted under her body and the other stretched out to the side. Her legs were spread wide like butterfly wings and then brought together at the ankles by the shalwar he had knotted around them. Her torso, bare and pale, gleamed as though made entirely of plaster. The kameez she had worn was rolled up to beneath her breasts, affording some modesty in death. The head . . . well, that's where the problem lay.

Kamran smoked his cigarette slowly as he considered his options. The call had been quite clear that the husband of the woman, whoever that hapless bastard was, should find her head separate from her body. He decided to search for more knives and stood up, tossing the half-smoked cigarette down into a puddle near his feet. It extinguished with a bloody hiss.

He returned a few minutes later, beaming like a child who had just been given the toy he had been asking for. He held up a much larger knife, looking at the serrated edge with satisfaction.

'Now, if only you had told me where this was, we wouldn't have wasted so much time,' he said to the woman's body, his voice playfully chiding. Kneeling beside her, he placed one hand on her chest and slid the blade into the gap in her neck. It glinted like a new moon against a night sky.

When he was done, he swept the clutter of cosmetics to the floor with a swipe of his large forearm, then placed the head on the dressing table. He closed one eye and studied the display for a few seconds, then made minor adjustments in the angle so that it was dead centre on the table. The small mirror behind it reflected the back of the head, fistfuls of hair stuck together in clumps with patches of bloodied scalp showing through. Satisfied with his placement, the man turned to consider the rest of the body. The caller hadn't specified what was to be done with it and he decided that as it currently lay, with thighs spread wide, it said all it needed to. Years earlier, when he was a young man in his teens and these jobs were new to him, he would wonder why he was never asked to leave a note or a message with the body. Now he knew the body was always the message. Whoever it was meant for – in this case, the husband of the woman he had just defiled and decapitated – would know exactly who did it, why it was done and what was required of him from now on.

He left the room and walked out of the house, pausing to shove the apron and knife into a dustbin near the entrance. The sky was darkening into night and he scanned the street as he walked through the gate onto the lane outside. Two boys were playing cricket at the far end, using stacked cardboard boxes as their wickets. A stray dog with light brown fur and a pink face watched them play. It turned to look at him when he got into his car, then lost interest. One of the boys waved to him as he manoeuvred the car carefully around their makeshift pitch, and he waved back. Kamran pulled up to the end of the lane and stopped the car. He killed the engine and waited, watching the view reflected in his side-view mirror.

After an hour of smoking cigarettes, he saw a single headlight swing into the lane from the far end and stop in front of the gate. The boys had left much earlier, the dog following them. The lane was mostly dark, this part of Karachi not being considered worthy of street lights. The motorcycle turned and parked on the incline and a man got off. Kamran couldn't make out any features from this distance, but the practised way in which the gate was pushed open was all the proof he needed that the husband was finally home. Kamran waited till the bike was rolled through the gates and then switched his car back on. He drove onto the main road ahead, turning up the volume of the radio as he did.

It took an hour for him to reach home, a featureless apartment building that rose six storeys. Just as he was getting out of the car, the blare of traffic was drowned by the amplified wail of the call to prayer. He reached into the back seat for his black turban, coiled like a python. The shalwar kameez he wore was clean, but his hands still glistened red, the fingers sticky with blood. The man shrugged and jogged to the mosque next to the apartment block, entering through a small gate with a crowd of men. He put the turban on, pressing it over his head as he entered. Around him, all the other men entering the mosque also wore identical turbans.

The taps dispensing water for wudu were all occupied, so he had to wait his turn. Finally, spying an available one, he made his way to the corner of the mosque and sat on the stone seat in front of it. Removing his shoes and socks and carefully tucking them in a corner under someone else's sandals, he rolled up his sleeves and began the ritual washing. The water from the tap in front of him ran red as he scrubbed meticulously. No one paid it any heed, nor did he bother to look up and see whether anyone was watching. At this particular mosque, the faithful were used to some of their number cleaning off blood before prayer. He ran water over his forearms, between his toes, around his ears and spat mouthfuls of it into the thin canal at his feet, then raked fingers through the tangles of his beard, teasing out knots of dried blood that had caught there. Then he got up and found a place inside the mosque, standing shoulder to shoulder in a phalanx of believers. They prayed as one body, bowing and standing in perfect unison.

Once they were done, he greeted the men on either side of him.

'Assalam o Alaikum, Kamran,' said the younger man on his left. They clasped hands and hugged. 'It has been a good day of work for you?'

'Jazak Allah,' replied Kamran, 'it has indeed. And you?'

'I have some work to do later tonight. You know how it is,' replied the younger man.

'I do,' said Kamran. 'Mashallah, I do.'

Once the crowd of worshippers dispersed, Kamran walked up to the elderly imam who had led them in prayer. The man had a beard so white it reminded Kamran of a fresh fall of snow on the hills of Swat. Swat had been good. When he had killed there, he had not had to do it in silent houses.

'You took long coming back,' said the old man. He was sitting on a chair which had a green cloth draped on it. He did not look at Kamran as he spoke, eyes weighed shut by wrinkled folds. Kamran sat down on the ground next to him, cross-legged.

'I did not have my tools. It slowed me.'

As the last of the greeters left, the old man turned to Kamran and appraised him.

'It is done then? Good.'

'Next time, at least let me take my tools with me. Why did you not just get one of these children to do it?'

The old man smiled.

'Because they ask questions. Always questions with these boys. Was he a Shia? Is she an Ahmedi? Did he blaspheme? What is to be gained? So many questions. They do as they are told, but always need to be told why. I have no patience for that. You never ask questions. You do as you are told. I wonder, does that make you obedient or stupid?'

Kamran shrugged.

'Does it matter?'

The old man chuckled at that, although it sounded more like a cough. He patted Kamran's cheek – it felt like autumn leaves were brushing past him. 'No, I suppose it does not. Go. Rest. If we have need of you, we will call. After all, there are still many messages we have to send.'

Kamran stood up, then bent to kiss the old man lightly on his forehead. Climbing the three flights of stairs up to his apartment, he unlocked his front door and walked in, flipping on the light switch. The narrow hallway inside his apartment brightened as a bulb came on, flickering slightly as it strained to find enough voltage. The hallway led into a room with a small TV, sofa and chairs all arranged neatly in a circle. On the sofa, regarding him coolly, was a man Kamran had never seen before. In a single, smooth motion, he lifted his kameez and pulled out the gun he had tucked into the waistband of his shalwar, levelling it at the man on the sofa.

'Who are you?' he said through clenched teeth.

The man raised his hands, palms out. Kamran narrowed his eyes, peering over the gunsight. The room was dim, the light in the hallway fading as it approached the stranger, leaving him nestled in shadows.

'Who are you?' Kamran repeated, moving into the room. He allowed himself a glance to make sure there was no one else in there, finding the corners of the room empty. Just as he was about to advance further, the gun was snatched from his grip. Kamran was a large man with big hands that were not used to releasing something unless he decided to give it up, but the gun was plucked so effortlessly, he might as well have been a child. Then the light bulb behind him flickered again and shorted. Darkness filled the room. Behind him, the bulb exploded with a crystalline pop.

None of this disturbed Kamran. His nerves had been blunted and set in iron long ago. Instead, guessing that whoever took the gun from him would be to his left, he swung out with the empty hand, still curled in a fist. It sailed through the air with speed and force, but finding nothing to collide with, simply caused him to stagger. The darkness was complete. The part of his mind that wasn't consumed by rage but always stayed cold and analytical noted that the room should not be so dark. He was used to the power failing, as was everyone else in Karachi. And always, within a few seconds, ambient light from outside – be it from distant signage or the moon – allowed for some relief. But this time there was none.

'What is this?' he bellowed. 'If you have come to kill me, then try already instead of dodging about in the bhenchod darkness.'

'Please, calm yourself,' said a voice, from the direction of where the man had been sitting. It was a soft voice, calm and conversational. 'If I had wanted you dead, then you would have been so the moment you entered.'

His fists still raised, Kamran stared into the darkness.

'Then what do you want?'

There was no reply. Instead, a match lit ahead of him. First one. Then another. Except the flames from the matchheads burned sideways, like small flickering eyes. Nor did they offer any illumination, their light seemingly contained entirely within them. More flames appeared, erupting all around. He lowered his fists and stared stupidly at the burning slits, as though the darkness in the room had somehow been cut in places with a fine knife and a blaze that existed behind it was peeking through. Kamran tried to move towards one of these, but found that neither his hands nor his feet would respond to his will. They stayed firmly in place, as though held there by taut chains he could not feel.

'Are you sure this is the one?' asked the man's voice, still relaxed and casual.

'The one what?' replied Kamran, straining against whatever had bound him, but finding no give. 'Who are you? Fucking let me go or I will tear off your head and –'

'Oh, shut up for a second,' snapped the man. It was said with mild irritation, as if to a noisy child. If Kamran could have freed his hands then, he would have wrapped them around the man's throat and pressed down with all his strength.

Then a voice replied to the man. It was a voice that Kamran didn't hear so much as feel. It resonated deep within him, like a vibration that hurt his teeth and buzzed in his skull. It was not a low voice, nor a high one, but seemed to be both at once. It sounded almost like two drills, one embedded in concrete and the other in wood, both working simultaneously.

'It is him,' said the voice. 'We saw him some time ago putting out a man's eyes with his thumbs in a room of a house that we had made our home. The victim cried and prayed for mercy, but this man gave none. Once dead, he cut off his cock with a knife.'

Kamran felt nauseous, just listening somehow disorienting him. The meagre contents of his stomach churned menacingly.

The voice continued, seeming to come from everywhere at once. 'Then, this one placed the genitals in the mouth of the dead man. It is him. We remember.'

'Well,' said the voice of the man who was still sitting in front of Kamran, 'that is quite the recommendation. You seem exactly like the kind of person I need.'

Kamran gave up struggling and relaxed his muscles. Turning his head in the direction of the man's voice, he said, 'You want my fucking help? Why should I help you? I will fucking kill you, kafir son of a whore.'

The man laughed in the darkness. 'I'm sure we can think of some way to convince you. Then you will find a boy for us.'

The flames grew larger as they moved closer and he understood for the first time that they were not suspended in the air at all, but were eyes on faces. Kamran screamed for the first time in his life.

X.

The rickshaw puttered to a stop in front of Wahid's house, belching grey smoke. Thinking about anything had been impossible on the ride back, the assault-rifle clatter of the engine, along with the mass quantities of exhaust he had inhaled, had left him with a pulsing headache and a growing constriction in his chest. He paid the rickshaw driver and felt in his pocket for the inhaler. He then realized he had left it in his room. It was the first time he could remember having left the house without it. That realization unnerved him more than he had thought it would. He'd always wished for the day when he would no longer be dependent on it. Yet now it just seemed like one more seismic shift in a world already careening recklessly around him. This was intensified when he looked around him and saw how empty and dark the street was. He rushed inside.

The sense of panic passed as soon as he entered the house itself, a visible shiver that was shed like wet clothes. He had seen Imran chacha's car in the driveway behind his mother's and could hear them talking in the drawing room.

Grabbing his inhaler off his desk and puffing on it deeply, he walked back down to find Imran chacha, Batool chachi and his mother sitting quietly. They all stared at him solemnly, concern written on their faces in neon lettering.

'Where have you been?' asked Mumtaz, motioning for him to seat himself on the couch next to her.

'I just had some things to check. I was with Hamza,' he answered, flopping down next to her.

'Wahid, beta, there is something we need to tell you,' said Imran chacha, putting down his cup of tea and leaning forward.

'Okay,' said Wahid.

Before Imran chacha could start, however, his mother began to weep. He turned to her and put his arm around her, telling her everything would be all right.

'Wahid, that girl –', began Imran chacha.

'Maheen. Her name is Maheen.'

'Yes. Maheen. She is still in a coma. I'm sure you know.'

'I heard,' he said softly.

'Well, her father is a retired general. He was the previous corps commander of Karachi, did you know that?'

His mother was still sobbing, he felt her shivering against his arm.

'I know,' he repeated, his voice still barely a whisper.

'Wahid … the father is, well, he's angry. Really angry. He wants the police to arrest you. And even if they don't, we … we don't know what else he might do. He is very powerful, Wahid. Do you understand me?'

Wahid nodded. 'What should I do?'

'You shouldn't do anything at all,' said Imran chacha, glancing at his wife who instantly stood up from her seat and crossed over to Mumtaz, crouching down next to her and squeezing her hand.

'I have a few friends in the police. They told me they're being pressured into arresting you. I delayed them until tomorrow, but I won't be able to do more than that.'

'Should I … should I turn myself in?' asked Wahid, fighting the dizziness that shaded the peripheries of his vision.

'No!' exclaimed Mumtaz suddenly, loud enough that they all jumped.

'No, no,' repeated Imran chacha, trying to bring his voice down to a comforting tone. 'Not at all. If you do that then Allah knows what will happen. No, you need to leave home for a while. Until I can calm things down.'

'Leave home ...' repeated Wahid.

'Yes. Maybe in a few days that Maheen girl will recover. It could happen. And I can talk to the General through some common friends, try to convince him that it wasn't your fault.'

'But ...' he began, 'but I can't leave. Not now. I ... I need to find a way to help her.'

'Wahid, please listen to Imran,' said his mother, finally composing herself.

'You aren't a surgeon or a doctor, Wahid, there's nothing you can do. Her father has a lot of money and he's getting top surgeons and doctors to care for her. In the meantime, you can help yourself and your Ammi by staying safe.'

'But where will I go?' asked Wahid. He started to think of characters in books and movies who fled their countries to escape threats to their lives. They all jumped on planes and flew to obscure European or South American countries. He didn't have any visas ready.

'I have a hut on the beach. It's a small house really. Bathroom, generator for electricity, even a fridge. You've been there a few times in the past, I think?'

Wahid stared at him, then at his mother.

'The beach? But can't the General find me there? The police can, surely?'

'They won't know where you've gone. We won't tell them and it will buy some time for me to sort things out. You'll be comfortable there, meanwhile. I have a housekeeper who can cook and take care of you.'

'How'll I get there?' asked Wahid, realizing that none of this was being offered to him. The decision had been made.

'You can go in my car. I'll have my driver drop you off. Just before morning, I think. Best time to not be seen. Rahat, the man who takes care of the hut, will meet you and let you in. Stay there for a few days. It's the best option right now.'

Imran, Batool and his mother stayed in the drawing room and let him go upstairs. Wahid sat on the edge of the bed in his room for several minutes, staring blankly ahead. Then he picked up his cell phone and dialled Hamza's number.

'I have to go into bloody hiding,' he said, trying to keep from letting his anger turn to tears. He explained the details as told to him by Imran chacha and found that repeating them only increased his rage.

'Look, I see what they mean,' said Hamza. 'Everyone I talk to from school is saying that Maheen's dad will probably have you picked up and shot or something. I don't know if it's true but who wants to stick around and find out, yeah?'

'But what about Maheen? What about what I saw? I need to … I need to find out what happened to her. I need to find the … the djinns and find out what they did to her. I can help her.'

'Well, you can't do that with some general kicking you to death,' reasoned Hamza. 'Look, don't get angry, but are you even sure that … you know, it happened that way.'

Wahid collapsed on his bed, pinching the bridge of his nose with his fingers and exhaling slowly.

'I don't know any more. I know what I saw and what happened. But it doesn't make any sense. The mullah at the mazaar said there aren't any djinns around. He said he could see them once, but not any more. But they must be around. They attacked me, didn't they?'

'Listen,' said Hamza, 'I just realized. You've been running around the city all day. Now you are off to the beach alone. What if they attack you again?'

Wahid considered this for a second, then softly said, 'I can kill them, right?'

Hamza giggled on the other end of the line.

'Boy, you suck at sounding tough.'

'Fuck you,' said Wahid, the smile feeling like finding something he'd lost long ago.

'And you can finally curse. Man! Arif would have loved to be here for this.'

'Yeah, he would,' said Wahid. 'I miss him.'

'I miss him too, man. We'll never know how Chantilly's adventures ended.'

'Probably with an orc head in one hand and a flagon of ale in the other. Bountiful bosom heaving.'

They laughed at that. Hamza promised to email Wahid as much information on djinns as he could find online, though Wahid pointed out that it was unlikely that Imran chacha's beach hut would be wired for Internet. Wahid said goodbye and began to pack his suitcase.

XI.

The drive to the beach took less than an hour, with Imran chacha's driver speeding through empty predawn streets. The skyline sloped downwards in a gradient curve; high office buildings and apartments giving way to factories that descended into shops and finally all of it resolving into flat stretches of sand. The roads deteriorated rapidly, the car bouncing over uneven patches of crushed rock covered with a thin veil of tar. The driver was finally forced to slow down when the road narrowed into a single lane, closed shops on either side. Everyone in Karachi made regular pilgrimages to the beach, although those journeys were usually longer affairs made later in the day, with much squeezing through gaps between container trucks and risking cell phone robberies. He knew that every shop had been purposed to serve the mass of Karachiites driving daily to the oceanfront and they all provided large tin iceboxes filled with soft drinks and neatly bagged food. He saw with some relief that there were even a few Internet cafes, never having noticed them before.

When the ocean did appear on one side, it was glimpsed mostly through the spaces between private huts. They pulled up in front of one such hut, raising a great cloud of dust around them as the car skidded to a stop. Wahid covered his nose with the crook of his elbow and got out, the driver having already sprinted around to the back of the car and pulled Wahid's suitcase from the trunk.

Wahid had been to the hut before, sometimes with Hamza and Arif, a few times with his mother when Imran chacha had invited them all for a barbecue. A rusted tin gate opened onto a courtyard just large enough for two cars. Beyond that was a single-storey brick house with a front patio that ran straight onto the soft brown sand. When the tide was high, the water almost reached up to that patio. Wahid could hear the roar of waves churning beyond.

Rahat the hut keeper was an old man, stooped forward not as much by age as he was by an impressively large nose. He easily hefted Wahid's suitcase and led him inside. The interior was cool blue, with a fine sprinkling of sand over every surface. They passed through a small kitchen and then climbed up a tightly spiralling staircase to the bedroom.

'You want breakfast now?' grunted Rahat in a voice raked over by a lifetime of cigarettes and tea.

'In an hour, please, I want to take a nap first,' replied Wahid. Rahat shrugged and walked out, closing the door behind him. Wahid sat on the bed and sighed, looking out at the ocean beyond the window. He was soon asleep.

XII.

'You know this is a dream, right?' Maheen said from the passenger seat. Wahid was gripping the steering wheel so tightly his knuckles had whitened. He turned to look at her, sitting next to him. She was dressed the way she had been when he last saw her, her face smiling and clean.

'He knowssh,' said Arif from the back seat. His voice was slurred, his speech slowed. It could have been because he was drunk, or possibly because his lower jaw was hanging loose, twisted to the side like a thermos lid. Wahid glanced at Arif in the rear-view mirror and saw him wink back at him with the eye that wasn't smashed and bloody.

'I know,' said Wahid. He turned his attention back on the road. Black asphalt raced above them, the sky below it. The car was travelling upside down, yet responding to every incremental adjustment to the steering wheel that Wahid made. The sun was rising slowly up towards the horizon that bisected his view.

'I'm sorry I killed you,' said Wahid.

'You didn't kill us,' answered Maheen, touching his cheek lightly with her fingers.

'I'm dead,' pointed out Arif, lying down and resting his feet on the gaping hole in the back window. One foot aimed upwards and the other was twisted round the other way, bone stabbing through the blood-soaked sneakers.

'But it's not your fault,' said Maheen reassuringly.

'I don't know what happened,' said Wahid, turning the steering wheel to follow a curve in the road above.

'Djinn came, car shwent boom, I go bluugh, Maheen goessh eeeh, and you walk away,' said Arif with a snorting laugh.

'But … I didn't mean for it to happen. I don't even know why it happened. And Maheen isn't dead. You aren't, are you?'

'No,' said Maheen, her voice sad. 'No, I'm not. I'm … well … what did they do to me, Wahid?'

'I think they … I think they stole your … your soul.'

'Djinns shteal shoul, Maheen goesh eeeh, now you go waaah,' summarized Arif.

'I'll fix this somehow. I promise,' said Wahid.

In the distance, he could see a black speck in the centre of the clean sky. He knew he had to avoid it and so turned the steering wheel around. The car didn't respond, instead continuing to cruise forward, the road above blurring as it picked up speed.

'Good luck with that,' said Maheen. He turned to look at her and saw her face was veiled in blood – a deep gash had opened on her forehead and another sliced across her cheek.

'Eyesh on the road,' said Arif.

Wahid looked ahead and saw a black wall that stretched in every direction. In the centre was a burning hole, like the mouth of a volcano seen from above. The car rushed towards it, moving so fast that both the sky and the road had become solid blurs. Wahid raised his hands to shield his face, screaming against the impending crash.

XIII.

Sunlight snuck in through a gap in the curtain, creating a patch of warmth on the pillow next to Wahid's head. He sat up, rubbing eyes that felt tender. He reached for his cell phone and checked the time. It was afternoon. His stomach growled. The room was damp, the air inside smelling like seaweed. Looking out of the window, he saw tea-coloured sand below, leading up to an ocean speckled with sunlight. A family was picnicking near the water, children splashing ankle-deep as their parents cheered from around a bowl of biryani. He watched them play for a few minutes.

'Your breakfast is cold. Should I heat it up?' asked Rahat from a large rocking chair on the patio below. He was also watching the family ahead, yet had somehow known Wahid was in the window overhead.

'Yes. Actually, no. There are shops nearby, right? I'll walk down. Stretch my legs.'

Rahat shrugged and went back to staring ahead. Wahid pulled on his sneakers and went downstairs.

'Which way should I go?' asked Wahid.

Rahat clucked in annoyance and then pointed north. 'Shops are that way. Fifteen-minute walk. Many places to eat there.' Then he pointed south and said, 'That way no shops. A few huts only.'

Wahid left, walking to the road behind the hut with his head down. Trucks careened past and a van full of riotous teenagers slowed just long enough for everyone inside to jeer and yell incomprehensibly at him. By the time he realized that it was too hot and the distance much greater than he had anticipated, it was too late to turn back.

It took him close to half an hour to reach the shops, after swallowing enough sand to coat his tongue, sweating through his T-shirt. There were convenience stores packed next to one another, an assortment of chai cafes, and even a gym advertised with a faded poster of Arnold Schwarzenegger. He found a small cafe with cane chairs arranged around plastic tables and sat down. A man with a Hitler moustache and purple shalwar kameez took his order and returned some minutes later with a plate of grease spotted with a few lumps of chicken. Steaming hot naans were piled onto another plate next to it.

After cleaning up the grease with the last scraps of naan, Wahid explored the rest of the shops. There was a small bookshop near the far end and he went inside, finding a narrow interior divided in half by a glass counter. Most of the books displayed were Urdu digests and religious texts, with hard covers in bright primary colours and curling typographic titles. The English shelves were mostly full of old Robert Ludlum and Stephen King novels. A stack of withering comics, most of their interior pages brown with dust and neglect, lay at the bottom of one shelf. He flicked through them absently, thinking of the rows of fanatically maintained comics that were probably still stacked up in Arif's bedroom.

'Is there anything you want?' asked the shopkeeper, glaring at Wahid accusingly from behind the counter. He was thin with large round spectacles and neatly combed white hair. He was looking at Wahid as though he had caught him in the act of trying to read every book in the store without paying for any of them.

'I'm looking for a book on djinns,' said Wahid defensively.

'Those are comics.' The shopkeeper sniffed. He turned to the shelf behind him and started scanning the titles arranged there. 'English or Urdu?'

'Either is fine,' said Wahid. He walked up and studied the books as well, clapping the dust off his hands.

The shopkeeper stared at his stock for a while and then pulled a thin book from a shelf just above him. He turned and handed it to Wahid, wiping the cover clean against his own kameez before he did.

'*The Signs of Qiyamat*,' read Wahid aloud. 'Sorry, I said djinns. Not this.'

The shopkeeper seemed to have lost all interest in Wahid. He had picked up a rag attached to a thin bamboo stick and begun beating at the books on the higher shelves. Great quantities of dust rose as he did. 'This is all I have,' said the shopkeeper. 'It has djinns in it. Leave it if you don't want it.'

Wahid paid in cash and took the book. Tucking it under his arm, he set off in search of a cybercafe. He found one tucked away between a soft drink shop and a small aqua-green mosque. Inside were a dozen computers on a single long desk, each separated by a small frosted glass partition. A few of them had men hunched in front, typing into Facebook chat windows. Wahid sat down at the nearest computer and logged into his own Facebook page. There were no new messages for him and so he wrote to Hamza, asking if there was any update on Maheen's health. Then, moving over to Google, he began to search for more information on djinns.

The same results opened up that he had read two nights before. He skimmed the Wikipedia entry, searching it for any relevant information:

Djinn

The **Djinn** (Arabic: جن ǧinn, singular جني ǧinnī; also spelled **jinn**), or **genies**, are spirits mentioned in the Qur'ān and Islamic theology who inhabit an unseen world in dimensions beyond the visible universe of humans. Together, the jinn, humans and angels make up the three sentient creations of God. The Qur'an mentions that the jinn are made of a smokeless and 'scorching fire', and they have the physical property of weight. Like human beings, the jinn can also be good, evil, or neutrally benevolent and hence have freewill like humans and unlike angels. The jinn are mentioned frequently in the Qur'an, and the 72nd surah is titled *Sūrat al-Djinn*.

He clicked on the hyperlink that led him to the Quranic surah and read a description of it. Wahid had studied the Quran, but the entire reading had been in Arabic. According to the Wikipedia summary, the Quranic chapter detailed how djinns also believed in Allah and how they were disgusted with humans for the acts of blasphemy that they committed. Then it explained that even djinns knew nothing of the Day of Judgement:

'I know not whether the (Punishment) which we are promised is near, or whether my Lord will appoint for it a distant term.'

Returning to the Google page, he read the IMDb summary of a French film in which soldiers in Africa come across a djinn and fight it. There were links to a brand of running shoes named Djinns Chunky, and some blogs written by people discussing personal experiences with djinns. Wahid read these and found nothing that was similar to his own. Most of it was someone claiming to have relatives who could talk to djinns or having seen them in trees or abandoned buildings. There were no descriptions of figures made of darkness, with eyes full of flame, that crushed cars and exploded when touched.

He tried another Google search, this time typing *how to kill a djinn* and ended up on a discussion forum for a role-playing game that featured djinns in the menagerie of mythical creatures. The illustrations showed genies emerging from ornate lamps, with curling beards and immense bellies wrapped in cummerbunds.

Wahid stretched in his chair, arching his back and rubbing his face. One of the boys next to him lit a cheap cigarette and the acrid smoke forced Wahid into a coughing fit. He paid for his Internet usage and left, stepping back out into the growing crowd outside. The smell of the sea was buried under a thick layer of petrol and exhaust, the street in front choked with traffic. Wahid set off for the hut, his book tucked under his arm.

XIV.

Kamran considered torturing the boy's mother. Any other time he would have. It was something he had been required to do before and he considered it a fairly direct way of finding out information. But to do so, this time, was more than he could bear. This was because of what the man and the creatures in his employ had done to him. When the lights had come back on and Kamran had been left alone, shivering in a foetal ball with his arms wrapped around his knees and vomit dripping from his chin, he had cried.

He believed in djinns; to not would have been against the dictates of Islam, and Kamran always considered himself a devout man. Yet, to have them play with his thoughts like children exploring a pile of old toys, their fingers pressing into his mind, into the very thoughts themselves … that was more confirmation of belief than he'd needed.

They'd picked apart his memories, leaving charred fingerprints across his life. Then, when they found the memory of a murder or rape that satisfied their needs, they had used it against him, branding him like cattle with the details sizzling on his flesh. He had experienced each kill, each violation, not as he remembered them, but as his victims had suffered them. He felt bullets tunnelling through his throat and eye, bullets that had killed an Ahmedi fruit seller with when Kamran was thirteen, under the instructions of the man responsible for the madrasa where he had grown up. His insides were cleaved by the recollection of a

Christian girl he had raped when sixteen, her skin soft under his teeth. The sensation of a knife slicing upwards from crotch to neck, mechanical drills biting and chewing through his kneecaps and elbows. More rape, so much more murder. He had screamed until all that came from his throat was blood, and shit and urine poured down his legs. When it was finally, mercifully over, the flames in the darkness had blinked out in pairs, eyes closing to leave him in pitch-blackness. Then the man had spoken again, loudly to be heard over Kamran's whimpering, and given him the name of a boy he had to find and kill. Kamran had begged then, asking that he never have to kill again, but the man had laughed and told him not to embarrass himself. Then Kamran was left alone.

Standing in the darkness of the boy's house and thinking back on what he had been made to suffer and how he had begged like the weak pieces of shit that he had killed so many times, Kamran hated the man. His anger needed vent and his hands itched to give it release, but contemplating more violence was beyond him for the moment. Walking in socks so that his footsteps made no noise, he waited in the dark. Once he was sure the boy's mother was asleep, he ascended the stairs carefully and went into the boy's empty room. There he found evidence of a hurried departure: a stack of clothes piled on the bed, a cupboard full of empty hangers. He turned on the computer, the brightness of the screen filling the room and stinging his eyes. He opened the browser and looked at the recent history. It was full of links leading to articles about djinns. He pulled the cord out from behind the computer, killing it suddenly and silently.

His torchlight scanned the rest of the room, stopping on a picture frame lying on his desk. It showed three young boys. He picked Wahid immediately, having researched the boy during the day. Of the other two, one he guessed must have been the friend who had died in the car crash, about which he had read in the news articles provided to him by a military officer in his employ. He plugged the computer back in and switched it on. Once it was connected to the Internet, he opened the browser and directed it to Facebook, praying for the password to be saved. He thanked Allah when he saw a series of asterisks displayed where the password was needed and hit the Enter key. The screen filled with pictures of teenagers. There was an unread message in the inbox and he opened it. The thumbnail photo accompanying the most recent message was that of the other boy, the one not dead. Kamran memorized his name, then scanned the content of the message. The message asked about the beach, which gave Kamran a location for Wahid. Still, he needed an address; there were thousands of huts and houses along Karachi's coastline. He considered walking into the woman's room and using her to fill the gaps in his knowledge. But he knew it was too soon for him to return to his habits.

Instead, he would talk to the boy named Hamza. It was easier to kill a boy than a woman. Women felt pain differently than men. That much he had learned. And he never wanted to experience that again.

XV.

Sleep didn't come easily to Wahid. He lay in bed and stared up at the fan paddling overhead for close to an hour. He tried to read the book he had bought, but found it poorly written and not very helpful. It was – as he had pointed out to the shopkeeper – not about djinns at all, but about how Judgement Day was nigh as confirmed by signs that were evident to any who were true to Islam. The writer seemed desperate to convey his concerns that the clock ticking down the hours of human existence was close to midnight. There were signs of Qiyamat quoted and then demystified: 'Naked, destitute, barefoot shepherds will compete in constructing tall buildings,' was one such prediction, recorded by those who had lived during the time of the Prophet. The writer had pointed hysterically at Dubai. Other predictions were more vague and thus even easier to explain, such as 'Knowledge will be taken away and ignorance will prevail' and 'Illegal sexual intercourse will become widespread'.

Wahid found the chapter on One-eyed Dajjal, the Islamic anti-Christ, interesting. He remembered the stories his Islamiyat teacher had furnished them with in seventh grade, of a creature with a single eye who would perform miracles that fooled those with weak faith. Only the true followers of Islam would be able to see through his deception. They would be able to see the letters KFR on his forehead, which stood for Kafir. Then she informed the classroom full of enthralled children that Dajjal was an analogy for the Israeli air force, which had KFR written on the tail of each jet. The writer, however, believed Dajjal to be a metaphor for television, with the large screens transmitting lies and sin serving as the single eye.

There was also a chapter on the Yajuj–Majuj, an army of savage creatures who would destroy everything in their path. They had been walled up by an ancient king and would escape when the final days were near. The writer explained that this referred to the Mongol invaders who pillaged the Islamic world centuries ago. Discrepancies in the timeline of events were not addressed. About djinns there was only the clarification that even they would be judged on the final day, their good deeds and bad stacked up before them just as they would be for the humans.

Kicking off the blanket to stay cool, he thought about the attack yet again. The djinns had seemed to be targeting Wahid and yet they hadn't returned. But he was still no closer to learning why they had come for him at all, nor why he could kill them with a touch.

'You know, you think too much,' said Maheen.

Wahid turned his head and saw she was lying next to him on the bed, her head resting on a pillow. She had pulled the blanket up to her chin and was offering a smile that was pure cheer. Wahid lifted himself up on his elbow and glanced around the room.

'Where's Arif?' he asked.

'Oh, he moved on,' she replied. 'Told me to tell you to avenge him, but more importantly to keep his comics safe.'

Wahid lay back down and faced her. Seeing her face filled him with a mad panic to undo whatever had been done to her.

'Oh please, you don't even know what the djinn did,' she said, sounding like a kindergarten teacher playfully scolding a child. 'And even if you did, what could you possibly do to help me?'

'I could find them and make them give back your … your soul.'

'Well, finding them seems a bit impossible. Besides, they tried to kill you. You should stay as far away from them as possible.'

'I don't care. I want them to try killing me again. Then I can find out what's going on. And I can save you and –' Wahid felt embarrassed by what he had just stopped himself from saying.

'And you can finally ask me out?' offered Maheen. 'Then we'll date and become college sweethearts and afterwards you can marry me and we will live happily ever after and have lots of babies.'

'That's ...' whispered Wahid, his ears growing hot, '... not what I was gonna say. I mean, kind of.'

'Oh Wahid,' said Maheen, sitting up in the bed. The blanket fell away and he could see a softly transparent body, ribs and spine glowing neon-white beneath the glassy skin. She pulled the edge of the blanket up to her neck and smiled at him, a grinning skull staring out from under the skin of her face.

'I'm just a dream and you're still too scared to ask me out. Maybe the djinns did you a favour by knocking me out.'

'You're not a dream,' he said firmly. 'I will save your soul.'

Maheen laughed. 'Okay, so if I'm not a dream, ask me something only I would know.'

'What's your favourite book?' said Wahid.

'Oh please, like you haven't stalked my Facebook profile a thousand times. It's *World War Z*, the original book, not that terrible movie. What if I had said, something by Paulo Coelho or *The Secret*? What would you have done then?'

'Probably given up the search for your soul right away.' Wahid grinned.

'Okay, let's try something only I would really know,' she said, raising an eyebrow. He found it irresistible despite the hollowed darkness behind her eyes. 'How about this? My name is Maheen I. Janjua. What does the I stand for?'

Wahid didn't reply but instead turned to consider the ceiling again. The rest of his sleep was dreamless.

XVI.

Two days of inactivity followed. Wahid would wake to the smell of salt and the sound of battering surf. He would eat breakfast served up by Rahat and then spend some time walking along the beach. Karachi's skyline could be seen clearly in the morning, geometric silhouettes set against the curving horizon, off to one side. The rest of his view was pure ocean, stretching for parsecs without interruption. Whenever he spotted a family playing in the sand, he would cut a wide arc around them. It was paranoid behaviour, but when you were being hunted by an enraged general, paranoia wasn't just an abstract concept. In the afternoon, he walked to the shops for lunch and to surf the Internet. He decided against logging into his Facebook account and email, maybe the General hadn't brought the full services of a tracking unit into place, but why risk it. He purchased the stack of withering comics from the unhappy shopkeeper, who glared at Wahid as though he was being asked to surrender some aspect of personal integrity. In the evening, he sat on the patio, cooled by the damp breeze to a marginal chill and read them. They were random issues of random stories, disconnected from their larger plots; two *Action Comics*, almost fifty issues apart; a selection of various *Spiderman* titles, each in the middle of their own storylines. It was like finding the fourteenth chapter of a novel and only having that to read over and over.

The Internet searches revealed no further information on djinns that could be of help. Imran chacha called once on Rahat's phone and told Wahid that Maheen was still in a coma and the police had finally taken out an arrest warrant. The stay would be longer than he had hoped and he would send some more of Wahid's clothes through the driver.

A fisherman's boat was moored in the sand near the hut, a hollowed curve of wood with chipped red paint, and Wahid climbed into it and brooded. He abandoned the boat when he spotted a sea snake creeping along its bow. At night, he walked along the moonlit beach, a haze of spray obscuring the pulsing lights of the distant city. He glared at them, willing them to turn into eyes of flame.

A storm appeared on the third day, rendering the sky gunmetal grey. Clouds roiled like immense snakes and the ocean reflected their mood, hissing waves snapping at the beachfront. By the time he finished eating breakfast, it was raining. A spastic drumming beat out against the tin roof, and Wahid sat on the balcony, watching shifting curtains of rain consume the horizon. The beach was empty and he knew it would remain that way – the roads connecting it to Karachi would be swallowed by water.

It occurred to Wahid that he was definitely going to miss the A-level exams. This realization added to the sense of panic that had become a consistent migraine. In the evening, with the rain persisting, he jogged up and down the stairs to alleviate the monotony. After his eighth descent, he felt out of breath and so he went to find his inhaler and sit on the balcony again. Wahid thought he would not last more than another day or two of this loneliness. It filled the air around him, not with silence, but the persistent hiss of a radio tuned to a dead channel.

The rain finally abated at night, leaving a cool mist that smudged the moon. He pulled on a jacket and told Rahat he was going for a walk.

'Do not go far, it is not safe at night,' said the old man, offering more words in that warning than he had said all day.

Wahid decided to explore the area in the opposite direction of the shops. The road had turned into a shallow river, trash swirling in its current and so he walked on the raised sidewalk, careful to avoid any bushes and rocks he might trip over. A single street light flickered ahead, haloed in the fine spray.

The road curved away from the beach, huts growing more infrequent. The evening had turned cold and he pushed his hands into the pockets of his jeans. After ten minutes or so he passed the last of the huts, metal gates attended to by a guard wrapped in a shawl so tightly that only his nose showed. Wahid continued past him, thinking only of exams he would not give and the home he could not go back to until Imran chacha had found a way to calm Maheen's father or Maheen woke up from her coma.

The road sloped upwards just as the sidewalk disintegrated to rubble, so he stepped onto it and picked up his pace. He turned around to see how far he had gone and saw that the route back was completely hidden behind a wall of mist. It had grown so thick that the last hut was no longer visible. Practised paranoia about running out of breath took hold of him and he focused on breathing slowly and evenly. He began to walk back, counting the crunch of his shoes on the wet road and trying to average a single deep breath for every two footsteps.

Then he heard a second pair of footsteps behind him. He turned and peered into the darkness. His entire body tightened, every muscle tensing, as he felt sure the fog would part to reveal figures made of blackness rushing towards him. Wahid braced himself, pulling his hands free of his jacket and bunching them into fists. A lone woman walked into visible range. He relaxed. She was moving carefully, head bowed and an ornately patterned red shawl pulled low over her forehead. She was dressed, despite the cold, in a sari made of the same red cloth as her shawl, golden trimmings sewn in paisley patterns all along the edges. Tiny bells on the hem of her shawl gave every step a tinkling applause. The hands that held the sides of the shawl pulled over her mouth were decorated with henna.

She reached him and looked up, a pair of wide eyes outlined with thick kohl emerging from under the shawl.

'Bhai,' she said in a sweetly soft voice. 'Is it safe to walk this way? I need to return home.'

Wahid tried to make sure he was smiling as pleasantly as he could and replied, 'If you like, baji, I can walk with you so no one bothers you. I was heading back that way myself.'

She nodded and they began to descend the hilly road together, their footsteps echoing loudly in the thick miasma. After they had walked in silence for some time – Wahid trying to observe the rules of propriety by not looking at her too obviously – she said, 'Why are you walking alone so late at night?'

'I just felt like enjoying the weather,' explained Wahid. 'Are you returning from a wedding?'

'Yes,' she said. 'I was at a wedding.' Her voice was thin and quivering, like a figurine made of fine blown glass that would shatter if held too tightly.

'Oh, that's nice,' said Wahid.

They walked on in silence, she a few feet behind him. Wahid returned to focusing on his breathing and counting his steps. It was more difficult as the sound of her footsteps distracted him from his own. She was walking, from the sound of it, much faster than he was, with each step coming almost instantly after the previous one. Yet, she seemed to be keeping a steady pace behind him, the soft padding of bare feet setting a metronomic rhythm. He looked up and saw the fog was thicker, so opaque that he could no longer even see the moon. If he was near the huts he had passed on the way up, he had no way of knowing; the world had become featureless. Wahid looked over his shoulder and found that the girl was no longer visible, swallowed by the dense atmosphere, though he could still hear the footsteps and the soft tinkling of bells.

'Baji,' he called out, 'the fog is very thick. I'll wait for you to catch up.'

There was no reply, just the sound of her walking towards him. Then even that stopped. It didn't dissolve as it would have had she passed him, but stopped abruptly.

'It was my wedding,' she said from behind him somewhere. Her voice was low yet clear and she could have been next to him or far away, there was no way of telling.

'Baji …' said Wahid again, his own voice betraying nerves that had begun to fray.

'I looked so beautiful,' she continued, her voice echoing. 'And my husband was handsome. So handsome.'

Fear coiled up Wahid's spine. He called to her again, but his own voice came out as barely a whisper. She continued, soft and full of mourning.

'He took me home.' She sighed. 'To his home. To our home.'

Wahid didn't want to hear the rest. His mind urged him to run, to flee into the fog with all the speed and strength he could find. But he could not move, rooted to the middle of the road as though the fog was holding him in place. *Maybe*, said a part of him, fighting back the panic, *maybe you've found what you've been looking for. Maybe she's a djinn.*

'Are you a djinn?' whispered Wahid, his throat clenched so tight he could barely even manage that.

The bells chimed again, not gently but with a frantic clamour. She came out of the fog, a blur of red and gold charging towards him, hands curled into claws. Wahid saw eyes black with hate and bared teeth. She'd been far away, but the distance closed in an instant. She ran on feet that Wahid already knew were twisted the wrong way. Screaming as she covered the last few feet between them, her voice was the growl of something old and angry. Wahid threw his arms up with a wail.

The impact never came.

Wahid lowered his arms slowly. She stood in front of him, perfectly still. The shawl had fallen off her head and she was staring at him. Long strands of black hair crossed her face like scars. Where there should have been eyes, were the deep holes of a skull. Her lips were pulled back in a snarl, showing jagged shards of pale glass instead of teeth. Dread and revulsion consumed every atom in Wahid's body. To his surprise, he didn't run.

'Are you a djinn?' he repeated.

The eyes, empty like a freshly dug grave, narrowed.

'What are *you*?' the creature in front of him asked.

'I … I am a boy. I mean, I am a man,' said Wahid. He could smell her, he realized. She smelt of old roses, withered and dying.

She moved towards him, hands still by her side. The hem of her sari lifted a bit as she did and Wahid saw a heel briefly peek out from under it. As she walked, most of the shawl that had been draped across her shoulders fell to the ground, revealing a blouse black as her eyes. Wahid stared at the skin on her neck and across her collarbones, white without any hint of blood beneath. She reached Wahid, standing just a few inches away from him. She was taller than he had thought, her eyes level with his. He could not bring himself to look into them, feeling that to do so would cause madness. So, he looked down instead and saw the gentle curve of a small pale belly, her midriff exposed under the high edge of the blouse.

'Yes. A man,' she said, the voice still that of a curious girl but blooming with menace. 'But not just a man. Something more. Something different. What are you?'

Wahid glanced up at her face, so close to his that had she any breath, he would have felt it on his face. Instead, there was just the stench of rotting flowers.

'I … I don't know what you mean. Please, are you a djinn?'

She raised one hand and traced the curve of his chin with her finger. 'No, not djinn. Djinns live. I do not.'

Wahid realized with horror that she was not burning. Her finger was not beginning to glow red-hot as the djinn's had when it had touched him. The panic returned in an instant, loud and urgent.

'I'm … I am looking for a djinn,' he said. 'Please don't hurt me.'

Her fingertip lingered on his neck, nail as fine as a blade tracing a line from his chin to his throat.

'Hurt? Men hurt girls.' She sighed. 'My man hurt me. Pressed a pillow to my face and held it there until I could scream and breathe no more. But you are not a man. What are you?'

Wahid closed his eyes and pushed the panic away. 'I'm sorry, I don't know what I am.'

She took a few steps back, again studying him with her head tilted to one side.

'Something new, something strange. You are looking for a djinn? Why?'

'A friend of mine … a girl. She was hurt by djinns. I need to find them to save her.'

Her features softened, the scowl fading so she became more of a woman and less of something that had been hungry.

She took his hand in hers. Her fingers were cold and the skin felt thin, the bones too close to the surface. Something small and hard moved under her palm, tickling his hand lightly. Wahid resisted the need to pull away.

'Tell me,' she said. 'Tell me of the girl.'

Breathing deeply and closing his eyes to keep from looking into hers, he did. He told her of Maheen, of how she had been torn in two by the djinn and now lay dying. How he felt it was his fault as the djinn did it to threaten and punish him. He told her he would do anything to save her and to do so he needed to find the djinn who had hurt her. He said these things slowly at first, but became more relaxed in the telling of it. Recounting the tale seemed to affirm the strangeness that had become his life and somehow – standing there with a woman who said she was dead, with eyes that were holes in her face and who held his hand with her near-skeletal fingers – it seemed more acceptable.

'You love her? Yet you have hurt her. You all hurt us,' said the woman, not with menace, but resignation.

'I guess I did. I didn't mean to, but that doesn't matter. Now I just want to fix things. I just need to find a djinn and I can fix things. I know … I believe I can.'

'Find a djinn,' repeated the woman. She lowered herself to the ground, sitting in the middle of the road on her knees, the sari blooming around her. She still held Wahid's hand and so he too sat down across from her, cross-legged. The gravel on the road poked him in the butt and felt damp. He looked around them, the fog had darkened until everything was shaded charcoal, yet he could see her clearly.

'How can you –' he began to say, when she grabbed his other hand in a movement that was too fast to see and then raised both his palms to her cheeks, placing them on either side of her face.

Wahid felt the forms and shapes of a thousand insects, all moving under the skin. A worm tracked slowly across the cheekbone, its path a raised ripple under his hand. Wahid felt bile rising in his throat and swallowed it.

'Do you know what they call me? Witch, they say. Chudail, sometimes. They think I come to eat their souls because I am evil. Do you know what I am?'

'No,' said Wahid softly. He had grown up hearing stories of women with twisted feet who killed men. Everyone had heard of them. They were said to haunt the roads at night, killing those unlucky enough to stop to help them. He had heard them called pichal pairees – women with turned feet.

'I am what is left of the woman who dies at the hands of men,' she said. 'I am her revenge.'

Her face changed. Eyes swelled in the empty sockets, brilliant white sclera unfurling like the petals of a lily. Fine arteries branched under the surface of her cheeks and forehead, purple and broken. Her cheeks puffed and neck broadened. Bruises patched her skin. She looked very much, Wahid realized, like someone who had just suffocated. The transformation had happened before him, yet it seemed as though it had happened in an instant.

'I am also other women. So many other women.'

The face changed. The bruises dissolved and the skin across her throat pulled apart, sliced by an invisible knife. Dead grey muscle peeked through the gash, which winked and closed again. One eye collapsed inwards, not into the dark well that had been there before, but became smashed, like an overripe fruit thrown against a wall. The eyeball in the centre was round and exposed, glaring out at him. More changes began but Wahid did not see them. Closing his eyes, he screamed.

'I am all these women,' she said. 'And so many more.'

Tears coursed down Wahid's cheeks and he opened his eyes, seeing her as she had originally been. He actually felt relief to see the pale skin and empty eye sockets again. She released Wahid's hands. A spider, as small as a fingernail, crawled out of one socket and she pushed it back in absently.

'I am sorry,' Wahid said, wiping his tears. 'Oh God, I'm so sorry.'

'We will find your friend. Before she becomes one of us,' said the chudail.

She lowered her head, crossed her hands over her breasts and began to hum. Her voice wrapped around them, swaddling them in a blanket of music. She swayed as she hummed. Wahid had never heard the tune before and couldn't seem to capture it in his mind when he tried. Every note was perfectly harmonious, yet it melted away from him the moment she moved on to the next. Wahid stared at her, at the bare shoulders with hardened edges of bone and the swell of the bosom under the blouse. He even found himself swallowing the sight of her midriff, with a dark navel and gentle folds on her stomach. He felt a longing for her and if the music continued much longer, he knew he would not be able to control his need. There was desire in him and with it something lower, something older and more primal. Something male. He wanted to be with her, to be in her. But that wasn't enough, he wanted to hurt her. To take her with force and take from her with anger. Take and take, again and agai –

The humming stopped. Wahid looked up, the haze of lust evaporating in an instant. He was shaking.

'What … what was that?' he gasped. 'Ya Allah, what was that?'

She smiled a knowing smile. 'That was the song of women,' she said. 'It is not meant for men to hear. That you are not dead means you are not a man.' Then, 'I know how you can find a djinn.'

'You do? How?'

'One of my sisters, dead in Kolachi for so long, told me. She died with a child still in her belly, killed by one of the six men who took from her what was not theirs to take.'

Wahid was about to start apologizing again, feeling the guilt of being a man even if she did not believe he was one, but then paused.

'Kolachi? That's … that's the old name of Karachi, isn't it?'

'It is the name she knew it by,' said the chudail.

'What did she say?'

'She says the djinns are gone,' the chudail said. 'The djinns are gone from Kolachi just as they are gone from everywhere. She says, maybe they have left forever. No one knows. But there is one who might help you find them. She says ask the king.'

'The king?'

The chudail stood up, looked down at her sari and began to brush at it with both hands. Wahid stared at her. Her concern over cleanliness of her clothes struck him as the strangest thing that had happened all night.

'You said the king? Which king? The mayor? A minister?'

She straightened up and smiled, cold blue lips curving upwards.

'The King of Karachi. Every city has a king. Just as the birds and rocks and the clouds have kings.'

Wahid rubbed his forehead with a fist, suppressing the need to cry out in frustration.

'But how will I find him? I don't even know who you mean?'

She flicked a speck of gravel from her sari and sighed. 'Ask for him. Ask the forgotten, the poor, the dredges. Ask them and he will find you. You are of Karachi so he will speak to you. Maybe.'

'Okay,' said Wahid contemplatively. 'Okay. The forgotten and poor. There are lots of those in Karachi.'

The chudail moved close to him. She raised her arms and rested her elbows on his narrow shoulders. Her hands pushed into his hair, fingers playing with the curls. She leaned forward, pressing herself against him and brought her lips to his ear.

'Now you must give me something,' she whispered. Her voice was playful and full of flirtation.

Any composure Wahid had dissipated in that instant. He began stammering and sweat broke out across his forehead.

'Did you kiss this girl of yours?' she whispered. The words tickled the inside of his ear and the smell of charnel house roses was overwhelming.

'No, I … I never …' said Wahid. He could feel the soft press of her bosom against his chest. 'I mean, I … no … I've never kissed.'

Her fingers unfurled his curls and then let them spring back. 'Your first kiss then. That is what I will take from you. A boy's first kiss is true. Only later does he learn to lie with it,' she said.

Wahid twitched, his whole body displaying the surprise he felt.

'Okay,' he said.

Wahid closed his eyes, promising himself he wouldn't vomit.

She pressed her lips against his. They felt soft and dry. A scaly tongue pushed gently into his mouth, caressing his own. He tasted dead flowers. Despite himself, he felt his mouth responding, his lips moving against hers. A moan escaped him.

She pulled away with a smile, a finger lightly pressed against her lips. Wahid opened his eyes again. His mouth felt as though all the moisture had been taken from it.

Then she turned and began to walk away.

'Wait,' Wahid called out, 'who … who was your husband? The man who hurt you? Maybe I can help?'

She stopped and glanced over her shoulder at him, pulling her shawl over her head as she did.

'He is dead,' she said, 'he died long ago.' Then, with sadness, she continued, 'I did not get to kill him.'

The fog swallowed her.

Wahid turned and ran back, not stopping until he reached the hut.

XVII.

Hamza screamed. Kamran pushed the tip of the knife into the brown flesh under Hamza's nipple. As he did, he imagined the tiny bursts of pain that must be popping in the boy's nerves and discovered that he too craved for this pain.

'Please, oh God, please don't,' gasped Hamza, a skein of drool across his chin and lips. He was hanging from a beam, a rope tied around his wrists. His hands were pink and swollen as the weight of his full body pulled against them. His naked torso was pinpricked with red beads and a thin line of blood tracked from the centre of his chest down to the hem of his jeans. His feet, dangling a few inches off the ground, dripped urine. Kamran had hung him up while he was unconscious and hadn't said a word to him yet.

They were in an empty room of an abandoned house he used for just such work. Kamran, since he first discovered the place some years before, had killed over a dozen men here.

'Why are you doing this?' pleaded Hamza. 'Who are you? Wh … oh God, why are you doing this?'

Kamran didn't answer, instead he took out a fresh pack of cigarettes from his kameez pocket. He pulled one out, closing one eye against the lighter's flame as he lit it. Hamza wept in high wailing sounds. Kamran pulled hard on the cigarette, then he took it out of his mouth, held it in front of his face and blew on the tip. Tendrils of smoke jerked and vanished under his breath, and the ochre glow of the burning cigarette deepened to a strawberry red. He moved forward, put one hand over Hamza's mouth and pressed the tip of the cigarette against the cut under Hamza's nipple. The boy screamed into his hand. Kamran sighed, ecstasy writ on his face.

Once the screaming died down, he removed his hand and examined it. Hamza must have bitten it because he could see a neat row of indentations on the side of his palm. Kamran sniffed, amused by how little pain it took for the boy to suffer.

'My parents aren't rich,' Hamza whimpered, 'but please, just call them. They'll give you whatever you ask for. Just … please don't hurt me any more.'

Kamran ignored the boy's cries and continued to examine the bite on his hand. It didn't hurt. In fact, he hadn't even felt it happen. He felt as though an opportunity for savouring pain had been lost.

So he bit his own hand.

He tried to line up his teeth with the marks. As his teeth pierced through the skin on his calloused hands, he tasted blood. The pain that followed was simple and weak, not like the complex buffet he had been force-fed by the djinns under that man's command. Kamran spat out a thick glob of red, then stared accusingly at the wound. Hamza stopped begging.

Kamran looked up at him, as though he had forgotten Hamza was there. Then he recovered his purpose.

'Where is Wahid?'

'What?' said Hamza.

Kamran looked up at the boy's face, red and swollen, glistening with sweat and tears. Then he reached out and put one hand on Hamza's crotch, cupping his groin. The boy's eyes widened with understanding.

'Nononono.'

Kamran squeezed, not with all his force, knowing his strength would cause the boy to lose consciousness, but enough to make the tendons in his wrist stand out like strings on a guitar. The sound that Hamza made was much like the air escaping from a tyre. Kamran let go and wiped his hand on his jeans, his palm damp with the boy's urine.

'Wahid,' he said again, his tone casual, 'where is he?'

'But I don't …' began Hamza, then started squealing *nonono* as Kamran's hand returned to cup his testicles.

'He's at the beach,' screamed Hamza, his voice high-pitched with desperation. 'Please, oh God, don't. He's at the fucking beach!'

Kamran accepted this information by squeezing once again, this time putting more force into it. Hamza gave a strangled cry and vomited all over himself. Kamran took a step back, faster than someone his size would be assumed capable of. Watching the boy retching, he pulled out another cigarette and lit it. Getting the rest of the information from Hamza would be easy, he thought. And so, he decided to take his time.

XVIII.

He had to find the King of Karachi. The fact that Wahid had no idea how wouldn't slow him. Slowing down, in any way, would probably lead to insanity. He had allowed himself a brief moment of consideration after breakfast, but it had almost brought on an asthma attack and left him filling the toilet bowl with the regurgitated contents of that breakfast. And so he decided to move forward, stay in motion until he found the djinns and made them release whatever aspect of Maheen they had taken.

He asked Rahat to lie if Imran chacha or his mother called by saying that he was out on the beach or sleeping, depending on the time of the phone call. It was unlikely to work, especially since it involved Rahat actually communicating with someone; but the fear of having their calls monitored meant they might not call at all.

Wahid left the hut on foot, walking towards the shops. He glanced up in the opposite direction but found, under the flat glare of day, it was just an empty road leading into dust. Finding a taxi was unlikely this far from the main city, but Wahid managed to convince a van driver delivering crates of bottled water into giving him a ride in exchange for a few hundred rupees.

The Suzuki van smelled of rusting metal and diesel fumes. Wahid sat in the passenger seat, struggling to tune out the tinny warble of Sindhi music playing through a broken speaker, and tried to think of the next step in his forward motion.

The chudail had said to speak to the poor and the forgotten, and ask them to take him to the king. The idea seemed counterintuitive; why would a king be best approached through his most wretched subjects? Besides, who exactly was this king? Karachi had many rulers, but none styled themselves as kings. At least as far as Wahid knew. There were politicians who had divided the city into private fiefdoms. There were probably many crime lords who controlled the underbelly of the city – all those stolen cell phones and cars had to be going somewhere.

'You are the most serious-looking boy I have ever seen,' yelled the van driver over his music. He kept glancing at Wahid as his vehicle trundled over ditches and boulders.

'Sorry, I've got a lot on my mind, that's all. Thanks again for taking me into the city.'

'No problem. Just be grateful to Allah that you found someone as honest as me. So why are … OYE! GET OUT OF THE WAY, BHENCHOD!'

A boy, perhaps Wahid's age, dressed in a ragged shirt and jeans was strolling down the middle of the road, blocking their path. The van driver blasted him with his horn and the boy leapt out of the way, tossing them a middle-fingered jab as they sped past.

'Bastard,' grumbled the driver, picking up speed. 'I tell you, chote sahib, never give them any money. It's all a scam. They're all actors, hired by these politicians and criminals. All the money goes there. No one is honest in this fucking country any more, I tell you.'

Wahid had heard this theory before. It was a commonly held belief, in fact, that all the beggars in the city belonged to a mafia of their own. He was never sure of the truth of it though. He chalked it up to a coping strategy developed by those with money when confronted by the continuous onslaught of those without. After all, there was only so much you could give out of guilt. It was easier to believe that the act of not giving was somehow more charitable.

However, there certainly was a behavioural pattern that fuelled this theory. An intersection near his house seemed to be the allocated workplace of a legless man with a long black beard, who pushed himself around in a small box with wheels, rowing through the traffic using his hands as oars. Another intersection nearby was frequented by a blind man escorted by a little girl, and a woman with a face that had been mutilated – presumably by acid – so severely that Wahid had never been able to bring himself to look at her. In fact, upon consideration, he could probably tell which traffic light he had reached on the roads he most travelled simply by a description of the beggars working there.

'Where am I dropping you?' asked the driver.

They had driven into the city proper, their progress slowed by the dense Clifton traffic. Wahid had decided it was best to stay away from any area where he might run into someone he knew – or worse, someone who might be looking for him. He also needed a place where beggars would be easy to find.

'If you can take me up to Tariq Road, I'd really appreciate it.'

'Very well.' The driver grinned. 'Tariq Road is out of my way, but you shall be my good deed for the day.'

Tariq Road was not just one road, but the general name given to an entire grid of intersecting streets, all buzzing with frantic commercial activity, far enough away from everyone in Wahid's world of Defence and Clifton.

They had to abandon the main route across the city to Tariq Road once they encountered rows of cars driving towards them on the wrong side of the road. One of the cars slowed long enough for the driver to explain that a suicide blast in an open-air bazaar nearby had created a small riot. Survivors and grieving relatives had blocked the main road with burning tyres and were throwing rocks at any passing vehicles.

'Only Allah can save this city,' said the van driver. 'Don't worry, chote sahib, I'll get you to Tariq Road. I know every side lane in Karachi.'

True to his word, the driver sped through a maze of narrowing alleys and soon brought Wahid to one of Tariq Road's entrances. Wahid thanked him and gave him an extra five hundred rupees.

All of Tariq Road was covered with shops. Cramped and cluttered stores overflowing onto the pavement, each displaying a headache-inducing onslaught of wildly patterned fabrics, walls of cheap plastic toys, and more shoes than there were feet in the world. Mobs of pedestrians crossed the road from shop to shop, streaming through the gaps between cars and motorcycles. Horns blared like a continuous siren heralding the end of the world. Wahid dodged to avoid a motorcyclist who swerved past him at a speed that shouldn't have been possible in the perpetual traffic jam, and found shelter in the entrance of a shoe shop. Standing between steel shelving units filled with white school shoes, he puffed on his inhaler as his lungs began to wheeze.

'I am very hungry, please,' said someone from below, startling Wahid. He looked down to find a man sitting on the ground next to him. It took Wahid several seconds to untangle the configuration in which the man had arranged himself. The emaciated upper body was resting against a pillar, naked up to the waist, while his legs – exposed by a shalwar that had been rolled up above the knees – were whiskers of bone and skin, worn thin as cellophane. Each leg was thinner than Wahid's wrist and had been folded backwards on either side of the man, so that at first he looked as though he was sitting with two wooden crutches. The man gestured to an empty clay bowl placed in front and repeated the plea for food. Wahid reached into his wallet and pulled out a ten-rupee note, placing it in the bowl. The man gave him a smile that showed a single, lonely tooth.

'Can you do something for me, please?' asked Wahid, crouching down in front of him.

'If it is in Allah's favour, then I shall,' replied the man.

'I'm looking for the King of Karachi,' said Wahid.

There was a long pause as the man considered the request. Then plucking the ten-rupee note and pushing it into the waistband of his shalwar, he replied, 'Who is he?'

Wahid's confidence in his plan dissolved. It was, in the brightness of day, utterly ridiculous. His mother would be furious and Imran chacha would stop helping them out of frustration. Then he would have to go to jail and Maheen would die.

'Uh … um … nothing,' he said, standing up quickly.

The beggar stared at him for a few seconds, then shrugged and began focusing his pleas on a woman who had just stepped out of a nearby shop.

Wahid stalked away, cursing himself loudly in language that would have made Arif proud. He barrelled forward, head down and seething, until he almost collided with a flock of children. They clearly lived on the streets, each one dressed in a filthy collage of second-hand clothes. Wahid caught himself before he fell over, but not fast enough to escape scraping his ankle against the edge of the sidewalk. He let out another stream of curses, then grabbed the arm of a boy he had almost crashed into and yanked at him. The boy, shiny eyes glaring out from behind a mask of dirt, shrieked and wriggled under Wahid's grip.

'Watch where you're going!'

'Go fuck your sister,' the boy yelled, trying to shove at Wahid with his free hand.

Wahid let the boy go and watched him leap into traffic, dodging between two cars and running up to his friends who were watching from the other side. When he reached them, the entire group of children turned to Wahid and yelled at him, their high-pitched voices describing carnal acts they would inflict on his mother.

'Fuck you and fuck the King of Karachi,' yelled Wahid back and stalked off in the opposite direction. A few people glared at him, but most didn't even notice.

He kept walking until his temper cooled. Then his stomach grumbled, reminding Wahid he hadn't eaten since vomiting his breakfast and it was well into afternoon by now. Spying a small chai shop in a side lane, he jogged off the main road. The narrow alleyway seemed to exist in a bubble of calm, somehow shielded from the cacophony of the road he had just left. It was shaded by high apartment walls, a thin stream of gutter water slithered down one side. Wahid held his breath against the stink of sewage and made his way to the chai shop. Hollowed out of the side of a building, the few tables inside were empty, the proprietor's attention focused on a small television on his countertop. Wahid sat down at one table and buried his face in his hands.

'What do you want?' said the man, sparing a glance from the screen for Wahid.

'What do you have?'

The man seemed irritated by this question, as though the responsibility was on Wahid to already have this information. He motioned to a white board hanging behind him that had a menu advertising dal, naan and a small range of chicken curries.

Wahid chose the dal and naan, and asked for a soft drink as well. The man continued to watch the match for a few more minutes and then walked out to get the food. Wahid stared at the cricket match, not really registering the details of the game. He had to go back to the beach, he decided. Stay there until Imran chacha could sort things out. Everything else was ridiculous and a waste of time.

He didn't notice the boy he had yelled at walking into the chai shop. Nor did he notice the other children all taking up flanking positions outside, like security guards protecting a dignitary. So when the boy spoke, it seemed as though he appeared out of the furniture itself.

'Hey bhenchod,' said the boy, with a grin almost as large as his face, exposing a mouth lacking several teeth.

Wahid turned and stared at him, seeing first the boy and then the others peeking in from outside.

'Look,' he said, 'I'm sorry I yelled at you, okay. Now leave me alone, please.'

'The bhenchod wants to be left alone,' the boy yelled out to his friends. They laughed loudly, sounding very much like crows cawing in delight upon finding a rat to feast on.

'Stop calling me that,' said Wahid in irritation. Then taking out his wallet he retrieved a fifty-rupee note and offered it to the boy. 'Here. Now please leave me alone.'

The boy snatched the note and shoved it into his shirt pocket, still grinning immensely. 'Why do you want to meet the king, bhenchod?' he asked.

Wahid stared at the boy in astonishment, his mouth hanging open.

'You know the king?'

'I might,' said the boy, his grin widening into that of a salesman. He held out his hand, curved like a begging bowl.

Wahid put away his wallet and sighed.

'Don't be sad, bhenchod,' said the boy with a shrug. 'I can take you to the king. All you have to do is ask.'

'Fine,' said Wahid in irritation, 'take me to him then.'

'Ask nicely,' demanded the boy.

Wahid glared. 'Will you please take me to see the King of Karachi?' he said. 'And stop calling me bhenchod.'

He never saw who hit him on the back of his head, as he lost consciousness and his face slammed onto the table.

XIX.

Maheen was standing in front of him, darkness all around her. She was watching him sadly.

'Oh Wahid,' she was saying.

'I'm sorry,' Wahid said to her, 'I'm trying.'

'I know,' she said, moving closer to him so that her face filled his view. It was the most beautiful face he had ever seen.

'I'm sorry,' he said again.

She smiled, tears appearing on her eyelashes and gliding like mercury down the soft curve of her cheek.

'Wake up, Wahid,' she said. 'Wake up, bhenchod.'

He opened his eyes. Shapes coalesced in front of him.

'He's waking up,' said someone nearby. 'Slap him again.'

Wahid moaned loudly, trying to form words of protest. He was in a small room, lit only by a dusty bar of sunlight streaming in through a high window on one side. The boy was standing in front of him, grinning triumphantly. The other children, three boys and two girls, stood shoulder to shoulder, crowding behind the boy. They were all watching Wahid, curiosity writ on their ash-smudged faces.

'Aye madarchod, are you awake? Or should I slap you again?' asked the boy.

Wahid was lying on the ground, looking up at all of them. The back of his head throbbed dully and he sat up, rubbing it with one hand.

'What did you do to me? Where am I?' he said, the words coming out slowly and sounding as though they were being said by someone else.

'We hit you, chutiya,' said the boy.

Wahid sat up fully, looking at the boy with an expression that was equal parts anger and astonishment.

'Why did you do that?' he exclaimed. 'Are you trying to kidnap me? What is this?'

The children all laughed, their high-pitched voices echoing so that it sounded like a hundred small animals engaged in a pitched battle of shrieks and squeals.

'This isn't funny!' screamed Wahid, amusing them even more. He tried to stand up, but discovered his ankles were tied together by rope. The laughter died down with a few final snorts and giggles.

'You wanted the king?' said the boy. 'Here he is.' He gestured over his shoulder with a thumb. Wahid looked and saw the same children smiling back at him. Just as he was about to let off a stream of creative insults, the children moved aside, pressing up against the sides of the room. From behind them, a boy younger than the rest, stepped forward. He was, at most, seven years old. If Wahid were standing, he might come up to Wahid's waist, but only with the help of thick-soled shoes. He wasn't wearing any shoes, however, standing on feet black with dirt. He was dressed much like the others, in clothes that were too large for him and drained of all colour. The only relief in the entire grey ensemble was a thin chain around his neck, made of red and orange threads wound tightly together. Dirty blonde hair curled like Wahid's, over a face that was handsome even for a boy his age, with green eyes set above a wide nose and smiling lips. The boy regarded Wahid silently, picking his nose as he did.

'Oh, fuck it,' said Wahid in irritation. He decided that, even with his legs bound, he might be able to fight off the children long enough to scream for help. Maybe even make it to the door behind the peculiar little boy. He started to push himself off the ground with his hands, when the new boy made a barely noticeable gesture to the one who had been insulting Wahid. The first boy lifted his shirt and showed a gun tucked into the waistband of his shorts, the grip comically large against his stomach.

'Sit down, bhenchod,' growled the first boy, placing a hand on the gun.

Wahid let the weight shift back to his butt, glaring at the armed boy.

'You were looking for me,' said the youngest boy. 'Well, you found me. What do you want … what did you say his name was again?'

'Bhenchod,' said one of the girls.

'Hurry up and talk, Bhenchod,' said the young boy, moving a step closer to Wahid with his hands clasped behind him. His posture was that of an elderly gentleman strolling through a library that contained no new books for him to read.

'My name is Wahid, now quit fucking around and let me go.'

The small boy sighed, then motioned to the one with the gun who pulled it out, gripped it by the barrel and smashed the handle hard into the back of Wahid's head. The whole thing happened so fast that Wahid barely had time to duck, the gun butt bouncing off him. He yelled out in anger and pain.

'You know who I am,' said the boy, deadly serious. 'You were looking for me. Now tell me why, Bhenchod, or I will have my friends beat you to death. They have done it before. Kulsoom here,' he motioned to the girl who had spoken, 'bit a man's throat just last week. Pulled his tongue out with her teeth.'

'I am … ow … I'm looking for the King of Karachi,' said Wahid, struggling to stay conscious as the pain in his head filled the world with creeping darkness around the edges.

'That's him,' said the first boy, tossing the gun in the air casually and catching it with both hands.

Wahid opened his mouth to speak, then found he didn't know quite what to say.

'I'm the King of Karachi,' said the young boy grimly. 'At least, I'm the king for now. The last one died some months ago. He stuck the wrong needle in his arm.'

Wahid stared at the boy. Eyes as green as the Pakistani flag stared back at him.

'Okay, if you're the King of Karachi, why are you so young?'

The boy laughed. It was a child's laugh, full of unrestrained joy. Then he motioned for the other children to leave the room. They all filed out obediently, even the boy with the gun, closing the door behind them. Wahid caught a glimpse of a brick wall a few feet ahead through the doorway, painted blue with shadows.

'Why, now? The last king was an old man. Old and stupid. Sometimes he talks to me,' said the boy, crouching down on his haunches and untying the knotted rope that bound Wahid's legs, with fingers already knotted with callouses.

Wahid stared at the boy, trying to decide whether or not to take him seriously. He looked very much like any of the beggar children who had just left the room, like any child who would rush to Wahid's car asking for money at traffic lights across the city. But the other children, all older, had shown him deference. From the interactions Wahid had seen over the years, children who lived in the street followed a code of authority based on seniority of age.

'Look, I just … I just need help. So please be straight with me,' he said, not exactly managing to keep the desperation out of his voice.

The boy looked up at him and smiled. It was probably meant to give his face a sweeter appearance, but somehow the smile made him look more menacing. It was like a baboon's grin, baring teeth.

'My name is Badshah,' said the boy, 'and I am the King of Karachi. Now what do you want from me, Bhenchod? Tell me or fuck off, it doesn't bother me either way.'

Wahid helped him pull apart the last knot on the rope, rubbing his ankle where the fibre had cut into skin. His head still felt heavy, tines of pain poking at him every time he moved.

Badshah stood up, reached into his pocket and pulled out a pack of cigarettes. They were the kind that Hamza had once brought over a year ago for them to try smoking hash with. When they had emptied the cigarette, rolling it between their palms, the tobacco that drizzled out had been mostly wood shavings. Badshah lit the cigarette with a box of matches he pulled out of the other pocket, sucking on it a few times and exhaled smoke from his nose. On any other boy his age, it would have looked grotesque. But on him, it looked as natural as the Marlboro Man.

Wahid stood up, grimacing as his knees popped loudly. The cigarette smoke unfurled slowly across the room, passing through the shaft of sunlight between them.

'I was told to look for the King of Karachi by a … I think it was a chudail,' said Wahid.

The boy pinched an eye shut against the smoke and took the cigarette out of his mouth.

'I was wondering how you had heard of me. Rich fucks like you don't come here ever.'

'I'm not rich,' protested Wahid, then reached behind him to feel for his wallet. It was, and he was not particularly surprised to discover so, gone. As was the cell phone in his front pocket.

'I ate only a single stale naan yesterday,' said Badshah, inspecting Wahid with disdain, 'and that's all I've had to eat since then. So to me you are a rich man.'

'I'm sorry,' mumbled Wahid.

'Fuck it, let's go outside. This room stinks of the last guy we killed in here,' said Badshah, walking to the door.

They exited into a thin alleyway between two high buildings. It was different from the alley he had sat down for lunch in. Whatever meagre sunlight made it down was poor in quality. Exposed brick gleamed with moss and sweated in the heat, frog-coloured puddles of gutter water reflecting the tangle of wires above. The alley was full of children, most of them sitting in clusters down its length. Some played with stone, trying to knock down piles they had assembled. A few played cricket with a broken plank and a balled up newspaper. Wahid could see the children who had been in the room with him, standing around a dead rat, which they poked with a stick, its innards spilling out onto the street through a hole in its side. The boy with the gun saw Wahid looking at them and stuck his tongue out.

Badshah walked with bare feet splashing through the filthy water and reached a pile of crates stacked up against the wall. He climbed onto them and perched on top like an alley cat, squatting with the cigarette between his lips. Wahid hopped across whatever dry surfaces he could find and stood in front of him.

'If you're the King of Karachi, why aren't you … richer?' he asked.

The boy gave that same smile that was too full of threat to be friendly and waved towards the alleyway.

'*This* is Karachi. Not those big houses and fancy fucking shops you rich fucks roam around in,' he said. 'There are more of us hungry and poor children than there will ever be rich fuckers in this city. So why should the king be rich.'

'Okay. So how did you become king?'

The boy sat down cross-legged on the crate, his face level with Wahid's. He called to one of the girls playing with the rocks. She was barely older than him and dropped her pebble and came running up. Her face was beautiful, with large eyes and pink lips.

'Bina, go,' said Badshah. 'It's your turn.'

Bina gave him a mock salute, her hand smacking hard against her forehead and stamping one foot on the ground. Then she ran off, disappearing down the far end of the alley.

'Where are we?' asked Wahid.

Badshah turned back to him and took a long drag on his cigarette. 'Very far from your rich home. This is my home. This is where we children live. I was born here.'

'Where are your parents?' asked Wahid, realizing that he had not seen a single adult in the entire alley.

Badshah shrugged. 'My mother died giving birth to me and I only met my father once, a year ago, when I killed him.'

'You killed your father,' said Wahid in a startled voice.

'He raped my mother. Fucked her in the back of his rickshaw. She was flung out of her house when she got pregnant. She was rich, much richer than even you can ever hope to be. She came here and lived on food that was thrown on the ground. When I was born, she died.'

There was no sadness in the boy when he said this. It was related as matter-of-factly as the description of an old cricket match.

'The previous king raised me. He helped me find my father. He was still driving the same rickshaw. I waited until he fell asleep in it one afternoon and stabbed him in the stomach with a broken bottle. When he woke up, I choked him to death with this.' Badshah pointed at the coil of threads around his neck.

'I'm … I'm sorry,' said Wahid. If Badshah appreciated this sentiment, he did not show it. He just kept surveying the boys and girls in the alleyway and smoking his cigarette.

'So, what do you want?'

Wahid breathed in deeply, anticipating the response. 'I'm looking for a djinn.'

'Djinn,' said Badshah. 'That's not so easy. I can find anything in Karachi. But the djinns, they've left.'

'You can see them?' asked Wahid. It was starting to seem as though everyone in the city could see djinns. As though seeing a djinn was as common in Karachi as seeing roadkill.

'No, but I know when they are here,' said Badshah. 'I know everything in Karachi. And I know that djinns used to live here. But a few weeks ago, they all left. Vanished. Poof.'

'Someone else told me the same thing,' said Wahid sadly. 'So, that's it then. They are all gone.'

'I said they left,' said Badshah, flicking his spent cigarette into a puddle near Wahid's feet. It hissed as it died, bobbing on the opaque water. 'I didn't say they were gone.'

'What do you mean?' asked Wahid.

'They all left, but a few of them come back from time to time,' said Badshah.

'Where?' asked Wahid, his voice rising in excitement.

'I could tell you, but then you have to do something for me,' Badshah said, jumping down from the crates and standing in front of Wahid.

'Please don't tell me you want me to kiss you,' said Wahid.

'What?' asked Badshah.

'Nothing, sorry. What do you want?'

Badshah's face softened and for the first time he looked sad. It made him look his age, like a seven-year-old boy who needed comforting.

'That girl, Bina. She'll be dead in a few hours. They'll toss her in a graveyard not far from here. Put a stone on her grave when you get a chance. She'd like that.'

Wahid stared in horror at Badshah, the pain in his head, that had receded, returned at full bore.

'She'll be dead?' he almost shouted. 'Why?'

'I told her to, that's why.'

'Why the fuck did you do that?' yelled Wahid.

Badshah stared at Wahid as though it was the most ridiculous question he had ever heard in his short life.

'She will let herself be run over by a bus. The bus driver will escape, which will cause an angry mob to burn his bus. This will turn into a riot, until the police will come. There will be fighting. Because of this the road where all this will happen will be closed. An ambulance, carrying an old man to the hospital, will get stuck in the traffic jam this will cause. He will die in that ambulance. I want him to die in that ambulance. I also want that bus driver to lose his bus. It will drive him to poverty and when he is needy I will find him.'

Anger and confusion fluctuated inside Wahid with a rapidity that caused dizziness. He could only sputter.

'That's my business. And Karachi's business. I told you. I am the King of Karachi and I need to get things done.'

Wahid leaned against the crates, not quite sure how to react. He wanted to hit the boy, but knew that would be a dangerous thing to attempt. As if sensing there might be just such a problem, the children in the alleyway all walked up and stood behind Badshah.

They stared at Wahid, daring him to attempt anything with their eyes. Promising him a painful death if he did.

'Now fuck off, Bhenchod, go to your djinn,' said Badshah.

'You … you haven't told me where to find it.'

Badshah pointed at the boy with the gun. 'He will show you. There is a sweet shop that the djinns used to visit every Friday night. The owner leaves a tray of sweets for them to eat. One of them still comes to that shop. I know it does because the owner still leaves the sweets and the windows of the shop see the djinn eating them.'

'The windows see the djinn,' said Wahid weakly.

'I am the King of Karachi, Bhenchod. Are you too dumb to understand that? Karachi isn't just the people. It is also the city. And I am its king. Now go.'

The boy with the gun waved for Wahid to follow him and ran off down the alleyway. Wahid stared at Badshah and then, mumbling a thank you, ran after the boy.

'Don't forget Bina's grave,' yelled Badshah from behind him.

XX.

The Sohni Brothers Mithai Shop first opened its doors in 1923. At the time, the Sindhi–Muslim neighbourhood was patronized almost exclusively by members of the British Raj. It stood proudly on the street between a tailorshop, specializing in suits worthy of Saville Row, and a small restaurant that sold lunch meals named after the monarchy. The Sohni brothers were Bilal Sohni and Akhtar Sohni and they took pride in the quality of Indian sweets that they produced. Every morning, Bilal used to take stock of the finest ingredients, collecting them from specialized wholesalers in Empress Market. He would check the quality of each ingredient himself before handing it all over to Akhtar, who would then conduct the staff of his cramped kitchen in the production of gulab jamuns that sweated saffron, laddus that dissolved the instant they were bitten, and ras malai that had been written about in letters sent back to England. By Maghrib prayers, when the shop would close, all the trays on all the shelves would be empty. All, that is, except one. On a single tin tray, the brothers would lay a cloth of fine silk and then fill it with rows of sweets. They would leave that tray on the countertop, protected from flies and vermin by a thick glass cover. Then they would lock the shop and leave for their respective homes, knowing that the next morning all the desserts would be gone.

It was a small price to pay for the shop's prosperity. The plot of land that they had built the shop on had been empty for a long time before their arrival, a rectangle of sand with a single mango tree growing in the centre. When they purchased the land and began the process of construction, they encountered some trouble in removing the tree. The first worker who approached the tree with an axe had been slapped by a hand he could not see but definitely felt. The blow had tossed him backwards and the axe flown from his grip, embedding itself into his shin. The next worker sent began screaming in fear after reaching the tree. Through hysterical shrieks he described a snake with the head of a man, glaring at him from the branches. The brothers, who had spent almost every penny they had on the plot of land, sought the advice of a Sufi. The holy man studied the tree from afar, leaning against a gnarled walking stick hidden in his robes. Then he advised the two men to approach the tree slowly, apologize for needing to cut it down and then offer the djinn who lived there a place in the shop they intended to build. The brothers protested, explaining that customers were unlikely to frequent a shop in which they would be slapped by invisible hands and frightened by snakes with human heads. The Sufi gave this a great deal more thought, and finally told them to make a gift of the finest desserts they made every day to the djinn. The tree had been cut, the shop built and every day they selected the best sweets from their kitchen and made an offering of them.

This practice had been continued by the shop owner's sons and then the sons' sons. Over time, the generation who inherited the business decided to expand. Two of them moved to Lahore and opened 'Karachi's Famous Sohni Brother's Mithai Shop' in that city, another one established a larger branch in a more affluent part of Karachi, and only one remained to keep the original store going. The area it was in had seen a gradual decrease in importance and affluence, with the tailor shop and restaurant on either side being replaced by a succession of failed businesses. Currently, it was flanked by a tyre repair shop on one side and a kabab roll assembly line on the other. Yet, Sohni Brothers Mithai still maintained its quality and reputation, enjoying patronage from dedicated customers. Everyone knew of the offerings that were made daily. Children would sit outside the shop at night, hoping to see someone moving around inside but never catching so much as a glimpse through the tinted glass windows. People living in the apartments above would lie to one another about a tall figure entering the shop at night and the current owner had long grown tired of answering questions about his peculiar customer. But he never failed to leave that tray of sweets out every night and was always grateful to find it empty the next morning.

Except for the last few weeks, when he opened the shop after Fajr prayers, the tray was still full. The first time he turned the lights on to find it still laden with dessert, he had thought perhaps there had been a mistake and the quality of sweets had not been good enough. Upset at having possibly offended the djinn, he screamed at his staff and threatened to fire all of them. The next day, when the tray was again as full as he had left it the night before, he began to worry. By the end of the week, he was gripped with panic. His family, when consulted, pointed out that after all those years perhaps the djinn had moved on. Maybe djinns do not occupy the same place forever. Still, every night he selected the finest of his day's produce and placed them in the tray. So two days before Wahid visited, when the sweets had started disappearing again, the shop owner felt relief, and had offered prayers of thanks.

By the time Wahid and the boy reached the shop, it had shut. They travelled by bus and then walked the rest of the way. During the journey, the boy had insisted on being called Commando. He, of course, continued to address Wahid as Bhenchod.

The street was lit by a large neon billboard, standing above the apartment that had grown over the shop. Stencils of green light splayed across the asphalt.

'This is the shop,' said Commando, pointing to the metal grate that barricaded the front door. Wahid stared in dismay at the large combination lock that secured the grate to a hook on the ground.

'It's locked,' he pointed out.

'Bhenchod, you are useless,' said Commando. He peered down each end of the street and then walked up to the lock.

'Are you going to shoot it?' asked Wahid.

'Do I look like your mother's cunt?' answered Commando with a grin.

The constant insults had stopped irritating Wahid, fading out of the conversation like background noise.

Commando crouched down in front of the lock and reached into his pocket, retrieving a small folded piece of tin. Wahid moved closer and saw it was shaped like a ring. Commando held it up to give Wahid a better look and then, with a proud grin, wrapped the ring around the shackles and pushed an extended bit into the space where the clasp disappeared into the lock. He fiddled with it for a few seconds and then gave out an exultant whoop as the lock sprang open.

'I can open any lock in Karachi,' Commando announced, dangling the lock from a finger. Wahid gripped the edge of the grate and pulled it up. It rattled loudly as it lifted. He raised it just high enough to crawl underneath, then turned to Commando.

'Coming?' he asked.

'No way, Bhenchod,' said Commando. 'You are on your own. I'll wait out here. If anyone comes, I'll rattle the grate and you hide.'

'Thanks,' said Wahid, genuinely grateful for having an accomplice. He got down on his hands and knees and crawled under the grate. Commando lowered it behind him, leaving the edge an inch above the floor.

The shop was empty. In the light seeping in from the front windows, he could make out the shapes of a few glass display counters and shelves behind them. He stood up and inhaled the smell of sugar and saffron, letting his nose lead him to the tray of desserts. His stomach grumbled loudly as he pressed his nose against the glass cover, staring down at the sweets underneath. They glistened teasingly. He considered lifting the cover and eating a few, but then decided not to risk alerting any djinns that might appear. Finding a spot – in a corner where he was sure the darkness would hide him – he sat down and waited.

Two hours passed in silence, with the only interruption being the sound of the odd car passing on the road outside. Each time the interior of the shop filled with light for a moment and then plunged into darkness again, forcing Wahid's eyes to have to readjust. Commando had fallen asleep on the sidewalk, curled up on the concrete with his back against the grate. Inside, Wahid dozed intermittently. Each time he fell asleep, he would force himself awake, although it was becoming increasingly difficult to do so.

The fourth time, he was woken not by his own need, but by a sound. It was, Wahid realized as he pulled his eyes open, the sound of someone eating. He peered into the darkness of the shop and saw a figure blocking his view of the dessert tray. It was tall, so tall that the head almost brushed the ceiling, which would make it at least two feet taller than Wahid. He could only see an outline and it took a few seconds to read it. The figure was standing in profile with half its body hidden from him. An arm as thin as rope reached for the sweets and picked one up, bringing it up to the face to inspect it carefully before popping it into its mouth.

It chewed noisily. He could see the outline of a ribcage, curving into the jut of a hipbone from which protruded a leg only slightly thicker than the arm. The whole shape was of a tall skeleton with skin stretched taut over it.

Wahid slowly stood up, unfolding his legs carefully and pushing himself upright with his hands pressed against the wall behind him. The distance between them wasn't much and he knew he could cover it in two quick steps. Holding his breath, he reached his full height and readied himself, poised on his heels and building tension in his calves to run forward.

A car passed outside. White light flooded the shop, throwing everything into stark contrast.

Wahid shrieked.

The figure was not standing in profile, he realized – it was halved. It stood on the only leg it had, with just one arm and even the head was incomplete. It was as though someone had sliced an emaciated human vertically down the middle and only one side now stood in front of Wahid. A half-head jerked sideways and a single eye stared at him. Then the car passed and darkness returned to the room. Wahid didn't wait until he could see again. Instead, he closed his eyes and leaped forward, arms outstretched. The creature shrieked, like a metal fork being dragged across a ceramic plate. Wahid collided with it and they both toppled to the ground. The floor smacked against Wahid's back but he ignored the burst of pain, instead rolling sideways to bring himself on top of the shape next to him, grabbing it at the elbow as he tried to lift himself up. It began to scream. The sound stabbed at Wahid's ears and he resisted the urge to cover them. Instead, he pushed himself into a sitting position without releasing the arm. He looked down and saw the creature writhing on the ground. The scream had gone beyond hearing now and the half-mouth that ended abruptly against a flat wall of skin was open wide. The arm, where he gripped it, was starting to sizzle, the creature's skin blistering under his fingers.

'Stop fighting,' Wahid yelled out. 'Stop it and I'll let you go.'

The single leg thrashed behind him, the knee slamming into the small of his back. He rocked forward, releasing the creature. It pulled its arm away but he managed to grab it again, this time placing one hand down on the narrow half-chest. It shrieked again, so loud that Wahid screamed as well, in surprise. The skin beneath his hand began bubbling and boiling instantly. Wahid pulled his hand back in horror, leaving a burned imprint of a hand.

The words it screamed were not complete, more like the echoes of words.

'Eese,' it begged, 'eese et it go.'

Wahid let go entirely, raising both hands off the creature, but keeping them hovering just a few inches above.

'Stop fighting then,' he said, pleadingly.

It fell still, staring up with the single eye shimmering with tears. The solitary nostril flared and half a tongue hung out of the incomplete mouth as it gulped air. The room smelt of burnt meat.

'Are … are you a djinn?' asked Wahid.

It began to cry, whimpering like a small wounded animal.

'Please answer me,' said Wahid. 'I'm sorry I hurt you. Are you a djinn?'

It watched his hands carefully.

'Es. Es.'

'Yes,' repeated Wahid carefully. 'Good. But, you look so … what kind of djinn are you?'

It shifted slightly and Wahid's hands moved with it. Seeing this it relaxed its body, lying flat on the ground. Tendrils of smoke rose from it as the burns cooled.

'Grine.'

'Grine? Are you saying Grine? Is that a kind of djinn?'

The djinn nodded.

'I need to ask you some questions, will you answer me? I don't want to hurt you again.'

It nodded. Then it said, 'Ungry.'

'Hungry? Okay. I don't care about the food you were eating. Just answer my questions, okay. I want to know why your kind … why the djinns attacked me?'

It stared at him, the expression on the half-face no longer that of fear or pain, but of surprise.

'Uu are im,' it said. 'Uu are im.'

'What? I don't understand what you're saying,' said Wahid.

You are him.

The voice came not from its mouth, but in Wahid's head, the words reverberating inside his mind.

'Him? What do you mean? Who am I?'

It raised its long thin arm slowly, careful to avoid Wahid's hands and placed bony fingers on the burns on its chest.

You are the end of us. You are why we withdrew.

'But you attacked me. Not you, but others of your kind. They were … full. Complete. And they were black. They killed my friend.'

Those were Marid. I am Grine. I did not do it.

Wahid decided to change tactics. He stood up and pointed one finger at the djinn.

'Stay there. Don't move,' he said. Then he stepped back to the tray of sweets and lifted it. Half the offerings had been eaten, sticky caramel stains left behind. He carried the tray with both hands and sat down next to the djinn, cross-legged, with the tray in his lap. Then he pointed to the desserts and said, 'You want them? Are you hungry?'

The Grine nodded warily, eye fixed on the food. Wahid gestured to the tray.

'Go on. Take one.'

The Grine's hand blurred and a gulab jamun disappeared from the tray. It swallowed the sweet whole and then smacked its lips noisily.

'If you answer all my questions, I'll give you more. Okay?'

It nodded eagerly.

'Why was I attacked?'

You does not know what you are? How curious.

Wahid glared at it in irritation and seeing his expression it continued, *You are the one who can hurt us. Can kill us. That is why we left. Our king told us to leave so that we can be safe from you. So you can kill no more of us.*

'I killed one of your kind,' said Wahid, 'but it attacked me. I don't even know how I did it. But if all the others left, why're you here?'

The Grine looked embarrassed.

Not supposed to be here. Not allowed to be here. But so hungry. Did not think anyone would know it came. But you knew. See, you do hunt us.

'But I don't hu – oh never mind. To hell with it. One of your kind. This Marid … it did something to a girl I know. It took something out of her. What did it do?'

Do not know, do not know, please. More. So hungry.

Wahid sighed and gestured to the tray. Two more sweets disappeared.

'You said the djinns have all left. Where have you gone? I need to talk to someone … some THING that knows and can help me.'

Gone to Kaf.

'Kaf? What is … where is Kaf?'

Kaf is where djinn are.

'Fine. How can I get there?'

Cannot, it cannot. None but us can.

'Shit,' muttered Wahid. 'Okay, wait. I don't understand one thing. You said all the djinns have left, right? Because I can hurt djinns? But I don't want to. Just go back and tell the djinns that I just want them to fix my friend and then we can leave each other alone. You can do that, right?'

The expression became a sullen one, childish almost.

Cannot. Just a Grine. Not important. No one listens. And if King finds it came here, will punish. Do not want to be punished. Then it said aloud, 'Ere is un.'

'What?'

There is one.

'What one? What is it?'

It looked at the tray hungrily and ran the half-tongue over its lips.

'Fine, here,' said Wahid, pushing the entire tray towards it. There was a blur of movement as its hand flew from the tray to its mouth and back again several times. In a few seconds, the tray was empty. Syrup glistened on its chin.

There is one who can help you. Maybe. If it wishes to. One who is not in Kaf. Who cannot go to Kaf. Never can be in Kaf.

'Who?' asked Wahid.

Azah-zeel. Call to Azah-zeel.

'Who is that? Is he a djinn too?'

The creature nodded. It spoke again, 'Eese. I go. Eese.'

'Fine, just one more thing. How do I call this Azah-zeel?'

Call to it. If it wants to, it will come. That is all this one knows.

The djinn shrugged. Then, seeing Wahid lowering his hands, it stood up slowly. Wahid stood up at the same time and they regarded each other in silence. It balanced perfectly on the single leg, staring at him with the one eye. Then it turned, hopped towards the metal shutter and passed through it. Wahid placed the tray back on the counter and made his way to the shutter as well. He pulled it upwards, waking Commando who was still sleeping outside.

The boy sat up, yawning and stretching as he did. 'Did you find anything?' he said.

'I … I don't know, honestly,' said Wahid.

'Where to now, Bhenchod?' said Commando, standing up and rubbing his eyes.

Wahid considered this carefully. He still couldn't go home, even though he felt an immense need to sleep on his bed and be under his own roof.

'I think I need to go back to the beach,' he said, then he turned and glared at Commando. 'Except you took all my money. So I can't.'

Commando slapped Wahid on the leg and laughed. 'Oh Bhenchod, you are pathetic.' He sighed. Then he reached into his pocket and took out Wahid's wallet. Wahid reached for it but Commando danced away.

'Uh, uh,' he said, wagging a finger at Wahid. He reached into the wallet and pulled out whatever cash was inside, then threw it at Wahid. Wahid tried to catch it, missed and then stooped to pick up the notes from the ground.

'Can I have my phone at least?' he said as he stood up again. But Commando was gone. With a deep sigh, Wahid began walking towards the main road.

XXI.

In a room wallpapered with blood, Hamza died. As Kamran sliced across his throat with a curved blade, the boy's last thought was *I don't want to die*.

Hamza died, but for some time he did not know it.

As his mutilated body hung from the ceiling by dislocated arms, Hamza watched as Kamran wiped the knife clean with a rag, then washed his hands in a basin on the far wall. Staring out from behind closed eyes, Hamza observed Kamran scrupulously scraping blood from under his nails, then wringing his fingers through steaming water.

'Please. Let me go. Please,' he said to his murderer through a mouth that hung broken and still. But the man seemed not to hear him. Instead, Kamran simply walked out of the room, closing the door behind him, the humming rising into a tuneless whistle.

'Come back!' screamed Hamza, although there was no sound. The door remained closed. A naked bulb hanging in the centre of the room was switched off. Hamza screamed into the darkness. He screamed curses and screamed for mercy and finally he simply screamed because it was all he could think to do. He didn't notice the flatness of his voice, how it was utterly devoid of echo and fell heavily in the room. Nor did he notice that as he screamed and shook, his body remained still. When he was done screaming, he did notice the absence of pain. Since he had woken in this room, the man had subjected him to nothing but pain. But, now, the pain was gone. He looked up at his bound hands, swollen and red like pomegranates, and tried to move them, hoping to slip them free of the knots that kept him suspended. They didn't respond, disconnected from his control as though they were someone else's. Hamza tried drawing in a deep breath, hoping to use it to give his body the strength needed to pull himself upwards. No air entered his lungs, however. He tried again, with the same result. His nostrils didn't flare, his chest remained impassive. The panic that was already streaming through him amplified. It was several minutes before he realized he didn't need to breathe. When he finally stopped trying, he instead attempted to cry, but felt none of the dampness of tears.

'I think I'm dead,' he said aloud in a voice that no living person, had there been any close by, could hear.

A rumbling began in the dark. At first, it was a low scraping, like mortar being worked against pestle. Then it grew, the sound of rocks tumbling, boulders crashing and finally the deafening blast of tectonic plates cracking. Hamza found himself calling to Allah for help, his voice barely audible beneath the avalanche of noise.

The ground before him crumbled. A mouth widened in the centre of the room, concrete falling away inside the yawning maw. Light, not white and bright, but infernal red, glowed within. It was like being on the lip of a waking volcano.

'I'm dead,' he thought. 'I'm dead and I'm going to Hell. Oh God, I'm going to –'

A voice cut him off. It boomed so loudly he felt its force, a surge of lightning crackling through him.

'Hamza bin Jamal.'

Hamza stared. If he could have, he would have vomited, but his body denied him that reaction.

'Fuck,' he gasped.

From out of the earth climbed two figures. Hamza first thought they were women, their forms hidden behind curtains of black hair that draped past their feet and trailed back into the hole from which they had risen. In their darkened faces, twin moons shone, eyes as round and large as plates, with light streaming so brightly from them that Hamza had to squint against it. They moved like reflections of one another, raising one hand each from under the hair to point at him. In the other hand, they both held whips, with handles as thick as Hamza's waist and python lengths of leather coiling in front of them.

'Hamza bin Jamal,' they both said as one.

'Yes,' shrieked Hamza, 'Allah save me! Who are you? Please ... what do you want with me?'

'I am Al-Munkar,' thundered the first.

'I am Al-Nakeer,' thundered the other.

'Please don't kill me,' wailed Hamza. 'Please don't take me to Hell. Please, oh Allah, please –'

'Answer our questions,' they said together, their voices buffeting Hamza. The whips slithered across the floor, their ends curling up towards his feet.

A stillness descended over Hamza. One instant he was crying and shrieking, the next he was calm and silent. His mind became as tranquil as a petal lying on a dead man's lips.

'Ask your questions of me,' he heard himself say in a dull tone.

'Mann rabukka?' asked Munkar.

'Maa deenuka?' asked Nakeer.

'Maa kunta taqul fee hajar rajl?' This they asked together.

In life, Hamza had studied the Quran as much as Wahid. A maulvi had taught him the Arabic pronunciations and intonations and he knew the more important of the surahs by heart. But, like Wahid, he had never understood most of it. When he heard the questions just put to him, he recognized them as Arabic immediately. But he also found he could understand.

Who is your Lord?

What is your religion?

What did you say about this person?

Hamza answered the questions without any need to consider them, fluent Arabic flowing from him in a clean stream.

'Rabbe-Allah,' he said. *My Lord is Allah.*

'Deenil Islam,' he said. *My religion is Islam.*

'Huwa Rasoolullah e sallalaho alaihi wassalam,' he finished. *This is Allah's messenger, embraced with Allah's mercy and my greetings to him.*

Munkar and Nakeer nodded in turn, then together. The light from their eyes grew, filling Hamza's entire world with a glare so intense he felt it would burn him into ash. Then it was over.

In a silent room filled with unbroken darkness, the body of a dead boy hung over a pool of his own blood.

XXII.

Wahid crawled into bed in the beach hut early next morning.

'Imran sahib called. I told him you had gone to the shops,' Rahat informed from outside the bedroom door.

He woke up when the afternoon sunlight cast a blinding patch over one eye. He felt so covered in dirt and filth that he was sure the water would turn black on contact with his skin. It didn't, but the soap was significantly worn down by the time he finished. Putting on an old T-shirt and jeans, which he took out from the small suitcase he had brought with him, he went down to ask Rahat for breakfast. After eating, he walked to the cybercafe.

The crowds were thick on the stretch of road in front of the shops and Wahid pushed and bumped his way to the cafe. He sat at the end of a row of boys playing Counter-Strike and cursing loudly at each other as they ran around pixelated streets with guns. Pulling up the browser, Wahid began searching for ways of summoning djinns.

A simple Google search for 'How to summon djinns' revealed a surprising amount of content. There were discussion forums detailing rituals, people sharing experiences and techniques and even YouTube videos with step-by-step instructions. Every message forum had the same format of someone asking how it could be done, someone else offering a technique that involved several days of praying, fasting and Quranic recitations followed by an argument raging for several pages over whether it was allowed at all. One method involved forty-five days in a graveyard, reading passages of the Quran that related to djinns. Apparently, during those forty-five days, the practitioner would be assaulted by horrific visions. If he persevered, a djinn would be under his control. If he didn't, he would die.

Another method involved red candles, sitting in a circle made of flour and reading passages of the Quran backwards. This was then condemned as blasphemy by other members of the forum. Insults followed, animated gifs showing anime characters exploding, and then a moderator closed the discussion thread before it melted the entire website.

All in all, it seemed as though almost everyone knew of a way to do it, everyone else had known someone who had done it, and they were all unanimous in their agreement that it was a terrible idea. Wahid gave up. The only thing that seemed to be common to most of the methods was recital of the surah Al-Jinn. He paid for his time on the computer and left the shop. It occurred to Wahid that he actually had no copy of the Quran itself and so he returned to the narrow bookshop with the surly shopkeeper. He was treated with exactly the same lack of consideration, despite being the only repeat customer the shopkeeper had had in weeks.

Wahid purchased a copy of the Quran, a small hardbound edition with a brown slipcase. The shopkeeper reverentially placed it in a cloth bag and then handed it to Wahid with strict instructions to carry it in both hands. Wahid did so, walking the entire route back to the hut with it held out in front of him.

Remembering the strict training imparted to him by his maulvi sahib as a child, Wahid first performed the necessary ablutions. He ritualistically washed his arms and feet, blew his nose and gargled. Then he sat on the bed and opened the Quran, placing it on the blanket in front of him. Each page was divided in half. On the left side of the page was the Arabic script, curling and flowing. On the right was the English translation, in strict vertical letters. It took Wahid close to an hour to locate the relevant surah, scanning each page as he searched for it.

The entire surah was scarcely a page in length. The translation followed the same poetic structure as the original Arabic text. Wahid first read the Arabic aloud and then the English. It described djinns coming to the Prophet and declaring their fealty to Allah and Islam. They then condemned those amongst them who sought to deceive believers and apologized for past attempts at lying and rejecting Allah. Finally, there was an agreement on the inevitability of the Day of Judgement. The Prophet was quoted as saying he does not know whether the day will be soon or if Allah means for it to be much later. It contained, to Wahid's dismay, no clear means of contacting djinns. He memorized the page, going over it again and again, until his eyes grew heavy with sleep. Then he closed the Quran with a deep, frustrated sigh.

'Not what you expected?' asked Maheen. She was leaning against the far wall, hands folded across her chest.

'No,' replied Wahid, standing up and staring down at the cover of the closed holy book.

'What were you hoping for?'

'I don't know,' he said. 'Something. Anything. What am I supposed to do? Couldn't there have been one line saying, "O Azah-zeel, come to me" or something like that?'

'Wahid,' said Maheen flatly.

'Yes?'

'Look out,' she said.

A boulder crashed into the small of his back. He was pushed to the ground so suddenly his head snapped backwards. He landed on his chest, the air gusting out of his lungs in a single rush. Pain, sharp and hot, exploded in his spine. If he screamed, he did not hear it.

His head was yanked upwards as a large hand pulled him by the hair and Wahid felt himself being lifted off the ground. Then he was thrown forward again. His face slammed into the brick wall and he felt his nose crunch loudly and lips mash against teeth. Tears filled his eyes and neon flashes stuttered his vision. Wahid put a hand to his nose and felt the broken shape, as though it had been twisted to one side. He could taste his own blood. He twisted his body and raised a hand out reflexively.

'Stop,' he groaned.

A hulking black mass was standing over him, blurred by his teary vision. He wiped his eyes and looked up at it again: a man, large and broad, but definitely a man. His face was as impassive as a wall, with an unruly beard below it. He wore a red kameez with a white shalwar and studied Wahid silently.

Wahid staggered to his feet, his mouth and chin thick with blood. His eyes burned and his spine felt as though it was made of shattered glass. He threw himself at the man, hands shielding his face as he toppled forward. It felt like colliding with a rock. He bounced off and crashed to the ground, lying there moaning at the man's feet.

Somewhere, far away, a high keening whistle sounded.

'You don't seem worth the effort,' the man said.

Wahid heard his voice distantly, the auditory foreground filled with the grating rasp of his own breath. He rolled over on to his back and looked up. Kamran had moved away and was sitting on the edge of the bed, not really looking at him but seeming more interested in the room around him.

'Why ...' croaked Wahid, his mouth filling with blood. He swallowed painfully and felt bits of teeth slide down his throat. One eye began to swell and close.

'Allah knows,' said the man. 'Someone wants you found. Took me fucking ages. Had to torture your friend.' Then he checked his watch, a large black hunk of rubber and metal on his wrist. 'Actually, he's probably dead by now.'

Wahid tried to speak again but the words were swallowed by a fit of painful coughs.

The whistling grew louder, becoming the wail of a suffering infant.

Wahid strained to hear the man – Kamran – but the ringing sound in his head made it difficult to pick out the words. Through one eye he watched as Kamran lit a cigarette, puffed it once and then stubbed it out on the side of his own neck.

Wahid began wheezing, every breath drowning in blood and phlegm. His hands moved to his chest and began clawing at the bloodstained T-shirt.

'What are you doing?' said Kamran, finally looking directly at Wahid. Then, 'Oh fuck.'

Wahid felt himself being lifted off the ground by large hands gripping him under his arms. He was upright, with his feet dangling above the floor, head lolling backwards as he gasped feebly.

'Don't die,' Kamran was saying, barely audible now. 'They didn't tell me to kill you. They want you alive.'

The siren was a scream. It roared closer, louder and louder.

Wahid's vision began to fade as his lungs surrendered. Kamran threw him onto the bed. Wahid landed like a marionette with its strings cut as Kamran began looking frantically around the room for Wahid's inhaler. Wahid moaned.

An explosion of darkness filled the room. Kamran threw up an arm to cover his face, shrieking as he did so. The lights were smothered in darkness.

It coalesced. Then it withdrew, light cautiously returning. With the fluidity of a receding storm cloud, it pulled back to the centre of the room, solidifying into a human shape.

'He's dying,' screamed Kamran. 'I didn't mean it!'

The figure moved towards Kamran, walking on feet trailed by wisps of smoke.

'He's over there on the bed,' Kamran said.

The black arm rose up, an arc of vapour following it.

'What are y –'

Black fingers pushed through Kamran's face. He screamed once and collapsed, the weight of his body creating a seismic event in the room.

The black figure turned towards Wahid, lying still on the bed. His arms were resting on his torso and he could have been sleeping. Only his chest was unmoving and the eye that wasn't a swollen purple bruise was staring unblinkingly upwards. The figure approached the boy and tilted its head to the side, regarding him with burning eyes. A book, lying on the ground amongst the mass of clothes, rose up in the air and sailed lightly towards it. The book hung in the space between the boy and the figure, rotating slowly. Then it began to smoulder. Pages first charred, then burst into flames. Fire rippled across the cover and it began to curl in on itself. The flames grew and the book blackened under the mass of writhing tongues. A large black hand gently curled around it and the crackling faded as the fire extinguished itself. A small ball of ashes settled in the palm of the hand.

The figure put one knee on the bed, the blanket singeing under it and leaned forward. With one hand, it gripped Wahid's jaw and pulled his mouth open. The other hand pushed the ball of ash down into it. Whatever force was holding the ashes tightly in place dissipated and the hot flakes of dead paper filled his mouth. They stuck to his teeth and lips and filled his throat. The figure moved its hand across the air above his face and some of the flakes caught in the currents created by the movement, spreading across the boy's face.

For a full minute, there was nothing. No movement, no sound. Just a djinn, full of blackness with glowing red eyes, that watched a boy, lying dead with a mouth stuffed with burnt paper. For a whole minute, there was just the silence of death.

Wahid's chest rose. Once, then again. And again. The gap between each rise and fall decreased until it reached a steady rhythm. He made a sound, soft and tired. The iris that had been staring up at the ceiling dilated. He sat up in one sudden motion, exhaling as he did so. What little ash was left in his mouth blew out.

Wahid gasped. He wiped his hand across his face, brushing grey flakes from it. They left dark smudges across his cheeks and forehead. He blinked once, then opened both eyes. He felt the contours of his face with trembling fingers and moaned softly as they traced an unbroken nose, the smooth ridges of his eyebrow and cheekbone around a healed eye. He breathed deeply, pulling air unhindered into his lungs and held it there for a few seconds. It tasted sweet, if lightly burnt – like caramel. Wahid wiped his lips with his hand and stared at the bits of ash that stuck to his skin. Then he looked up at the black figure standing in front of him.

Wahid scrambled backwards with a shriek. His voice was hoarse and tired. He stood up on the bed, hands bunched into fists and held in front of his face.

'Don't come near me. I know I can hurt you,' he said.

The figure seemed to shrug and then raised one hand, pointing at the prone body on the ground near its feet. Wahid looked down at the large man who had attacked him, lying face down.

'Is it ... did I do that?' he asked, his eyes wide and round with astonishment.

A mouth opened in the black face, a furnace roared inside and it began to laugh aloud. It was the sound of a million hornets raging simultaneously. The laughter echoed in on itself, as though it rose up from a deep chasm and became many voices laughing at once.

'Who are you?' Wahid asked.

'I,' said the figure, bowing grandiloquently, 'am Azah-zeel. Some people call me Shaitan. But I prefer Iblis.'

XXIII.

Wahid gaped at Iblis, trying to form a sentence and then realizing he had none in mind.

'You called me, boy, and so I came,' said Iblis, his mouth curving into a smile. The tip of a flame poked briefly out of the corner of his mouth, like a snake tasting the air.

'I … I didn't … I didn't know,' stammered Wahid.

'Well, now you do,' said Iblis. The voice still echoed and buzzed and made Wahid's teeth grind.

'Will you attack me? I can … fight you. I'm not scared of you,' said Wahid.

'When it is time to fear me, you will. But I will not attack you,' replied Iblis, waving a black hand dismissively in the air. Black vapour trails drifted off his fingers.

'How did … did I heal?' asked Wahid, gesturing to the man on the ground. 'He beat me up. Badly. Then I woke up and I was fine. Can I just … heal … like that?'

Iblis stood up and walked over to where the man lay, playfully nudging him with his foot.

'I healed you,' he said. 'You can't heal yourself. You can barely take care of yourself it seems.'

'How?'

The djinn laughed again. 'You do not know what you are?' Then he looked up and gestured at Wahid. 'Allah! He actually does not know!'

'What … what am I? What do you mean?' asked Wahid.

Iblis moved closer and Wahid instinctively moved backwards, catching himself from toppling over the side of the bed.

'You,' it said, 'are a djinn.'

Then, as Wahid stared at, it continued. 'Well, half-djinn anyway. Half-fire, half-earth. Your father was a djinn. Or your mother. Although, if your father was a djinn, you would be more fire than earth. So, it must be your mother.'

'No,' said Wahid. 'That's not … my mother is a … she's a human. And so is my father. I mean … I know they are. My father is dead. He died when I was ten years old. But my mother isn't a djinn. She's Mumtaz. Her name is Mumtaz.'

The djinn leaned forward and looked directly into Wahid's eyes.

'Oh, your mother was a djinn,' Iblis whispered. 'I can see it in you. You weren't carried to term in a belly made of mud. You were pushed out of a djinn womb, boy. I can see the fire inside you. Stronger now than when I first laid eyes on you. But I knew right away.'

The djinn sniffed him.

'How interesting,' he said. 'You are truly a unique creature. One of a kind.'

'That doesn't make any sense. And you're really Iblis? The Shaitan? I mean … the Devil?'

Iblis nodded. 'I am many things, boy. Yes, I suppose the Devil is one of them. I like the name Iblis though. It is what I was known by before the time of men. Sometimes I am called Azah-zeel, but that is mostly by my kind. Other names I have are … less flattering.'

Wahid stepped off the bed slowly, fists still raised.

'Okay … okay, Iblis. Fine. Shit. Fine. But, how is my mother a djinn? Because that –'

The man lying on the ground moaned. Wahid looked down at him, then looked closer. The kameez that he had taken for red in colour, was soaked with blood.

' – he's bleeding. A lot. Did you do that?'

The djinn didn't bother looking down. 'He has carved words into his chest and flayed his back. I think the words are names. He is … insane. I think that is the nice way to put it.'

'He said he'd killed my friend. I think … I think he's killed Hamza. Oh God. He's fucking killed Hamza.'

Iblis shrugged, black smoke drifting off his shoulders and dissipating around him.

Wahid's mind rifled through all the information he had collected on djinns in the last few days.

'So,' he said, 'I summoned you, right? I must have, I mean. That's why you're here. Which means I can control you, right? Doesn't it?'

More laughter from the djinn. It hurt Wahid's ears.

'Stop it! Please, you have to help me.'

'I did,' said Iblis. 'I saved your life. Although, I admit it was out of curiosity.'

'I'll … Look, I just want to know. This man said he killed my friend. I just want to know if Hamza is safe.'

'So considerate,' said Iblis in a sing-song taunt. 'Oh all right, let's amuse ourselves some more.'

Iblis walked to Kamran and bent over him. Then he dipped one finger into Kamran's head, passing it through the hair and skin of his scalp as easily as though it were passing through the air. He held the finger there, submerged into the side of Kamran's head for several seconds. Then he pulled it out. It was coated in a thick silver liquid that dripped as he raised his hand up. It shimmered like mercury. A thin strand stretched from the side of Kamran's head to the finger. Iblis opened his mouth and sucked on his finger. When he pulled it out, it was clean again.

He spat. A glob of lava sizzled on the floor.

'I see your friend. This man tortured him to death. Yes, his name was Hamza.'

Wahid let out a wail. He pressed his fists to his face, screaming. Then he threw himself on top of Kamran's unconscious body. He began to punch the face beneath him, fists colliding against cheek and forehead. It seemed to have no effect, except to hurt his hands. He grabbed the bloodied shirt and ripped it open, buttons popping as he did so. One flew up and hit him in the eye. He let out a startled scream. Then he fell backwards, scrambling away from Kamran's unconscious body. Dried blood coated the exposed chest and the shirt had ripped in places, leaving patches of cloth still stuck to the skin. Carved into the flesh were words, names formed by narrow canals of sliced muscle. They were scrawled chaotically, running into each other. Where they intersected, whole chunks had been gouged out. From breastbone to navel, it looked like a grotesque attendance sheet.

'What … the …' gasped Wahid.

'Fuck?' offered Iblis.

Wahid turned slowly and stared at Iblis, his eyes still wide.

'Whoever is after you, boy, they have some strange men in their employment,' said Iblis.

'Can you find out where Hamza is? Where is his … his body?'

Iblis shook his head. 'I took one taste of his memories and have no intention of doing it again. You were lucky. The boy he killed was close to the surface. To find detail, however, would lead to madness. Even for me.'

Wahid stood up abruptly. 'We should kill him,' he declared.

'Go ahead. He has done nothing to harm me. I just put him into a sleep that won't end for a full day or so. That is enough.'

Wahid looked around the room for a weapon of some kind. He knew there would be knives in the kitchen downstairs, but the moment the thought occurred to him, he realized he could not visualize himself using them. His anger and hatred of the man was deep and wretched, but he was not able to kill.

'So what shall it be, boy? I am getting bored and I am sure you did not call me here for lessons on murder.'

Wahid turned to Iblis and wiped the tears from his cheeks with shaking hands.

'I need your help. The Grine said you would know about … about Maheen … about how I can find the djinns. I need to stop this. I need to stop it now. Please.'

Iblis gestured to Wahid. 'Let's go outside. I like the air there.' Then he passed through the balcony door.

Wahid opened the door and followed him. The air outside was cool and damp; it was like passing through a fine netting made of dew. The balcony was lit by a shard of moonlight and in the distance, Wahid could see the city lights shimmering and dancing. Leaning against the railing, like a patch of night, was Iblis.

Wahid squinted, trying to make out which way Iblis was facing. The head, he realized, was looking away from him and at the dark waves roaring beyond.

'I can't see you. It's dark out here.'

'Ah, perhaps you would prefer another shape then?'

The djinn changed form. There was no visible shifting, just that one moment he was a tall figure made of black and the next he wasn't. What he was, was a cat, with orange fur and a thick swishing tail. It stood on the edge of the banister and stared at Wahid, purring softly.

'What are … I … Iblis?'

The cat changed. It was a woman, old and stooped. She was wrapped in a dull grey shawl with a leathery face and a large hooked nose. She laughed once, a high cackle that was exactly like the voice of every witch in every cartoon he had ever seen.

'Would you prefer this?' she rasped.

The old woman was a tall, thin woman, young and beautiful. She stood naked, with long black hair that covered her breasts and slender hands resting where her legs met. Her stomach was flat and her skin was the same colour as the moon.

'Or this?' she said, her voice low with lust.

The beautiful woman was Wahid's father. Looking as he did the day before he died.

'Stop it!' yelled Wahid.

The creature that looked like Rehman chuckled. Then it shifted again. Iblis was a man, one that Wahid couldn't recognize. The face was young, with a neatly groomed black beard outlining the hard edges of a firm jaw. Short black hair was parted on one side. He was dressed in a black shalwar kameez, and a flame red shawl curled around his shoulders.

'I read about this,' Wahid said. 'Some djinns can change shape.'

'Is that how people get information on djinns now? By reading about us?' said Iblis. 'Was it online? I bet it was. No one reads books any more. There was a time when if you wanted to know about a djinn, you would ask a djinn.'

'I am asking a djinn,' said Wahid. 'Now, please, tell me if you'll help me.'

'I might. Just because I'm bored. Depends on what you need.'

'I need to stop the djinns from attacking me again. I want to know why I was attacked in the first place. And I want to know what they did to my friend.'

'A girl?'

'Yes.'

'Of course. Describe it to me.'

So Wahid did. Iblis listened and then, once Wahid was done, he approached him.

'They stole her soul. You were right in guessing that. It is a terrible thing to do and doing so damns the djinn who did it to Hell. I have not heard of it being done in a very, very long time. They must fear you a great deal to have done that.'

'But why did they attack me?'

Iblis shrugged. 'I don't know. Very few of them talk to me. Besides, they have all gone now.'

'To Kaf? The djinn in the sweet shop. The one who told me about you. It said they have all gone to Kaf.'

'Yes. All of them withdrew from this world simultaneously, a few weeks ago. All of a sudden, after thousands of years, I was the only one of my kind left here.'

'But that doesn't make any sense. Why would they do that?'

'Someone who can kill us? That sounds like the kind of thing that would frighten those fools.'

'But I wasn't even bothering them. I didn't know anything about djinns. I just want to save Maheen,' said Wahid, his voice rising in desperation. 'And now Arif and Hamza are dead and I'm screwed. What can I do?'

Iblis seemed to consider this for a while.

'It seems to me,' he said finally, 'that you need to find a way into Kaf then.'

'How the fu … how can I do that?'

Iblis laughed loudly. 'You really are a good boy, aren't you? Your entire life is crumbling before your eyes and you can't bring yourself to say fuck.'

'Will you help me? Will you tell me how? I mean, you are … if you are Iblis. The real Iblis, aren't you the Devil?'

'The Devil *you* know,' said Iblis.

XXIV.

Hamza was standing in a universe of nothing. Pristine white stretched around him in every direction, brilliant in its clarity.

'Hello?' he said.

Silence swallowed the sound of his voice.

Hamza looked down. He was standing on more emptiness, a single speck on a blank page. He was about to take a tentative step forward, when he noticed his clothing. When he died, he had been wearing nothing but a pair of jeans, stained dark with blood. The jeans were gone and in their place he saw a clean white skirt, which ended just above his ankles. A second length of cloth, just as pure white, was loosely draped around his shoulders, covering his torso. He had never performed hajj, but recognized the ihram worn by those who did. The cloth was as white as his surroundings, so that it almost looked as though his hands and feet were disembodied, floating below him.

'Is this … is this Heaven?' Hamza said aloud, 'Am I in Heaven?'

'Yeah, I thought that too at first,' said a voice. Hamza whirled around with a yelp. Arif was standing behind him, dressed in the same white ihram, a grin stretching across his face.

'Oh my God, Arif!' screamed Hamza. He threw his arms around his friend and when he felt the solidity of Arif's body against his, Arif's arms squeezing him tight in response, he began to cry.

'What a pussy you are.' Arif laughed and Hamza pulled away, punching him on the shoulder, then wiping his tears.

'You're here. Am I dead?' asked Hamza.

'Yeah, sorry,' said Arif, shrugging. 'I don't know which one of us died worse.'

'I'm really dead. Fuck.' Then, 'Oh God, is this Heaven? Can I swear in Heaven? I probably shouldn't say the F-word in Heaven, right?'

Arif laughed hard, meaty guffaws ending in a snort.

'Oh Barslow, you are too fucking funny.'

'Fuck you, Chantilly. So I'm dead. Wow. Shouldn't I be more, I don't know, traumatized? Like in shock or something?'

'You'd think, right? But I don't think anyone ever is. Not when they get here anyway. The trauma probably happens just before death. Mine was too quick for me to notice really. I felt it in the grave afterwards. Did you see those two angels? Monkey and Nonkey, or something?'

'Oh God, yes,' said Hamza, rubbing his face as he recalled the experience, 'Mankar and Nakeer, I think. Those were angels? I thought they were demons from Hell. You saw them too?'

'Yeah, they came to me in the grave.'

'They came when I was still hanging in the room where that man killed me. I didn't even realize I was dead until I saw them.'

Arif began to walk, motioning for Hamza to follow him. They started walking through the emptiness, feet finding firm ground with each step even though none could be seen below.

'Not for me, man,' said Arif. 'I woke up in the grave. It was horrible. I think I woke up as soon as they closed it over me. I remember it was completely dark and I could hear the footsteps of people walking away. Were you there? At my funeral, I mean?'

'Yeah.'

'How was it?'

'It was … it was a funeral, man. What can I say?'

'You could tell me three virgins threw themselves on a pyre in lamentation or something. That's why you never became DM.'

Hamza slapped his forehead. 'The man who killed me. I think he was insane. He kept hurting himself and then hurting me. He wanted to know where Wahid was.'

'Yeah,' said Arif. 'A lot of people are after Wahid. Well, some of them aren't people. That's kind of why I'm taking you to meet someone.'

'Meet someone? Meet who?'

'You'll see,' said Arif with a wink.

Hamza realized slowly that the whiteness was not a void so much as a fog. As they walked, others began drifting out of the obscuring veil. Men and women, all dressed in the same ihrams, began appearing around them. He saw a gathering of fifty or so people, sitting cross-legged in a circle as a woman stood in the centre, delivering an animated oration.

'Who are –' Hamza started to say, then tripped.

Arif grabbed him by the shoulder and steadied him. 'Watch yourself,' he said as a little boy, no more than four years old, bumped past them with a ribbon of laughter trailing behind him.

'Who are all these people? Are we in Heaven?'

'This is Barzakh,' Arif said.

'Barzakh?'

'Yeah. Heaven and Hell are empty right now. They won't be filled until after Qiyamat. That's when Allah will judge everyone and send them to wherever they deserve to go. Barzakh is more like, well, it's like a waiting room.'

'A waiting room? So all these people are dead like us.'

'Yeah. Everyone who has ever died is here. I met my grandparents. It was cool.'

The crowds of people began to grow thicker. Knots and clusters of the dead spread out around them. Hamza looked for someone he might recognize. Instead, his search was abruptly halted by a mass of people standing off to one side. Several hundred men and women, young and old, grouped in a tight circle. Unlike everyone around them, their ihrams were black and they stood in silence, heads bowed. They created a stain on the purity of the environment that seemed almost blasphemous.

'Who're they?'

Arif lowered his voice to a whisper. 'They're people who failed the exam that those two angels take. Basically, they are going to go to Hell after Qiyamat. That's why their clothes are black. It kinda marks them out. Everyone stays away from them.'

'So they aren't Muslims? Is that it?'

'Oh no, getting the shiny white outfit has nothing to do with being a Muslim or non-Muslim. It's about what kind of person you were when you were alive. Good people get white and bad people get black.'

'There must be a lot of people wearing black then.'

'Not as many as you'd think. In fact, I've hardly seen any. This is the second group I've seen since I got here. I guess Allah's called All-Forgiving for a reason. Ah, here he is.'

A man walked up to them. He was dressed in the same sinless white ihram.

'You must be Hamza,' he said, with a smile. 'Assalam o Alaikum.'

'Walaikum as Salam,' replied Hamza. 'I'm sorry, do I … I mean, did I know you?'

'This is Wahid's father,' said Arif, patting the man on the shoulder. 'I found him, Rehman uncle. He just arrived a little while ago.'

'Wahid's father?' repeated Hamza, 'Oh! Yes! Salaam, uncle! Wahid used to talk about you. Uncle, Wahid is … he's in danger. Like, a lot of danger. You need to help him!'

'No beta,' said Rehman, his face becoming grim, 'I can't. I've been here too long. Which is why I've come to ask you to do so.'

'Me? How can I help? I'm dead too.'

Arif smiled, it was a smile devoid of joy. 'You just died. Like, literally just died. You can still go back. You won't be alive when you do, but we … well, we got special permission. Think of it like a hall pass, I guess.'

'What do you mean I won't be alive?' asked Hamza, his voice rising. 'Will I be a zombie?'

Rehman took Hamza's hand in his and patted it. When Hamza looked at him, he could see Wahid's eyes staring back.

'Beta, your ruuh, your spirit, is still linked to your body. If we hurry, we can send it back. The body may be dead, but the ruuh can keep it moving. Can make it do things that only the dead can do.'

'I really don't understand,' said Hamza.

'Think of it like having superpowers,' said Arif. 'You'll be Zombie Superman. That's better than being just a dead guy who can walk around.'

'So what then? I go back and save Wahid? What if I can't find him?'

'You'll find him,' said Rehman. 'You'll be able to go to him if that is what you choose to do. And you will be able to save him. If you agree, of course. We can't force you.'

'Look, if it means I can save Wahid from that psycho, then yes. Absolutely. Send me back right now. How do I go?'

Rehman pulled Hamza forward and hugged him, planting kisses on his cheeks. 'Thank you, beta, thank you. Allah be with you always.'

'Allah could probably have helped me not die in the first place,' said Hamza.

'Really?' Arif laughed. 'You choose this place to try blaspheming in? You got balls, man.'

'Oh, shut up, Chantilly. So how do I go back?'

Rehman stood back, holding Hamza at arm's length. Arif put an arm on his shoulder too.

'The Malak al Maut will send you back. It agreed to let you go when we approached it. Only it has the ability.'

'The Angel of Death? Do you mean those two angels with the long hair again?'

'No,' said Arif softly. 'Look up.'

Hamza looked up. He realized he hadn't looked up since he first found himself in this place and wondered how he could have missed doing so. The white surroundings ended high above, a ceiling of dark night sky sealing them in. Millions of stars sparkled constantly, each one flaring and fading as if struggling to escape the darkness.

'Whoa, didn't notice that. Where is he? Is he in the sky somewhere?'

'Look closer, beta,' said Rehman.

'That's no sky,' said Arif.

Hamza squinted, searching through the darkness above. He saw just the rippling of clouds, violet and deep blue curves swelling gently and the frantic sparkle of stars.

Except.

Except the clouds hinting through the darkness weren't softly smooth the way clouds could be. They rippled, like fur on the underbelly of an immense beast. Like fur, thought Hamza, or feathers.

The image presented above him coalesced in his mind and he staggered backwards, steadied himself and then sat down, head still tilted back to stare upwards in slack-jawed horror.

'Oh God,' he said.

'I know, right,' said Arif.

Feathers, millions of them, each one black and vast, stretched for miles overhead. It was like staring into the wings of a raven, only considering the size of the complete wing made Hamza's mind start whirling and his vision blur. In each feather, what Hamza had first mistook for stars, were eyes. They speckled the darkened plumage like grains of white sand, millions of eyes rippling as they blinked over and over.

'It's … it's a wing. Oh Allah, it's a wing,' gasped Hamza. 'How big is it?'

'Each wing is as large as the universe,' said Rehman, 'and he has many wings.'

Tears stung Hamza's eyes, curling down his cheeks, 'It's … Allah … oh Allah … it's beautiful.'

'To us,' said Arif with a smile, 'to us it is beautiful.' He motioned with his head to the blot of men and women wearing black. 'To those poor bastards, it's horrifying. That's why they keep their heads bowed. Too scared to look up. I don't ever want to know what they see when they do look.'

Hamza stood up, eyes still fixed above. 'So how will he send me back? Where is he? I just see the wing. How big must he be?'

'They say he is big enough to cup the Earth between his hands. But he knows you're here. Just close your eyes and he'll send you back when you are ready.'

Hamza closed his eyes, then opened them again. 'Will I … will I be able to return? Will I see you again?'

'You'll be back when it's done. When you want to come back, you can. And I'll be here. Just save Wahid, man. It's important.'

'I love you, Chantilly,' said Hamza, closing his eyes.

'I love you too, Barslow.'

Then a sound began, growing louder with such speed that Hamza had barely understood it before it drowned him. It was the sound of wings beating.

XXV.

'Aren't you supposed to be evil?' Wahid said to Iblis.

A part of his brain was screaming at him. It was telling him he had gone insane and this was all a grand hallucination. That he was lying on a hospital bed in a coma, caused by smashing through the windshield of a car that crashed while driving back from a party.

Iblis leaned against the railing, arms crossed as he smiled back at Wahid. 'That's just bad PR,' he said. 'And not everyone thinks I'm evil, you know. There's a group of people in Uruk who started worshipping me some centuries ago. They created a whole religion around me, declared me a Peacock and said I gave birth to the Universe in the form of an egg. I saw some of them in Dusseldorf a few years ago. Nice people. Persecuted for their beliefs of course.'

'So you aren't evil?'

Iblis laughed. It was, thankfully, a human sound.

'Only if you piss me off,' he said.

'My father once told me that when he went for hajj he threw stones at the Devil. At a rock that represents well … you.'

'Yes, I've seen that. They used to be pillars. Three of them I think. Now they are walls. And all the good little Muslims throw pebbles at them. Do you know why?'

Wahid shook his head.

'Because they believe they're re-enacting a story in which your Prophet Ibrahim threw stones at the Devil who appeared before him thrice. They believe the stones drove the Devil away because Ibrahim was acting under the guidance of an angel, and by doing it again they hurt me now.'

'Do they?'

'Not at all. Besides, like everything else, they got the details of that day wrong.'

'You were there? You *did* appear in front of Hazrat Ibrahim?'

'Yes,' said Iblis, 'and you know what? I didn't run away because the stones had some magical angel-given powers. I ran away because no one likes having stones tossed at them. Yet … today, people still toss stones at a wall. That part of the hajj has killed over a thousand people over the years, crushed or suffocated by the crowds. Yet I'm the bad guy.'

'So why do you want to help me then?' asked Wahid suspiciously.

'Because I'm bored, I suppose. I've existed since before mankind. And after a while, there are almost no new things to see and experience. But you are something new, something unique. That's what your name means, after all. You can be a fun distraction indeed.'

'So what do we do?'

Iblis shrugged. 'Beats me.'

Wahid decided he preferred the possibility that he was hallucinating all this from the depths of a coma.

'But you said you can help me? You said that.'

'Whoever your mother is, she must be deeply disappointed by you. The part of you that is a son of Adam is to blame, I suppose. He never did pay attention to what he was told. I said I can help you figure it out. So let's get figuring, boy.'

The wind picked up and growled as it rushed across the ocean. On the road behind the hut, a car drove slowly, casting a false moon against the sky with its headlights.

'So what do you know about Kaf?' Iblis asked.

'Nothing,' Wahid said, yearning for a computer and a high-speed Internet connection.

'Kaf is not of this world. It is connected to it though. Djinns can use many paths to get from here to there and back. But those paths are closed to me, since I am an outcast. *The* outcast. And I'm not sure they would work for you either. You are still too human.'

'So, then what?' asked Wahid.

'I know of one way. It is an old route and not without some dangers, but it might still be open.'

'How do we get to it?'

'Well, we begin by walking,' said Iblis.

'What about that guy,' said Wahid, glancing towards the room behind them.

'What about him?'

'What if he wakes up? We should call the police?'

Iblis laughed again. 'Oh? I haven't spent much time in Karachi recently, but has the police here become magically competent?'

Wahid hung his head, sighing in exasperation. 'No. No, they haven't. Plus, I'm supposed to be in hiding. I don't know, maybe we should at least tie him up.'

'Do you have any rope?'

'No.'

'You really have no solutions to any of your life's problems, do you? Well, since you have no rope and we obviously cannot call the police, might I suggest we leave him there? He won't wake until morning and I can assure you he is quite deranged. Maybe he will do you a favour and kill himself.'

'You think he'd do that?'

'I've seen humans do stranger things.' Iblis shrugged. 'Look, I'm starting to get bored. Do you want to go to Kaf or not?'

'I do,' grumbled Wahid.

'Well, then let's start walking, please. We have a journey ahead of us.'

They exited the hut and made their way to the road, walking side by side through the night. They passed the shops, all shuttered and silent. Iblis kept a fast pace, bare feet moving silently over gravel and rocks. A truck rumbled past once and before Wahid could ask if they should stop it and ask for a ride, Iblis shook his head.

Cool ocean spray was freeze-framed in the buzzing neon signage of a petrol station ahead. As they walked towards it, a motorcycle carrying two men pulled up in front of them. One of the men jumped off, lifted his shirt and pulled out a revolver. He aimed it at Wahid and grinned.

'Oye, phone and wallet,' he snapped, then he levelled the gun at Iblis. 'You too. Hurry up.'

There was a standard operating procedure to being robbed and all Karachiites knew to follow it. Wahid instinctively looked down so as not to meet the thief's eyes and reached for his wallet, then paused as realization flared inside him.

'Uh … I've already been robbed,' he said.

'Fuck you, give me your phone and your wallet. You too, asshole, if you don't do it now, I'll shoot you.'

Iblis stood silently, his eyes closed as though he had fallen asleep standing.

'Look, I promise I –' Wahid began, then the man punched his shoulder with the butt of his gun. Wahid cried out in pain.

'That'll be enough,' said Iblis, opening his eyes. Fire burned inside them, casting a glow over his face.

'Ya Allah,' shrieked the man with the gun. There was a sharp explosive sound and Wahid saw the muzzle of the gun flash in the dark. Iblis didn't flinch even though the gun had been aimed at him. Instead, with one smooth movement, he stepped forward and wrapped a large hand around the gun. There was a snapping sound and the man screamed.

'Oye!' yelled his accomplice on the motorcycle. He leapt off and began running at them with his own gun pulled out. Wahid crouched down and wrapped his hands around his head, just as the stutter of gunshots crashed around him. There was more screaming, then the sound of dry wood snapping. Then there was silence.

Wahid looked up. Iblis was standing, brushing his sleeve. On the ground in front of him lay the two men. The one who had tried to rob them was curled in a foetal ball, whimpering as he stared at his hand, shards of metal stabbed through it. The other lay flat on his back, staring up at them through bulging eyes. The skin on his face had melted and ran like thick paint in a puddle around his head, the surface bubbling.

'Can you ride a motorcycle?' Iblis was asking. Wahid tried to shield himself from the stench of burning flesh and managed to gag only slightly as he shook his head. A dull ringing in his ears made it hard to hear.

Iblis sighed, lifted the bike and straightened it. He sat down and revved the engine. The silencer had been removed and the bike roared, punching through Wahid's deafness. Iblis grinned. Wahid clambered on behind him.

'Be careful not to touch me,' Iblis yelled over the engine. 'I have no interest in burning.'

Wahid put his hands behind him, gripping the edges of the seat and pressed his legs tightly against the motorcycle.

Iblis spun it around and aimed it at the road, then twisted the accelerator, lurching them forward. Wahid bit down on a scream as they blasted through the narrow streets, Iblis swerving around every ditch and breaker. Soon, they were speeding across the wide road that connected the outlying beach to Karachi. Even late in the night it was thronging with traffic and they had to slow down to find passage between cars and trucks. They crossed over into Clifton, passing closed restaurants and high-rise offices. At a traffic light, a group of policemen tried waving them down. Iblis slowed the bike enough to let the closest cop see his eyes. The man flinched and stumbled backwards as they sped away.

'Where are we going?' he screamed in Iblis's ear.

'Almost there,' yelled Iblis back over his shoulder.

They took a side lane, diving into the bowels of a suburb.

'I really can't be seen here,' Wahid yelled over the roaring bike.

Iblis ignored him, instead accelerating so that they turned into another lane at such an angle that Wahid almost fell off. He did tumble off when it came to a screeching stop, landing on the road with just enough balance in place to keep from crashing down.

'What the hell, man,' he snapped at Iblis.

Iblis killed the engine and pushed the bike to the side of the road, letting it drop to the ground near the sidewalk.

'I thought time was of the essence for you,' said Iblis.

'Yeah, but I don't want to die along the way.'

'I'm quite sure you are tougher than that.' Iblis smiled.

Wahid swallowed a few choice curses and looked around. He had driven through here many times and recognized the gate just ahead of them.

'That's the entrance to the graveyard,' he said. 'Is that … is that where we're going? In there?'

He knew the graveyard well. Had stood many times amongst the rows of marble headstones. His father was buried there.

'No. That is just a graveyard,' said Iblis. 'We are going there.'

He pointed across the road. Wahid turned to see a broken wall, fractured brick facade exposing an empty plot of land just beyond.

'What's there?' he asked.

'What do you see?'

The boundary wall had fallen in places, piles of brick strewn across the sidewalk in front. Through the gaps he could see nothing but dirt and a few strangled bushes. Despite the explosion of development in Defence, there were still a few untouched spaces left. They belonged, he guessed, to people who had not yet decided to make the move across the city or were locked in property disputes with warring relatives.

'It's an empty plot. I've driven by it many times. So what is it really? Some sort of magic portal or something?'

'Ah, you are catching on. Well done,' said Iblis.

'Yes, well, it's kinda typical, isn't it? In fantasy novels, you walk through a place like this and end up in Narnia or Tanelorn or some such place. So what? We walk in and end up in Kaf?'

Iblis crossed the road and stood in front of a gaping hole in the brick wall, motioning for Wahid to join him.

'No. Not Kaf. Kaf is still far. But yes, this is a … what's the word you used … portal. I suppose that's right. It's a forgotten place. Abandoned. And it leads to other forgotten and abandoned places. And through there we will find our road to Kaf.'

'Let's do it then,' said Wahid, stepping forward. He climbed through the hole, bricks crumbling when brushed by his feet. Iblis followed, passing through the wall.

They were standing on a moonlit field of dirt, ground flattened by shadows. It wasn't a particularly large area, with houses blocking it in on three sides. Scraggly bushes hunched over the walls, thick with thorns. A rat ran past them, disappearing under a rock.

'Well, this is anticlimactic,' said Wahid.

'Quit whining,' growled Iblis, 'follow me.'

The ground crunched loudly under Wahid's sneakers as they made their way towards the far wall. On the other side of that wall stood a small bungalow, rising one storey above with darkened windows.

'Here,' said Iblis.

They had reached the centre and Iblis was looking down at the ground. Wahid looked as well and then looked back at Iblis.

'I'm really not sure I'm ready to climb down into a sewer,' he said.

At their feet was a circular manhole cover, a pancake of concrete almost entirely hidden under a thick layer of dirt.

'Just push it aside,' said Iblis.

Wahid crouched down and put his hands to the edges of the lid. It slid with surprisingly minimal effort. Underneath wasn't the darkened canal full of shit and muck that Wahid pre-emptively held his breath against, but a flight of stairs curling in a tight spiral.

'Huh,' said Wahid. 'Where does it go?'

The entrance was just barely large enough to fit a grown man. The stairs were made of steel and not particularly neglected either, they seemed as if they had been used frequently enough to avoid any build-up of dust, their surface gleaming dully in the moonlight.

'It goes to Kaf, but it is the long way there,' said Iblis.

Wahid stared at Iblis. He was silhouetted against the full moon, red eyes staring down from out of the darkness.

'Now, come on.'

Iblis pushed past Wahid and climbed down the stairs. Wahid followed, the metal frame wobbling slightly with each step. As he descended round the first narrow curve, the meagre moonlight seemed to shrivel and darkness gawped below. The stairs seemed to disappear into it, with no evidence of how far below the eventual landing would be.

'Iblis?' hissed Wahid.

'What?' called out Iblis from somewhere below him.

'How far down does this go?'

'Stop being such a coward and climb down already,' grumbled Iblis.

Wahid descended into darkness, taking each step cautiously by feeling it with his foot first. The darkness turned out to be just a wedge, brightening abruptly after a few feet. Wahid emerged through it and found himself at the end of the stairs. He blinked in confusion, then looked back up the way he had come and then again at the surroundings he found himself in. It seemed as though the stairs had led nowhere at all. He was still standing in the same flat, empty field of dirt and rocks that he had left above. There was a sky overhead, with a moon glaring balefully in the distance. The only difference was the spiral staircase behind him, whose top seemed to disappear into the night sky; much longer when viewed from below. Iblis stood a few steps ahead of him, staring at the boundary wall that they had entered through. An identical hole created by the decay of bricks gave a view of a road ahead.

'What's going on?'

Iblis looked at Wahid with his fiery eyes and grinned.

'Oh, come on! Just tell me!'

'Fine, fine.' Iblis laughed. 'It's not that complicated. Especially for a brilliant mind like yours that has clearly achieved a higher state of intelligence by reading books about dragons.'

'I never said that.'

'Oh hush, now is not the time for wounded egos. I told you, Kaf is close to your world, but separate. Think of it like, let's see, two hands pressed together.' Iblis placed his hands flat against each other in demonstration. 'One hand is your world and the other is Kaf. They both come from the same body but are separate, yes? Well, there is a distance between them, even when they are so flat against each other. The distance might be as fine as an atom, but it exists. We are in that space, in that distance between the two worlds.'

Wahid turned it over for a few seconds in his head. 'So, who put the stairs here?'

'In every city of the world, a place like this exists. Places where reality is thin. They tend to be abandoned areas, forgotten by the people of the city and so worn down that their existence becomes, well, vague. But in Karachi, a place was set aside for just this purpose by your government.'

'By the government?'

'Well, by the army to be exact. Your army is your government after all, even I know that much about your politics. This is the only country in the world that has diplomatic relations with Kaf.'

'Hang on,' said Wahid, rubbing his face as the information settled in him. 'You're saying we have a … what? An ambassador for djinns?'

'Yes. Honestly, it surprises me it took so long to happen. In the centuries before, when the Islamic empire was spread across the world like an immense hand, the various Khalifas used to meet with djinns on an official basis all the time. But when the empire disintegrated, especially in the years after the horse archers from Mongolia chewed up Baghdad, the rituals of communication were lost. Muslims still believed in djinns, but they did not speak to them as equals or with respect. But your army decided it was in its best interest to set up a channel of communication. So they consulted every scrap of knowledge they could find. It probably wasn't easy, but eventually they discovered a way. They created an entire space in the city, several miles of houses and developed land, and then sacrificed the whole area. Wiped it out quietly and took it out of any maps that might exist. It's an incredible achievement really. And so that space became a forgotten path, a passageway between Karachi and Kaf.'

'So they use it? Like, do army people come down here?'

'Not just anyone is allowed. Most cannot see the stairs, even if they look for them. But there is probably one person in the army who can see it. Who has been given the ability by my kind and he comes here whenever he must speak to djinns.'

Wahid leaned against the frame of the stairs and was silent for several seconds. Then, recomposing himself, he said, 'Okay. Fine. If you say so, then fine. Fuck it. I've been attacked by djinns, kissed by a chudail and called bhenchod by a boy who claims to be the King of Karachi. If the army wants to have diplomatic contact with the djinn world, then sure. Why not? So where are the djinns? I don't see any.'

'Like I said, this isn't Kaf. If the djinns have withdrawn to their world, they will not be here. This place is always mostly empty anyway. It is not particularly safe. To get lost here would be a dangerous thing indeed. Whichever human is given access will never walk beyond that boundary wall. Not if he wants to ever find his way back again. Fortunately for you, I'm an excellent guide.'

'How do I know I can trust you?'

'You don't.' Iblis smiled. 'But then you don't seem like a boy with many choices. Now come on.'

They walked to the boundary wall, Wahid glancing back at the staircase every few steps. It did not disappear, as he had expected it to.

EARTH BOY

I.

Wahid and Iblis walked through the hole in the wall, and into another world. On the other side was a double-lane road, stretching ahead of them into the distance. The closely packed houses of a Karachi suburb were gone, replaced with empty stretches of sand on either side of the road. Wind carried fractal patterns of dust across their path and the moon lit their way with a clean brilliance.

'Stay close,' said Iblis, 'this is not the kind of place we want to get lost in.'

'Yeah, yeah, you told me already,' grumbled Wahid.

'And why are you in such a foul mood?'

They were walking at a steady pace along the road, their voices the only sound, other than the low whine of the wind.

'I don't know. I'm sorry. Look, I've had a lot to digest in a short time, okay. Gimme a break.'

'True. What bothers you the most?'

'Honestly?' Wahid sighed. 'You said my … uh … my mother is a djinn. But that would mean my father would have known about it, right?'

'Perhaps. It's not impossible for him to donate his seed without realizing he'd done it. But even if he did not know, your adopted mother would. After all, you certainly didn't spring from her belly.'

'Then who's my real mother? Which … I mean, is there a djinn out there that gave birth to me?'

Iblis shrugged. The length of red shawl draped across his shoulders trailed after him like a stream of blood.

'I don't know. It's something that has not been done before. It isn't even considered possible. A thing such as you has never existed. Who did it? Why was it done? I cannot say.'

They walked for several minutes in brooding silence. Finally, Wahid felt the strength go out of him. It left him like air rushing out of a deflating balloon.

'Can we take a break? I'm kind of exhausted,' he said.

'I suppose so. It will be night for some time still. We can probably just settle down right here and then start again in the morning. Best to stay on the road, sleeping in the desert on either side isn't considered safe.'

They sat down right where they stood, on the hard tarmac of the road. It looked freshly laid, surface still black as a beetle with painted white dashes dividing its length. Wahid sat cross-legged across Iblis and stared at him. Then before he could begin to speak, Iblis cut him off.

'Yes, I am the Devil. Yes. Satan. Shaitan. Iblis. If you ask me one more time, I am going to leave you here. See if you can find your way back then.'

'I know, I know, it's just, well … how? I mean, I get that my life has become weird, but the Devil himself? I mean, if my life is going to become some weird fantasy adventure, then I think I prefer magicians and dragons and orcs and stuff. Those I understand. Those I've read about.'

Iblis cocked an eyebrow at Wahid. 'Your complaint is that you cannot deal with the creatures you have met? But why not? They are of your own people, are they not? Dragons and orcs and such are of foreign lands. I've never seen a dragon and I doubt they exist. Djinns, chudails, even me – we are all things that you are supposed to believe in. Yet when faced with them, you are filled with horror and doubt? I do not understand the Muslims of the modern world. Your faith is only worthwhile if it is never confirmed, it seems.'

'Look, give me a break, okay. You can understand why this is all a bit much. I mean, come on. At what point do I go back to having a normal life?'

'A normal life? Why would you want that? I doubt you can go back to it even if you tried now.'

Wahid sighed. 'I'd like the choice, that's all. I think that's not too much to ask. So if you're really the Devil, or Shaitan or whatever, why aren't you in Hell? Aren't you supposed to be busy running Hell?'

Iblis lay down on the road. Raising his arms upwards towards the dark blue sky, he exclaimed, 'Oh Allah! And you threw me out of Heaven! These idiots don't even know their own history any more.'

'What?' said Wahid, defensively. 'What is it?'

'There is no Hell,' Iblis said. 'Not yet. Not until after Qiyamat anyway. Then Jahannam will be created and filled. So no, I am not there, nor will I be for a long time. Nor will I be running it. Honestly, don't they teach you anything now? After Qiyamat, I too, like so many others, will face my punishment in Hell. Allah has no need for servants to rule on his behalf. Although, given how I'm already being punished, perhaps I'll be offered some reprieve on the end days.'

'How are you being punished?'

'You want my story? Fine then, it's not a bad way to pass the time, I suppose. That's how people did it in the past, after all. Now everyone just watches porn and masturbates.'

With Wahid struggling to get into a comfortable position, Iblis began his story.

Iblis's Story

For a million upon million years before the sons of Adam, the world was only for djinns. They existed when the Earth was nothing but flame and rock, created by Allah from the fiercest of fires. Djinns thrived in that world. They danced in the air, flitting across the currents of scorching heat, bathed in molten oceans, and made love on the lips of volcanoes. The world was theirs and, in this knowledge, there was rejoicing.

None was thrilled with their existence more than Iblis. He was the oldest of the djinns, created first from the stuff of fire by Allah. None was wiser than him and none more devoted to prayer and praise of the Creator. When the djinns found their disagreements too evenly split, he was their adjudicator. When they needed guidance in moral judgement, his was the advice they sought out. So beloved was he by all, that there was neither surprise nor jealousy when Allah gifted him the opportunity to live amongst the angels.

Just as djinns are made from fire, angels are made from light. Theirs was an existence of complete and utter devotion to the divine, for Allah had not granted them the freedom of thought and intellect in the way that he had given to the djinns. Amongst them, Iblis was truly happy. For with them he could serve his creator as well as revel in the peace and solace he needed for meditation on the nature of the universe that had been gifted to them all.

Over time, the Earth cooled. What was fire became ice. Then ice melted into water. Rock softened into mud and clay. Lava drowned under oceans and volcanoes eroded into islands. The djinns found the changing environment not to their liking and so they petitioned Iblis for help. He, in turn, begged Allah for a home suitable to his people's needs. Allah granted the wish, dividing the world in two. From that moment on, there were two earths, two universes, separated by a membrane as fine as skin. The djinns could choose their home and naturally they chose the one they were best suited for, though they did pass from their world of sand and heat to the world of oceans and green whenever they wished to do so.

Then, one day, when the continents on the new world were still fused together like the plates of a skull, the Creator summoned all the angels and Iblis. They stood in his divine presence, separated from him by hundreds of thousands of miles, for to be any closer would scatter their forms, so great was his light. Then he showed them that which he had newly created.

It was a single figure, standing upright as Iblis was, though not as tall. Its skin was not as black as Iblis's, but brown as clay. And Iblis could see that though what lay beneath the skin was red, it was not made of fire but of water. Iblis stared in wonder at this newest invention and praised the Divine Creator for his limitless ingenuity.

'O Allah,' he called out, 'such a sweet yet fragile creature. What is to be his nature?'

And the voice of Allah was heard everywhere, both outside and inside Iblis, just as the angels too felt it coursing through them. Allah told them this was Adam and he was the first of his kind. There would be another to join him and together they would live in Heaven, this place of eternity and serenity that was granted to those closest to Allah.

This rankled Iblis. He had been granted this proximity to the divine through epochs of devotion and prayer. Why did this new creature enjoy the same privileges in such a short time? But Iblis knew better than to give voice to this question. Instead, he approached Adam and smiled as best he could, forcing his irritation from his mind.

'Welcome to the world,' he said.

The man smiled and looked around, first at the glorious light of Allah that filled their surroundings and then at the Earth below.

'What are those?' the man asked, pointing down.

Iblis looked. Streams of winged creations were sailing through the blue skies underneath. They had existed for an age, given form by Allah.

'Those are creations of the Divine,' said Iblis. 'Like you and I and all that is.'

'Birds,' said Adam, 'I shall call those birds.'

'Birds,' repeated Iblis, watching them wheeling across the world, wondering why the naming had come so simply to Adam, yet never even occurred to Iblis as a possibility, or a need.

Then the voice of Allah filled them all again. It commanded them to press their foreheads to the ground, all but Adam, for it was to him that they were submitting. He was the best of all creation, said Allah. The angels did as instructed, for their will was bound to the words of Allah. But Iblis did not.

Allah demanded to know why, when all had been instructed to declare their inferiority to Adam, did Iblis still stand tall.

'O Allah,' Iblis cried out. 'How can I accept him as my better? He is made of clay, that which is soft and easily destroyed. I am made of fire, consuming and relentless. He is not even my equal, much less my better.'

This enraged Allah. He declared Iblis disobedient and cursed him to an eternity in Jahannam. Then, to add to Iblis's horror, Adam intervened. He asked that Iblis be given clemency, that his pride not be regarded as so damning. Allah agreed, changing Iblis's sentence so that he was cast out of Heaven and condemned to Earth below, barring him entry from even the world of his own kind.

For years did Iblis wander the Earth, his heart so full of rage, he could have killed all of its creatures had he the power. He swore to avenge himself and to show Allah that the creation he had been so proud of was flawed and weak. That Iblis was better. Djinns should have been the favoured ones.

When, on occasion, the man came to the world below, Iblis hid from view and observed. He saw that Allah had given him a companion, a female. They laughed and played in the grass and amongst the trees, having descended to Earth for exploration and to, no doubt, continue naming things as though all the universe was theirs to do so with.

Iblis noted a pattern in their visits. They were free to swim in the waters, play in the grass, and even climb any tree they wished. But there was one tree they would not approach. It stood alone in a meadow, the branches stretching wide and thick with leaves. From the tips of each branch grew apples more round and more red than any Iblis had ever seen. He studied these for some time, pulling one down and marvelling at the perfect skin, unblemished and polished. He took a bite, tentatively at first. Thick syrup ran down his chin and the immeasurable sweetness that filled his mouth staggered him. Then he understood what the fruit was.

He spat out the bite and threw the rest of the apple into a stream nearby. After that, he planned.

'You look so happy,' he said to them, the next time they were on Earth.

'We are,' replied the man. The woman sang her agreement.

'Truly such joy can only come of the complete and utter freedom to do as you wish for all eternity,' said Iblis, walking with them, but also subtly leading them.

'Yes,' agreed the man. 'Our freedom is a wonderful thing.'

They entered the meadow and he pretended surprise when they both halted at the edge of the clearing.

'Come, we shall celebrate your existence. This tree bears the sweetest of fruit. They are my favourite. Let us eat them together.'

But the man and the woman did not move. Instead, they looked first at the tree, then at Iblis and finally at each other.

'What is the matter?' inquired Iblis, his tone weighted with sincerity.

'We are not permitted to eat the fruit of that tree,' said the female. Her eyes were downcast when she spoke.

'Really?' said Iblis. 'That is odd. No such prohibition has been put on me. Nor on anyone else in all of this world.'

'It is on us,' said Adam. He sounded firm and confident, or at least attempted to be so. Iblis was sure he could hear confusion stirring in the soul beneath.

'Not even a bite?' said Iblis, pulling down two apples. They were both perfect and identically large. His back was turned towards them as he picked the fruit from the tree. Then he dropped one on the ground, letting it land softly in the thick grass below. He tutted at his own carelessness and bent down to retrieve it. Then he returned to the pair, biting one apple as he did. They watched as he closed his eyes and moaned in pleasure, the apple crunching noisily between his teeth.

'It is the finest apple I have ever tasted. Surely, nothing can come of eating just an apple,' he said. 'After all, how free can you be if you cannot eat an apple?'

The man and his companion looked at each other and in their glance was Iblis's victory. He handed the apple to the man who took a large bite and then gave it to the female who did the same. They both smiled as they chewed, wiping the nectar that dribbled from the sides of their mouths with their hands. The man finished his bite first and sighed. The woman did so as well.

Iblis smiled.

II.

'You switched the apple.'

'Hm?'

'When you dropped it, you switched the apples. You hid a safe one in the grass and that's the one you picked and bit into, and gave them the other one. Right?'

'Yes. It's a simple trick and now you couldn't even fool a child with it. But back then, it was the first cheat ever performed.'

'So now you're trapped here.'

'It's not so bad,' said Iblis. 'I have gotten used to it, I suppose. After all, humans are trapped here too. Until Qiyamat anyway.'

'And when is Qiyamat?'

'Only Allah knows. There are signs that will foretell its arrival. Some have come to pass, small ones. But those occurred centuries ago. The major signs, however, are still to come.'

'I read about those. Recently, actually.'

Iblis yawned, then grabbed a fistful of sand from the roadside and tossed it in Wahid's direction. 'Go to sleep, half-djinn. Even I am tired.' Then he turned his back to Wahid and almost instantly began to snore.

Wahid lay with head resting on his crossed arms and stared up at the night sky. He was just considering how sleep seemed so far away when he too began to snore.

III.

Hamza woke up in the same room in which he'd died. He broke the stillness with a cry, his voice raspy and tinged with whistles as air escaped through the gash across his throat. He was still hanging where Kamran had left him, arms stretched above his head and feet dangling inches from the ground.

Hamza growled, saliva flecking around his mouth as he strained at the rope around his wrists. He pulled down with strength that felt more than any he had ever had before. The rope broke with a snap and he landed nimbly on his feet.

He stepped forward, bringing his arms down in front of him. The rope had snapped above the knot, leaving thick cords still bound around his wrist. Hamza stared in astonishment at how easily it came undone when he pulled his hands apart, falling to the floor around him.

Hamza looked at his surroundings, his eyes finding the darkness in the room easy to penetrate. There was the empty chair his killer had rested on, a washbasin in the corner and a table next to it. He walked over to the table and inspected the items lying on it. An assortment of knives, their blades crusted with skin and blood, and a hand drill, the spiral tip just as thick with gore. Looking at them reminded Hamza of his own wounds and he took a step back, as if afraid the weapons might still be able to hurt him on their own.

His fingers traced the gashes and gouged parts of his torso, trembling more with each discovery. He refused to look down at himself; he could not bring himself to. When he felt the gaping grin curving across his neck, fingers barely touching the peeling lips, Hamza screamed. It was not a scream of pain – there was no physical pain at all – but of fury.

After several seconds, he brought himself under control. Still shivering with anger, he grabbed a knife and stomped towards the door. He slammed his palms against it. The door snapped off its hinges and crashed in front of him, breaking in two.

'Oye!' yelled someone at the end of a long hallway. It was dimly lit, with a single flickering bulb, and a man was running towards Hamza from the far end. The man was not his killer, but was dressed in the same white shalwar kameez as his killer, and had the same black turban on his head. He was carrying a machine gun in one hand. Hamza recognized it as a Kalashnikov, having seen it in so many movies when he was alive.

'When I was alive,' Hamza thought. Then he screamed.

The man didn't slow his pace. Still running towards Hamza, he raised the gun up to waist height. A rattle of shots bounced off the walls and bullets spattered around Hamza. Two of them punched into his chest and he screamed in surprise. He flung the knife at his attacker. It sliced through the air between them and rammed into the man's chest, burying itself up to the hilt. The force of the impact lifted the man off the ground and threw him back, an arc of blood curving after him, following him down to the ground.

Hamza threw himself on top of the man, screaming with rage as he brought a fist down onto the shocked face beneath him. It felt like punching an overripe tomato. The head exploded under Hamza's blow with a wet sound, brains and skull fragments spreading like butterfly wings across the floor.

Hamza stared at the bloody mess and fell backwards, scooting away on all fours.

The silence that followed was so sudden it seemed almost a force of its own. Hamza looked away from the man's remains, feeling tears course down his cheeks. He wiped them with his clean hand and saw that they left black smears across his palm.

'What the fuck,' said Hamza, each word hitching on jagged sobs.

After several minutes of struggle, he brought his emotions under some measure of control. Standing up, he allowed himself a glance at the man behind him. The body lay sprawled awkwardly on the dirty ground, ending violently at the neck. It was definitely not the man who had killed him; this one was smaller and thinner. Hamza prayed for the opportunity to do to his killer what he had done here and then walked towards the end of the hall. He absently felt the bullet holes in his chest, barely registering that they were dry.

IV.

A wet finger on his face. Tracing the curve of his cheek. A sound, so far away. Like the rumble of a distant engine. The finger drew a slick pattern across his forehead. The engine growl grew louder.

Wahid brushed at the annoyance, trying to stay inside the warm cocoon of sleep.

Breathing. Heavy and fast. Hot stinky breath on his face.

Wahid slurred a soft protest, pushing out his hand. The hand pressed against a tangle of hair.

'Maheen?' he murmured, opening his eyes slowly.

A grunt and then a laugh. Not gentle and playful, but coarse, like bark being ripped from a tree. Wahid opened his eyes and sat up.

At first he thought it was a large dog, or perhaps a small bear. Bent over on all fours, its body was covered in a thick matting of fur. Except, it wasn't fur. Fur would have been short and these hairs were long, dangling low like the beard of a mullah. The creature's entire body was so densely carpeted that he could not see the face beneath. The animal padded away from him and then began to move in a wide circle, sniffing at the air with a nose hidden behind the heavy shag.

'Iblis,' Wahid hissed. 'Iblis! Wake up!'

He glanced at where Iblis should have been lying and saw no one. The road was empty on either side of him and there was no sign of his companion. He turned back towards the creature, ambling gently around him. It stood up, not clumsily like the bears he had seen at the zoo, but easily and with comfort. It stood straight, long arms dangling by its side. Wahid revaluated his first impression, wondering if it was an ape of some sort. But the back was too straight and it stood too tall.

'Hello?' he said.

It was a man, or at least shaped like a man. There was the curve of the head and the widening of shoulders. The arms and legs were indeed longer than the small torso should have allowed for and it only stood as high as Wahid's chest. The hair fell flat against it, too thick for Wahid to see eyes or any other feature. He had the peculiar realization that had he not seen it moving, he would not have known which way it was facing.

'A visitor,' it said, the way a goat would speak if it were able to. There was an effort involved in combining the syllables, the words stitched together with warbling pitches. 'None for ages. And now so many.'

'What are you?' asked Wahid, crawling back a bit and then standing up as well.

'Al Jassasah,' replied the creature.

'Jassas ... what?'

'A servant,' it said, long thin hands rising out of the tangles of hair. The fingers were edged with curving yellow nails that came to jagged ends. It raised its hands to the sides of Wahid's head, and he tried not to flinch too obviously as it clasped him. The head tilted upwards and he heard it sniff wetly. 'First to come since Tamim al Dari, yet different from what came before. Different from all.'

'Tamim al ... I'm sorry. I don't know who that is,' said Wahid.

'A follower of Iisa, become a follower of the unlettered Prophet. Many years ago.'

Wahid could now smell the creature. It was the smell of freshly cut meat. He was reminded of the goats sacrificed on Eid, of standing as a young boy at the butcher shop with his father and covering his nose with his hands to shield himself from the stink of animals growing rank with fear.

'Iisa?' Wahid said. 'That's Jesus? So this Tamim was a Christian. And then he converted to … to Islam. The unlettered Prophet would mean Prophet Muhammad, Peace Be Upon Him, right?'

Jassasah let go of Wahid's head and turned, facing away from him. A hand pointed towards the side of the road. Wahid followed the direction it was pointing in and saw a small structure in the distance. It glimmered in the darkness, a cube of moonlight just at the edge of where it grew too dark to see ahead.

'Come,' said Jassassah in its broken voice, 'he is eager to meet you.' Then it bent over, going down on all fours, and began trotting towards the small building. It paused after a few metres, turned back and called to Wahid.

'Come, come. He waits. Must see you. Must meet you.'

Wahid cast around for Iblis again and then cursed when he saw no one. Perhaps Iblis had also gone into the structure. Wahid made a quick prayer to Allah for safety and then followed Jassassah. It kept up a fast pace and Wahid had to jog to keep up.

The structure was a perfect cube, with hard edges and unblemished walls. It was larger than Wahid had first guessed it to be, rising several feet higher than him. Even in the gloom of night, light reflected off it so brightly that Wahid had to squint against it. An entrance had been cut into the side facing him. It had no door. Jassassah reached the entrance and sat down on its haunches, like a large dog.

'Go inside,' it said. 'Go, go.'

Wahid walked in, taking each step tentatively.

'Hello? Is … uh … is anyone there?'

There was no reply. He was blocking the only source of light in the large room and his shadow merged with the darkness in the interior. Wahid's eyes adjusted after a few seconds and he noticed someone at the far end.

Directly across, crumpled on the ground, was a naked old man. He was sitting against the far wall, bent over so low that Wahid was presented with the top of his head – a bald pate ringed with long white hair, fine as a spider's web. Legs that were just loose skin hanging on bone crossed each other and seemed as though they would snap if any weight were put on them. Both arms lay limp on either side, hands resting on the ground. There were large metal shackles on each wrist, attached to thick chains that were buried into the wall. The ankles were bound similarly and Wahid could make out a metal collar clasped around the man's neck. The effect of so much being used to restrain such a feeble and pitiful figure was almost comical.

Wahid was about to speak, when the head rose. The chains clanged loudly as they shifted. The face was older and more haggard than any Wahid had ever seen before. Sunken eyes, lidded by folds of spotted skin, stared at him. A silken beard trailed down to the man's navel.

'Wahid?' asked the man. It was a voice so dry it seemed to pull the moisture from the air.

'How do you know my name? Who are you?' asked Wahid. He stepped fully into the room and was instantly swallowed by the smell of decay.

The old man made an effort to sit straighter, his spine making terrible snapping sounds as he did. The skin on the torso was as thin as tracing paper, ribs like bony fingers almost visible beneath.

'I,' rasped the old man, 'am Allah.'

He didn't say this with any pride or dignity, but whispered it as if a shameful confession were being shared. Wahid stared, mouth agape.

The old man raised his hands, pressing them together in front of him as though in prayer. The thick manacles seemed to gleam with menace. They were so large, it was a miracle they did not break his wrists. Wahid could see, despite the dim interior, Arabic carvings on the metal. Words had been set into the surface, not just of the bindings, but also of each hand-sized link in the chains welded to them.

'I know you. I know all. I am the Creator, trapped here by my creations.'

Wahid walked to the man and crouched down in front of him. 'But, how can you be Allah? Allah is …'

'I am Allah,' the old man said again, his voice dusty and flaking. 'I am trapped, little Wahid. Little boy who is half-djinn and half-man. I am Allah, trapped here by Dajjal.'

Wahid made several attempts at speaking, each time the words drying up in his throat. Finally, with great effort, he managed to squeak out a question.

'Dajjal? But … I don't … how is that possible?'

The old man lowered his head again and Wahid could see a teardrop splash on to his swollen ankle.

'Dajjal is free. Has been free for a thousand years. He trapped me here in the bonds I created for him and he roams the world, rules it like I should have.'

'But that doesn't make any sense,' Wahid gasped. 'Allah is supposed to be out … out there. Everywhere.'

The old man stared out at Wahid, yellow-tinged eyes swimming in tears. 'Out there? Everywhere? The world I was forced to abandon is full of terror. This is not the world I created.

This is the rape of my world. This is the world of Dajjal. Won't you help me, Wahid?'

Wahid sat down cross-legged in front of the man, massaging his temples.

'How can you be Allah? If you are Allah, how can you not free yourself? Didn't you create everything? Even Dajjal?'

'None believe in Allah,' mourned the old man. 'They have not for an age. They pray to me but do not do it with their hearts and souls. And so I am weak. Dajjal seized this weakness. Turned it against me. He bound me here and now the beast that will end creation runs free.' He fixed Wahid with a stare as forceful as a fist. 'But you are here. You can free me. You can believe in me.'

Wahid's mind didn't race so much as break into a panicked leaping gallop. Dajjal was the anti-Christ of prophecy. Dajjal had one eye and the letters KFR on his forehead. Dajjal was trapped by Allah and would only escape when the end-times were near. He knew all this because he had read it and had been taught it.

'It's … it's not possible.'

'Half-djinn, you should not be possible either. Yet here you are. I am Allah. How can I prove it to you?'

'What … what's my father's name?' asked Wahid. It was the first thing that came to him.

'Wahid bin Rehman, son of a merchant. You too doubt me? Will no one believe in me any more?'

The old man began to weep, tears flowing in a convoluted path down his ragged face.

Wahid stared at the thick chains, at how they were swallowed by the brick of the wall. He considered the strength needed to pull them out, or to break them. Then he thought of Iblis. Maybe he could run back and ask Iblis to help him. Except that Iblis was the Devil. Maybe he would not want to free God. Maybe he bore a grudge. Maybe he had helped Dajjal.

'I'm sorry. I'm trying. Okay … okay. My mother? Who is my mother? Just answer this and I'll believe you if you do.'

The old man's sobs wracked his fragile body. Wahid thought if he cried any harder he would break, the bones inside shattering like flutes of glass.

'First answer questions for me, little Wahid, please. I beg of you,' rasped the old man.

'What questions?'

'Tell me about the wombs of women,' he said.

'What do you mean?'

'Do they still bear children? Do pink babies still sleep within them for nine months and then emerge, wet and squealing?'

'Wombs? … Yes? I mean, of course. Babies are born. Why wouldn't they?'

'I don't think they will for much longer,' said the old man. Then, 'Tell me about the spring of Zamzam. Are followers of the Prophet still cleansing themselves in its waters?'

Wahid said they were, thinking of the bottle of Zamzam water gifted to his mother a few years ago by a friend of hers who had returned from hajj. It had sat in the fridge for several weeks, his mother blowing prayers over glasses of it and making Wahid drink it for his health. It had had no effect on his need for a inhaler.

'It will run dry soon,' said the old man. 'And finally, have the arrows tipped with broken atoms been loosed upon the world?'

'The what?'

'The arrows. That spread a fire that kills millions and hides the sun behind a cloud of ash and snow. Do they fly through the air like birds and then build nests as high as mountains?'

'I don't … do you mean nukes? Broken atoms. That's atom bombs, right? Are you asking if the atom bombs have exploded?'

The old man nodded.

'Not yet. Actually, wait, no. There have been two explosions. In Japan. But that was like sixty or seventy years ago.'

'Not two. Have there been hundreds, maybe thousands?'

'A war with that many? No, no, that definitely hasn't happened.'

The old man sagged. 'It will happen. And when it does the other signs shall also come to pass. Then Qiyamat will come and it will be too late. Now ask your question of me, Wahid. If I answer it true, then please free me so I may stay the influence of Dajjal.'

'If my mother is a djinn, who is she?'

'Your mother? Your mother is Mumtaz, little Wahid,' said the old man, seeming to grow exhausted with the effort of answering. 'You know this. But the djinn who gave birth to you, its name was Balasa.'

'Where is she now?' pleaded Wahid.

The old man didn't answer. The sobbing took over again and he folded in on himself, a jute sack filled with broken sticks collapsing inwards.

Wahid looked at the chain closest to him. It was attached to the manacle around one of the old man's wrists. Each link was thick and heavy, the kind he imagined could be used to carry the weight of an anchor. He grabbed the chain and yanked it hard. He couldn't even wrap his hands fully around the metal and he felt no give.

'Please,' moaned the old man, his voice drifting slowly away as he slumped sideways.

Wahid strained again, pulling with all his strength. Sweat beaded on his forehead and his arms began to burn, as though they would tear at the elbow. The old man was completely flat on the ground now, barely moving at all. Wahid gritted his teeth and felt a deep roar building inside him. He let it loose and doing so somehow gave him access to a reservoir of strength he didn't know he had.

'Come on,' he screamed and almost let the chain go when the wall behind it cracked. A jagged line split through the rock surface, then another line bisected it. Each crack was announced by a sharp splintering. Smoke was rising from where he gripped the metal and tiny ripples of flame coursed across his hands. His eyes widened but he didn't let go, just kept on pulling.

Arteries of fire criss-crossed across the surface of his hands and then climbed up the chain, darting like adders towards where it was embedded in the wall. When they struck rock there was a burst of smoke. Wahid fell backwards, tumbling across the floor with metal clanging deafeningly around them. The chain was free, a large chunk of the wall lay on the ground between him and the old man.

A blinding white light filled the room. Wahid threw up his arms to shield his eyes. It strobed so brightly that it pushed through his eyelids and he could actually see his hands X-rayed in front of him.

'Finally,' boomed a voice.

The light snapped off, as though a switch had been thrown. Wahid opened his eyes, neon worms floating in his vision. The old man was standing upright. He seemed more substantial to Wahid, muscle thickened under his skin.

'I did it,' exclaimed Wahid.

'You did,' said the old man, looking up at him. 'You have freed me.' He grinned, showing teeth, long and sharp. The eyes that stared at Wahid were brighter, strength emanating from behind them. Then the old man reached up and placed his hand against his face. Fingers as thin as twigs curled and pushed, piercing the skin around his left eye. They sank deep into his head, twisting as he gripped something inside. When he pulled them out, thick ropes of blood and membrane trailed after them, leaving behind an open and bloody maw under his brow. The eyeball made a wet plop as he threw it to the ground.

Wahid stared. He tried to scream but his voice had left him entirely. Not even a whisper came out. The old man stared at Wahid with one eye, cleaning his bloody hand by wiping it on his own belly.

If Wahid could scream, he would have screamed the old man's true name. The name he had learned belonged to the creature with one eye that would begin Qiyamat through blood and fire. Instead he scrambled backwards, found his legs, spun around and began running towards the small door that he had entered through.

'Come back, little Wahid,' roared the old man, his voice like the hungry call of a pack of wolves.

Wahid glanced over his shoulder to see the old man walking after him, the bloody maw on one side of his face making sucking sounds as he drew closer with each stride. Wahid finally found his voice and screamed, looking in front just in time to see the doorway blocked by the animal thing that had led him here. The creature snarled, yellow blades flashing in its mouth. Before Wahid could stop his forward charge, it leaped at him claws outstretched, just as fingers grabbed him around the back of his neck. He screamed again. Then darkness crashed into him.

Interlude a.

Karachi does not need djinns and chudails for all its horrors. The city breeds violence, acts of murder feeding like maggots on a discarded corpse. People walk like troglodytes, hunched over with Karachi's pressure draped over their shoulders. Karachi feeds.

At night, Empress Market's Victorian clock tower is a fountain pen nib, scratching the sky stained with street lights and neon glare. Ochre brick walls that have stood for over a hundred years are splashed red with betel-nut spit. If you look closely though, you might see that some of the ragged graffiti spray isn't day-old spittle, but still-wet blood. It glistens under the jaundiced lighting, just above the head of a man that passers-by might think is asleep on the pavement. At dawn, a child will try to pick his pockets without waking him, only to discover that he is curled over a mattress of his own intestines, spilling from the wide gash across his belly. No one will ever know who he was nor why he died.

Far across the city, on Tipu Sultan Road, a crowd will wait for the police to open a large gunnysack on the sidewalk. It is resting against a lamp post, a burlap stomach pregnant with death, jute fibres turned velvet by the bloody contents inside. It is the third one in as many days.

In Lyari, where children have grown bored with watching a gang of men play football, a six-year-old boy walks away from the cheering field. He runs home through bullet-scarred streets and climbs the stairs to his apartment. Inside, he finds his mother dead in a pool of blood, one side of her head caved in. His father is on the sofa behind her – still holding the bloodied hammer – face blue, a foam of spit covering his chin like a beard, syringe dangling from his arm.

On Zamzama, the expensive coffee shops and designer boutiques are dark, their thick glass windows staring like the hollow eyes of a skull at the massage boy. Just turned fifteen and already raped more times than he can remember, he climbs into the passenger seat of a car. It is larger than the squalid hole he shares with seven other boys when each night's work is done. The man who is driving will take him some place private and will pay him for sex. Or he might not be paid at all. Some of them just beat him. One even wanted to be beaten by him. Maybe this one will drive a knife into his guts. The boy isn't surprised to find he doesn't care much which it is.

On Tariq Road, an old man locks the small imambargah that he has cared for his entire life. It has been the responsibility of his family for generations and he has cared for it since he was a boy. It runs on donations given by Shia families and even though he has no sons of his own, he hopes his grandson will inherit it when he is old enough. As he fits the lock over the gate he hears a motorcycle come to a stop behind him.

'Forgive me, but I am closing it for the night,' he says as he turns around. 'Perhaps you can come back in the morning?'

He sees the gun an instant before it roars. It is the last thing he sees as bullets channel through his chest and puncture his heart. The men on the motorcycle cheer as he drops to the ground. They shoot his corpse again and again, each bullet heralded by cries of 'Shia Kafir!' A juice shop next door still has a few customers who run away with practised speed. The men on the motorcycle ride away, leaving the old man where he fell.

The dozen men in an apartment on Boat Basin have not yet committed the murders they came to Karachi for. Travelling down from the mountainous north, they have all gathered here over the last month. Each is battle-hardened; trained in camps, in Afghanistan, by cruel men with promises of a bloody jihad. They have rained down hailstorms of gunfire on American troops outside Kabul, seen their brothers explode in marketplaces in Quetta, and hung women from poles in Swat. They are so used to the stink of death that they barely even notice the heavy gutter reek of a sewerage canal next to the apartment building they are now in. An open pool of filth as wide as a football field, its surface a black jelly fogged with mosquitoes. It's rumoured that up until a few years ago, hospitals nearby would dispose of unclaimed dead babies there. Sometimes, when the wind howls across its surface, residents in the apartment complex think they can hear the ghost screams of forgotten infants.

None of this matters to the dozen men in the apartment though. To them, all that is important is the mission they were sent here for. They burn with a feverish need to accomplish it. In the morning, they plan on taking the guns and armour they have been given and laying siege to a mosque nearby. To even call it a mosque angers them, for it belongs to a sect of people who dare to believe in something other than the finality of the Prophet. They will begin their attack when the infidels gather for prayer and kill as many as they can. Some of these men have done the same before in Lahore and the rest are grateful for the opportunity. Just as they are done making all the preparations – loading their guns with ammunition, handing out grenades and checking the bulletproof armour – there is a knock at the door. They are expecting one of their number to return with food and so think nothing of it.

Karim Farzad, who had led the assault in Lahore and will lead the next one too, gets up and walks over to the entrance. Just as he is about to look through the peephole, all the lights go out in the apartment. Failing electricity is not surprising to any of them; it is a common feature in every city they have lived in. But the darkness remains. They had fitted backup generators that should have blinked the power back on. Karim curses at one of the younger men and commands him to go and see what the problem is. There is a second knock on the door and he grumbles as he opens it.

'Wait, you bhencho ...'

His voice gives out abruptly. The hallway outside is lit blue by a buzzing tube light. Karim begins to puzzle over the blackout being localized to their apartment when he sees the figure standing in front of him. The silhouetted shape is so completely black that he can't make out any features. Except the eyes. They seem to glow. Karim has never screamed in fear and isn't given the chance to do so now. None of the men are.

V.

'Wahid.'

Iblis's voice, like a silken rope, pulled him out of the darkness.

'Wahid. Wake up, it's time to go.'

Wahid's eyes opened to a blur of light and shape. He tried to speak but only managed a disoriented 'Guh.'

'Indeed,' Iblis said, standing over him. 'Now can you please get up?'

Wahid sat up. The world pulled into focus around him. He was sitting on the black tarmac that they had lain down on. Every bone in his body seemed to thrum with exhaustion and his muscles were stiff and aching. He looked around, rubbing his face with dirt-caked hands as he did so. Iblis was standing to one side, a mast anchored against the wind that whipped his black kameez and red shawl around him. He was looking down at Wahid, fire eyes burning in a human face. Wahid looked past him but saw nothing in any direction. Flat, featureless land stretched as far as the horizon. No white cube. No Jassassah. No Dajjal.

'What are you looking for?' asked Iblis.

'There was … I think I had a dream,' said Wahid, pushing himself up and stretching. His back hurt, in the way it should after sleeping on a hard road for several hours.

'Oh? Was I in it?'

'No. Actually, you weren't. But there was something else.'

He tried focusing on the details but they drifted away from him, evaporating in the sunlight like dew.

'I think there was a … a place. And a dog. Or something.'

'Sounds fascinating. You should write a book about it. Now come on.'

Wahid searched overhead for a sun but found nothing. The sky was a faded Levi's blue, stretching for parsecs in every direction, and as devoid of feature as the land around them.

'Where's the sunlight coming from?' asked Wahid. 'I don't see any sun.'

Iblis shrugged. 'Like I said, this is a place between worlds. It exists according to its own whims, I suppose. We're lucky there is a day now. Sometimes the night here can go on for years. This day might stretch until the end of the world for all we know. In case it doesn't, let's use it while we can.'

They began walking along the road, a black scar slicing through the face of the empty land.

'Iblis,' said Wahid.

'Yes?'

'Do you know which djinn gave birth to me?'

There was a name, haunting the edges of his mind. He couldn't make it out exactly, but grasping for it was like trying to listen to an echo of an echo of an echo.

'No. It's not believed to be possible. A human can bear a djinn's child. That has happened before, although those children do not live long. The heat they carry within burns them from the inside out. But never has a djinn birthed a human before. Whoever did it was very determined. Maybe she died as a result of it. I can't imagine it would have been easy.'

'Djinns die the same as people?'

'Some do. The weaker ones can be killed. Not so easily by a human though. By another djinn maybe. But the older and stronger djinns, like a Marid or an Ifrit, they do not die at all. Except, apparently, at your hands.'

'Can you die?'

Iblis laughed. 'No. Although I'm not about to try finding out if you can kill me, thank you very much. No. My curse is to live until Qiyamat. After Allah has judged everyone and reduced the world to the same stuff of nothingness he created it from, then I will die. And then I will go to Jahannam.'

Wahid thought about this for several minutes in silence, both of them walking side by side.

'I never wanted to kill anyone. I've … I've never killed before,' he said softly.

'Yes. Yes, that is tragic. But now you have to deal with the life you have, not sit around pining for the life you lost, right?'

'I suppose. You know, I didn't even really believe in djinns until … you know …'

'Oh? But you believe in Islam, yes?'

'I suppose. I mean, I'm a Muslim so I believe in Islam. I always thought that if I was born a Christian, I would probably just believe in Jesus. I didn't really have a choice.'

'Such conviction. Well, what do you think of the djinns now that you know we exist?'

'I kind of wish you were the type that granted three wishes and went back into the lamp.'

Iblis laughed at this, a full-throated laugh that filled the air around them. Just when Wahid thought he was done laughing, he stopped walking and hooted even harder, bending to rest his hands on his knees as his body shook with snorts and guffaws. Finally, he composed himself enough to continue.

'Yes, that must have been disappointing indeed,' he said with a giggle.

'Well, I don't know. The only djinn I'd ever seen before this was the big blue guy in the *Aladdin* cartoon as a kid. Or he was a genie … Same thing, right?'

'*Aladdin?* That's from those stupid *Arabian Nights*, yes? Was he the one with the forty thieves?'

'No, that was Ali Baba, I think. I don't know. I never really read it. Every fantasy book I've ever read that had djinns in it was all about the *Arabian Nights*. But I've never actually read the *Arabian Nights* stories themselves.'

'I did,' said Iblis. 'Centuries ago. I remember enjoying it. But yes, that's why most people probably think djinns live in lamps and grant wishes dressed in turbans. It certainly stops them fearing us. Not like they used to in the old days.'

'I'm scared, if that makes you feel any better.'

'Thank you, I suppose it will have to do.'

As they walked, a wind picked up, howling across the desert.

'You know, I always thought that if djinns existed, they would be in, like, the Middle East,' said Wahid.

'I don't understand.'

'Like in Egypt or … or Iran, or Saudi Arabia or some place. That's where Islam started, right?'

'Yes. I suppose it did. Mecca is where the revelation first came to your Prophet. But that was long ago. Those places are the history of Islam. The future of Islam is being decided in your country.'

'I don't understand.'

'Religion is a changing thing. It evolves, if you will. The core belief may be the same. The Quran is unchanging after all. But the interpretations? Those shift and morph according to the moods of the time. I remember when Islam was all about scientific discovery. Where Allah's revelations were seen as a demand for innovation and ingenuity. Now, they are seen as an abandonment of the same.

'The factions and groups that each define what the future of Islam will be are all gathered in Pakistan. All of them live in the city we have just come from. They fight over it, kill over it. Whichever group is left standing when it is all done will be the final decider. There are many, myself included, who believe that Qiyamat will start in your country. Maybe even in your city.'

Wahid was considering this, when a sharp echo began to sound from the distance. It was, Wahid realized, a horse clip-clopping on the road ahead. The way in front of them had been flat and clear, yet suddenly there it was – a horse, moving at a relaxed trot towards them, ridden by a single rider, silhouetted against the horizon.

'Who is it?' asked Wahid.

'I don't know,' replied Iblis, coming to a stop. The two of them watched the figure grow larger as it covered the distance between them.

It was, Wahid could see, a beautiful horse; so white it gleamed like porcelain. It was larger than any horse he had ever seen, much larger than the starved creatures that gave tourists rides on the beaches of Karachi. The rider was a man who seemed as though he was the only one who could ride such a beast. Tall, broadly built and exceedingly handsome. He had thick black hair and a face that seemed to be of every age between eighteen and forty. It had the hardness of wisdom earned through years of seeing and inflicting violence, and the beauty of a child who was experiencing everything for the first time and enjoying it thoroughly. He was wrapped in a purple cloak with intricate patterns embroidered across it in gold. His legs were bare up to the shins, feet protected inside thick boots made from the hide of some impenetrable animal, and fastened with black cords. He drew up in front of them, the horse stamping the earth with powerful hooves.

Iblis spoke first, raising his hands when he did. What he said, Wahid had no way of knowing, since the words were in a different language. The man replied in the same language, leaning forward as he spoke. Wahid plucked the word 'djinn' out of the alien conversation. Iblis nodded and then asked a question, to which the man gave a long answer. Then they both turned to look at Wahid.

'What? Who is he?'

'He's asking the same about you,' said Iblis.

Wahid stepped forward, extending a hand. 'My name is Wahid. Nice to meet you.'

The man looked at his hand, then at Wahid's face. He nodded his head in Wahid's direction then turned to address Iblis again. They spoke some more and then the man kicked the horse lightly. It neighed once, before breaking into a sudden gallop. He raced off into the distance behind them. Then he was gone. Faded from view even though there was no horizon to dip over.

'What the hell was that?' asked Wahid.

Iblis watched the man ride away, then sat down on the ground. Wahid crouched next to him.

'That was a man from a long time ago. His name is … or was … Dhul-Qarnayn.'

'Dhul-Qarnayn? Who's that? What was that language you were speaking?'

'Greek. Not as it is spoken now. But as it was spoken some two thousand years ago.'

'So he was Greek. Dhul-Qarnayn doesn't sound very Greek.'

'Oh, and all of a sudden you're an expert on Greek names, are you? But you're right, it isn't Greek. It's the name given to him in Syriac. In Greek, he was called Alexander.'

Wahid didn't sit down as much as fall backwards onto his butt.

'The Great? That was Alexander the Great? But how is that possible?'

'We're in a place outside time,' said Iblis. 'Here it's the past, the present and the future all at once. That was Dhul-Qarnayn, or Alexander, as you know him. He came here in his dreams. He knew he was dreaming. He said when he awoke he would be in a tent in Gaugamela, resting after a battle he had just won.'

'So, what was he doing here?'

'Allah's bidding, I assume. He said he came here to find a great army of terrible people ready to wage war on the world. So he built a wall between two mountains and trapped them behind it. He thought he had been here for several years. I told him he would wake just a few hours after he fell asleep.'

'So what was he looking at me for?'

'He asked if you were my lover.'

Wahid opened his mouth but no sound came out.

'If it makes you feel better, he said a scrawny boy like you could not satisfy me for very long. I agreed.'

'Thanks,' said Wahid, not sure if he was grateful at all. 'So these people he trapped behind a wall … those were Yajuj–Majuj, right? Gog and Magog, I think they're called in English? They were in the book on Qiyamat I read. He trapped them there and they won't get out, right?'

Iblis stood up and peered into the distance, in the direction Alexander the Great had ridden up from.

'This presents us with a problem,' he said.

'What?'

Iblis cocked his head to one side. 'Listen.'

Wahid did, and realized there was a low whistle of a wind racing towards them. It took several seconds for him to comprehend that if there was a wind, he could not feel it.

'That sound …'

'It's them,' said Iblis.

It grew louder. A howl that wasn't singular, but a thousand screams all compressed into one continuous keening. It rose with every step, wretched and mournful wails that burrowed through Wahid and rattled against his brain. He covered his ears and turned to Iblis, who was pointing ahead.

A wall had appeared in the distance. It hadn't been there before, but was now very definitely blocking their way. Wahid gawped at it: a smooth black plate so high, if there had been clouds they would have broken against it. Like everything else so far, first it hadn't been there, then it was.

'What is it?' screamed Wahid, trying to be heard over the incessant howling.

Iblis screamed into Wahid's ear, each word hollered slowly so it could be heard.

'The Yajuj–Majuj are behind the wall. We have to go through.'

'Why can't we go around?' Wahid screamed back.

Iblis motioned, first in one direction, then in the other. Just as the wall was high – it seemed to have no actual top – the same was true of its length. It went as far as the desert went. There was, Wahid saw, the road on which they were walking, bracketed by desert, and it all ended up ahead at this seemingly infinite obstruction. He understood Iblis then. There was no 'around'.

The sound began chewing at his sanity. Screaming, wailing, moaning, crying, all too loud to allow any other thought.

During the first ten days of the month of Muharram, Wahid would accompany his mother for the daily Shia gatherings. They would sit in their car on a wide street glutted with cars, all filled with families like theirs listening to the imam's voice broadcasting through speakers strung to lamp posts, as he narrated tales of the Prophet's family being martyred. The imam was inside the imambargah next to the road, its interior filled with young Shia men. As the story wound to its tragic conclusion – with the Prophet's grandson killed by his enemies, his relatives murdered one by one before his life was eventually taken – the men inside would start crying loudly. Wahid's own mother would weep in the car, as would the occupants of other cars around him. And the sound of everyone's grief, accumulated by microphones and broadcast into the Karachi night, would become a fog of lamentation. That sound was a whisper compared to what Wahid heard now.

He pulled off his T-shirt and wound it into a thick cord, then wrapped it around his forehead, angled low to cover his ears. Iblis watched him do this with a smile. He seemed entirely unperturbed by the sound.

They approached the wall carefully, studying the smooth surface. Wahid noted that there were no scratches on it, not even any dust on its surface. How, he wondered, had a black wall in the middle of a desert stayed so clean? He placed a hand on the surface, cool, metallic and gleaming. It thrummed, a vibration travelling across his palm.

He turned to ask Iblis what next. He wasn't there. Wahid was about to open his mouth, when a face emerged from the wall. Iblis had, Wahid realized, walked into it. Phased through it, like Kitty Pryde. A hand emerged, and Iblis motioned for Wahid to follow him. Then he turned and was swallowed by the wall entirely.

Wahid gawped. The metal was perfectly solid under his hand. Maybe if I think it isn't there … he thought.

He tried again. No change. The wall continued to exist with an infuriating tangibility against his fingers. Wahid opened one eye and stared at the expanse of black in front of him. He sighed and tried again, eyes pinched shut. It isn't there. But it was. He lowered his hand, feeling the echo of the vibration still tickling his palm. It isn't there, he thought again. The tips of his fingers pressed harder against the metal. The wailing on the other side was louder, he decided. The metal might as well be as thin as paper, given how ineffectively it was blocking whatever was creating the sound on the other side. It doesn't matter if it is there, he thought. And if there was metal still under his hand, he could no longer feel it. Wahid opened his eyes slowly, to see his hand submerged up to the wrist inside the wall. He pressed his eyes closed again and began to chant his last thought in his mind. It doesn't matter. Then he took a step forward. Another step. It doesn't matter if it is there. It doesn't matter if it is there.

Again and again he repeated the line, each time taking another step forward with his arms stretched out in front of him. He felt cool air rushing through his fingers, and decided that as long as that was all he felt, he would be fine. Which is why when something wet and rough scraped against his hand, Wahid opened his eyes with a shriek.

A face was staring at him. It was the face of a man – not Iblis's – and it looked as shocked to see him as he was to see it. Wahid lowered his hands and glanced behind. He had emerged on the other side of the wall; it was solidly pressed against his back. He turned back to the man in front of him. Features flat as a shield, with small eyes set far apart that stared at him. The face was framed by a thick red beard that climbed upwards into long hair. The lower half of the face was coated with blood, soaking the beard so it was as dark as the wall. Wahid glanced down at his hand and saw it had a streak of blood across it.

There were more faces staring at him, on either side. They were close by and he could feel their breath on him. All of them were identical, with the same configuration of small eyes and blood-soaked chins. Some of the faces were female, although the only discernible difference was the absence of a beard. They were all of the same height, level with Wahid. But their bodies were broad, with thick round shoulders and heavily built chests. None of them wore any clothes, their skin fair except for graffiti sprays of blood. Even the women had builds as impressive as the men's, their breasts flattened by the tight stretch of muscle.

Wahid then noticed the source of the blood. Those that hadn't turned towards him had their faces pressed against the wall and were licking it. Not tentatively as a child might lick an ice cream, but with the aggression of an animal using its saliva to tenderize meat. Swollen and torn tongues left smears of spittle and blood on the metal. As they licked the surface, so hard that their lips were mashed against it, they moaned their suffering. From each one of them, the sound rose independently, forming a fog bank above their heads. Wahid realized in horror that where the blood was thickest, the wall had eroded by several inches. Small grooves had been pressed into it by each person's tortured effort, and each lick seemed to drive the depression in deeper. He turned back to look at the man in front of him, who grabbed Wahid and yanked him out of his way. Wahid was thrust out of the dense crowd of muscle and flesh, landing on the ground behind them, sprawling in the dirt. The man who had tossed him so effortlessly glared down at him, before he went back to licking his portion of the wall. He did not seem grateful for the break in his task and instead was licking faster than the others, his miserable wail a rapid hiccup.

Wahid crawled backwards, his mouth hanging open and eyes wide with horror. Those that had noticed him had turned their backs on him as well, their muscular bodies pressed against the wall. He staggered to his feet, fighting the wave of dizziness that threatened to topple him. If he had had food in his stomach, he would have vomited it up. Instead, he dry-retched twice and coughed up a few gobs of spit. Turning, he saw a city, with towers and streets and homes, all built of packed earth. A narrow alley curved ahead of him, between two towers as high as any in Karachi, so he scrambled into it.

The light was dim inside the alley, shaded as it was by the immense buildings. The sound too was squeezed to a thin squealing as he moved deeper inside the tangle of lanes. He was running, choosing lanes and side lanes at random, diving deeper until the panic subsided. He had been wiping his hands on his jeans the entire time, he realized. Stopping to lean against a building, Wahid caught his breath. Then he looked around.

The streets and everything on them looked old. Not worn down, but from another era. He was reminded of pictures he'd seen of streets in Morocco, or some of the more ancient parts of Lahore. Brown walls and brown floors, all created from evenly sized bricks cemented with mud. And they were empty. None of the strange, muscular people were here. He hadn't, he recalled, seen any during his panicked dash either.

He could hear them, of course. The sound trailed after him, and whenever he stood still it wound around him. He called out to Iblis, barely able to hear himself over the din. Wahid turned another lane and came to a clearing, emerging out of the warren and into a clear patch. The thicket of buildings was behind him now. Ahead was another wall, as high and black as the one he'd run from. And pressed against it was the same seething mass of people.

There was a louder groaning and he could see the wall starting to sway. They all stopped their licking and looked up at it. It rocked backwards slowly, the metal rending and screeching. Then it swayed back and settled as it had been, though this time seeming a great deal less stable than when Wahid had first seen it.

The Yajuj–Majuj began to cheer. Loud, ululating cries of joy rose up as they hugged and clapped. They began dispersing, all of them striding purposefully away from the wall. Hoping not to be seen again, Wahid receded into an alleyway. He would wait until he was sure he would not be noticed, then try passing – phasing – through the wall ahead.

'Who are you?' said a voice from behind him and two large hands thudded on his shoulders. Wahid spun around to see a man standing there. He was identical to all the others that Wahid had emerged in front of, with the same blood-soaked beard and dirty red hair. Beads of sweat freckled the broad chest and Wahid was uncomfortably conscious of his nakedness as a thick, flaccid penis hung from beneath a nest of red curls.

'I'm Wahid,' he said. 'I just want to pass through the city. I've got no … no problem. I mean, I don't want any trouble.'

The man grabbed Wahid's wrist in a hand that was large enough to snap his arm like a dry twig and began to walk towards the exit of the alleyway. Wahid ran to keep pace, stumbling once over the edge of a broken ladder lying across the ground. They emerged into the clearing between the buildings and the wall. It was still full of people, all of them identical in size, physique and nudity. Some of them were carrying large troughs of water to wash off the blood. They seemed cheerful, despite the ragged tongues that flapped like torn sails every time they opened their mouths. None of them seemed to notice him. The man dragged Wahid through the crowds, circling around several towers and making for the largest one. It stood closest to the wall, with a broader base than the others and rising too high for the peak to be visible. A wide door had been cut into the rock.

The inside was an immense cavern, a curved ceiling sloping overhead as though the entire space had been excavated from a solid mountain in a single scoop. The light that made its way inside through the doorway and high windows was compressed by the interior gloom until it seemed as though they were standing in perpetual dusk. Men and women moved around in accumulations of dense shadows. The air inside, cooled by the rock walls, was syrupy with the smell of sweat and blood.

'Where are you taking me?' asked Wahid as he was lurched forward into motion.

'The king. He will want to see a curiosity like you,' said the man. His words were slurred, but not as badly as Wahid thought they would be with a torn tongue.

Wahid wondered why there were suddenly so many kings in his life. Did the supernatural worlds not have democratically elected governments, with presidents and prime ministers elected through a parliamentary system? He decided it was a question best kept to himself, because considering it threatened to make him break into hysteric giggles which he knew would be unwelcome here.

In the centre of the cavern was a stone stairway, spiralling upwards into a gap in the ceiling. They ascended it, with the man taking two steps at a time and Wahid stumbling repeatedly, banging his ankles against the edges more than once and eventually just letting himself be pulled along. The stairway opened onto a smaller room. A man and woman were copulating on the floor in the corner, their frenzied actions like those of two wrestlers grappling for domination. Their animal grunts echoed in the room, punctuated by the metronomic sound of muscles slapping together. Wahid blushed and looked away as he was dragged past them. He seemed to be the only person who noticed them. The half a dozen or so other people on the same floor as them were all resting, some sprawled flat on the bare ground and others leaning against the walls. The man deposited Wahid in the centre of the room on a large block of stone that must serve as a chair. In front of it was a table – also of stone – attended by more chairs on either side. The man stood next to Wahid, crossed his thick arms across his chest and stared at the couple in the corner. Wahid, who now had a clear view of them, instead chose to inspect his feet.

A thick layer of grey dust from the desert had accumulated on his sneakers, and crusted into a sole on the underside. He picked at it lightly with a finger and the edges crumbled under his touch.

'Stand up,' said the man next to him. 'The king is coming.'

The king, it turned out, was the male participant in the coupling that Wahid had been audience to. The female lay on the ground, panting with satisfaction as her partner stood up and began walking towards them. Wahid noticed this man was taller and wider than all the others he had seen, even though his features were identical to theirs. The muscles on his arms and thighs were swollen so large that their contours could be seen moving under the skin. Every vein that stood out across his body was as thick as a rope and despite the ferocity of the sex he had just had, he breathed as easily as someone who had been engaged in nothing more strenuous than reading a book. The king noticed Wahid when he was halfway across the room, his body visibly jerking to attention when he did.

'Who is this?' he bellowed, his voice the sound tectonic plates make when they shift against each other.

The man who had brought Wahid was about to speak when Wahid stood up and took the lead in the conversation.

'I'm Wahid. I come from outside. I just need to pass through.'

The king slumped into a chair across from Wahid and stared at him with eyes ignited by interest.

'Outside?' he rumbled. 'Were you sent by Dhul-Qarnayn? Did that coward send you to inspect his fucking wall?'

'No … I don't … I mean, I saw Dhul-Qarnayn, but I am not … associated with him. I came with a … a friend. I don't know where he is, but I just want to pass through. I'm going somewhere else.'

The king leaned forward, resting his arms on the table. 'Do you know who we are?'

Wahid considered his answer carefully. 'You're the Yajuj–Majuj. Dhul-Qarnayn trapped you behind a wall because Allah told him to, right?'

'Correct.' The king grinned. The man next to Wahid laughed, and Wahid glanced at him, long enough to note that his tongue had healed entirely.

'We are the Yajuj–Majuj. We are also known as the people of Gog and this city is Magog. We are built for war and that is all we know how to be good at. We are the best. It's what we have always done and when we tear this wall down, we will do it again. Tonight, the wall is weakened. Tomorrow, it will fall. Then we will go out into the world again, and crush all, eat all, rape all and kill all.'

Wahid tried to speak again, but the words dried up inside his throat. He croaked once and then coughed and tried again. His hands, he realized, had begun to shake visibly, so he hid them behind his back.

The man standing next to him laughed loudly. 'The boy is afraid of what is to come, my lord.'

The king smiled. It made him look hungry.

'Don't worry, little boy,' said the king. 'You will be dead long before that. We have been trapped here for an age now and I have not eaten someone different from our own kind in a very long time.'

Wahid stepped back but was shoved forward again by a pair of large hands.

'No! Please! I just ...' Wahid began to scream for Iblis.

The king stood up, his knuckles cracking like thunder as he flexed his hands. The man grabbed Wahid and threw him against the edge of the table. The side slammed into his gut and he collapsed onto it, his legs behind him. He tried to turn but the king was behind him now, pressing down on his back with one hand. Wahid screamed and the king laughed. Fingers, so large and strong that they felt mechanical, grabbed his neck. Wahid tried to scream again, but the words were choked out of him. He felt his head being pulled backwards, his spine arching painfully and then the rush of being slammed into the table.

If there was impact, he did not feel it. Instead, the room turned red. There was a roar, so loud that Wahid could no longer hear his screaming. He thought blood had filled his eyes, until he realized the red that had painted the world so suddenly was undulating, like fabric caught in the wind. He raised his head, finding that the king's hand was gone. The roaring grew louder behind him. It was continuous and did not waver in pitch or tone. He turned slowly, trying to see through the red veil.

The king was on fire. Not just him, but the entire room. Flames licked at everything and there was no surface that wasn't blanketed by them. The roaring, however, wasn't from the fire, but from the king. He was standing behind Wahid, hands raised as the fire curled around his body in rings. His hair and beard were gone and Wahid could see his skin bubbling. Wahid scrambled onto the table, then looked down to see that his own shoes had burnt off. The table was also alight, and Wahid was standing in a nest of fire. Yet he felt no heat, nor any other effects. As far as his body was concerned, the temperature of the room was quite serene. He could feel the flames – they licked at his hands like kittens searching for milk – but none of the energy affected him.

The fire swallowed the king entirely and the roaring trailed off. Wahid leaped off the table and ran for the stairway, reflexively shielding his face even though it was unnecessary. He slipped on the first step and almost fell down the stairs face first, but managed to catch his balance in time. As he ran down, a horde of red-haired men and women were charging up towards him. Wahid braced himself, but they barrelled passed him, disappearing into the burning room. He continued running down until he reached the cavernous entrance he'd been brought through.

Wahid ran towards the doorway that led out onto the street. A shout from behind made him pause and turn. A man was standing high up the stairs, pointing at him and screaming unintelligibly. Descending the length of the stairs and then trailing across the floor behind him were burning footprints. Each bloomed on the ground, a step apart. Wahid looked down at his feet to see petals of flame unfolding where he stood. More people appeared at the top of the stairs, all of them pointing at him. He turned and ran as they began to descend.

Wahid exited the tower, launching himself straight onto the street. A crowd of people had gathered, alerted by the screams, and they turned as one to stare at him. He spun in every direction, looking for a gap through which he could reach the wall. Seeing one, he charged, throwing himself into a mad dash. The buildings around him began dissolving, first into clouds of dust, then those clouds began coalescing into more people. All of them were streaming after him, not physical so much as dust whorls, a sandstorm with roiling shapes within it surging towards him.

Hands clotted next to him, large fingers forming in the haze. Behind it, a face emerged, lacking distinct features but growing more and more detailed with each breath. Cavernous eyes stared out at him, hollow like on the face of a skull with a gaping maw beneath, sand hardening into jagged rows of teeth. Fingers grazed against him as though he was being scraped with a pumice stone. Wahid leaned forward into his run, trying to increase his speed. He had never been athletic but his height afforded him giant strides so that he was almost leaping between each footfall. He frantically considered how running towards an immense deadend made any sense, but changing direction would slow him down. The wall drew closer with each step, looming high above.

The hand touched him again and Wahid almost fell trying to dodge out of its way. He put too much weight on his right leg in an effort to balance himself and felt the impact jar against his hip. Then he felt heat. A furnace blast whooshed behind him and the thunderous snarling turned to shrieks. A gust of heated air lifted him several inches off the ground and Wahid landed a few feet ahead, legs still pedalling as he came down, his momentum unbroken. Still propelling himself towards the wall, he looked over his shoulder – a sheet of fire rose behind him. Flames rippled and clashed as they flowed off the ground and slammed into the chasing sandstorm. The entire barrage of claws and faces had come to an abrupt stop, almost entirely hidden behind the dam of fire. A rooster tail of flames was spreading out behind him, leading up to the fiery barrier.

Just then, a stitch in his side flared and caused him to look ahead again. The wall was close enough now that a few more bounding steps would bring him right to it. But he stopped abruptly when he saw what was at the base of the wall. He stumbled and went down face first on the hard earth, rolling the last few metres, arms and legs crashing until he came to a stop. Jumping up in a mad panic, he stared in front. Level with him were more of the Yajuj–Majuj.

These were solid in appearance, with their muscular backs towards him, faces pressed against the wall. The screams of pain were rising again, and he could make out the individual threads of suffering from inside the blanket of noise. The one right in front turned and looked at Wahid. Wahid stared at him and then at the others next to him, their faces still flat against the wall. The one looking at him opened its bony mouth, and Wahid saw, unfurling down its chin, a ragged and bloody tongue like a strip of raw meat.

Then Wahid was yanked backwards and spun around. Large hands gripped his shoulders as he looked up into a mouth filled with gleaming shards.

'Food,' it hissed, and he could smell rotted meat on its breath.

Wahid screamed. Then the creature holding him screamed as well. It released him and fell backwards, shrieking in agony as flames enveloped it. Blades of fire sliced out from inside its head, puncturing its eyes and wagging from its mouth. A flower of orange and yellow unfurled around Wahid. He saw it happen, saw waves of flame spreading outwards from his body and washing over the creatures around him. They screamed hideously, falling to the ground in writhing masses. Behind him the fire extended all the way to the wall and crested against it, rising up the surface like a sheet of locusts. More than a dozen bodies burned around him and as they did, more of the creatures began to focus on him. The air between Wahid and the gathering crowd of howling Yajuj–Majuj simmered and he could see fangs gleaming through the haze.

Suddenly, claws squeezed his shoulders, stabbing through skin. Wahid shrieked and tried to break free of the vice-like grip.

'Hold still, fool,' said a voice from above him.

Wahid looked up and saw wings, black and vast. A raven's shiny beaded eyes stared down at him, the head as large as his. Talons had buried into his flesh and he felt them tighten on muscle and bone.

'Would you prefer I leave you behind?' said the raven, its beak clacking as it spoke.

'Iblis!' screamed Wahid, gratefully. The wings beat downwards once and Wahid felt himself being lifted off the ground. Another push of the powerful wings and he was soaring over the heads of his pursuers, their hands grasping at the air. A swarm of faces glared up at him, identical in their fury. As he watched, they shrank away, a seething mass that dissolved into a sandstorm batting against the wall below.

The wall had a top after all, and they soared over it. The raven's wings widened like sails and they drifted down to the other side, coming to a tumbling stop on the desert floor. Wahid lay there for a few seconds, gulping air hungrily and staring up at the sky. Next to him, Iblis was once again his original shape. Not that of the man he had let himself look like for Wahid's comfort for all this time, but the actual figure made of blackness lit by a smokeless fire from within, that only found vent through his eyes and mouth.

'They grabbed me as soon as I appeared. I just broke free myself,' said Iblis, his voice no longer human, but the droning of propellers, like a fleet of kamikaze pilots cresting the horizon.

'They … they tried to eat me,' gasped Wahid, 'but then I … I think I set fire to everything.' He turned to look at the wall. It loomed over them, no longer seeming as substantial. The cries and howls of rage made by the Yajuj–Majuj on the other side were sifting through it and Wahid felt as though it was no more than a muslin shawl that would catch in the wind, leaving him at their mercy.

'Yes, that is something I didn't know you could do. I knew you'd be able to pass through the wall, given you are half-djinn. But the fire is something else. To create fire on that scale, fire that can hurt things as impervious to pain and harm as the Yajuj–Majuj, that is something new,' said Iblis.

Wahid stared at the wall. It was swaying. Only slightly, but enough.

'Will it …'

'Fall? No. Not tonight. Not tomorrow either, it seems. If it had to fall, it would have fallen by now. No, they will tire and they will sleep, and in the morning all the progress they have made on the wall will be erased. It will be as strong and new as ever. Then they will begin running their tongues across it again. This has been happening since … since Dhul-Qarnayn built it. More than two thousand years ago.'

'But they … why don't they give up?'

'You saw them. Did they seem like the type who could give up? They know only war and they won't stop until they can spread it. One day that wall won't repair by itself. It will fall and stay fallen. Then they will ride out. They will drink rivers dry and bury cities under dust and blood. That's been preordained as a sign of the Day of Judgement.'

'Why don't they just climb over it? I saw a ladder. We just flew over it.'

'They don't have the imagination. They aren't human. They aren't even djinns. They are just weapons that move. They're singular in their goals.'

Wahid sat up, turning his back on the wall and the city full of warriors it held at bay and stared at his hands mournfully.

'What's the matter, boy?'

Wahid began to cry, despite his efforts not to. He hid his face in his hands and dissolved into great heaving sobs. Iblis stood next to him quietly, looking away. When Wahid was done, he wiped his nose on his forearm and stood up.

'I'm sorry,' he said, with a shaky laugh.

'I've seen worse,' observed Iblis. 'Now, are you done?'

'Fuck off,' said Wahid, trying to smile.

Wahid stood up, staring at his hands, then aimed one hand, palm outwards, ahead of him. Nothing happened. He punched the air with his other hand, also aiming it at the horizon.

'What are you doing?'

'I'm … I'm trying out my powers.'

'Powers?'

'Yeah. See if I can make blasts of fire again. It's like a superpower, right? Why isn't it happening?'

Iblis shrugged. 'I don't know. I didn't even know you could do it at all.'

Wahid closed his eyes and tried again, this time putting all his strength into pushing his hands out.

'Still nothing,' said Iblis. 'Now can we move on? I want to get as far away from this damned place as possible.'

Wahid was about to say something in agreement but retched instead. His insides churned and he burped once, a declaratory 'braap'. Then, just as he began to look embarrassed, he vomited. He managed to lean forward in time to stop the vomit from spewing all over himself, bending double as he heaved onto the desert floor. Finally, when all that he had left was noisy gagging sounds, he straightened up. His vision was bleary with tears and he rubbed his face on his arm and spat.

'Are you okay?'

'Yes. Sorry. I … I think, it's the adrenaline. And, you know, almost dying just now. I was really scared back there.'

'So was I. Those things are frightening, even to me. There's no shame in it. But we are safe and if I'm correct, then we're close to the entrance to Kaf.'

VI.

They found the road again. After an hour's walk, drifts of sand began encroaching upon the black tar, until soon it was entirely hidden. By the time they saw the first dunes over the horizon, the sky had become a dark splash of wine.

'I think it's close,' said Iblis with a smile.

'Really? Because I'm exhausted.'

'There,' said Iblis, pointing ahead.

The landscape undulated, all the edges blurred by thick sand. Directly in front though, the earth was cracked, sand having given way to a jagged crevice. They walked to the mouth of the fissure and looked down into it. It was as large as a car, a puncture in the landscape, sand drizzling down into the hole. If there was ground below, it was too far to see through the dark inside.

'This is the Majlis al Djinn,' said Iblis. 'It's an entrance into Kaf.'

'So how do I go down? I mean, I don't have any rope. Are you going to fly me down there?'

'No,' said Iblis. 'I am not allowed access to the world of djinns. I was barred from there when I was barred from Heaven. But you can go down on your own. You have that much of our kind in you. More than when we first met, for sure.'

Wahid got down on his hands and knees and crawled to the edge, peering inside. A thin wind was screeching up out of it.

'Don't worry,' said Iblis, 'it's quite safe.'

'Yes, but how do I get down?'

'You jump.'

Wahid stood up and regarded Iblis.

'Okay.'

'Well, then. This is as far as I go.'

'Look,' said Wahid, 'I … '

'You are terrible at saying thank you. Here, I'll do it for you, "Thank you, Mister, The Devil, for being so nice to me."'

Wahid grinned. 'Thank you, Mister, The Devil, for being a great deal nicer than your reputation would have me believe you capable of.'

'Like I said,' Iblis said, smiling, 'bad PR. Now jump already.'

Wahid looked into the crevice. It was large enough for him to leap through easily. He stood on the edge and stared into the darkness beneath.

'I … I don't think I can. How deep does it go?'

'Only one way to find out,' said Iblis, then he pushed Wahid into the empty mouth.

Wahid's scream trailed behind him, the black entrance opening into a vast cavern. His senses struggled to contextualize the immensity of the belly of rock inside which he was plummeting. His cry was echoing around him and cool air buffeted upwards against his body, as if trying to lift him back out.

After a few seconds of free fall, when he didn't feel his bones shattering upon impact with a floor, he opened his eyes to find he wasn't falling through a vast cavern at all. He was still dropping, but now it was through emptiness. It was as if he were diving across the surface of a white page; the only way of confirming that he was indeed falling were the tears squeezed out by the slipstream and pushed up past his face. He stopped yelling when his throat began to burn and then there was just a silent rushing through nothingness. First, he thought it was a cloud that had enveloped him, the way you see a world devoid of colour and shade through the window of a descending plane, but after several minutes passed he gave up that theory.

After an hour of falling endlessly, he lost consciousness.

When he awoke – before he opened his eyes – he thought it had all been a dream. For a moment, there was comfort in knowing that he had never left his bed and was still curled under a blanket with the simplicity of exams ahead of him, and a world still filled with friends, and girls he had to confess feelings to. Then he woke fully and found he was still falling, the only blemish in a pristine white universe. He tried to call out but the sound was swallowed by a wind that he could not hear but could feel streaming around his body. The muscles in his arms and legs burned, as though he had been lifting weights for too long. Moving them was an effort and he found he did not have the energy for it. After another hour, he lost consciousness again.

The next time he awoke, before opening his eyes, he prayed. He called out to Allah for an end to the freefall and it seemed, for once, that Allah had heard his plea. He opened his eyes to see he was lying on his back on an ocean of soft black sand. There was a cloudless sky overhead. It wasn't blue, but the brown of mud that had been rained on. The sky looked as though, if he could touch it, he would find the same thick and viscous texture of a bog and be sucked into it, like a wounded animal drowning in quicksand. A flattened sun shone grimly through the murky backdrop. Yet, the powder beneath him was comfortable and his body had settled into it easily. Wahid lay there for several minutes, just digging his fingers into the fine sand and finding he had never been as grateful to be on the ground as he was just then.

He eventually sat up, grains of sand sticking to his back, and looked around. The air simmered with heat, there were geysers in the distance that burped out pure flame every so often, and the black sand caught what measly light there was and glimmered menacingly.

'I am so sick of fucking sand,' Wahid grumbled. He stood up and dusted himself off. While the landscape was even in every direction, there was a cluster of palm trees in the distance ahead of him, so he trudged towards it. It took him half an hour. The trees, it turned out, were rock formations, growing in parabolic curves out of the ground. Wahid's stomach was beginning to grumble loudly and his throat was sore from thirst and the screaming. As he contemplated his condition, a wave of dizziness overcame him and he had to sit down with his back against the rock. Exhausted, he fell into a deep sleep.

VII.

In life, Hamza had liked reading *The Economist* and the *Incredible Hulk* comics, smoking copious amounts of hash, playing Half-Life, fantasizing about his one-true-love Emma Watson, watching Hong Kong cinema, masturbating to Pakistani models, masturbating to a few girls in A levels with him, masturbating to his English teacher, and reading Neil Gaiman's novels. He had hoped to become a successful lawyer one day, even though he knew lawyers didn't ever end up fighting morally glorious cases. Still, he was good at elocution, had been captain of the debate team in school, and had once even represented Pakistan in an international debate competition held in Singapore – he lost but it was a near-run thing. His father was a surgeon and so was rarely home, but Hamza loved him enough not to resent his absence. His mother loved him a little more than she loved his elder sister, something he knew she would never admit. Hamza had found happiness in the simple things: when his mother, after a little emotional blackmail, made her special khao suey for dinner; when he had no homework, just a sleeve of Oreos and a night of gaming on the console ahead of him; and when Wahid took them through an imaginary world, detailed only by Wahid's vivid descriptions and a handful of dice. Each game would begin with Wahid saying, 'You find yourself in …' and then the room around them would melt away and Hamza was Barslow, the elven thief, who was raised in the gutters of the city of Muldoon by a retired criminal mastermind Halfling, and was as likely to slit your throat as pick your pocket. On a good night, there would be a story involving at least one dragon that needed slaying, two trap-filled dungeons that had to be crawled through, zombies to be evaded, goblins that needed slicing, a few cups of ale and a pot of gold to end it all. The settings were never that remarkable, almost predictable sometimes. But it was the way Wahid described them that made them real. When he got into it, Hamza could feel the splash of dirty water pooling in cobbled streets, see the twin moons suspended in a clear night sky, and feel the twang of his bow releasing yet another arrow between an opponent's eyes. Hamza had loved those nights of Dungeons & Dragons with Wahid and Arif.

The realization that there would be no more nights like that filled him with fury. It was the kind of fury, Hamza discovered, that could only be quieted when he killed more of those bearded fucks with black turbans who kept spilling out of the mosque next door and running at him with their guns spitting. Hamza had killed the first one in the corridor outside the room he had died in, punching his head like an overripe grapefruit. Since then, he had killed two more in front of the exit. They had been running towards the fading echoes of gunshots when he stepped out of the shadows and snapped their necks as easily as pushing the heads off his old action figures. It was only when they lay twitching on the ground, heads bent at harsh angles, that he considered how they hadn't seen him even though he was standing right next to them.

'You will be dead,' the Angel of Death had told him, whispering to him through the smothering blanket of black feathers and blinking white eyes. 'The dead do things the living cannot.'

The angel had told him one more thing. It had told him he would be able to find Wahid just by looking for him. He hadn't had a chance to test that ability yet though. After exiting through the steel doors of the house he had woken up in, he discovered it abutted a mosque. Through the gates of the mosque, more young men had come charging, shooting at him with machine guns. He found it easy to dance around the bullets though, once he understood how to move through shadows. He could enter one patch of darkness and walk out through another. By the time he killed his seventh attacker, he was focused less on the task and thinking more of the things he would never do again. Then he thought of the things he would never be able to do for the first time. Have sex was topmost on that list. A bullet thudded into his shoulder, bringing him back to the present. Five more men had emerged from the mosque, screaming and rushing at him. He lifted a body near his feet and threw it at them, using the confusion it created to disappear into the shadows once again. When he emerged behind them, he heard himself scream, 'Taste zombie death, bitches!' as he pushed his hands into their backs, shredding spines and slicing lungs with his fingers. When he was done, a total of fifteen men lay dead around him. The air stank of blood and gunfire. Hamza wiped his hands on one of the men's kameez and then stood up. Karachi was surprisingly quiet. No sirens could be heard in the distance and any traffic near the mosque had cleared out when the shooting started. Other than the bodies all around him, Hamza thought, it was quite peaceful.

'Wahid,' he said to the night sky, 'where are you?'

There was nothing. No instinct, no psychic knowledge, no voice emanating from the darkness above.

Spying a flat blade of shadow against the wall next to him, Hamza walked towards it. He would wait, he thought. And while he waited, maybe his killer would come back. As he disappeared into darkness, Hamza flexed his fingers hopefully.

VIII.

'I'm so close,' Maheen was saying. She was made of a cloud of white sand that swirled and danced in front of him. Her face was a mass of glittering powder; her hands left trails of dust in the air that floated softly around them.

'I'm sorry it's taking so long,' said Wahid, wanting to touch her but scared that his hand would plunge through her form and she would turn into an accumulation of sand drifting through his fingers.

'Don't worry,' said Maheen, then she kneeled in front of him. She bent forward, bringing her head down to his feet as if praying to him. She opened her mouth and a white tongue emerged from pink lips. Her face moved closer and the tongue, dry and rough, traced a line from the heel to the tip of his toes. Then Maheen shrieked.

Wahid jerked awake. Maheen continued to scream. The sun had descended to a point directly in front of him, and so he thought the silhouette writhing in pain at his feet was her. It took a second for Wahid's eyes to adjust and he leaped up in horror. The high scream was from a thin figure, pale as the sand around it. As it lay on its side kicking and twisting it seemed as if it was constantly trying to merge with the desert and was repeatedly vomited back out. A bald head thrashed from side to side. It had eyes that were melted puddles of red wax, which stared at Wahid whenever they faced him. From the mouth poured a purple ribbon of tongue, slithering across the desert floor like an angry snake. The creature clutched the tongue in two bony hands. It seemed to be the source of its suffering, as smoke unfurled from between the fingers. The skin of the tongue sizzled audibly.

Wahid took a few steps back and put the tree between himself and the creature. It managed to get its knees under it and bent over, taking the length of tongue and laying it on the ground in front. Then it pushed piles of sand over the tongue, focusing on the burning tip. The screams diminished, settling into cooing whimpers.

'What are you?' stuttered Wahid from behind the tree, his voice still hoarse. The creature paid him no heed, consumed by the need to soothe its pain.

'It is a Palis,' said a voice from behind him. Wahid turned, expecting to see Iblis but found a cat instead. A black tabby, as large as a small dog with fur like the night. It was sitting a few feet away from him, curled on the sand and regarding him with burning red eyes.

'It tried to feed on you. But it was burned by your skin,' said the cat, as naturally as if it was the most common thing in the world.

'And what are you?' asked Wahid, finding he wasn't surprised by what he saw, just mildly curious at most.

'I am not a Palis, thank Allah. I am a higher order of djinn. My kind are called Qarin.' The cat stood up on all fours and stretched, its back flattening as it pushed its front paws out ahead of it, dragging claws through the sand. 'And you should not be here.'

'Well,' said Wahid, 'I'm here nonetheless.'

The Palis was mewling softly now, slowly massaging its tongue. Wahid glanced at it and then back at the Qarin that began pacing in front of him.

'So, are you going to attack me now or what? Because I should warn you, so far it hasn't turned out very well for anyone who has tried,' said Wahid.

'No,' said the Qarin. 'I will not be doing that. If what they say about you is true, then it would be foolish to try it. But I am still curious as to why you are here.'

Wahid smiled broadly. 'Oh, isn't it obvious? I want you to take me to your leader.'

He thought he could make out a shrug, then the Qarin turned and started padding away from him.

'Follow me,' it said.

Wahid walked after it, more impressed by his own composure than the strangeness of what was occurring.

'Why did the … Palis lick my feet?'

'That is how they feed. In the desert, they drink blood from the feet of Bedouins while they sleep. Since we withdrew from your world, it has been hungry. I convinced it that you would provide a worthwhile meal.'

'Why did you do that?'

The Qarin stopped and turned to face Wahid, a hungry smile curling on its feline face. 'Because I was curious.'

They travelled for several minutes in silence until Wahid, finally finding his thirst unbearable, asked for water.

The Qarin seemed genuinely apologetic for not having provided better hospitality, as though it hadn't just tried to have Wahid's blood drained by a vampiric djinn. It raised a paw and a portion of sand on the desert floor began to part. A puddle of clear water rapidly filled the shallow hole left behind. Wahid bent down and tentatively tasted the water. It was warm and sweet. He cupped both his hands together and brought up as much as he could to his dry lips, gulping it noisily. It felt like a salve had been rubbed on the inside of his mouth and throat. He drank more and then splashed it on his face, even running it through his hair.

'Thank you,' he said, wiping his face on his forearm.

'You are welcome,' said the Qarin, and it waved its paw, the puddle disappearing as sand filled in.

The landscape gradually began to shift, with soft powdery sand giving way to hard grey rock that was uncomfortable to walk on. Wahid's ankles began to hurt and his calves felt as though they would swell and explode like balloons filled with too much water. Just as he was about to ask to rest, Wahid heard the flapping of a canvas. He and the Qarin rounded a small hill to find a tent on the other side. It was as large as a room and made from fraying material that had probably once been olive green but was now too faded to hold any colour. It was worn thin in places, so that the cross-hatched weave of the fabric was visible, with diamonds of negative space between the threads showing darkness within. As they approached it, the front flap of the tent lifted and a bare foot emerged, followed by a muscular leg. A naked man stepped out, easily two heads taller than Wahid and with a body that was taut with defined musculature. The entire surface of his body was covered with a matting of fine grey fur. The even growth of hair started at the top of his scalp, ran over his face and neck and ended at the tips of his toes. The only break was in the red eyes that surveyed Wahid and the Qarin, and the large teeth that sprouted from either side of his mouth and curved upwards to a point beneath his eyes.

'What the fuck is he doing here?' he growled at the Qarin.

'I don't know. I am taking him to meet the Ifrit.' Then the Qarin turned to Wahid and said, 'He is a Ghul. Be careful of him. They hate your kind.'

'My kind?' asked Wahid.

'Bani Adam,' said the Qarin.

'Haven't you heard,' said Wahid with a confident grin, 'I'm only fifty per cent human. The other half is djinn.'

'That's more than enough for me to hate,' the Ghul grumbled from behind, falling in to lock step with them.

Some way ahead, they crossed a group of Grines, a dozen half-formed creatures hopping slowly in procession. They took one look at Wahid and after a brief conversation with the Qarin also fell in behind him. Over the next hour, they accumulated a small crowd composed of several Ghuls, Grines, even a few Marids who glared menacingly at Wahid when they first saw him and then walked behind everyone, shouting curses at him for killing one of their kind. Wahid ignored them all and kept walking silently.

The landscape shifted from desert to rock floor to desert again, interrupted sporadically by pools of bubbling lava and the odd geyser. Waves of heat drifted lazily over them, and Wahid found it oddly refreshing. Every so often, he noticed they would pass something quite out of place. The first was the empty shell of a small house, the brick frame crumbled in places to show a hollow interior. It stuck out of the sand at an angle, as though it had been carelessly dropped from above and left there. It was from this house that two Ghuls emerged and joined their procession. The incongruity of the tilted house was enough to make it noticeable, but Wahid initially put down the transparency of the structure to a trick of the light. The whole thing somehow seemed less substantial than everything around him.

Some minutes later they passed by a single room, similarly laid over the desert. It had four walls and a door and through the gauze-thin walls he could see a chair, a desk and a bed. The entire thing just sat uncomfortably on the sand. Inside it was a creature with human legs and a human waist, but the chest was covered in black feathers, the arms were wings folded back and the head was that of a crow, with a large beak and black eyes. The creature saw the crowd passing by and joined in, attempting to strike up a conversation with one of the Marids who swatted it away. It cawed in disgust and relocated to a different place in the crowd.

Wahid saw several more oddities; a broken elevator, a kitchen with a sink full of rusted pans and broken dishes, even a small yacht lying on its side on the hard rock ground. From each one a djinn would appear and, after inquiring about the reason for the growing procession and having Wahid pointed out to it, would join in. Wahid was beginning to feel the burden of attention as close to fifty creatures were now following him, all watching him with burning red eyes. His face flushed and his ears grew red and warm. They all seemed to keep a fair amount of distance between him and themselves. He thought about how he had created a blaze without even meaning to and wondered if he could kill so many djinns if he lost control somehow. Wahid hoped he would never have to find out.

'That is where the Ifrit sits,' said the Qarin. It was the only djinn in front of him, and it had stopped and was pointing at a large tree ahead.

Wahid saw a mango tree, with thick sinewy branches and a canopy of lush leaves.

'In the tree?' asked Wahid.

'Yes, that is the home of the Ifrit.'

The crowd behind Wahid had stopped, but as he began to walk towards the tree, they spread out in an arc around him. Wahid tensed, worrying that they would rush him from both sides but their focus seemed to be on the tree, and trying to find the best positions from which to observe what was about to happen.

Wahid reached the thick round trunk that rose from the rocky ground. This tree was not afflicted with any transparency, yet had somehow grown out of hard earth, with no visible mud or grass in which to bury its roots. As he looked up into the branches overhead, a ghost of a memory flitted inside him.

There will be a man sitting on the branches above, thought Wahid.

There was. On a strong and wide branch, with his legs dangling below, sat a tall man with bright eyes dressed in a shalwar kameez.

'Are you the Ifrit?' asked Wahid.

The djinn hopped off the branch and landed on the ground, then sat against the trunk of the tree, long legs crossed like a yogi.

'I am Ifrit. I am also an Ifrit, and for as long as anyone can remember, I am the Ifrit,' said the djinn in a voice that was deep and calm. 'How did you get here, Wahid? Why are you here in Kaf?'

Wahid sat down as well, feeling relief as he took the weight off his feet.

'It doesn't matter how I got here,' said Wahid, hoping his voice sounded as confident as he wanted it to. 'What matters is why I'm here.'

'And why are you here?' asked the Ifrit.

'For Maheen. Her soul. Two djinns, two Marids, attacked me. They killed a friend of mine and I killed one of them. The other took the soul of a girl I was … who was with me. I want to rescue her.'

'And then what? Let's say I give her soul back to you. Then what will you do?'

'Nothing. I'll take it away from here and never come back. That's what you want, right?'

'What we want?' said the Ifrit with a hand sweeping towards the assembly of djinns around them. 'What we want is to be left alone. Yet djinns are disappearing and some are dying. It is no simple thing to kill us and yet it is being done simply. Are we not to defend ourselves?'

Wahid punched the ground and when he spoke his voice was trembling with anger.

'I'm not killing the djinns. I only killed the one that attacked me. If you had bothered to ask me instead of trying to kill me, you would know that. And you killed my friends, so … so fuck you. You even sent a bloody psychopath after me, or did you forget that?'

'What are you talking about?' asked the Ifrit, leaning forward.

'The man. That man who attacked me. He would have killed me if not for … if not for luck.' Wahid omitted Iblis from his narrative, not knowing exactly why, but knowing it was best to do so.

The Ifrit considered this for a few seconds then waved his hand dismissively.

'I sent no human to kill you. It is not our way. If there is killing to be done, we do it ourselves. No. That had nothing to do with us.'

'But that … well, then who sent him?'

'I don't care. It isn't my problem. You say you are not hunting djinns. If not you, then who? You are the only one with the power to do this to us. You can kill us with a touch. Burn us with a touch.'

'How did you even know I could do that?' asked Wahid. 'I didn't know it myself.'

The Ifrit held up his hands, palms facing Wahid. The skin on each hand was seared, the flesh charred like burned meat.

'You do not remember?'

Wahid was struck with the memory of fingers closing around his throat and of a figure in the darkness, receding with smoke drifting off his hands.

'That was you!'

'Yes. I knew then that you would be dangerous to us. A few weeks ago, when djinns started dying and disappearing, I did what I had to. As their leader, it's my duty to protect them. Perhaps you are correct and I should have sent someone to talk to you first. Maybe even come myself. But what is done is done. You say you have not been stealing our kind? Killing our kind? Then who has? Who but you has power over us? Not since Sulaiman has this been allowed.'

'Who's Sulaiman?'

'Hazrat Sulaiman,' said the Ifrit, then turned and spat. A gob of lava spattered on the ground and sizzled. 'He was a slaver. He used his ring and bent us to his will. Made us build his palaces and his walls, as though we were labourers.'

'Well, I don't know anything about him. Nor do I know anything about djinns disappearing or dying. I just need to save Maheen. She didn't deserve any of this.'

The Ifrit stood up slowly, seeming less imposing to Wahid now and more like a tired man who finds the weight of responsibility too heavy to carry.

'We dare not venture out of our world into yours. My people are too frightened. You say you are not doing this to us? Maybe I believe you. So now we have a mystery. Who is doing this to us? Who is stealing and killing djinns?'

'I don't give a fuck!' screamed Wahid. 'Just give me Maheen!'

The Ifrit stood up and Wahid did too, unsure if he was about to be attacked.

'Might as well.' The Ifrit shrugged. 'It was a foul thing to do. To steal a soul like that. And it was done to keep us safe from you. Yet, here you are.'

The Ifrit turned and plunged his hands inside the gnarled wooden trunk. Then he stepped back and held his arms in front of him.

Maheen lay delicately in his hands.

The distorted shape of the tree trunk behind her was visible through the glassy surface of her skin. Her eyes were closed and her features expressionless. She looked as if she were dead.

'Is she …?' asked Wahid softly.

The Ifrit turned to face Wahid with Maheen draped over his arms.

'Souls are neither alive nor dead. They exist forever. The bodies they inhabit are limited to those two states. That she is here and not ascended to Barzakh means her body is alive.'

'Can … can I hold her?'

The Ifrit stepped forward and held her out. Wahid placed his arms under her back and lifted her carefully. There was no weight, nor could he feel any texture to her skin. It was as though he was holding nothing.

'Maheen?' he whispered to the soap bubble, shaped like the girl he last saw smashed inside a car.

There was no response. He looked up at the Ifrit, trying to tamp down the anger that was growing inside. That they had done this to her. That they had cost him so much. He forced himself to stay calm.

'What do I do? How do I return her to her body?'

'Just release her. The choice is hers. If she wants, she will return to her body and awaken. If she does not wish to live again though, she will allow herself to drift off into the place where we wait for Allah's judgement after death. It will be her decision.'

'I just let her go?'

'Yes.'

Wahid looked down at her, lying still in his arms. He felt the need to cry bubbling inside him, but was too conscious of the mass of djinns standing around to follow through.

'I hope you choose to live. I want to see you again. I want to tell you I'm sorry,' he said to her.

Then he bent down on one knee and laid her on the ground gently. She slid slowly onto the rock surface, lying perfectly straight like a princess in a fairy tale waiting to be awakened. Then she dissolved out of view.

Wahid sat slumped, staring at the space where she had been. His eyes stung and his lungs burned, each breath struggling under the weight of exhaustion. For the first time in ages, he felt like he needed his inhaler, as if breathing would be too difficult an accomplishment without it. The yearning for it took him past the last few days and back into the moment before the car crashed and it all changed. He could see her sitting next to him, Arif snoring in the back seat. He could see himself dropping her home and then meeting her the next day. Maybe studying together. Maybe even asking her out eventually.

'What did she choose?' asked Wahid, palming away tears.

'I do not know,' answered the Ifrit with a shrug. 'I suppose you will find out when you return to your world. Although, I still have not decided if I will let you go.'

Wahid bunched his hands into fists. 'You're going to try to stop me?'

The Ifrit laughed, making gestures of placation. 'Relax, relax. I am not going to attack you. You might be strong enough to defeat me, but you would also die in doing so. And I have no interest in killing.'

'Then what do you want?'

'I want your assurance that you will solve this mystery. You will find out who is stealing djinns and what they plan on doing with them.'

'Why should I do that? I just want my life back and I can finally get it.'

'Well, if you don't agree, we will just keep you here. How did you find your way in anyway?

'I jumped. Into a cavern.'

'The Majlis al Djinn? That is an entrance into our world, but no Bani Adam can use that. But you are not Bani Adam. Not completely. Which is why you are perfect for this task. You can go back to your world and find whoever is behind this. After all, it was because of that confusion that we attacked you in the first place. Wouldn't you like the mystery to end?'

'I don't really care much actually. I just want my life back.'

'But your life isn't going to get back to you. Not if I don't let it.'

'How will you stop me?' said Wahid, raising his fists.

'Stop threatening me, boy. You may have power but you are still just a boy. I have the entire assembly of my people at my command. There are more djinns in Kaf than children of Adam ever existed. You do not think you can kill all of us, do you?'

'I can try.'

'You can try and fail. And then die. Which is what I should let happen since you are a threat to our existence. But I am not going to do that if you are willing to make a deal with me.'

The djinns around them had formed a complete circle and that circle had begun to slowly tighten. Wahid glanced at them, at the grotesque forms and myriad shapes that all watched him with menace.

'So what then? You want me to go back to Earth and find whoever is doing this to your kind?'

'It is your kind too. Do not forget your parentage. Whether you like it or not, you are half-djinn. That cannot be simply cast aside. So, will you do it?'

Wahid lowered his hands, glaring at the Ifrit.

'Fine. But how?'

'I have a means of helping you.'

'What's that?'

'Your government. We've had contact with them for some time. Not often, but just regularly enough for them to know that we have no ill will towards them. Frankly, they are a bit paranoid. They worry endlessly that we will be employed by their enemies to steal their weapons or attack them. As if djinns are simple mercenaries. There is a man who knows of us, and I can send him a message. Have him meet you.'

'Whatever. Okay, so if you are in touch with them, why can't you ask them to help?'

'Because they cannot see our kind. Not unless we choose to let them. But you can. And with your eyes you might be able to find those of us who have been stolen faster.'

Wahid rubbed his face. He decided that swallowing the information whole would be easier than picking it apart and studying each morsel. He was too tired to do so anyway.

'Fine, then, have them get in touch with me.'

'Good. It is agreed. Now to get you home.'

'Do I go back the same way I came here?'

'There are better routes to and from our world. We use them all the time.'

'Oh? Which ones?'

'Abandoned places. Some trees. There are pathways between the worlds that we djinns can travel on.'

'So those things I saw, the house, the room, an elevator. Those are pathways?'

'They are. When a place has been left empty for too long it belongs to us. We can inhabit it and live in it. And if we choose, use it to enter into your world from ours.'

'And trees?'

'Some trees. Old trees exist in both worlds. We make our homes in them as well. This one has been my home for several years now. If you were a djinn you simply had to choose one, or find an empty place and then walk through it, as long as the djinn who lives there gives you permission. Where do you need to go?'

Wahid didn't need to think about his answer. 'Home. My home in Karachi.'

The Ifrit looked at the assembly around them. It had grown during their conversation, with many more djinns in varying shapes and sizes adding to the number.

'Who here has a passage into Karachi?'

Several djinns raised their hands. Some did not have hands and so raised the closest approximations: wings, paws with curved and glinting claws stabbing the air, and one column of dust that rose out of a larger whirlwind. The Ifrit scanned them all and then pointed at a djinn standing near the front. It looked like a boy, rounding on ten years of age, with a chubby face, pale skin and thick black hair. The only evidence of its true nature were the burning eyes.

'You, Si'lat,' said the Ifrit.

'Yes, my king,' said the boy in a voice that was as old as a continent.

'Where is your home?'

'It is an old hospital. It juts into an old part of Karachi. I can take him, though the journey will take some hours. It is some distance away.'

'Do you mind the journey?' the Ifrit asked, addressing Wahid.

Wahid sighed. 'At this point? No.'

'You know,' said the Ifrit, studying Wahid with interest, 'I am amazed. You do not seem scared. Throughout the ages, when humans first saw djinns, they would piss themselves in fear. Some would go insane. Others turned to Allah for protection. But you? You have seen an entire host of us standing around you and you barely bat an eyelid. It is strange.'

Wahid considered this, once again looking at the throng of creatures: human shapes filled with darkness; animal–human hybrids; half-formed hopping djinns that leered at him with their only eye.

'They aren't really scary, I guess.' Wahid shrugged. 'Maybe in the past, but you know, they look kind of like, well, animation. I know a part of me should be frightened of them, but I've seen scarier things in movies and read about them in books. Most of what I see here is like … bad video-game character design or something. It's not particularly imaginative I guess is the right way to describe them. I'm sorry if that's rude but it is what it is.'

'I can scare the fucker,' growled a Marid from nearby, taking a step forward. Fire blazed behind the clenched teeth.

'There's no need for that,' said the Ifrit. 'Now go, Wahid.'

The Si'lat motioned for Wahid to follow him. He was about to set off behind it, then turned and called out to the Ifrit.

'My mother. If she is a djinn, then who is she?'

'It is not me,' said the Ifrit with a laugh. 'I am sorry to disappoint you. It should not be possible to give birth to a human child. It has never been done before and I have not heard of whoever managed it.'

IX.

Wahid and the Si'lat left the crowd of djinns behind and started out across a vast desert. They passed several more abandoned places and the Si'lat told Wahid where each one led.

He pointed to a large crab shell made of red bricks. 'That is the basement of a house in Quetta. It has been there for several hundred years now. The people in the house above do not even know it exists under their floorboards.'

'Who lives there?'

'A family of Qarin, they steal food at night, and sometimes spy on the women of the household,' said the Si'lat.

'Is this your real form?' asked Wahid.

'No. I am a Si'lat. We have no real form. All forms are ours. This is the one I choose to keep for now. It is the form of a boy I killed some years ago. He was exploring the hospital with some friends and he got separated. I took the form of a nightmare he had had a few days before. His heart stopped when he saw me. I ate his body and stole his shape. Do you like it?'

Wahid made an obvious show of not looking at the Si'lat when he turned and preened in front of him, a little boy strutting with his chest puffed out and pride on his face. The boy-shaped creature's laughter was like the crumbling of rocks.

After half an hour of walking, Wahid stopped and gaped at the shape of a city in the distance – high modern towers gleaming through drifting clouds of sand.

'What is that?'

'Dubai.'

'But Dubai isn't an abandoned place. People live there, right?'

'Perhaps. But some of it has come here. Large towers full of empty rooms. They are our playgrounds now.'

The towers faded from view after some time and Wahid began to feel his legs ache from the walking. Hot pins stabbed at his calves and his feet felt as though the skin had been scraped off them.

'How much further?' he gasped after pausing to stretch out the beginnings of a cramp.

'Almost there,' said the Si'lat, pointing to a rectangular building that appeared ahead.

As they drew nearer, Wahid could see a squat, two-storey building. A tree grew out of one side, branches having pushed their way through the broken exterior. The entrance sagged inwards as though it had been punched by a gigantic fist. The Si'lat walked towards the heavy wooden doors that hung loosely on their hinges like rotten teeth ready to be pulled.

The inside smelled of dust and emptiness. Despite every window frame being empty of glass, very little light seemed to make it indoors and most of the interior was a thatch of shadows. A steel gurney lay on its side near a doorway that opened into a large room that must have once been the reception area. A ceramic countertop had melted like a wax candle, dripping down to the warped floor. The Si'lat waved his small arms around grandly and sniffed.

'Home,' he said proudly.

'So how do I get from here to Karachi?' asked Wahid, eyeing a tilting chair. He tested it with one foot to see if it could bear his weight. It crumbled the moment he touched it with his toe.

'You don't.'

The shadows took shape. Four Marids walked out of the corners of the room, surrounding Wahid.

'You do not go any further, human bastard,' said one of them.

Wahid groaned and then held up his hands. 'Look, I don't want to do this. I'm tired and I just want to go home. You know you can't come near me.'

Another Marid snorted loudly and then walked over to the collapsed gurney. It grabbed the long metal railing and wrenched upwards. The railing snapped off easily with a loud crack. The Marid turned to face Wahid, brandishing the jagged-edged railing like a sword.

'We don't need to touch you to hurt you,' it said. The other Marids also made makeshift weapons from the furniture lying around the room. One lifted an entire chair over its head. The other two picked up bricks and held them in their large hands, ready to hurl. The Si'lat waved at Wahid and ran off giggling, disappearing around a corner.

'You don't understand, this isn't going to turn out well for you,' said Wahid, standing his ground.

'No,' said the Marid with the metal rod, 'it will turn out exactly the way we want it to.'

It flew at Wahid with surprising speed, covering the distance between them with a large leap. The rod swung through the air, whistling towards impact. Wahid barely had time to flinch.

There was an explosion. A ball of fire engulfed the rod and the Marid wielding it. It screamed in pain and fell to the floor, writhing as it burned, a black toffee inside a wrapping of red and orange. Wahid turned to face the other djinns.

'Your eye,' said the one with the chair, sounding stricken.

A small gout of flame erupted from Wahid's right eye. It curled in the air and swooped towards the chair. The wood caught fire on contact and turned to ash in the Marid's hands. The other two dropped their weapons and ran for the exit. One leaped out of the door while the other passed through the wall. Wahid stared at the remaining Marid who stood shivering in front of him, hands clasped over its face.

'Lower your hands,' said Wahid. 'Lower them and look at me.'

The Marid looked up into the face of a teenaged boy, with one eye full of fire. The air between them shimmered.

'I can kill you. It's easy for me,' said Wahid.

The Marid howled.

'But I won't do that. I'm tired of death. I never wanted to kill anyone. So get lost and don't ever come near me again.'

The Marid almost fell as it turned to run and escaped out of the front door on hands and knees.

'Where are you?' asked Wahid, grimly.

The boy walked back into the room. It did not seem afraid.

'You set a trap for me,' said Wahid, the air around his hands sizzling.

'The Marid asked me to. But this is a far more interesting result,' said the Si'lat.

'I can kill you.'

'But you will not. You just said so. And you have nothing to fear from an old djinn like me.'

'No more killing children,' Wahid said, his voice flat and loud.

The Si'lat cocked its head to one side and studied Wahid.

'You know, the last person who tried telling me what to do was Sulaiman. I stole the ring that gave him his ability to control my thoughts and actions, and made a beggar of him. Then I sat on his throne for many years, killing the children of his land. He took it back in the end, but I had my fun. And when he looked upon what I'd done to his kingdom, he wept like a child. I'll find a way to hurt you as well.'

'No, you won't,' said Wahid, faltering a little. The fire in his eye sputtered and began to fade.

'Perhaps. Perhaps I will be content to live in this beautiful home of mine. Perhaps not. But you should leave now. Unless you want to stay in Kaf, and I do not think you do.'

'How?'

The boy pointed to the door they had entered from, the same door the Marids had escaped through. 'Just walk through it. It is an entrance and an exit to both worlds.'

Wahid considered saying something more but the rage had left him and exhaustion began to saturate every joint and muscle. He flipped a middle finger at the boy-shaped djinn, and walked through the door into the light of a Karachi morning and a gun staring him in the face.

Interlude b.

Dajjal waited on the edge of reality. He had walked to the foot of the winding staircase and each step had left a black print. Tar bubbled in his wake, oil seeping from the ground under him, rising to the surface like sweat. With his single eye, he peered up into the swirling metal column, waiting for the doorway above to open.

Dajjal could wait. Patience was an easy virtue. After so many thousands of years, chained inside the small cube by Allah's angels, he had learned to control his own hungry anticipation. It was an ever-present thing though, lurking around the edges like a starving beast. He had always known he would be set free, that he would break his bonds when the end of days began. That even he did not know exactly when that would happen meant he had spent every moment of every day believing Qiyamat was just a breath away.

Anticipation. It could drive you insane.

But Dajjal had learned to cope with it. The first thousand years had been the toughest. He had screamed in rage, pulled on his chains and bashed himself against the floor. The next thousand years had been spent in contemplative meditation. He had sat quietly on the floor, cross-legged, with his eye closed so that he could turn his mind inwards. Dajjal had examined every atom of his being over that time. Yet even then, even in that utter silence, his skin burned with expectation. When your freedom could be granted at any time, it was hard to not constantly expect it.

As the millenniums passed, he noticed the iron bonds had begun to weaken. Ever so slightly. They had started to rust and crack at the same speed at which continents drifted apart. When he first noticed the decaying, the starving beast that was his anticipation surged forward, baying and thrashing inside him. But straining against the chains proved as futile as ever, and it had retreated to the fringes of his mind, growling and spitting in frustration.

Then the djinn had come to him with a plan. And then the boy had come to him, in the unfolding of that plan. No man or djinn could free him from those chains, so had Allah decreed. But a symbiosis of man and djinn, that was a new thing. That was neither and both. And the boy had freed him unwittingly.

Now Dajjal stood, waiting for the world above to be burnt enough for his arrival. He was free of the bonds but still not free to walk outside. For that there needed to be fire and death, and pain and suffering. There needed to be desperation in the sons and daughters of Adam, a mourning as deep as the deepest winter. A nuclear winter. Then he would walk amongst them and create miracles, make them believe that he was Allah, so that they would turn their backs on their true Creator. He would feed on their belief and grow stronger with each prayer until the world was his and none could stand above him.

The one eye blinked in anticipation as Dajjal watched and waited.

X.

The gun was several inches away from Wahid's face, a dark tunnel almost entirely filling his view. The man who held it was dressed immaculately: a shirt so crisply white it seemed as if it was lit by a spotlight; black pants with unforgiving vertical creases along each leg; Ray-Bans that reflected Wahid's face. His hair was neatly combed to one side, gleaming with gel. Behind him was a second man, identically dressed. He was casually carrying a large rifle, while leaning against the side of a grey Pajero with tinted windows. Both their faces were devoid of expression. A low rusted gate barely clinging to its joints separated the man with the rifle from the one holding a gun to Wahid's face. Beyond was a desolate alleyway with rubbish heaps on either side, contents spilling out onto the cracked road.

'Wahid Husain?' said the man with the gun aimed at Wahid.

Wahid nodded.

The man lowered his gun and stuck it in the holster clipped to his belt. Then he grabbed Wahid by the arm and started dragging him towards the car. Wahid stumbled, but found his momentum unaltered as they passed through the gate.

'I don't … who are you?'

The men stayed silent. The one with the rifle opened the car door and got inside. Wahid was lifted and pushed in next to him and was almost instantly joined by his captor. The door slammed shut and a third man sitting in front gunned the engine.

As the car lurched forward, Wahid tried to repeat his question with a greater amount of authority. Just as he was beginning to voice it, the first man pulled out a small black cloth bag from the pocket of the back seat in front of him, and in a single smooth motion, slid it over Wahid's head. Wahid tried to struggle but his arms were held down. The surprise that had paralysed him began to turn into anger, and he screamed from inside the bag. Then he felt a sharp stab like a bee sting on his neck and lost consciousness.

It was a black and dreamless sleep – the kind that swallows the consciousness so completely that waking from it is an endless effort, that may never be accomplished. Eventually he woke up, grudgingly opening eyelids that felt like stone doors rolling back on ancient hinges. He raised his head and was hit with a sickening sense of vertigo and he had to fight back nausea as his equilibrium realigned. His head had been resting on a steel table, a puddle of drool on the surface connecting to his cheek by a silken strand. He was sitting on a chair, alone in a small empty room with white walls. The single door on the facing wall was closed.

'Hullo?' slurred Wahid. His throat felt dry and itched when he spoke. He cleared it and tried again, louder. 'Hello? Where am I?'

The door swung inward abruptly as a whipped salute and a man entered. Wahid hadn't spent much time around anyone from the army, but the bearing was universally recognizable. He was dressed in a dark blue suit and maintained a strict posture, despite carrying a sizeable belly under his jacket. His face was an accumulation of circles, with large cheeks, a bulbous nose and even concentric rings around his eyes. He walked into the room, slammed the door behind him and sat down on the chair across from Wahid. He placed a plain black T-shirt on the table and motioned to Wahid to wear it.

'Who are –' began Wahid, only to be cut off by a hand being held up as the man took out a notebook from the inside pocket of his jacket. He studied its pages for a few seconds, then spoke.

'You are Wahid Husain,' he said, not asking so much as informing.

'Yes. I don't understand why –'

The hand cut him short again.

'Your father was Rehman Husain. Your mother is Mumtaz Husain. You are their only child.'

Wahid gave up speaking and nodded instead.

'Wahid, do you know who I am?'

Wahid knew the answer as soon as the question was asked.

'ISI?' he asked.

The Inter-Services Intelligence, Pakistan's spy agency. Except, in Wahid's imagination – as well as the imagination of most of the country – it was the country's secret power that knew everything about everyone and could make anything happen. He had heard stories about the ISI since he was a child. Each varied depending on the source. If the story had come from someone his age or slightly older, the ISI was the most wretched group of people in the country responsible for everything that was wrong with Pakistan, from terrorism to corruption. If, however, it came from any of his elder relatives or teachers, the ISI was the only thing standing in the way of Indians marching across the border, and deserved all credit for making Pakistan a nuclear country. The common tenet in each belief was that the ISI controlled Pakistan and very little happened without its say-so.

The man gave no impression of having heard the response.

'What do you know about djinns, Wahid?' asked the man.

Wahid sank in his seat, exhaling slowly as he leaned his head back against the chair.

'Too much. But it's not my fault.'

'What isn't your fault?'

'Whatever you are going to say. None of this is my fault. Ever since djinns entered my life, it has gone to shit. I have dead friends … Wait, did the djinns contact you? Did they talk to you about me? What did they say?'

'Have you met with djinns recently?' the man asked, finally looking up from his notebook at Wahid.

'Yes, I have. They told me that someone was kidnapping them. They thought it was me, but it isn't. That's what they were supposed to tell you. And that you would help me find whoever it was actually doing this.'

The man stared at Wahid blandly. 'Why would djinns think you were kidnapping them?'

Wahid slammed his hands onto the table. 'Look,' he yelled, 'I just want to be left alone. Instead, in the last few days, I've been attacked by djinns, seen shit that you wouldn't believe and had my friends die. I tried to save a girl so that one bloody life that intersected with mine could be restored, and I don't even know if I've managed that. And now I'm sitting in this room and you're treating me like a fucking criminal.'

Wahid slumped in his chair, deflated by the exhalation of his outburst.

'I just want to go home. Please.'

A silence stretched out between them, with Wahid staring at the table and the man watching him.

'My name is Major Ibrahim Daulat,' said the man finally. He reached across the table and placed a hand on Wahid's. 'I am the ambassador to Kaf, the world of the djinns.'

'I know what Kaf is,' grumbled Wahid.

'I know,' said the major softly. 'Would you like a glass of water?'

'No, thank you.'

'The Pakistan government has had a working relationship with djinns for some years now. I am the fourth ambassador to Kaf, which should give you some idea of how long this arrangement has been in place. We do it so that we do not ever need to worry about our enemies using djinns to attack us. It's paranoid, I know, but this is a world which rewards paranoia.

'A few weeks ago, the djinns withdrew from our world and we lost all contact with them. I tried to reach out to the djinns through all the normal channels, but there was no response. Then, a few hours ago, I received a message. It informed me that a boy named Wahid was going to appear soon and that he would know what happened. There, I have been honest with you. Does that help?'

Wahid stared at Major Daulat in astonishment. 'Yes. That's what I know.'

'Good, now we are on the same page. The question is, why do you know about Kaf? How did you get there and why are the djinns so interested in you? Can you please help me, Wahid? I can't do much for you unless you are honest with me.'

Wahid decided he did need the glass of water and when it was brought to him, he gulped it down. Then he detailed his experience, from the moment he was attacked in the car up to exiting the empty hospital. He left out Iblis and the Yajuj-Majuj. That seemed like information best kept to himself. When he finished, Major Daulat let out a low 'Ya Allah'.

'Do you … do you believe me?'

The major stood up and paced around the small room once, his hands clasped behind his back.

'I suppose I do, Wahid. I don't know about this entrance you used to get into Kaf. Across from Defence Graveyard, you say? I'd very much like to see that. But still, it's too ridiculous a story not to be true. And you say you are … what? A half-djinn?'

'Yes. Apparently. It lets me do things. Like kill djinns. Not that I want to. Ever again, I mean. Just, yeah, that's what I am I guess.'

'Very interesting,' said the major, rubbing his chin. 'Mashallah, you are quite a miracle.'

'So will you help me? I mean, with what the Ifrit asked for? To find out who is kidnapping djinns?'

'Well, it explains their disappearance. It is something I will consider for sure.'

'So how should we, y'know, proceed?'

The major walked to the door and opened it, standing with his hand on the doorknob. 'You will be staying here.'

'What?' said Wahid, leaping out of his chair.

Two soldiers, dressed in full uniform with rifles held against their chests, walked into the room behind Major Daulat. They levelled the guns at Wahid.

'Sit down, Wahid,' said the major calmly. Wahid lowered himself into his seat, glaring at the major. There was an impulse, an urge building inside him, to let the fire come through him again. It coiled inside him, a burning snake unravelling somewhere in his stomach and rising upwards. Wahid wondered if he could burn the soldiers before they managed to shoot him. It seemed a fatal question to ask. Wahid tamped his rage down.

'Like I said, you will be staying here until I figure out what to do with you. If you can kill djinns, your ability to do so might come in handy. We should probably put that ability to the test once we find some djinns. In the meantime, sit down and don't raise a fuss while I deliberate.'

'This is bullshit,' said Wahid.

'Maybe. But I need to know if I can trust you first. Here, this should help calm you down in the meantime – just before I got here, I heard from one of my friends. A retired general. His daughter had been in a coma for the last few days after a car crash. We were all very upset. I've been informed that she has woken from that coma. She seems to be okay. I thought you might like to know that.'

Wahid stared at the major, then down at his feet.

'Thank you … for telling me that. Thank you.'

'You're welcome,' said Major Daulat, then turning to the guards, 'Stay outside.'

Interlude c.

Karachi screams. The sound rises upwards as though Karachi is an inverted storm cloud, streaming rain towards the sky. The people have learned to block out the noise, tuning out the constant suffering in an effort to keep themselves sane. And so, they do not hear the story behind each cry, ignore the origin of every shriek. On this night, the screaming is louder than normal. Ambulances race through the city, their sirens a melancholy fugue.

In Clifton, outside the mazaar, an addict wakes from a terrible dream. He rolls over, his arm numb from being pressed between his head and the hard concrete sidewalk. The feet of another addict twitch close to his face and he is offended by the blistered soles he is forced to stare at. His answer is to climb on top of the unconscious man and push his thumb into that man's eye. None of the other addicts sprawled around him stir and so he sits alone, staring at the final twitches of the dead body and smiles at how the single eye that stares blankly up at the sky looks so much like the single eye he saw staring at him in his dream.

In an apartment in Gulshan, a woman returns from a twelve-hour shift at a call centre, walks into the house without greeting her parents, takes a knife out of the kitchen drawer and plunges it into her own left eye, carving a hole under her brow. Then, before she loses consciousness, she smears a word onto the wall with a finger coated in blood.

Screams course through the city, a river of sound with a tragic undertow. Tributaries contribute to the flow, pain streaming through them like shoals of black fish.

At a traffic light on Tipu Sultan Road, a man hands his wallet and cell phone through the car window to a teenager on a motorbike. The teenager takes it, and as he is about to put the gun back into the waistband of his jeans, he thinks he hears the man say a single word. The sound startles him and he flinches, his finger still curled around the trigger flexing. A bullet punches through the man's eye, tunnelling through his skull. The boy on the motorbike speeds away, repeating the word to himself, over and over.

In Korangi, outside a biscuit factory, three boys are run over by a truck. The driver stops and reverses over them, then drives forward again. Reverse. Forward. Repeat. And again. Until he is pulled from the truck by a crowd of horrified bystanders. As he drowns under a hail of fists, the word he is screaming over and over is transferred to them like a virus, until they are all screaming it.

Everywhere in Karachi, death screams its name triumphantly. The same name over and over. By murderers and killers, by old people feeling life slip away, and by the sick who cannot struggle against their illnesses any longer.

'Dajjal!' they say.

'Dajjal!'

So close that he can smell the blood – but still too far to taste it – Dajjal smiles.

'Soon,' he says.

XI.

There was no clock in the room and so Wahid had no way of knowing how long he paced. The air conditioning had been cranked to the lowest temperature, and he was grateful for the T-shirt he'd been given. Eventually, more exhausted by a sense of despair than exertion, he slumped down in a corner and buried his head in his hands. He tried to cry, hoping tears might relieve the frustration, but none came. Twice he called out to Iblis, first whispering the name and then saying it louder. No one appeared. The room stayed as brightly lit and empty as before.

After some time, when he was nodding off from boredom, a soldier brought him food. He devoured the mountain of steaming biryani, shovelling large bites into his mouth with barely a breath between them. Eating reminded him of his mother, and he realized she would have found out about his disappearance by now. Eventually, with a full stomach and a mind stretched thin with worry, he fell asleep.

A distant booming pulled him awake. Muffled thunder crashed in the distance, the first blast followed by another. Wahid lifted his head off the table and stretched his arms, stiffened joints popping loudly. The sound continued when he stopped moving, a rattle of firecracker replies to the deeper rumbling thunder. Just as his mind cleared enough to recognize it as gunfire, the entire room shook violently. Wahid's chair jolted, the walls thrummed and the table clattered noisily as it danced across the floor. He got up and ran to the door, thumping on it hard.

'Hello,' he screamed, 'what's going on? Hello?'

From the other side came the voice of a man, sounding aggressively commanding. 'Oye! You aren't supposed to be here!'

'But you put me here,' Wahid yelled into the flat steel door. He was about to thump his fist against it again when the cacophonous crash of gunfire punched through, loud enough to startle him away from the door. It was followed by screaming, that started in the lower registers of rage, and then peaked as it switched into a yelp of pain. There was a wet crunching sound and then silence.

Wahid cautiously approached the door again, 'Hello? What's –'

There was another boom, sounding closer than the previous ones. The door shuddered on its hinges, a bulge popping in its centre. Wahid stepped back, taking several steps until he was against the far wall, his fists raised to chest height.

The door swung open so hard, it smashed against the wall and bounced back shut again. A hand pushed against it and it swung in, staying open this time. Framed in the entrance, wearing only a pair of blood-darkened jeans, his skinny torso riddled with punctures and deep gashes, was Hamza.

''Sup?' He grinned.

'Hamza!' Wahid shrieked and ran across the room, throwing his arms around his friend. The two of them stood there, hugging each other tight for several seconds.

'God!' said Hamza. 'You smell terrible. Get off!'

'I thought you were dead!' said Wahid, wiping away tears as he held Hamza at arm's length.

'I was,' replied Hamza.

That was when Wahid realized how cold Hamza's skin was under his grip. The flesh lacked any warmth and felt raw, like frozen meat. Wahid took in the damage done to Hamza's body: the clean puncture wounds in his chest and stomach went so deep that he could see nothing but darkness inside each, and the jagged slice across his neck that still looked fresh enough to be bleeding. There was blood smeared across his face and his hands glistened red, but Wahid could tell that none of it came from Hamza.

'I don't understand,' Wahid said.

'Look, I can explain later. In detail. For now, yeah, I died. I was killed by some sick fuck looking for you.'

'I know,' said Wahid, 'he tried to kill me too.'

'Yeah, sorry,' said Hamza, looking embarrassed. 'I think I might have told him where you were … when he was torturing me. I tried not to but …'

'It doesn't matter. You're alive. That's all that matters. I thought you were dead.'

'I still am, I think. I died and I went to … a place. Arif was there. And your father. They sent me back to save you. But, I don't think I'm alive technically. I guess I'm trying really hard not to say the "z" word right now.'

Wahid took a step away from Hamza, still holding his hand. 'My father? You saw Abba? What do you mean?'

'Like I said, man, later. We gotta get the fuck outta here first.'

Wahid followed Hamza out into the corridor. The soldier who had brought him the plate of biryani lay face down on the ground. His gun was shattered next to him.

'Did you do that?'

'Yeah.' Hamza grinned. 'I'm like a super ninja zombie now. It's quite cool actually.'

There was another distant rumbling, then two loud blasts somewhere overhead. The entire hallway quaked in response, Hamza and Wahid barely keeping their balance.

'Did you do that too? What is that?'

'No. That's not me,' replied Hamza. 'I don't know what it is. It was happening when I got here. Come on, let's get out this way. I think there's an exit ahead.'

Hamza led Wahid to the end of the corridor, blocked by another steel door. He tried the handle, found it unyielding and then pushed it down. There was the wail of metal complaining and then the door sprang open. The two stepped through and found themselves at the foot of a wide stairway leading up. They raced up it, taking two steps at a time as the thunderous blasts continued somewhere in the distance, growing louder the higher they got. Hamza reached the landing first and almost slipped back down the stairs as his foot slid out losing grip. Wahid, coming up behind, grabbed him in time.

'Fuuuuuuck,' said Hamza, staring at the puddle of blood he had stepped in.

A pair of soldiers lay on the ground in front of them. The side of one's head had been excavated in a messy scoop. The other lay face down, even though he was on his back, his neck twisted around so neatly that the skin was barely creased. Hamza and Wahid looked up from the bodies in front of them to the man standing ahead. Their first impression was of a *Star Wars* storm trooper, except dressed entirely in black. Black-tinted goggles over a black gas mask, black jacket behind a black bulletproof vest, even black pants behind black thigh and shin pads. The figure stood utterly still, regarding them, with a massive assault rifle clasped in both hands.

'You,' said the man, his voice muffled by the gas mask.

Then, from inside the man's head emerged a Marid. A skull full of night, with burning crescent eyes, erupted from behind the mask, streaming out like a soul evacuating a body.

'You,' the Marid hissed.

Before it could say any more, flames exploded around it. The fire had arced from Wahid faster than even he could see. As the man housing the Marid fell to the ground, flames curling around his writhing body, Wahid leaped over the dead soldiers in front of him. Skidding in blood, he regained his balance and raced over to the burning man, just in time to grab hold of the Marid as it climbed out of the body and tried to throw itself away from the reach of the flames. Black skin sizzled under Wahid's grip and the Marid screamed in agony.

'What the fuck is going on here?' roared Wahid, raising a fist against its face. The Marid gasped as Wahid released the arm, smoke rising thickly between them, all but obscuring Wahid's vision. The man whose body the Marid had been inhabiting let out a single subdued sigh and then stilled, fire still dancing across his form. The ski-mask over his face had caught, and his head was a twisting mass of orange streamers.

'What the fuck was that?' screamed Hamza, still standing on the topmost step.

'Please,' wailed the Marid, 'I didn't want to.'

'What. Is. Going. On?' growled Wahid, fire crackling hungrily in one eye.

'I was forced to. We all were. He has the ring. We have no choice,' the Marid whimpered.

Wahid, so full of anger that speaking was an effort, repeated his question. Somewhere in the distance, explosions and gunfire continued.

'The man. He has Sulaiman's ring. With it he forced us to come here. We found bodies to fill and he made us attack this place. There is something he wants from here.'

'Does he want me?' yelled Wahid. 'Who is he? Where is he?'

'How did you do that?' Hamza shouted, pointing at the burning body and then at Wahid.

'Bombs,' the Marid cried out, 'he wants the nuclear bombs.'

A door ahead of them swung open and three soldiers ran into the hall, guns levelled at Wahid.

Then everything happened at once.

'Stop,' one of the soldiers screamed. Wahid looked up just in time to see the flash of gunfire. By the time he registered the deafening clatter, the first bullet sliced across his cheek. The rest would have made several entries into his face had they not thudded into Hamza. He crouched in front of Wahid, a wide grin on his face as the bullets punched his back. Then he blurred. A smudge of movement, too fast to track, that leaped backwards and slammed into the closest of the soldiers. Wahid clutched the side of his face, feeling blood trickle from a thin gash just below his burning eye. The Marid stole the opportunity and shoved Wahid, pushing him backwards with immense force even as its palms seared on contact. As Wahid landed on his back, sliding towards the dead bodies behind him, the Marid bounded at the wall next to them, passing through it as effortlessly as if it were fog. Wahid screamed in anger as it disappeared into the concrete, just as the last of the three soldiers collapsed to the ground.

An abrupt silence filled the hallway; both friends stared at each other with wide eyes.

'How did you do that?' said Wahid, still on his back.

'I told you, I'm a ninja zombie. More importantly, how the fuck did you do that? Your eye was on fire and you set that guy on fire, and what the hell was that black thing?'

Hamza walked over and helped Wahid to his feet.

'You're not the only one with powers.'

'No shit. What was that?'

'I don't know. I think I can make it happen, but the two times it's happened before, it kinda happened by itself.'

'Dude, that was like … like Cyclops from the *X-Men*. You blasted that guy with your eye. And what was that black thing?'

'It was a djinn. It turns out I'm half-djinn. My mother … you saw Abba, you said, did he say anything? About my mother being a djinn?'

'Auntie is a djinn?'

'No. Not my mother. I mean –'

Another blast, much louder than any of those before. The force of it splintered the ground and threw both of them against the wall. The lights overhead flickered, then died.

'What the hell is going on out there?' said Hamza, reaching out for Wahid in the dark.

'I don't know but we really need to get out of here fast. I can't see anything.'

Hamza found Wahid's hand, cold fingers wrapping around Wahid's wrist.

'I can see a bit, come on.'

They stumbled through a series of corridors, feeling their way up two more flights of stairs. No one else appeared in their path, the only evidence that they were headed towards the exit being the steadily increasing sounds of gunfire and explosions. Finally, they pushed through yet another door and stepped out into the night.

XII.

Wahid's first thought was that the sky was burning. A low ceiling of flame roiled over their heads, painting the world a violent ochre. Heated winds buffeted them, burning the air in Wahid's lungs so that it felt like he was breathing in charcoal fumes. Hamza said something but Wahid couldn't make it out over the immense roaring that sounded like every motorcycle in Karachi was gunning its engine simultaneously. Flat tarmac stretched out ahead of them, its surface reflecting the overhead blaze. Hamza grabbed Wahid by the shoulder and pointed in front. Before them lay the skeletal remains of what must have been a cargo plane. A cumulus of black smoke fumed from the wreckage, metal ribs jutting from the undulant mass, glowing neon bright.

Another plane some yards ahead of it was still whole, its green camouflage skin charred by proximity. On the ground beneath it were several bodies. Even from a distance Wahid could see that they were not whole. More fires rose from craters around the planes, massive holes gouged out and filled with pools of lava.

Despite the continuous static roar, the staccato pop of gunfire from one side pulled their attention. They had emerged out of one of a series of buildings shaped like hangar bays, with flat, high walls and angled roofs. Wahid and Hamza turned and saw more black-clad storm troopers, all raining hell down on a building several hundred feet away. They were crouched behind barriers, rows of low cement blocks jutting like teeth in front of the buildings. Wahid could make out almost a dozen men, all of them simultaneously unleashing a relentless volley of gunfire. A hail of bullets spattered in a line in front of him and he pressed himself against the wall, crouching. One bullet sliced through Hamza's thigh, erupting from the other side. He staggered, caught his balance and then crouched next to Wahid.

'The Marid!' Wahid yelled to Hamza, pointing out a black ribbon of smoke that emerged from the ground ahead of them. It snaked through the air, reached the first of the storm troopers and hardened into a human shape, turning and pointing back towards Wahid. All at once, the siege came to an abrupt halt and each man turned in Wahid's direction. He saw a dozen black faces appear out of the bodies, eyes shimmering like candles. Then they all ran. As one, the storm troopers fled across the tarmac, crossing diagonally past the planes and towards a high boundary wall in the distance. Wahid saw puffs of bloodied vapour erupt from the heads of two of them and their bodies slumped to the ground, the djinns inside leaping out and continuing their pace without slowing at all.

'I'll nab one before they get away,' Hamza cried into Wahid's ear. Then, before Wahid could stop him, he dissolved. The churning orange sky was throwing abstract shadows in patches across the tarmac and Hamza appeared to hop through them, leaping from one to the other as though they were rocks above the surface of a pond. The largest shadow was cast by the intact cargo plane. Just as the last of the Marid-possessed storm troopers stepped onto this patch of darkness, Hamza surged up and out from inside it and blocked the terrorist's path. The lone storm trooper skidded to a halt, then exploded. Despite the distance, a supernova of sound slammed into Wahid. The plane, under which Hamza and the terrorist had been standing, was blown apart.

Wahid struggled to his feet, swaying clumsily. He knew he was screaming, could feel his mouth making the shapes of Hamza's name, but all he could hear was a continuous siren keening in his ears. He stumbled forward. The world was doubled in his vision, layers of blurred images shrouding everything. It was like looking at multiple realities simultaneously, all of them burning.

Some of the terrorists had been flattened by the explosion; their bodies discarded by the djinns who kept running towards the wall. The ones who had survived scaled the wall with ropes, while the djinns simply passed through it.

Wahid shook his head, smacking his palm against his ears until the ringing faded a little. He turned in time to see soldiers, recognizably human soldiers, trying to edge around the burning planes, their path blocked by debris. They were chasing after the escaping storm troopers, firing wildly in their wake. Wahid considered running to Hamza, not knowing if his friend could have survived the explosion. Then he saw some of the soldiers turn in his direction. Deciding he had no interest in being stuck back in a cell, he ran towards the wall the attackers had disappeared over and managed to make it across the tarmac without falling, even though the ground swayed underneath.

Climbing over the wall was more difficult. He grabbed a rope that had been left behind and used it to pull himself up and over, fighting to concentrate through surging waves of disorientation. When he crawled over the top and half clambered, half fell down the other side, he had to push back a swell of nausea that almost toppled him. Leaning against the wall, breathing slowly to steady himself, he looked around.

He had emerged into a narrow lane filled with bushes. Beyond it was a wide two-way road thick with traffic. Ambulances screeched past, careening around the cars and buses that had slowed so their occupants could gawk at the smoke and fire that hinted at the destruction on the other side. Wahid was obscured by foliage and so he made his way to the sidewalk ahead, emerging into a crowd of spectators, all their eyes trained at the black columns overhead.

Feeling steadier, he looked around for any sign of the attackers but his view was completely blocked by the press of onlookers.

'Bhai, you're bleeding,' said a man standing next to him, tapping at his own nose.

'I fell,' mumbled Wahid, wiping his face on his T-shirt. There was a bloody smear across it.

'Did you see any men in black running away from here?' he asked, but the man had already turned back to stare at the smoke. Wahid looked up as well. A glowing mountain of flame, almost too bright to look at directly, had appeared behind the wall. The sky above it was a bubbling lake of tar, a swarm of embers whirling inside it.

'Hell,' said the man next to Wahid. 'It looks like Hell.'

But to Wahid it looked like something else. It looked, he thought, like a million eyes embedded in an immense black wing, all glaring at the destruction below.

Can the dead die? he wondered. Had Hamza completely evaporated in the blast? Maybe he was strong enough to survive it. But if not, did his soul return to Barzakh? Thinking about it filled Wahid with a grief too large to comprehend. It erupted inside him and he felt as though, if given vent, he would create a blaze that could dwarf the one in front of him.

Moving through the crowd, in search of the escaped Marids, Wahid recognized where he was. Any chance of finding the djinns diminished rapidly. He had just come out of a naval airbase, situated close to the Karachi airport. If they had transport waiting for them, which they would have if they had used the possessed bodies to get there, they could already be hurtling back into the guts of the city. Or they could simply have found refuge in any of the towering apartment blocks that fenced the road on the other side. Finding them would be impossible. They could be anywhere in Karachi.

'Anywhere in Karachi,' said Wahid slowly to himself. 'Bhai,' said Wahid, patting the man next to him on the shoulder, 'can I use your cell phone please? I need to make an important call.'

The man turned and glared at Wahid. 'No scene, boss. You think I'm an idiot?'

Wahid ignored the response and turned away from the airbase. He waited for a gap in the traffic and then ran across the road, almost colliding with a motorcyclist and bringing one car to a screeching halt. The apartment buildings on the other side loomed high, every balcony filled with residents trying to get a better view of the carnage. Below them were all manner of shops, their trades advertised in painted boards and neon signs. Even before he made it all the way across, Wahid could see one that specialized in phones. He ran towards it, relishing the surge of strength that inspiration brought.

The shopkeeper was standing in the doorway, staring at the airbase. Wahid had to shake his shoulder hard to break his attention.

'Bhai, I need to make an important phone call and my cell phone has been stolen. Can I use a phone, please?'

The shopkeeper grinned sympathetically, waving him inside then turning his attention back across the road. Wahid walked into a narrow shop, display cases filled with a clutter of phones on one side. At the end of the small room was a table with a landline phone lying next to a small TV. The screen showed a reporter standing in front of the airbase and screaming into the camera.

'Local calls only,' said the shopkeeper over his shoulder.

'Yes, bhai. It won't be a long call, don't worry,' said Wahid. He picked up the phone and whispered a small prayer, then dialled his own cell phone number. It was answered on the third ring, by a young boy.

'Badshah?'

'Chutiya!' exclaimed the voice on the other end.

'Badshah, please, I need your help,' said Wahid, trying to keep the panic out of his voice and failing.

'Help? Why should I help you? Your phone isn't that nice and your wallet was almost empty. I'm busy.'

Wahid breathed deeply and tried to speak as coherently as possible, 'The attack. There's been an attack on the airbase, the one –'

'Yes, chutiya, I know about the attack. What is it?'

'The attackers were djinns. Djinns who had possessed people. I saw them and chased them, but they got away. I need you to help me find them. They are after nuclear bombs. If we don't stop them, they will definitely try again. Please, just tell me where they went. If they succeed the next time, there won't even be a Karachi for you to be king of.'

'You and your djinns. I really should just kill all of you.'

'I'll pay,' promised Wahid again, weakly.

'Yeah, yeah. You better. Stay where you are. I'll be in touch.'

An hour passed. The shopkeeper told Wahid that unless he was planning to buy something he should get out of the shop, and so Wahid found himself sitting on the sidewalk, watching police disperse the crowds around the airbase. Ambulances, police cars, and news vans created an impenetrable ring around the exterior wall, with a claw of smoke in the middle.

Just when Wahid was beginning to despair, a rickshaw screeched to a stop in front of him. A small boy, his clothes and face so filthy they were both the same grey, sat in the front seat, beaming at Wahid.

'Hello Bhenchod,' yelled Badshah over the popping of the rickshaw's engine.

'Thank you, thank you,' said Wahid, racing up to him.

'Okay, no need to try fucking me, I'm here,' grumbled Badshah, leaping out of the rickshaw. Then he kneeled and pressed his lips to the road, and began whispering.

'What ... what're you doing?' asked Wahid.

'Asking it to show me where they went,' said Badshah, standing up and wiping his mouth with the back of his hand. He clambered back into the rickshaw and motioned for Wahid to climb in, the entire vehicle clattering impatiently.

'Are you coming? The longer it takes, the harder it is to find them,' said Badshah.

Wahid climbed into the back. Badshah grabbed the handles and revved the engine, the rickshaw roaring as it leaped forward. Wahid grabbed the thin iron bar at level with his knees as the rickshaw swerved around a corner. Badshah drove with a frightening recklessness, forcing the small vehicle to go much faster than it was built to. Wahid felt the continuous scream of the engine in his head and his entire body vibrated like a tuning fork. They swerved through the congested traffic, Badshah manoeuvring the rickshaw through gaps that Wahid would not have believed large enough for a motorcycle and yet somehow they made it through each time. Often, pedestrians had to leap out of the way of the charging three-wheeler, trails of abuse fading behind them. They ran several red lights and were on to Shahrah-e-Faisal, the main road that cut a straight line through the length of central Karachi. Twice Badshah narrowly avoided colliding with buses. They blitzed across the main road and then swung onto a narrow street. Badshah brought the rickshaw to a jerking halt, then jumped out.

'Are we there?' asked Wahid, his ears ringing with phantom engine roars.

'No, the trail gets muddled a bit. I just want to make sure,' answered Badshah. He inhaled deeply and then took a few smaller sniffs. 'I need to make sure I can follow the smell of their van.'

'You can smell it?'

'I told you. This is my city. I can find anything in it if I want to,' Badshah said, hopping back onto his seat. 'They're in a Suzuki van. It runs on diesel, so the fumes are stronger, thankfully. Plus, one tyre is wobbling. It's left tracks on the road wherever they turned too fast.'

Wahid considered asking how seeing or smelling anything in a city with several million cars simultaneously on the road at any time was possible, then decided his life had moved far beyond such questions.

'So can we catch them?'

'Watch me.' Badshah grinned. 'No djinns fuck with my city.'

They accelerated again, this time coursing through side lanes and narrow streets lined with houses. Wahid tried to superimpose the route they were taking over his own internal map of the city and realized where they were headed a few minutes before they reached.

The gates of Karachi University stood closed before them.

XIII.

'I was here a few days ago,' said Wahid.

'That's exciting. Lots of people come here, man, now come on.'

Badshah killed the engine and they climbed out of the rickshaw.

'The gate is locked,' Wahid observed.

'So?' said Badshah.

He grabbed two bars of the thick grill and began to pull himself upwards, climbing with the ease of a cockroach running up a pipe. Wahid watched him negotiate the spikes on top and then lower himself down on the other side. Badshah grinned at Wahid through the thick bars, showing a row of crooked yellow teeth that looked much older than he was.

A chain had been wound around the handles of the gate and sealed with a large padlock. Badshah rummaged around in the pocket of his kameez and pulled out a long nail, its end flattened. He inserted it into the padlock and after several seconds of careful jiggling, they heard a satisfying click. He unravelled the chain. Wahid pushed the gate and it swung inwards, wailing loudly on its rusted hinges.

Badshah ran back to the rickshaw and roared it back to life. They sped across the roads winding through the large campus.

'No … but that's … no,' whined Wahid, his hands bunching into fists.

The physics building seemed larger at night, its square pillars and flat walls giving it the appearance of a concrete fortress.

'What's the problem?' asked Badshah.

'This is where I had come. There was a professor. It can't be him. It can't be.'

'Well, this is where they came and there's the van, see?'

An old Suzuki van was parked in front of the building, its exterior a piss yellow, with almost every inch of the body covered in dents and nicks.

'If it's him, then I know where he'll be,' said Wahid. The tinted glass doors to the department building were unlocked and Wahid and Badshah entered the darkened lobby. Badshah took out a cell phone and pressed a button at random, causing the screen to light up. The meagre light created a small halo that extended only a few feet around them. Wahid glanced at the phone.

'Hey, you can afford to buy another one,' said Badshah.

Wahid didn't respond, instead jogged up the stairs and into the hallway that he remembered led to Professor Rahim's office.

The door to the office was closed, the frosted glass window dark. Wahid tried the door and found it unlocked, pushing it inwards. He and Badshah stepped into the room with Wahid finding the light switch after some fumbling. A tube light flickered alive, showing the desk, chairs and bookshelf exactly where Wahid had last seen them, but no one inside.

'Maybe it isn't him,' said Wahid.

Badshah began to speak, but whatever he was about to say was drowned out by an explosive bang. His brains splattered on the side of Wahid's arm and face and Badshah fell forward. Wahid started to spin around when a heavy blow struck him on the back of his head. He too collapsed, landing on Badshah's body, his head slapping wetly in the blood.

XIV.

Slowly Wahid drifted out of darkness, with light spreading like a migraine. There was a moaning that grew louder as his senses sparked.

'You hit him too hard,' said a voice from far away.

The moan was his own, and he quickly stopped. His hands were tied behind his back, fibrous rope cutting painfully into his wrists. He was sitting on the ground, his back against a wall. Wahid ignored the clawing pain across his scalp and looked up. Crouched in front of him was the man who had attacked him in the beach hut. Wahid had last seen him unconscious on the floor, his shirt pasted to his chest with blood. He did not remember the face being so grotesquely scarred. Deep grooves curved across his features, starting from his chin and spreading outwards like a fan across his cheeks and nose before ending at his forehead. The flesh inside them was deep pink, like tyre tracks through a field of clay. He was shirtless, with his torso also a road map of cuts and scars. The stink of dried blood hung on him like a loose shirt.

'Wahid, hello,' said Professor Rahim, peering over the man's shoulder, a friendly smile on his round face.

'Professor?'

'Wahid, it's a pleasure to meet you again. So sorry it had to be this way,' said the professor.

'What … what are you doing?'

'Oh, I am sure you can guess most of it yourself. Stole a ring. Caught some djinns. And now trying to steal a nuke.'

Wahid stared as the professor held up a pudgy, liver-spotted hand. On his middle finger, he wore a large ring that gleamed brightly.

'I don't understand,' said Wahid.

'Ah,' said the professor, scratching his fine beard, 'is this the part where I act the idiotic villain from an American film and detail my plan? Then, while I am talking, you figure out how to escape? Yes, I do know I am the villain here. There is nothing heroic about my actions. I am not so deluded that I believe them to be the will of God or some such nonsense. I may be the first man who tries to kill lots of people and knows he is insane for wanting to. But first, let's show you how deeply fucked you really are.'

Kamran grabbed Wahid's head and pushed down until he was folded double. There was a tug at the ropes around his wrists and he was released. Kamran and the professor stepped back away from him.

'Get up. Get up and attack us. Do to us what you want to. What you can do to djinns so easily.'

Wahid slowly brought his hands forward, watching Kamran as he did. He pushed himself off the floor, standing up straight with the expectation that the large man would jump forward and shove him down again. When there was no reaction, he became emboldened. The rage inside him began to burn white-hot. His right eye ignited. A tongue of flame rose out of it, tasting the air. Wahid screamed and lunged forward.

Or, he tried to.

Every muscle in his body strained to move at his captors, but he was rooted to the spot. He tried again, this time his scream was replaced by a grunt of effort and found the results just as futile. His body refused to respond to him. The paralysis was so complete that not even his fingers moved. The fire in his eye faded and the iris filled in again. Wahid strained uselessly one more time.

Kamran stalked forward, swallowing the distance between them in two easy steps and raised a hand high. Wahid had a moment to notice the pink flesh where fingernails should have been and then the back of the hand struck him across the face hard enough to knock him to the ground. He lay there, fighting the darkness that threatened to overtake his sight.

'How …' he gasped.

'The ring, it's quite amazing. I believe it's Hazrat Sulaiman's. At least that's what the djinn who gave it to me said. It gives you the power to control djinns. And since you are half-djinn – so I have been told – it should work on you as well.'

'But what do you want?' spat Wahid.

'Oh, isn't it obvious by now? The end of the world.'

'That's … that's insane.'

'Yes, I suppose it is,' said the professor with a smile. 'But quite a majestic insanity, I believe. I suppose you would want to know what drove me to this point, yes? What made me so stunningly mad?'

Wahid didn't answer, just glared with bared teeth.

'I suppose it all started when my wife was diagnosed with cancer. Or maybe it was the stress of not being able to afford her treatments on my shitty teacher's salary. Maybe it was the fact that in the end, it wasn't the cancer that killed her at all, but a thief who shot her in the head when she didn't hand over her phone fast enough. He did it in broad daylight, and no one tried to stop him. No one even went near her body, do you know? She was still lying on the road when I reached an hour later …'

Interlude d.

Three months after his wife's death, Professor Rahim still had not slept a full night. His dreams were a montage of memories of his wife's life, and then her death. They always ended with him sitting up in bed, his cheeks glistening with tears like polished stone. This night he got up and went to the cupboard, opened it and buried his face in an armful of her clothes, still hanging where she had left them. Once he'd inhaled enough of her fading scent, he turned to look at the bed. He could not, he realized, sleep there any more. The absence of her body next to his would seep into his dreams. So, he locked the doors of the bedroom in which they had spent nearly forty years together and moved into a smaller guest room.

Three more months passed, with dreamless sleep, but sleep nonetheless. During this period, he returned to work, the daily rituals of living practised with the same hollow precision of a student mechanically reciting a physics concept, sans any actual engagement with its meaning. He would smile and talk and teach, but it always felt like a performance being viewed from afar.

Then one night, lying in bed he wondered if her clothes still smelled of her. He unlocked the bedroom for the first time since he'd walked out of it that night, many months ago. The room smelled of dust and abandonment. A cobweb barred the doorway, its silver filament catching the moonlight just in time for him to duck under it.

Against the opposite wall a djinn sat on its haunches, silently regarding him, with large black hands dangling over its knees. When he saw it, he thought it was a trick of the light, until it stood up. The top of its head brushed the ceiling and it watched him with eyes that burned. Professor Javed Kamal Rahim – despite his outward expressions of faith – had always been a man of science and reason at heart, and he did not scream. Instead, he recited aloud three times the Quranic dua that provides protection against djinns, blew softly once, then clapped thrice. It was what he had been taught to do as a child and something he did every night before going to sleep until he had reached his late teens when the ritual had started to feel ridiculous. If it had any effect on the djinn, he could not tell. It continued to stand utterly still and stare at him. Professor Rahim retreated from the room and locked the door behind him with trembling hands. It wasn't until he returned to his bed that he realized he had been saying 'Ya Allah' over and over.

In the rational light of the next morning's sun, he'd fancied it all a particularly vivid dream and would have left it at that. That night, however, scraping sounds started coming from the locked room. It was the sound of furniture being dragged slowly across the floor, of heavy wood on marble. He unlocked the door and found the room empty, but the large bed that would have taken several men to lift stood on its side. He flicked the light switch and swore softly when he realized the bulbs had died. Surveying the room in the dim light of a faded moon, he saw no sign of anyone, so he locked the door and walked out of the house. He spent the rest of the night sitting in his car reciting the same protective dua like a chant.

On the third day, he returned to the room and waited for the djinn. It did not appear. The room was silent every night after that.

Professor Rahim forgot about the djinn, considering it a brief lapse in his own sanity. He refocused on his daily duties: students needed educating, funding needed procurement, the house he lived in needed maintenance, and friends and family needed their respective attentions. And that is how he would have lived out the last of his days if not for the appointment of a new education minister.

Professor Rahim had heard of the religious scholar given the role. He was a famous man, made so by his standing as an authority on all things Islamic. Any who dared doubt him or question his authority had their own faith questioned publicly and were quickly branded kafir. Professor Rahim remembered him from an earlier time too, from when the religious scholar was younger. In an effort to raise his profile during the Zia years, he had been particularly judicious in calling people out on their lack of faith. Many of Professor Rahim's colleagues had been imprisoned by this man. Most had had their lives destroyed by the accusations.

When the education minister visited the university, Professor Rahim did not look forward to shaking his hand. But shake it he did, and even managed to smile as best he could when introduced. The education minister paused, smiling back at Professor Rahim.

'I heard about your wife. I shall keep her in my prayers,' he said. And then he moved on.

Professor Rahim had stood there with the fake smile fixed on his face, watching the man work his way down the faculty line. He kept his hands behind his back so that no one could see how tightly his fists were clenched, his knuckles turning ivory white.

That night Professor Rahim went back into the old bedroom, sat down in the centre of it, and waited. He waited there all night, then into the next day, until night came again. He fasted the entire time, with only a jug of water to keep him alive. By the second night, his stomach mewled and his strength began to wane, but he stayed there. By the third night, he was no longer sitting, but lying sprawled on the ground, clothes drenched with sweat, a bucket of urine stinking in the corner of the room. On the fourth night, drifting in and out of consciousness, he saw the djinn sitting in the same corner again.

XV.

'It told me about the ring. It told me that it could get it for me. So, I asked it to. And once I had it, my plan became real. I caught these djinns. Used the ring to trap as many as I could before they all disappeared and then set them to finding me a nuclear bomb.'

'Why? Why do you want a nuclear bomb?' asked Wahid.

'Because I am done with this world, Wahid. It's a terrible world, created by an unfair God, and it's a world that should no longer be allowed to continue. That people like that mullah should be allowed to pray for my wife's soul, that he should continue prospering, is an affront. You cannot lie to me, Wahid. You live in this city, in this country. Does it seem like the kind of world where good things happen? No.'

'So why … why me? Why did you send him after me,' asked Wahid, staring at the hulking mute crouched next to him.

'Oh, I need more djinns. Clearly. I only have a handful. The attack on the base proved they wouldn't be enough. There is no point sending the djinns in their true form, since the army is paranoid enough to expect that. The bombs are guarded by Qurans and prayed over by mullahs, day and night. You being there was just a happy coincidence. Or maybe it was kismet. Maybe Allah wants my plan to succeed. But now that you're here, with you and with what you can do, I can send you into Kaf and you can bring back an entire army of djinns. Then we can go after those nukes properly. No matter where they try hiding them. The djinns can possess as many bodies as needed and keep attacking until it's all done.'

'I won't do it.'

'Oh, you won't be able to stop yourself from doing it,' said the professor, waving his ring hand in front of Wahid. 'Besides, don't you agree with me? You must. Look at this world. Do you know, I didn't even have to work very hard to find armed terrorists for possessing? One of the djinns knew of a cell already preparing to attack a mosque. They had the guns and armour and everything. The idiots had chosen an empty apartment to hide in. If they hadn't died doing what I made them do, they would have killed Allah knows how many people. That's the world we live in. Aren't you tired of watching it all go to shit all the time? Every day? And the bad guys never get caught. The thief who shot my wife will never be found. No one ever gets caught or punished.

'But, I can see you will be reluctant,' said the professor with a sigh, 'which is why I have the ring. And if that doesn't work, pain will,' he said, gesturing at the horrifically scarred man standing next to him, the stink of menace radiating off him.

While Rahim spoke, Wahid took the time to study his surroundings. They were in a classroom, with chairs stacked on either side, and a chalkboard hanging on the far wall. Against that wall, watching him, were several djinns. Wahid counted three Marids, a pair of Grines, and a large dog with black fur and red eyes that he guessed was a Ghoul.

'You're ridiculous,' said Wahid, surprised by the boredom in his own voice.

The professor tapped Kamran on the shoulder lightly and a punch pounded into Wahid's midsection. The air rushed out of him and he felt the contents of his stomach in his throat.

'Behave yourself,' said the professor sternly, as though he were talking to a student who had disrupted his class.

'Those are your choices,' said the professor. 'Do as I say and maybe eventually you go free. It won't matter much, once I get the bombs, but at least you can say goodbye to your mother. If you don't aid me, I'll hurt you. Maybe I'll send the djinns after her. Maybe I'll test the ring and send you after her.'

Kamran grinned at Wahid, baring teeth stained with blood. Wahid realized his tongue had been cut out, a raw stump lying flat inside his mouth.

A smile returned to the professor's face. He turned to say something to the djinns, but his words were cut off by a child's voice.

'You tried to kill me,' Badshah said. He was speaking from all around them, resonating from the walls and rising from the ground.

Kamran and the professor spun around, trying to pinpoint the source.

'Who is it?' screamed the professor. 'Where are you?'

'I'm here. You tried to kill me. But you cannot kill Karachi. I am the city. I'm its spirit, and until it chooses another, or dies itself, I cannot die,' said Badshah from under them, and around them, and above them.

Kamran pulled out a gun with one hand and a knife with the other. He screamed wordlessly in fury.

'Yeah, fuck you too, buddy,' said the walls and the chairs and the fan and lights and the ceiling and the floor.

Kamran fired his gun into the air, a burst of explosions deafening them all. Chunks of plaster and concrete fell from the ceiling. He spun around and levelled the gun at Wahid. Wahid heard the professor scream the word 'No'.

Badshah rose out of the ground, almost too fast to see, shooting through Kamran like a guillotine, slicing him in half with his own small body. The top half of Kamran's body landed on the ground heavily, entrails arcing behind it like speed lines in a comic illustration. The legs stayed standing for a second longer, then they too toppled over. Badshah was covered in blood and thick chunks of muscle. A few knots of vertebrae lay on his shoulder like a macabre epaulette. They all stared at him, paralysed by their individual states of shock. Badshah spun around and grabbed the professor's hand. He pulled it towards him and the entire hand came free of the wrist as easily as a flower being plucked from its stem. The professor looked down at his blunt wrist, blood spurting out of the torn arteries, and let out an operatic cry before crumpling to the floor.

There was an abrupt silence in the room. Badshah stood with a severed hand in his grip, the djinns were utterly motionless, and even Wahid didn't move, his mouth agape. Only the professor twitched, lying on his back and moaning as he tried to stem the flow of blood with his other hand. It spewed out between his fingers in syrupy pink fountains.

'Hey Bhenchod,' said Badshah, dropping the hand to the ground, the golden ring still wrapped around the middle finger.

'You're alive!' Wahid smiled. Whatever control the ring exerted over him had been lost when it was disconnected from the professor.

'What about him?' said Badshah, pointing to the professor. The old man was still on the floor, rapidly losing consciousness. The flow from his wrist had slowed to a thin trickle and he was lying in a spreading pool of his own blood. His face was pale and he was moaning softly as he held the wrist to his chest.

'I don't know. Should we call for help? Maybe we should take him to the hospital,' said Wahid.

'I think they have other plans,' said Badshah.

The djinns had begun to converge on the professor, moving cautiously in the beginning and then, once they were confident of their freedom, stampeding towards him. Wahid got to the man first. The djinns stopped, watching Wahid. He ignored them and bent down in front of the swollen hand. It looked like a prop from a novelty store, the kind that sold costumes and sneezing powder. The ring slid off easily and he wiped it on his jeans before putting it into his pocket. Then he turned to the professor. The old man was staring at him with pleading eyes.

'Please,' he was whispering. 'Don't let them … please.'

'Don't touch him,' said Wahid, managing an approximation of a commanding tone.

A Marid glared at him. 'He controlled us like slaves. It cannot be done. He must be punished for it.'

'I don't give a shit what can and cannot be done. I'm telling you not to touch him,' said Wahid, stepping forward. 'You know what I can do.'

The Marid growled, the low rattle of a beast being denied its prey, but it did not move forward. Wahid kneeled next to the professor.

'Rahma,' slurred the professor in a fading voice, 'oh Rahma, my love.' His eyes closed and the breathing slowed until his chest stopped rising entirely. The body shivered once, as though giving up something, and then was still.

Wahid looked up at the assembled djinns.

'I'm sorry,' he said. 'No more of this. Go back to Kaf. Tell the Ifrit it's over. It's done.'

Then he got up and walked out, Badshah following him to the rickshaw.

XVI.

Major Daulat was waiting for Wahid at his home. Red and blue lights splashed across the street as a contingent of police cars, army jeeps and one dark Mercedes stood outside the gate. Badshah deposited Wahid near the start of the lane and turned the rickshaw in a tight arc until it was facing back towards the main road.

'You'll be okay?' Badshah asked.

Wahid had been in awe of the boy and what he represented, but now the King of Karachi suddenly looked very much like just a small child driving a comically large rickshaw.

'I'll be fine. Will you?'

'I am Karachi,' he said, thumping his chest proudly. 'I'm always fine.'

Then he revved the engine of the rickshaw loudly and sped off into the traffic. A group of policemen noticed Wahid and dispersed the smokers' circle they had formed, passing on word of his arrival to a soldier. Major Daulat climbed out of the Mercedes, looked at Wahid, noticing all the blood on his clothes, and raised an eyebrow.

'I swear it's not mine,' said Wahid.

There were kisses from Mumtaz, who had run out to meet her son. Wahid cried with her, both leaning on each other to keep the other from falling. Major Daulat followed them into the house, politely opening the door as mother and son stumbled in, manically alternating between laughter and tears.

'Are you okay, Wahid? I can have a doctor brought here,' Major Daulat offered.

Wahid refused with a tired smile. He sat next to Mumtaz and kissed her on the side of her head, pressing one hand between his.

'The attack on the base. I had nothing to do with it,' said Wahid.

'I know. But the – ' He looked at Mumtaz. 'Perhaps we should talk somewhere else, yes?'

'It's okay,' said Wahid. 'Ammi needs to know. Especially now that the man responsible for all this is … it's over.'

Wahid then detailed the evening's events, making last-minute improvisations to omit Badshah from the story. Once Major Daulat was completely informed, he recalled for Mumtaz the rest of the story. He told her of his mixed parentage, and how Hamza had come back, albeit briefly, after having met Wahid's father. When he was done, everyone in the room seemed drained.

'So now what?' Mumtaz asked.

'Now?' said Major Daulat. 'I don't know. Wahid's experiences are unique. I am sure if others in my chain of command find out, they will want you brought in for questioning. Detailed questioning.'

Wahid's shoulders sagged and Mumtaz started marshalling her anger.

'That is,' continued Major Daulat, 'if I tell them. I'll have to, but not right away. I think you might be more valuable to me out here than in some prison. If you promise to keep me informed of anything that ever happens again that you think I should know about.'

Wahid's face brightened. 'Thank you! Yes! I will! I promise!'

Major Daulat stood up and bowed slightly to Mumtaz.

'Baji, you have a good son. I will be leaving two guards outside your house for tonight, to make sure you are both safe. They will leave tomorrow morning.'

Wahid sprang up and considered the handshake on offer. Instead, he wrapped his arms around the surprised major and hugged.

After he had left, Wahid helped his mother upstairs to her room and asked her if she needed anything.

'Just some rest, beta. You need to go and shower.'

Returning to his room, Wahid undressed and threw the clothes in the bin. The stains on his jeans and shirt were black and sticky. There was a soft clinking sound as he tossed the jeans and he bent down to find that the ring had fallen to the floor. He picked it up and placed it in his desk drawer. After the shower, once he was sure the stink of blood was off him completely, Wahid returned to Mumtaz's room.

'Ammi,' he said knocking on the door. He found her shivering on the edge of her bed, fingers gnawing at a string of prayer beads.

'I don't understand what happened,' she managed through chattering teeth.

Wahid sat next to her and held her to his chest, promising to explain it all in the morning if she went to sleep first. He got up and found a couple of sleeping pills and gave them to her with a glass of water. She fell asleep in a few minutes and Wahid did too shortly after.

XVII.

He was in an enormous white room. The walls of the room stretched so high that clouds drifted overhead, dissolving against them. Wahid was walking across an endless ivory floor. He had been walking for some time before he understood that he would not be able to stop, even if he wanted to. A small tree was growing in the centre of the room, just a few feet higher than him. Every leaf was on fire, small flames blossoming on the thin branches.

If the tree had spoken to him, he had not heard it. But information filled him nonetheless, new information that he had not known a moment ago. He turned this knowledge over and inside out, letting the understanding it brought slowly spread through his mind.

There was only a little more to do, he was told. Just one more task to fulfil. After that it would be over. And then, if he survived, he might have a life to live. Maybe it would be the life he had been torn out of, or maybe it would be something new. But it would be a life worth wanting. Just one more thing to do.

The flames grew larger, each meeting with the other like a crowd holding hands until the whole tree was one single blaze. A tremendous heat emanated from it and Wahid knew that standing there a second longer would reduce him to ashes. And so, he awoke, knowing he had one last thing to do, and that he had to figure out how to do it himself.

The Ifrit was at the foot of his bed.

XVIII.

Standing at the blurred edge of realities was a man, whose name was Impostor to some, Deceiver to others, who had been waiting for the world to fall to ruin so he could ascend the staircase that led to his rule. With a single eye, protruding like a grape, he regarded the djinn in front of him.

'You promised I would be free of this place by now,' growled Dajjal. 'Free to roam, and free to rule.'

'You will,' said Iblis, not threatened at all by the creature's ire. His black form stood tall, curls of smoke rising off his shoulder. 'Things have been delayed, that's all. It'll happen. I'll find a way to make it happen.'

'You know, Azah-zeel, it's starting to seem like a good idea to kill you,' said Dajjal, snapping his teeth together to emphasize the point.

'There won't be any more killing,' said Wahid.

Iblis spun around and stared at the boy, walking towards them. Wahid looked tired and thin, but his face was calm.

'How did you get here?' Iblis asked.

'I brought him,' said the Ifrit, stepping out from behind Wahid. 'Assalam o Alaikum, Azah-zeel. What you did was very dangerous.'

'You're real,' said Wahid, pointing to Dajjal. 'I thought you were a dream.'

'I am indeed real.' The one-eyed creature shrugged. 'What will you do about it?'

'Wahid, get away from here,' snarled Iblis. 'This doesn't concern you.'

'It does. And I'll deal with you later,' replied Wahid.

'Wahid –'

Iblis stopped abruptly, staring at the ring loosely hung around Wahid's finger.

'You have Sulaiman's ring,' he gawked.

'Yes, and it controls djinns, right? So stay still and shut up.'

Iblis had a great deal more to say, but at that point all the strength he had couldn't will him to speak, nor to move.

Wahid turned to face Dajjal.

The man in front of Wahid stood taller than him by at least two feet. Wahid's head barely reached the heavily muscled chest. Under the pale sunlight of the desert, his skin was blood red, and menace twitched in every muscle. On his forehead, written in black scar tissue above the single eye, were the Arabic letters ك ف ر. Wahid recognized them as KFR. Kafir.

'I am not some little fire creature that you can bend to your will. Do not bother trying to control me with that little bauble of yours.'

'I figured that out,' said Wahid. 'But what are you exactly?'

'I am Dajjal. I am older than djinns, older than angels, older than the universe even. When the time is right, when the trees no longer bear fruit and the rivers run dry, then I shall walk among the people.'

'Yes,' said Wahid. 'But not if I stop you first.'

Dajjal laughed, showing several rows of sharp white teeth that went all the way down into his large throat.

'Try,' he said.

Wahid closed his eyes. Inside him, somewhere deep within, burned a single flame. He reached for it, imagined catching it between two fingers, closing a fist around it. Then he let it go. It grew, blazing wings spreading as they filled the inside of his head. Wahid opened his eyes. Gouts of flame erupted from both, like the windows of a house being swallowed by an uncontrolled blaze. He opened his mouth and fire surged from his throat in a column. Jets of flame punched through the air, blasting out of him and whirling towards Dajjal. For a moment, they were connected by a bridge of fire arcing between them. It poured from Wahid, gushing from his entire body in a single orange blade and smashing into the immense form of Dajjal. Flames crashed against him, surging until he was swallowed whole. Dajjal made no effort to move out of the way and when, after several seconds, the flames receded, he stood exactly as he had been. Wahid, on the other hand, collapsed. The fire trailed back towards him, like a shamed pet. He was still struggling to sit up when the last gulps of flame climbed back into his eyes.

'Quite the spectacle,' Dajjal said. The only evidence of the conflagration was the smoke drifting off him. 'Did you know he could do that?'

This last part was addressed to Iblis, still standing statue-like off to the side. The Ifrit was seated on the ground next to Iblis, legs crossed and watching Wahid with an obvious mix of fear and awe on his face.

'There's … thuh … there's more wuh … where that … oh fuh … fuck, I can't breathe,' wheezed Wahid. His chest was heaving as though he had just finished running a great distance and his face glistened with sweat.

'Enough, you're wasting your time and mine, boy.'

Wahid staggered to his feet, bent over with hands on his knees. He looked up at Dajjal through clumps of sweat soaked hair, taking deep breaths to calm his jackhammering heart.

'That's not true though, is it?' he said. 'You don't have anywhere to go. Not yet. You need nuclear war to start up there before you can get through. Why?'

'Because, little Wahid, I am Dajjal. My arrival has been foretold under specific conditions by your Allah and his unlettered prophet. The rivers must be dry; the trees must bear no fruit; the wombs of women must be as barren as the desert we stand in.'

As he had said each qualifier, the world around them changed. Wahid straightened up in shock as the entire desert evaporated in a mist and was replaced by a different environment. Shapes coalesced out of the fog and sharpened into distinct images. He and Dajjal were no longer standing on a flat dirt field, with an empty brown desert stretching endlessly around them and a spotless sky overhead. Instead, it was snowing. That was the first thing Wahid noticed. White flakes drifted around him, catching on his shoulders and hands. He looked up into a blizzard, great wheels of pale petals spinning overhead in a darkened sky. It was like looking up into a cyclone of static.

Dragging his gaze away from the snow, he looked around. They were still standing on a road, but this one was decrepit compared to the smooth, flat surface they had just been on. On either side of the road were the shattered husks of buildings, crumbling faces that were more wire skeleton than solid concrete. Some had been entirely reduced to rubble, while others were like skulls that had been stamped on by a giant boot. There were also actual skulls, knee-high mounds of them piled along the roadside like macabre barriers. Thousands of grinning teeth under hollow eye sockets were all around them. A snowflake landed on Wahid's palm and he held it up.

'It's ash,' he said. 'All this is ash. What did you do?'

'Nothing yet,' said Dajjal, plucking a skull from a pile near him and tossing it playfully from one giant hand to the other. 'But when the world is like this, then I will walk through it.'

'Are we … is this a dream? Or like a hallucination?'

'Not at all. This is just your mind. I'm showing you how the world will look when my time will come. See? See those people and how desperate they are.'

Dajjal was pointing over Wahid's shoulder so he turned to look, instantly wishing he hadn't. A crowd was approaching them, dozens of people all zombie-shuffling up the road. Wahid could see his mother in the front. Her face was burned, half of it melted to a puddle of wax. Both her eyes were pale, unblinkingly fixed on him. Around them he saw more people from his life: distant relatives, classmates from school, and family friends he recognized from Eid dinners. They all bore similar evidence of torture.

'This isn't real,' said Wahid through gritted teeth.

'It can be. It will be,' said Dajjal from behind him. Then he waved a hand. The drizzle of ash that had been consistently growing around them gusted, then swirled upwards, returning to the sky in a flowing river of particles. Light sliced through the darkness overhead, a beam of pure sunlight stabbed across the sky, picking out the straggling group with a brilliant spotlight. The illusion of Wahid's mother cried out in joy first. Illuminated by the solitary shaft of radiance, she was fully healed. She brought trembling fingers to her face, tears welling in the iris-spotted eyes. All the others were also restored. They were hugging each other and weeping joyously, some of them falling to their knees as they wailed in gratitude.

'You saved us!' cried Mumtaz.

Wahid started, then realized she wasn't addressing him but was pointing to Dajjal. She ran right past Wahid, not even slowing to glance in his direction and prostrated at Dajjal's feet, pressing her forehead to his toes. The others followed, streaming around Wahid and throwing themselves before Dajjal. Wahid saw a girl who looked like Maheen take his hand and press his knuckles to her eyes. His school principal was there, a stern woman who always reminded Wahid of jagged glass; she tried to reach over a cousin of Wahid's to touch Dajjal's chest. Several boys and girls he recognized from tuitions were crouched at Dajjal's feet, just like his mother, laying kisses on his ankles.

'See?' Dajjal bellowed to Wahid over the noisy obeisance. 'They are hungry for miracles. Allah does not give them miracles any more. I will. And in return, they will worship me.'

Wahid looked away, turning his back to Dajjal and staring down the fractured road. It disappeared into the darkness ahead.

'Why are you showing me this?' he screamed.

Dajjal appeared in front of him. The worshipping mob was gone and it was just the two of them again.

'Because I want you to know that I can perform miracles for you as well. When Qiyamat comes – and it will come one day – you and yours need not suffer. In fact, you might even enjoy it.'

Maheen stepped out from behind Dajjal.

'Don't do this,' Wahid said.

Dajjal smiled. 'She'll be yours, Wahid. I know how you love her, and what you did for her. She will know it too, and her gratitude will be complete.

'Just bow your head to me, that's all I ask. Accept me as your god and you can have so much,' said Dajjal. 'You can be my prophet abroad. Be my messenger to the people. Help them see me as their god. Spread my belief. And in return you can have all the women and all the wealth you can dream of.'

'Please. Stop it, please, please,' moaned Wahid, discovering he was turning towards Maheen despite every effort not to. It was like trying to steer a car that had run into a skid, careening in one direction uncontrollably. This isn't real, Wahid thought. This isn't real. This is just in my head. In my imagination. Dajjal said so.

A memory took shape inside his closed eyelids. An old *X-Men* comic that he had read once, sitting on the floor of Arif's room. Professor Xavier creating a psychic world which he could control, and trapping someone inside it. Was it Magneto? He could see the panels of the comic vividly, the pop blast of colour and inked lines as a bald man in a wheelchair floated in a blank space. Pink lines of psychic energy radiated off him and formed the details of a prison inside which the villain-of-the-issue was trapped. The memory startled him, appearing in such detail with utter suddenness. He felt a sad longing for those days which now seemed impossibly far behind him. Days when he would sit with Hamza and Arif and talk comics or play a game of Dungeons & Dragons.

Lips pressed against his own. Refusing to open his eyes, he felt Maheen's breath in his mouth, her tongue passing over his teeth.

It's just a psychic construct, he thought to himself. This is your mind. You can do whatever you want with it.

In the distance from a great height above him he could hear Dajjal speaking. 'Come, Wahid. Enjoy what your mind so clearly wants to give you. Take her and become mine. I will be a better god to you than you have ever had. What do you say?'

Wahid opened his eyes. Maheen pulled her face away from his, her lips glistening with his spittle.

'No,' Wahid said as calmly as he could.

Maheen dissipated. A cloud of ash danced in front of him, then caught in the wind and blew away.

'What do you say?' said Dajjal, standing in front of him, the single eye watching Wahid like a moon.

'I say,' Wahid said, grinning wildly, 'I say you find yourself in a room with white walls.'

Before Dajjal could respond, the shattered road and broken houses around them were blocked from view. Under their feet, the ground became flat concrete. They were back where Wahid had first met Dajjal.

'Don't waste my time, Wahid,' said Dajjal, although Wahid noticed something flicker in his single eye, a brief contraction of the large pupil perhaps. Dajjal motioned and the walls bulged outwards, bending like sheets of paper midway through being folded over. But they didn't complete their collapse, springing back upright after a moment. Dajjal winced visibly.

Wahid was no longer in that room with Dajjal, not as far as he was concerned. His body was in an imaginary room in a forbidden place between worlds, but his mind was somewhere far away, somewhere enjoyably mundane. He was imagining – no, remembering – sitting on a thick carpet, patterned with stains and cigarette ash. He sat cross-legged, a thick journal lay open on his lap, its pages filled with the outpourings of a teenage boy's imagination. In front of him sat his two best friends, hunched over in anticipation. Chantilly and Barslow were about to go on an adventure, their journey mapped by their Dungeon Master.

Wahid opened his eyes, pinning Dajjal with the glare of his focus. 'You find yourself in a room with white walls.'

Dajjal charged. Roaring, his mouth opening so wide the lower jaw somehow stretched down to his navel – inside was a field blossoming with razors. He closed the distance between them in three large steps. Wahid felt the heat of his breath, a furnace blast of rotting flesh. A clawed hand rose, and as it sliced towards him, Wahid screamed out the next description.

'Chains grab you.'

Dajjal roared as massive chains erupted from the walls. They snagged his wrists and curled around his thick neck. He pulled at them, hurling himself forward but they had little give and he found himself jerked backwards, crashing to the ground as the chains clanged around him.

'I will give you the world, Wahid! Don't do this!' Dajjal shrieked.

'I don't want the world,' Wahid said. Then he gave one final description, 'That which you fear the most seals you in.'

There was a door behind Wahid, the desert outside visible through it. As he turned towards it, words carved themselves into the space above the door. Each letter's appearance was heralded by a pained howl from Dajjal, his voice collapsing until the final letter's appearance was met with just a whimper.

'There is no God but Allah,' read Wahid, then shut the door behind him as he exited.

Iblis was still standing frozen where Wahid had left him. The Ifrit, seated next to him, stood up.

'It is done?' asked the Ifrit.

'Yes,' said Wahid. 'But I have one more thing to do. Do you mind leaving me alone with Iblis for a few moments?'

'Don't take too long,' the Ifrit grumbled, but walked away until it had reached some distance from them.

'You can move now, by the way,' said Wahid to Iblis, rubbing the ring on his finger with his other hand.

'Wahid –' Iblis started.

'You are my mother,' said Wahid.

Iblis smiled. 'You figured it out. What gave me away?'

'When you grabbed me. Over the Yajuj–Majuj. When you were a bird. You didn't burn at all.'

'It took you long enough to realize.'

'But why? I don't understand.'

Iblis drew in a long breath and smiled. It was the smile, Wahid decided, of an artist about to unveil his greatest work.

'Do you know what my name means? Do you know why they call me that?'

'No.'

'It means "He despaired". And it's true, Wahid. I lived in Heaven. I was chosen by Allah, and I lived in Paradise. And then I was thrown out of it. If that is not cause for despair, then what is? No one in all creation can know my suffering. My yearning to return. It was decided the day I refused to bow down to that clump of mud on legs. To be exiled to this world for the entirety of its existence. My only escape will be after Qiyamat.

'On that day, my judgement will be Hell. Of course, I know that. But not for an eternity. He is All-Forgiving, after all. Even I, even Iblis, will be forgiven eventually. I will make my way back to Heaven. That's my hope, Wahid. To start my suffering, so I can be purified by it.'

'So why didn't you bow down to him? Why were you so proud? None of this would have happened to you if –'

'It wasn't pride!' Iblis screamed. 'It was fear!' Then, softly, he said, 'It was the birds. For thousands of years they had flown above us djinns. They had nested and had taken wing, soaring with us and eating from our palms. And we never knew to call them birds. We didn't have that capacity. We still don't. To create. To imagine and then turn that imagination to reality. It was something we were never given. But to him, it came so easily. So effortlessly. He saw them and he named them. I knew then that we had been cheated. I had been cheated. Despite all my devotion and all my adoration, it was this new … thing that had been given the greatest of all Allah's gifts. I could see then that the men and women who would come after would be able to do more than we ever could. They could and did create. They created tools and they created art and music and even their own religions.

'They blasphemed. Do you know what an act of will that is? Of imagination? To turn your back on your own creator and then create other gods? To believe in them just as strongly? No other creature in all existence can do that. You have seen the djinns. You have seen Kaf. They have existed longer than humans and they have no buildings of their own creation. Instead they wait for humans to discard places and then crawl into them like insects living in a corpse. They spend their time amusing themselves by haunting and possessing and by hanging from fucking trees.

'I knew that then. And it filled me with anger. So I spurned Adam and was punished for it. You tell me, is that fair?'

Wahid rubbed his forehead, 'But why me? What does that have to do with me? Why did you give birth to me? How did you do it?'

'I first thought of you – or had the idea of you – hundreds of years ago. I tried so many times. In the form of a man, I tried to fill women with my seed. To have them bring forth a child like you. A child that was unique to the world. That was new. I bedded queens and princesses. Scholars and women of wisdom. And it did not work. All of them died once the child in their womb began to form, burnt from the inside by it. Eventually I understood what I had to do. So, I took this form.'

Iblis changed then, shifting from the form filled with darkness to a woman with dusky skin, wrapped in silk that shimmered like dew.

'I seduced kings like this. I took the greatest warriors mankind ever had in this form. I was even the wife of some of them, for a period. All the children I gave birth to died before they could draw in their first breath, and one grew up insane and cruel, so that I had to kill him myself.

'Eventually, I gave up. When I saw your father, I didn't plan on getting pregnant by him. I took him because his pure honesty and religious devotion irritated me. I thought it would be funny to corrupt such a simple man with an act of lust. Nine months later, unplanned and unconsidered, you were born. Not the son of a king, or a warrior, or a scholar, but of a simple merchant.'

The woman that was Iblis leaned over and cupped Wahid's chin in soft hands. The smile was maternal.

'The plan? What was the plan?' said Wahid, brushing the hand away.

'To bring Qiyamat. That is all. I found that old man who had the same wish. That mad little professor. Such imagination. All I knew was that I would use you and your strength to free Dajjal. Other than that, I had nothing. But to find the ring, to use it to control djinns and steal bombs and start a war. That was all the old man's plan. These humans can think of things we never could.

'And now you have it. But it isn't too late. You can still help me. Still give me what I crave. Go to Kaf with it and lead the djinns. Start the wars and let loose the forms of destruction that Allah has made. Start Qiyamat.'

'And you?'

'I will be next to you. I will advise you and serve you. Like a mother does. And then, finally, I will be free. Do you not want that for me? Is that too much to ask?'

Wahid rubbed his face as he considered Iblis's words. 'You gave the ring to the professor. You knew what he would do and you gave it to him. The djinns thought it was me, and two of my friends are dead. My mother was almost hurt. Maheen was almost killed.'

Had Iblis had human eyes, he would have rolled them then. He flapped his hand dismissively.

'Do you know how many humans I have seen die? From the first ones ever born till today. Even now there are thousands dying across the world. Humans die all the time. But you don't need to care about that any more. It shouldn't matter. Your friends would have died eventually. The woman you call your mother will as well. Even that girl. If you stay here, you will see them all die. But you won't die. Unless you are killed, and you are not easy to kill. My kind does not die easily, and you are stronger than us.'

'I didn't want this. I didn't want to start Qiyamat or any of that shit. I wanted to sit for my exams and fall in love and maybe go on a date. I … I like that. I miss that.'

'It's too late for that now!' snapped Iblis, reverting to his true form, a black silhouette with a mouth of fire. 'The girl will never love you. After what happened, she will never be comfortable around you. You will frighten her and she will not understand why. And after everything that you have seen, you won't be able to return to your normal life. It will be impossible to do so. Come with me. I am sorry about your friends, but in time you will forget them. I promise. There is so much you don't even know about yourself. I can show you how to travel anywhere. How to change your shape. To control the fires and to pull thoughts from men's minds. I can teach you to possess them. Please. Come with me. We can find some other way to do this. I know we can. You have the imagination to do so.'

'No,' said Wahid, rubbing the ring on his finger. It felt cold to the touch. 'I don't want to do those things. I never did. Maybe I am your child, but I'm not your son. I … I guess I am my father's son. And my mother's.'

Iblis's eyes blazed, his mouth a volcanic maw. There was rage there. And, Wahid later realized, pain too.

Wahid continued. 'You shouldn't have let my friends die. You didn't need to. If you had just come to me, maybe I would have helped you in some way. But you tried to trick me. I'm sorry.'

Then, lifting his hand up to show Iblis the ring, Wahid said loudly, 'Go away and don't ever come near me again.'

Iblis wailed. It was the sound of a great wind rushing down across a vast plain; of a thousand infants in pain; of a woman mourning betrayal. Then he was gone.

'It's over?' asked the Ifrit walking back towards him.

'Just one more thing,' said Wahid. He pulled the ring off his finger, looking at it as it shone in the palm of his hand. He made a fist around it. After a few seconds, smoke squeezed out from between his clenched fingers. He opened his hand again. The ring had melted into a puddle of gold. Wahid tipped his hand over and let it all flow onto the sand. Then he scuffed it with one foot.

'Now it's over,' said Wahid, 'take me home, please.'

XIX.

The next day he visited Arif's family and they greeted him without blame or anger. Arif's brother let Wahid sit alone in Arif's room for almost half an hour. It looked as though it had never been unoccupied. Wahid sifted through a pile of comics absently. He did not cry, although he wanted to. On the way out, he whispered to Arif's brother about a stack of porn DVDs that Arif had hidden under a false floor in his cupboard.

'It's probably best if you get rid of those before Auntie finds them.'

The brother agreed and thanked him.

At Hamza's house, there was less sadness. His family, sure that Hamza had been kidnapped and might still be returned alive, were fuelling their hopes with a forceful positivity. Wahid's guilt manifested itself as nausea and he spent only a few minutes there.

There was one more body to mourn, a promise he had made to Badshah that had to be kept. Finding the place had been difficult, but he eventually recognized the snarl of alleyways and roads near where he had first met the boy. An immense graveyard stretched behind several blocks of crowded tenements, and it took several hours before he found someone who knew where a little girl had been buried just a few days before.

'A lot of children are buried here,' said the caretaker. A young man with fresh mud on his hands, he led Wahid to a small mound of dirt. Wahid paid him to place a white marble headstone over it.

'Her name was Bina. Please write it on the marble,' said Wahid, bending down to touch the cool mud and bringing the fingers to his lips.

'Did you know her?' asked the caretaker.

'No, but someone should remember her still,' replied Wahid.

A week later, a small crowd of boys and girls gathered outside his gate. Wahid took as much cash as he and his mother had, and distributed it among them. They snatched it from his hand and ran off, cheering. He heard one of them call him chutiya, and Wahid laughed.

XX.

On a sweaty afternoon, Wahid and Maheen sat across each other in a restaurant. He had sent her several messages on Facebook, and she'd finally agreed to meet him. He prayed the reluctance he read in the tone of her response was his own paranoia.

She looked thinner than the last time he had seen her in person. Her skin was bloodless and her eyes were ringed by the tell-tale signs of insomnia. Wahid recognized them because he had them as well.

'Hi,' he said nervously.

'Hello,' she replied, trying to smile and almost succeeding.

'Do you want anything to eat?' asked Wahid.

'No, thank you, I'm not very hungry,' she said.

'Neither am I actually. Must be the heat.'

'Yeah, I guess so.'

They both stared at the menu cards on the table.

'Maheen,' Wahid said finally, 'I'm sorry.'

'Don't be. It's not your fault. I don't think … I mean, it was an accident. We were all there. I heard it was maybe a truck or something. I know you weren't drunk like everyone keeps saying.'

'What do you remember?'

'Not much actually. I remember leaving the party with you and … and Arif. And then nothing after that. The doctors said it's common. Trauma and all that. I'm sorry about Arif.'

'Thank you.'

'And I heard that Hamza has disappeared too? He was your friend as well, right? You guys used to hang out together. Do they know what happened?'

'I think they're saying it was a kidnapping. I don't know.'

'I'm sorry, I didn't mean to upset you.'

They returned to a studious scrutiny of the menu cards. Wahid sipped a glass of water just to do something.

'You don't remember talking to me at all? After the crash?'

Maheen played with a fork, poking the tines under her nails as she spoke. 'No. I mean, how could I? I was in a coma. Did you come to see me? I … I heard my father was very angry. I'm sorry if he blamed you.'

'No, it's okay.'

The waiter came up with a bread basket and placed it between them. Neither touched it.

Finally, Maheen spoke. 'I almost didn't come today. I don't know why. Every time I think of you, I get uneasy. Like I should hate you or fear you. I don't understand it. Even now, it's taking all my strength to sit here. What happened, Wahid?'

'I'm sorry. For all of it. I wish it wasn't like this. You can't imagine how much I wish that. But it is and I can't do anything about it. If you want to leave, I understand.'

Maheen stood up slowly, as if she was fighting with herself. Eventually, whatever debate was occurring in her mind seemed to resolve itself, and she took a step back from the table.

'Goodbye Wahid,' she said with a great deal of gentleness.

'Goodbye Maheen,' Wahid replied. Then, as she turned to walk away, he said, 'Your middle name is Imtiaz, right? That's what the I stands for.'

Maheen turned and looked at him, confusion on her face.

'Yeah,' she said in a slow, drawn-out manner. 'My full name is Maheen Imtiaz Janjua. What's your point?'

'It's a question you asked me once,' said Wahid, with a smile that hurt her to look at.

'I don't remember.'

'Never mind. Goodbye Maheen. I'm sorry.'

'Thank you, Wahid.'

She walked out. A few minutes later, Wahid left the restaurant as well.

'How'd it go?' asked Hamza, as Wahid got into the car. His friend was translucent, a tracing paper mould sitting in the passenger seat.

'About as bad as can be expected,' said Wahid, buckling his seat belt.

'Win some, lose some,' Hamza said, passing his hands through the dashboard experimentally. They disappeared up to the wrist.

XXI.

Iblis was right. Try as he might, Wahid could not slip back into his previous life. He saw Maheen one more time, although she did not seem to notice him and he didn't approach her. It was during the A-level exams that were held six months later. They had both had their exams deferred and were sitting across a large hall in a hotel, a mass of students nervously chewing their pens and furiously scraping answers onto sheets of paper between them. Wahid had made many valiant attempts at studying and failed every time. He would stare at the textbooks and although he read every word, they somehow failed to connect to each other and form full sentences. Sitting under the baleful watch of a phalanx of invigilators, he stared numbly down at the sheet in front. He managed to write his name and the date, but nothing else. After trying to reread the questions, he sighed, stood up and walked out. He didn't bother returning for the rest of the exams.

More and more, he began to see djinns. At the Sunday bazaar, while buying vegetables with his mother, he saw a Marid crouched under a table watching everyone go by. In a mosque, during Friday prayers, he saw a variety of djinns bowing their heads with the oblivious believers. None of them approached him, nor did any of them acknowledge him.

His previous life had begun to feel like an ill-fitting jacket that he kept trying to pull on. Six months passed like this until one day, while sitting with his mother and watching a pair of politicians arguing on TV, he decided it was time.

'Ammi, I need to go,' he said.

Mumtaz was watching the TV while flipping through a magazine about furniture. 'Hmm?' she said without looking up, 'where do you want to go, beta?'

'Away, Ammi. I've been thinking about going to Kaf. Where the djinns are.'

Her body jerked. 'Wahid, no!'

'Ammi, I have to. If I'm half-djinn, then I want to learn about that half. I want to find out more about what I am and what I can do. I'm not sure I fit in here any more.'

'But what if something happens?'

'Nothing can happen to me, Ammi. I'll be safe. And I'll come back from time to time, I'm sure. I need to do this.'

'But how will you go?' she said, tears filling in her eyes.

'There's an empty house a few streets down. I keep watching it. It's been empty for a few years now. I saw a djinn enter it a few days ago. I think I can use it to go to Kaf.'

'When?'

Wahid was silent for several seconds, then taking his mother's hands between his, he said, 'Right now.'

'So soon?' she whispered, her voice trembling.

'I'm sorry. I just need to,' he said.

'Should I pack your suitcase?'

Wahid smiled and kissed her on her forehead, hugging her tightly.

'I don't think I'll be needing it. But if I do, I'll come back for it. I love you, Ammi. I really do. Just think of this as if I was going away to college.'

'I love you, my beta,' she said.

He hugged her again, then got up. He went to his room and put on a pair of sneakers, then walked out of the front door.

The abandoned house was a five-minute walk away and he could hear his footsteps crunching on the gravel as he made his way towards it. In the distance, an ambulance wailed through the city.

'Are you ready for this?' asked Hamza, walking beside him.

'Sure,' said Wahid. 'Besides, who will mess with me. I'm quite powerful, right?'

'You still suck at sounding tough.' Hamza grinned.

'Yeah,' said Wahid, coming to a stop in front of the house. On either side were empty plots of land overgrown by weeds and thick grass. It stood like a single tooth in the open maw of the night.

Somewhere in Karachi, a boy who wasn't so much the king of the city, as the city itself, was smoking a cigarette while teaching another boy how to stab a man in the neck with a pen. It was the kind of lesson that would keep the student alive for longer than he would have otherwise managed.

On an empty street, a woman walked in search of a man. The hem of her sari hiding her twisted feet.

In a sweet shop, the owner left a tray of the finest desserts under a glass cover, knowing they would be eaten by morning.

And on a moonlit street, a boy who was half-human and half-djinn, entered an empty house, with his best friend's ghost, and walked through it into another world.

Acknowledgements

This book wouldn't exist if Ayesha Raja hadn't asked me to write her something to represent. She moved on, but the book stayed with me. So for that initial push, I will be ever grateful.

Ishma Alvi read multiple drafts, called bullshit on most of them, and if it's any good now, it's because she had standards to which my writing aspired.

Richard Walsh, Mahvesh Murad, Sara Amjad, all read the various versions and gave me patient advice on what to fix. If anything makes sense now, it's because of them. If it doesn't, it's because of me.

Fantastica, in Sydney, published me, because they're the only ones who will put money to mouth when it comes to publishing diverse genre fiction in a Western market. Thomas Wilson edited this with patience and care, sensitivity and consideration.

Once it came out in Australia, as a small two-part series, Kamila Shamsie championed it, as she champions so many lost souls. It was she who passed it on to Diya Kar Hazra at Pan Macmillan India, who then convinced everyone else there to risk their reputations. Sushmita Chatterjee put up with my petulance when asked to make sensible changes. The mistakes are mine, the corrections hers.

And finally, I would be remiss in thanking all the people in my life who shared their stories with me, the stories that formed so much of my imagination growing up in Karachi. From my cousins who told me about the shop where the owner leaves syrupy sweets on a tray for djinns to eat at night, to the variations on the pichal pairee tale. So many of them I couldn't even work into the book, no matter how I tried, and every South Asian who reads this will have so many more that they will wish had been mentioned.